ALSO BY LEO J. MALONEY

Termination Orders

Silent Assassin

Black Skies

Twelve Hours

Arch Enemy

A Dan Morgan Thriller

Leo J. Maloney

KENSINGTON PUBLISHING CORP.

www.kensingtonbooks.com

LYRICAL UNDERGROUND BOOKS are published by

Kensington Publishing Corp.
119 West 40th Street
New York, NY 10018

All Kensington titles, imprints, and distributed lines are available at special quantity discounts for bulk purchases for sales promotions, premiums, fundraising, educational, or institutional use. Special book excerpts or customized printings can also be created to fit specific needs. For details, write or phone the office of the Kensington sales manager: Kensington Publishing Corp., 119 West 40th Street, New York, NY 10018, attn: Sales Department; phone 1-800-221-2647.

PUBLISHER'S NOTE

First electronic edition: March 2016

ISBN-13: 978-1-61650-977-4
ISBN-10: 1-61650-977-5

First print edition: March 2016

ISBN-13: 978-1-61650-978-1
ISBN-10: 1-61650-978-3

Printed in the United States of America

With respect and honor I dedicate this book to the Mission K9 Rescue organization that has recognized and aided thousands of military and contract working dogs. These canines have served valiantly alongside their human counterparts to keep our country safe. The dogs and their handlers are heroes and should be treated as such.

Chapter 1

Dom Watson kept his gaze fixed on the watch face, gold against black, as the second hand ticked toward twelve. His striped button-down was soaked through with sweat, clinging like ice to his lower back. He tapped a pen against the desk, drawing his eyes away just enough to cast them up and down the open-plan office, the row of cubicles holding plants and word-a-day calendars and *Dilbert* comics. All that stupid, workaday normality, dead for the weekend. Watson wasn't going to miss it.

Now, with seconds to go, he was itching to have it over with. Eyes on his watch, *Breitling, five grand, not that anyone is asking*, he fiddled with the plastic and metal gadget in his pocket, tracing its contours with his fingers.

The two longer hands reached twelve in unison. He held himself still for five more ticks out of some unknown scruple, and then he drew the blue plastic parallelepiped from his pocket. He looked over his monitor and the wall of his cubicle at the dim space beyond. A few screens were still glowing, a few desk lights were still on, but anyone here at the office at 6 A.M. on a Saturday would not be concerned with what he was up to.

He bent forward in his chair, aligning the little device with the USB port on the CPU that whirred away under his desk and pushed, but it wouldn't go. Somehow, having been an IT specialist for almost a decade, he still managed to get the orientation wrong more than half the time. He turned the drive 180 degrees in his fingers and held it against the slot. Throughout this process he kept a wary attention, as if inserting a thumb drive into his computer were in itself suspicious in the slightest.

He was no good at this cloak-and-dagger bullcrap.

Last chance to give up, he told himself, knowing there was already no going back.

He thrust against the faint resistance until the device settled. It came to life right away, the once dark circle on its body blinking blue. His computer showed no activity at all, but he knew the little device was hard at work burrowing into the hard drive, laying the groundwork to offer up free access to the company servers to—he didn't know exactly who, or even whether they were white hats or black hats. He didn't want to know. They could keep him safe. They were his last hope. That was all that mattered.

Too anxious to keep seated as the worm did its work, he stood and looked out through tinted floor-to-ceiling windows behind his chair. Even from the seventh floor, Acevedo Tower had a gorgeous view of downtown Boston, of the Custom House still illuminated in the predawn light, dividing the skyscrapers to the right and the dark water of the channel to the left. Little flurries of snow drifted against the window, and he laid his hand against the glass to feel the cold. If there was something he'd miss about this place, it was this view. That and—

"Hello, Dominic." He nearly jumped at the singsongy voice coming from behind him. "Goodness, I didn't mean to startle you!" Violet Zanger, carrying her enormous cat-pattern purse. "Silly me, I forgot my theater tickets for tonight at my desk. I was in the neighborhood and thought I'd swing by. I didn't think there'd be anyone in the office this early on a Saturday."

"Just finishing up some security updates." *Stupid. Stop looking guilty.* "You know how it is. Can't leave until that progress bar reaches one hundred percent."

"Well, don't exhaust yourself. It causes premature aging, you know."

"Don't worry, Violet. I'll take care. Should be going soon."

Her painted-on eyebrows screwed up in a frown of put-on concern. "You know, I've noticed that you've been looking very tired. Have you been getting enough sleep?"

"Been sleeping just fine, Violet," he said, jaw set in irritation.

"Maybe you need to go to the doctor. You know, I had this friend in college—now what was her name—"

"Violet," he interrupted through gritted teeth, "I'm sorry, but I really can't talk right now."

A puzzled expression came over her face, more, he thought, at his daring to interrupt her than any concern about his strange behavior. "What's going on with you, Dominic? I'm beginning to get very worried."

"I'm fine, okay? There's nothing here for you to worry about, so just go ahead and go home, have a nice weekend, and don't worry about me." He was nearly yelling by the end of it, the stress of the day leaking out in spite of him.

"Well okay then," she said with a phony beam. "You have a wonderful weekend. Make sure you get some rest. It really looks like you could use it."

"Will do, Violet. All right. Okay. Good-bye!"

He shouldn't have snapped at her. He shouldn't have let it affect him like this. She would know something was wrong when he didn't come in on Monday. He ran his fingers through his short black hair as he watched her waddle to the elevator.

He glanced down at the device. The blinking circle had turned into a steady, penetrating blue, announcing that its inscrutable work was done. Watson braced his trembling hand and pulled it out. He surveyed his desk with the awareness that it would be the last time. It occurred to him that it should feel more poignant than it really did. He wondered whether there was anything he would regret leaving behind and came up empty. Even from his apartment, all he had taken was a little more than an overnight's bag worth of stuff—basic necessities and nothing more. Nothing personal, nothing sentimental. There was nothing that he cared about.

He shut down his computer and stood, pushing in his chair. He straightened the stuff on his desk one last time, wondering whether they would scrutinize his calendar, the contents of his drawer, looking for any clue to his disappearance. By the time they did, he would be far away, never to return.

Duffel bag in hand, he walked toward the elevator, but his eyes were drawn to Andrea's cubicle, across the aisle from his. There was one thing about this place he would miss, after all. He thought about her flowing blond curls streaming down her back, now and then a precious peek at her profile, her delicate upturned nose, and her pouty lips. He remembered how often he would sneak a glance at her during the day as she worked. Now, standing at her empty desk, a whiff of her perfume still lingering, it gave him a pang to remember, and to think that he would not see her again. But maybe he could do something for her. Nothing definite, but maybe something that would allay the creeping guilt of bailing and leaving her behind.

He tore a page from a yellow legal pad from a nearby desk and, hunched over her chair, scrawled in black Sharpie:

GET OUT WHILE YOU STILL CAN—D

Below that, he wrote a phone number and then slipped the sheet into her top drawer.

That being done, Dom turned on his heels toward the elevator. Standing at his perennial station was the ancient security guard, always a friend, always there.

"Burt," he said, in terse greeting. Burt tipped his hat and preempted him in pushing the call button.

"Late one today, Mr. Watson?"

"You know it."

"Only three more weeks till spring. Maybe you should take that vacation when it comes. You're not looking so hot, if you don't mind my saying so."

"I hear you, Burt."

"The elevator on the left's been acting up for the last hour or so," he said. "They've got it shut down."

"Good thing we have two."

The elevator car reached the seventh floor with a soft electronic *ding*, and its doors rolled open. It sagged as Dom, thick with muscle and grit, stepped onto it. A monitor on the elevator wall played a commercial for men's deodorant as part of the usual endless loop of ads. He pushed the button for the lobby, and the last thing he saw as the doors closed was the name Acevedo International in metallic letters on the opposite wall, shrinking to *ceved*, then *eve*, and finally closing on that final *v*.

Expecting a momentary weightlessness of downward acceleration, he instead felt a weight on his feet as the elevator went up.

"Goddamn it," he said out loud. Something about this unnerved him. The elevator never moved up after being called up to a floor, only down—unless someone had pushed the button for the same floor inside, but in which case the call button wouldn't have gone dark when the elevator arrived. Did it? He couldn't remember.

"Get a grip," he said to himself, shaking his head.

Then something in the monitor caught his eye. The image had gone static. There was no ad, nothing except two words, stark white against a black background.

HELLO, DOMINIC.

"What the hell?" He rubbed his eyes and looked again. The text on the screen changed.

YOU THOUGHT YOU WOULD ESCAPE US?

He looked at the floor display. *9.* He pushed 10, 11, and 12. The elevator ran straight through to 13 and kept going. He pushed the button to open the door. Nothing happened. He tried the emergency button. Nothing.

BUT YOU CAN'T. NO ONE CAN.

He pushed all the buttons, open-palmed, getting as many as fast as he could. The elevator wouldn't stop its constant ascent. If anything—*could the elevator be going faster?* He picked up the emergency phone. Dead.

YOUR RECKONING HAS COME.

He banged on the elevator door. "Hey!" he called out. "Help! Get me out of here!"

GOOD-BYE.

The screen turned to a commercial for the new Sentra, making smooth turns on a snaking, picturesque road.

"Hey! Can someone hear me?"

The elevator was coming up on the twenty-first, the final floor. The counter hit 20, then 21. But the elevator kept moving.

And then it crashed, knocking Dominic off his feet. The light fixtures were knocked loose, left hanging by their wires. The cables groaned above him as the elevator jerked without moving.

Then something snapped, and the car went into free fall. Dom was lifted, weightless, off the floor, flailing for a handhold as he hurtled toward the bottom of the shaft.

Chapter 2

T he car lurched, and Dan Morgan braced himself against the trunk lid. A sliver of light filtered into the sweltering darkness where an accident had opened up a crack between the lid and the body of the decrepit old Dodge. Morgan looked out from time to time, but all he got was the alternating blue and green of sky and canopy.

It got old fast.

He blinked and slapped his face against the drowsiness that permeated him. Wiping sweat from his brow, he shifted his weight again, trying and again failing to avoid a bulge that had been digging into his back for the entire ride.

At the end of said ride would be Jorge Saavedra, head of the cartel that bore his name. Well, it was either that or violent death. The suspense made the ride that much more unpleasant.

Being stuck for two hours in the hot trunk of a car driving north out of Cartagena, Colombia, on a pothole-pocked highway, possibly on the way to his death, really gave a man time to think about his life choices.

Diana Bloch hailed him on his comm, a hidden, skin-toned plug that went in his ear that communicated with a transmitter hidden in a button on his khakis. The beep lasted about half a second, followed by her voice. "Checking in. We still have a lock on your position. The chopper's twenty miles behind you."

Morgan knocked twice on the car's metal frame, giving the wordless signal that he had understood the message. It was a bumpy ride, and no one inside the car would notice.

"Copy that."

He shifted his weight again and was wondering how much longer it would be when he felt the tug of deceleration, pulling him toward the seat back. He braced himself until the car came to a complete stop. A voice outside put him on high alert. Men argued in heated Spanish, too muffled for him to make out anything.

No more than a minute later, the trunk opened to a figure silhouetted against the harsh light of day. Fresh air poured in, fat lot of good that did on such a muggy, hot day.

Morgan squinted, and his eyes adjusted enough for him to make out a bored-looking uniformed policeman, whose eyes widened in surprise upon seeing him there, but glazed over again just as fast. He was getting paid not to make Morgan his problem, and he wasn't going to let curiosity get in the way of profit.

He slammed the trunk door down. Morgan's ears popped. With a word from the officer, the car was moving again.

It was about twenty minutes before Morgan felt the deceleration again, this time followed by a left turn onto a local road. The car halted, and Morgan heard the whir of the motor of an electric gate. The car eased forward with a rumble of tires moving over cobblestone before coming to a final stop. The car doors opened and then the trunk lid, and the first thing Morgan saw was the ugly mug of Paco Ruiz grinning down at him.

"We are here, *gringo*."

Morgan ignored the hand Paco held out and instead braced himself against the rim of the trunk to hop onto the cobblestone, pulling behind him the button-down shirt he'd brought along for the meeting. He stretched out his aching limbs, cracking his neck and taking a moment to survey their surroundings. The driveway made a wide circle by the side entrance to the Saavedra villa, at the end of a mile-long road from the outside gate. A field of coconut trees stretched to either side as far as the eye could see. The 1987 metallic-blue Chevy Silverado carrying the crate was parked behind them. The two men who had driven in it, plus the three others who were in the car— cocky young assholes, all tattoos, gold chains, and shaved heads— were joshing each other and laughing.

Morgan didn't get much of a look at the house, but he could tell that even for a mansion it was huge, all colonnades and white walls gleaming in the early morning sun, the best in contemporary-rustic taste that blood money could buy.

Paco showed his two gold teeth again. He had one of those faces that invited an uppercut to the jaw. "I hope the ride was not so bad."

"Beats flying coach."

Paco was a greasy bastard, hair slicked back, forehead pocked with beads of sweat, shirt with at least two more buttons undone than was necessary, baring a hairy chest. He wore his two custom pearl-handled Magnum .50 Cal Desert Eagles on side holsters, cowboy style. Never mind that it was maybe the most vulnerable way to carry a gun. It made him look *badass*.

"The boss takes his security very seriously. He does not want outsiders to know where he lives."

Of course, a bag over his head would've done the job. But Saavedra wanted to flex his muscles, showing that he was powerful enough that men would come to him in the trunk of a car if he demanded it. It was the first volley in their negotiations.

Two security guards in pastel suit jackets and tieless button-down shirts came out of a service entrance, one wielding a metal detector wand in one hand and a handy little appliance for detecting RF signals in the other. The detector was designed to sniff out bugs and happened to suffer from a fatal flaw: it couldn't detect anything that wasn't turned on. Pretending to scratch, Morgan clicked the button that held his transponder once to shut it off. His earpiece emitted a demoralized beep acknowledging the shutdown.

The guard scanned him with the wand first.

The wand warbled as it passed over his crotch. "Don't enjoy it too much." The guard made no sign that he'd understood. Next, he scanned Morgan with the RF detector, which didn't make a sound.

"*Está limpio.*"

"All right, Señor Bevelacqua," said the other guard. "Come with me please." To Paco: "*Tú también.*"

The guard ushered the two of them inside through the service entrance (another attempt to put Morgan in his place), past an industrial kitchen where women in hairnets plucked chickens and stirred vats of broth fragrant with spice to the sound of salsa music. They crossed a swinging door into a living room appointed with rustic hardwood furniture. A uniformed maid laid out a silver tray of coffee and water for them.

Excusing himself, Morgan ducked into a bathroom, where he

clicked the button again to turn on the radio transmitter. The earpiece chirped.

"Contact reestablished," came Bloch's voice. "Are you in Saavedra's compound?"

"I'm in." Morgan took off his T-shirt and wiped as much sweat as the fabric could handle from his hairy chest and his back.

"The chopper's holding, two minutes away. Let's try to avoid having to call it in."

"I'll do my best." He ran his fingers to straighten out his thick black hair and then along his mustache and goatee. Then he pulled the light blue button-down over his solid muscular frame. His pants still had a caramel-colored grease stain from the trunk of the car, but there was nothing to be done about that.

Morgan walked back out into the living room and sat in the worn leather safari chair. "*Muy guapo*," Paco said, then leaned forward and spoke in a conspiratorial whisper. "When we go in, don't forget that with Señor Saavedra the most important thing is to show respect. Avoid eye contact, don't raise your voice, and *por joder* don't laugh. If he thinks you disrespect him, they find both our skins nailed to a bus stop in Cartagena. I don't think that jaw would be so handsome if it was not attached to any bones."

Having made his point, Paco leaned back and whistled some damn song for the fifteen minutes it took a secretary to come and whisper in his ear. "Come on," he said. "Saavedra is ready to see us."

The secretary opened a set of rough-hewn doors to a spacious office whose broad bay windows opened up to a palm-framed sea, admitting the sound of the surf and the caws of seagulls outside. Flanked by two uniformed bodyguards was Saavedra, double-chinned, sporting a thick head of near-white hair and a mustache to match, in an eggshell suit over a light pink shirt and a bolo tie, sitting in a high-backed leather chair, his own little throne in his own little kingdom, sipping tequila from a whiskey glass.

He did not acknowledge Morgan. "*Quién es?*" he asked Paco instead.

"*El hombre de las armas, señor*," said Paco, head bowed in deference. They had an exchange in low tones, of which Morgan caught only a word here and there. Then Saavedra turned to face him.

"So, Señor Bevelacqua." He hit a palm against his desk with enthusiasm. "Please, please, *siéntate*."

Morgan sat on one of the wicker armchairs across the desk from the drug lord.

"Quite a mouthful, your name." Saavedra removed a hand-rolled cigarette from a case—silver inlaid with gold. "You say you have guns for me?"

Showtime. "I have a supplier in Eastern Europe sitting on a small mountain of hardware. I'm talking Kalashnikovs, submachine guns, handguns, RPGs, grenades." He counted off each one on his fingers as he listed them. "He's desperate to unload, which means I can get you a price on it nobody is going to beat."

Saavedra sat back on his chair with a creak and set two polished wingtips on the desk. "You have my attention."

"It's worth more than your attention. This is the offer of a lifetime. But there is a catch."

Saavedra lit the cigarette and took a deep drag. His voice went deep as he exhaled smoke. "Paco tells me you don't have a transporter."

"Not in the region, no. Building up those kinds of connections takes time I do not have."

Morgan tensed as he watched for Saavedra's reaction. The whole game pivoted on this point.

The cartel boss sipped at his tequila. "And what do you think I should do about it?"

He was trying to throw Morgan off with his skepticism, by asking questions he damn well knew the answer to. "What I told Paco. And I'm sure he told you. I'd like to arrange a meeting with your logistics people and work out a deal to get the guns into the country."

"Maybe we can do that, or maybe not." Saavedra was acting aloof, like a cat. "What have you got?"

Morgan looked at Paco and nodded toward Saavedra. Paco pulled a folded-up sheet of paper from his back pants pocket and smoothed it out with his hands on the desk. Then he slid it across to Saavedra.

"That's everything," Morgan said. "A full list."

Saavedra held up a pair of gold-framed reading glasses as he scanned its contents. Then he tossed it on his desk. "I'm interested in the rifles and the explosives. That is all."

"That's not a catalog," said Morgan, leaning forward in his chair and resting an elbow on the desk. "It's a package deal. All or nothing."

Saavedra stared back at Morgan with fire in his eyes. Paco squirmed at Morgan's defiance. He was a lackey. He would never understand. But Morgan knew what men like Saavedra respected.

The boss puffed at the cigarette without breaking eye contact. "You are wasting my time."

"I saw what your men carry," said Morgan. "Your close lieutenants might have their fancy weapons, but your foot soldiers carry junk. And I know the other cartels are champing at the bit to move into your territory. You need better hardware. You need what I have."

"I don't need anything." He sipped his tequila with one hand, waving a dismissive gesture with the cigarette. "Men who forget that live to regret it. What's your price?"

Morgan stood, wrote a figure down on the list with Saavedra's Mont Blanc, and slid it back across, leaning forward and resting his hands on the desk.

Saavedra laughed, his porcine face going red, his double chin going triple. He crossed out the figure and replaced it with another, closer to half what Morgan had proposed.

"No good," said Morgan. "I'd be better off going to the Sudanese warlords at this price."

Saavedra crossed it out again and pushed it up another twenty percent. "Final offer."

"I'll take that without the handguns."

Saavedra raised an eyebrow. "What about that package deal story?"

"You pay this, you don't get handguns. I'll take my chances trying to find another buyer for those."

"I don't like your bullshit, Señor Bevelacqua." He crossed out the figure and wrote one a quarter lower. "This is my price now."

Morgan balled his hand into a fist and cast a glance at the bodyguards trying to look tough with scowls on their faces. If he let that slide, Saavedra would own the negotiation and Morgan wouldn't get what he was really after: face time with his smuggler.

Saavedra's lips curled into a victorious sneer. This couldn't stand.

Morgan swept his hand across the desk, knocking the glass of tequila from the table, sending it flying to shatter on the floor along with a stack of papers and a crystal ashtray. Paco gasped. The bodyguards' hands moved to their holsters.

Saavedra held up a hand, and they backed down. "You play a dangerous game."

"Don't screw with me. You and I both know my initial offer was a bargain even undelivered. Now can we make a goddamn deal?"

The bodyguards watched Saavedra's hand. Outside, seagulls shrieked.

Saavedra lowered his arm and wrote a new figure. The highest one yet, some ten percent below asking. "Will this do then?"

Morgan sat down and crossed his legs. "I think we can do business."

Saavedra addressed one of his bodyguards. "*Llame el Señor White*." He then stood up, took another glass from a leather-bound tray on a buffet table and poured himself another drink. "If Señor Bevelacqua will kindly agree not to smash it, might I offer you a glass? It is very smooth. Goes down like honey." Saavedra puckered his lips for emphasis.

"Don't drink."

Saavedra shrugged. "Let us go and see these guns of yours."

Behind Morgan, the door creaked open. A man, wearing a gray tailored suit and tie, balding, so thin and bony that he gave the impression of having been stretched, bowed in deference to the big boss. "Señor Saavedra." American. Morgan studied his face, committing the features to memory.

"White. This is Bevelacqua. The man with the guns."

The suit turned to Morgan with a cheerful businesslike demeanor. "Mr. Bevelacqua. You can call me Mr. White."

This would be Acevedo International's point man for their gun-smuggling operation. If their intel was correct, he knew enough to bring the whole corporation down.

"I look forward to working together," Morgan said, shaking the man's hand. "We were just about to—"

A frantic knock reverberated from the office door. Saavedra motioned to one of the bodyguards, who opened it and admitted a younger man in shorts and a T-shirt. Deferential even to the body-guards, the man knew his place at the very bottom of the totem pole. He spoke into Saavedra's ear, and *el jefe* stood. "We have a situation outside." Then, he addressed Morgan. "Come. This may be instructive to you."

Saavedra led the procession out through a veranda and onto a manicured lawn. A commotion of cartel soldiers had gathered around a central point on the grass. As the party—Morgan, Paco, Saavedra, White, the bodyguards, and the messenger—approached, Morgan saw that it was a man, beaten to the point of missing teeth, held up by his armpits by two cartel enforcers. His face was a mess of blood, which had trickled down to soak the chest of his worn yellow T-shirt.

"Miguel here is a snitch," said Saavedra. "He has been reporting our activities to the government authorities. I lost a good shipment to his interference."

The man moaned in pain. With a twitch of Saavedra's hand, one of his men kicked Miguel in the gut. He fell to the ground, writhing in pain, too beaten down to offer any resistance.

"Tell me, Mr. Bevelacqua. You are a tough man. What should I do with him?"

Morgan didn't respond. He looked at the face of the doomed son of a bitch. He was young, with a wisp of beard that wasn't done growing in, and not enough life lived to meet an end like this. Here was a brave man dealt a bad hand. Caught between justice and the cartel, he chose justice. And now he was going to pay.

Morgan knew what was about to happen. He knew he was powerless to stop it, even if he tried.

"You know how to deal with a rat."

Saavedra nodded. "That I do," he said. Then: "Elvis."

A man stepped forward. A man with dead eyes. Morgan could tell right away there was something off about him. He had seen his kind before. The kind of man who had no ambition, no pleasure in his life but to inflict pain on others.

Someone handed him a machete. Miguel caught sight of it, his eyes widening in fear. He tensed and squirmed, but the two gorillas held firm and pulled him along, the entire company of onlookers moving after them like a crowd of jeering chimpanzees. The men pushed Miguel's head and neck down against a tree stump bearing the gashes of countless strikes of the blade. One put his boot on his head so that he couldn't move, but had a clear view of Elvis making his practice swings with the machete, making a show of feeling its balance as if he were a goddamn martial artist. Miguel gurgled in desperation.

Morgan couldn't look away—Saavedra would be watching him carefully. He tamped down the anger that was growing inside.

Elvis stepped forward, and Miguel emitted wretched animal sounds. Legs apart like a golfer's stance, Elvis held the machete two-handed over his head. The blade glinted in the hot sun. The bastard was taking his time, enjoying the moment.

Then he swung, metal hitting flesh and bone. Not even close to a clean cut, the blade was no more than a quarter of the way in. Miguel's desperate cries turned to a bawling shriek as Elvis pulled out with a spurt of blood and swung the machete again and again. It took five or six swings to sever Miguel's spinal cord, silencing him, and as much again to do the butcher work of hewing the head free of the body.

Elvis picked up the head by the hair and raised it, beaming like a child during show-and-tell. The crowd whooped and jeered. Paco looked bored. White maintained a façade of professionalism through-out. Saavedra had the nonchalance of an aristocrat at a gladiatorial game.

Elvis carried off the severed head while two of the lackeys dragged the body behind him. The remains would be mutilated and displayed in Miguel's hometown as a warning. Maybe along with his family's.

Morgan's nostrils flared as he tried to contain his rage. He looked down to see that blood had spattered on his boots.

"Now," said Saavedra, "I was told you had a sample to show me."

Morgan shook off all emotion. It was time to get to work. Their party, along with three of the younger men and the two bodyguards, walked across the lawn to the driveway where they had left the old Dodge and the pickup truck.

The three men pulled the crate off the pickup truck, holding it by its rope handles. They strained and grunted at the weight of the thing and set it down, too hard, on the cobblestones.

"*Cuidado!*" Paco yelled.

He took a crowbar from the backseat of the Silverado and pried open the crate with a crack of the wood. After the men pulled off the lid, Paco swept aside the packing straw. Underneath was a neat row of black AN-94 rifles—Russian military standard, confiscated from an arms dealer two months before. Under Paco's instruction, the men removed the top rack, which held the rifles, and placed it on the driveway next to the box.

One of the men took a rifle to inspect it. White did the same with another. Saavedra just watched.

"You got these in," he said to Morgan. "Why do you need my guy?"

"Cost too much, risked too much," said Morgan. "And that's just for this one crate. I can't get the entire shipment in by myself."

"This is crap," said White, tossing the rifle to clatter on the cobblestones. "Third-world knockoffs. If this is what you're looking for, I can get you the same for half the price."

Morgan glowered at him. It was bullshit—he knew these were the real deal, and far better than what Saavedra's foot soldiers were used to. The asshole was sabotaging the deal. And if Saavedra had no more use for Morgan—

Saavedra looked to Morgan, questioning. "This is quality hardware," said Morgan, without taking his eyes off White. "He doesn't want competition."

"This is good stuff," Paco broke in, and then spoke in frantic Spanish until Saavedra held up one hand and looked at his other man, who was inspecting a rifle, for his opinion.

"*Es bueno*," the man said.

"My man says they're good," Saavedra said.

"Señor Saavedra," said White, "could we speak in confidence for a moment?"

Saavedra motioned for White to follow him down a small path toward a set of wrought iron chairs under a sprawling Mexican elm.

Goddamn it. The Acevedo bastard didn't bite. He was going to blow the whole deal. Morgan kept an eye on Saavedra's reactions as White spoke.

"What's happening?" asked Bloch through the comm.

"What do you think Saavedra and White are talking about over there?" Morgan asked Paco, for Bloch's benefit.

"Maybe they are negotiating terms for transporting the guns."

Idiot. White was speaking, a hand on Saavedra's shoulder, and the drug lord was nodding. "No. That is the sight of us losing this deal."

"You don't know that," Paco insisted.

"Steady," said Bloch. "We're not getting Acevedo this time, but you can still ID this Mr. White for us. It's progress."

Yeah. Progress.

Morgan looked at the drying blood on his boots. He couldn't get the image of the dying kid, Miguel, out of his head. He was hardly much older than Morgan's daughter Alex, come to think of it. Twenty, maybe twenty-one. Probably had a similar headstrong idealism, too.

Saavedra and White returned from their little conference. White shot him a self-satisfied smirk.

"Señor Bevelacqua," said Saavedra. "Your offer is appreciated, but we do not have a deal. I apologize for making you come all the way here. I will have my men put your sample back on the truck."

"Keep it," said Morgan.

He would survive, at least. Whatever White offered him, Saavedra needed Morgan alive if he was to be a bargaining chip with Acevedo.

"Just get out of there, Morgan," said Bloch.

Paco was still pleading with Saavedra, the idiot. Morgan's eyes were drawn to the tree stump, some fifty yards away, where Miguel had lost his head. A maid had brought a hose and was now washing away the blood, as if it were nothing more than a spilled drink. Morgan turned back to the smug, tranquil face of Saavedra and then cast his eyes down to his blood-spattered boots.

Paco was bent over the crate, nestling the F1 grenades to make room to repack the rifles, the pearl handles of his Desert Eagles sticking out on their hip holsters.

Oh, hell.

Morgan grabbed the two guns, pulling them from their holsters. He undid the safety with a flick and, before anyone had any time to react, opened fire.

Chapter 3

The IMI Desert Eagle Mark XIX is among the most powerful semiautomatic handguns money can buy. Paco's particular ten-inch variant carried eight .44 Magnum rounds each. Its extra-long triangular barrel makes it an iconic gun, popular in movies and video games and, as a result, among idiots like Paco.

It packed a hell of a punch.

Morgan took out the bodyguards first, one shot each, close range to the head—he couldn't miss at this distance. Then he turned the twin hand cannons to the other armed enforcers, six shots fired, three men down, too fast for anyone to do anything about it.

As for Paco, Morgan settled for breaking his leg with a well-placed downward kick to his knee.

White ran off into the house. Much as he might want to, Morgan wasn't about to shoot him down in cold blood. He could still be useful.

That left Saavedra, frozen in place.

"Need backup!"

The gunfire drew others from the house. Men with AK-47s, coming out to the veranda.

"Morgan, report!" said Bloch.

Morgan discarded the gun from his left hand and grabbed Saavedra by the collar, holding him hostage with the remaining semiautomatic in his right—four rounds left against the small squadron of gunmen that was approaching. Morgan counted eight, and more emerging from the house.

"Stay back or *el jefe* gets it!" Morgan called out. He didn't know whether any of them spoke English, but the Desert Eagle pressed against the boss's temple seemed to be getting the message across just fine.

Of course, this still didn't put him in a *great* position.

"You will die," Saavedra hissed.

The men were creeping forward, all eager to save the boss and just as scared of putting a bullet through his skull by mistake. Through his peripheral vision, Morgan felt them flanking him. He could only hold the stalemate for so long.

"Back! Move back!"

"Chopper's on its way," said Bloch. "Hold tight."

What he needed was time. Morgan inched forward, prodding Saavedra toward the crate of weapons.

"Back!" he screamed against the small army gathered around him. Sweat trickled down his forehead and from the back of his neck under his shirt. He pulled on Saavedra's collar. "Tell them to move back."

"Screw you."

Morgan knelt before the crate, yanking Saavedra down with him. Nine pairs of eyes were on him, eighteen hands gripping their weapons. The only sound was Paco moaning in pain on the ground.

Releasing Saavedra's lapel, Morgan reached in and drew out one of the lemon-shaped grenades. The cartel lackeys tensed up, raising their rifles. He stood, pulling Saavedra along with him.

Here goes.

He pulled the pin and released the grenade back into the crate with its twenty-three brothers. It seemed to fall in slow motion. For a split second, there was no reaction at all. But before the grenade had covered half the distance to the crate, some of the men were turning around to hightail it while the most loyal or reckless lunged forward to help the boss.

Morgan took two steps back and kicked Saavedra in the spine, forcing him to stumble forward, against the crate. Then Morgan spun around and darted like hell in the opposite direction.

Gunfire cracked as bullets whizzed past him, and then yells to watch out for Saavedra. Counting off the five seconds to detonation, Morgan ran as far as he could and dove headfirst onto the grass behind an ornamental stone.

Then came the fireworks. An eruption of death and mayhem.

Feeling the wave of heat pass, Morgan didn't even turn to look at the damage. He just ran, feet pounding the grass, now scarred with grenade fragments. Ears ringing and legs unstable, he dashed into the vast field of coconut trees.

After a three-second lag, renewed gunfire. Others were coming out of the house, drawn by the explosion. A Jeep packed with security guards was driving in from the gate.

Morgan stumbled. He had misjudged how competent he was to run—the blast had compromised his balance. He lost and regained stability only to step on a coconut, which sent him flying to the ground, kissing the grass.

Saavedra's men surrounded him. He waited for the bullet that would kill him, but instead what came was a kick to the gut and another to the face. Morgan spit blood. Four heavy arms picked him up and dragged him back.

Morgan surveyed the scene of destruction as they passed. The driveway was riddled with bodies around the blackened bloom of soot radiating from the splintered crate. One belonged to the poor bastard Paco, unable to run away with his broken leg. The Dodge and the pickup truck had caught a hail of shrapnel and were as torn up as any of the corpses except for one.

Saavedra. There wasn't much left of him.

They hauled Morgan all the way to the bloody stump where Miguel had lost his head. Elvis, Morgan was less than thrilled to see, had survived the explosion, with a couple of nasty cuts on the right side of his face. He was already standing by the chopping block, brandishing the machete that was to cut his head off.

Morgan knew the drill.

They kicked the back of his knees and forced his head against the stump. A heavy boot came down on his temple, sodden with blood and dirt, to hold him in place.

Elvis came forward, the rage in his eyes not quite eclipsing the relish he had in the prospect of his second beheading of the day. A short stride at a time, running a finger against the cutting edge of the machete, he approached until all Morgan could see were his hairy, blood-spattered shins.

"*Adiós, gringo,*" he said, raising the blade.

And then Elvis's head erupted in a mist of blood and brains.

Morgan had to admit, Diesel was one hell of a shot.

The boot came off Morgan's head as the men scattered, looking for the source of the bullet. Morgan ran low as the chopper burst onto the scene and Bishop rained beautiful death from the sky from the side-mounted M60D heavy machine gun. Crouching next to him, Diesel loosed single shots from his custom H&K PSG1 Precision Rifle, a surgical counterpart to Bishop's hack-and-slash approach.

The two other members of the tac team rappelled down, providing covering fire as Morgan ran, head low, toward the chopper. As he came closer, he made out Spartan's more slender outline to his right, made bulkier by her Kevlar vest, her close-cropped blond hair hidden by her black ballistic helmet. To Morgan's left was Tango, thickset, face painted with black streaks, gritted white teeth showing through a grin as he shook with the recoil of his Colt M4 Carbine.

"I have to hand it to you," said Spartan, between three-round bursts from her FN SCAR MK 17, "nobody raises hell quite like you do."

The landing skids of the UH-72 Lakota touched down on the grass, the scream of the rotors punctuated by cracks of gunfire. Bishop held out his hand, and Morgan, wincing against the wind whipped up by the blades, took it and hopped onto the corrugated metal floor. He held onto an overhead strap as Tango and Spartan boarded after him. They lifted off, Bishop spraying bullets at the handful of men who were still shooting at them from behind the carcasses of the cars. Within a few seconds, the chopper was out of range.

They circled around and flew north over the Caribbean Sea as a thin billow of smoke still rose from the mansion, leaving the world one drug kingpin lighter.

Chapter 4

Alex Morgan opened her eyes and was assaulted by the light glaring in through the unfamiliar window. She screwed her eyes and blinked, trying to get her vision to functional sharpness, but everything remained blurry and her eyelids seemed to stick together. Her head pounded, and her breath was absolutely heinous.

Hangovers. She was still getting the hang of those.

She shivered and noticed she had no shirt on. Only then did she feel the bulky presence boxing her in against the wall, emitting faint wheezy snores.

Oh, right.

Alex felt an immediate desire to get the hell out. Normally she'd be able to get up and out without as much as a creak of the bedsprings, but the blue fiberglass cast on her right leg wasn't helping. She'd have to wake him up.

At least she still had her pants on.

She pulled up the sheets to cover her bare chest. "Hey," she stage-whispered. "Hey, Devin."

He stirred and mumbled, but gave no sign of waking.

"Devin, wake up," she said in her normal speaking voice.

He opened his dark brown eyes, startled, and smacked his lips. He turned his head to look at her and smiled, crinkling his half-closed eyes.

Damn it.

"Good morning," he said, meaning it just a little too much for her taste.

"Hi," she said, tipping cheeriness into the word to the point of saturation, avoiding, she hoped, any hint of sexiness.

He stretched his arms, yawning, and stroked her hair, curling the frayed tips between his fingers. "That was amazing last night. I've never been with anyone so . . . *passionate*."

"Ha. Right," she said. "Yeah, I haven't—yeah."

He leaned in to kiss her, mashing his lips against hers, morning breath and all. Nausea rose in her stomach and Alex had to hold back vomit. She lay a hand on his chest. "Listen, I really should get going."

"Oh." Disappointment was palpable in his puppy-dog blue eyes.

"I just really need to get to the library at some point today, and with this thing"—she motioned toward the cast that enveloped her leg with a nod of the head—"it can kind of take a while."

"Sure, okay." He got up off the creaky bed and stood as far away as he could in the cramped bedroom, flat against his dresser. Inching her bad leg over the side of the bed, she sat up, holding onto the sheet covering her chest.

"Could you . . . ?" She indicated the door with her eyes.

"Come on. It's not like I haven't seen it already."

"It doesn't mean you get to see it again."

He shuffled out into the hallway in his boxers, closing the door behind him.

She fell back on the bed, exhaling in exasperation. From the ceiling, a banner depicting the creepy baby from *Family Guy* leered down at her.

As a junior, Devin had a right to a single room, which he had decorated floor to ceiling with posters paying homage to various TV shows and bands as well as to the concept of drinking. She scanned the floor among the many shirts and Bermuda shorts for her shirt and bra, diminutive, vanishing next to his enormous dirty shirts and pants. Finding both at the foot of the bed, she stretched her arm, nearly toppling to the floor in the process. She clasped her bra and pulled on her shirt. She adjusted the bobby pins in her hair, which kept her bangs, long overdue for a trim, out of her eyes. Next were her crutches, resting against the footboard. Everything ached as she hoisted herself to her feet.

She opened the door to find him waiting just outside. He held it for her as she came out into the hallway of his dorm, all fluorescent lights and ratty blue carpeting. She paused to say good-bye, and he leaned in for a kiss. She didn't have the energy to stop him, but when he tried for tongue, she kept her lips sealed.

"I'll text you, I guess," he said.

"Sure," she said, packing in as little enthusiasm as she could manage. "Why not?"

She turned around and walked down the hallway without looking back, passing a jaded junior girl in her towel, headed for the bathroom with toothbrush in hand. With her limp, Alex's fifty-foot toddle to the elevator seemed interminable. At least her own dorm, Prather House, was right across the quad. The walk of shame would be a short one.

She never heard him close the door. He must have watched her until she disappeared into the elevator.

Alex cast a guilty glance at the fresh fruit that made up her breakfasts in the beginning of the fall semester, back before she had broken her leg. On this day, she loaded up on bacon and pancakes, acutely aware of the tightness in the waist of her pants. Healthy living seemed like another life for her. She took her tray to the tables, where she spotted her roommate, Katie, sitting alone with a bowl of Frosted Mini-Wheats and a cup of diet cola, clad in her usual yellow sweatpants–Springhaven University hoodie combo, wild brown hair reined in by a pink headband. She waved her spoon in the air when she saw Alex, sending droplets of milk flying at a passing girl who looked down at her and scowled. Alex set her tray down and began the laborious task of lowering herself onto her seat.

"A little birdie told me you disappeared with Devin Monroe last night." Of course, Katie somehow would have heard about it already.

"All we did was make out." She played with a slice of crispy bacon on her plate, running it along the syrup.

"Yeah right, you slut." Katie said the word with sibilant relish. She shoveled a spoonful of cereal into her mouth, milk dribbling down her chin, and spoke with her mouth full. "So, how was it? Juicy details now, please."

Alex didn't bother to argue. "It was . . . *meh*."

Katie swallowed through her indignation. "I *cannot* believe you, Alex Morgan. Do you know how many girls would kill—*kill*—to hop into the sack with the star pitcher of the Springhaven baseball team? I mean, those arms." She emitted a sort of shudder-groan.

"He's kind of a . . . sloppy kisser." Alex felt the heat bloom on her cheeks as she blushed. "And he didn't really seem to know what he was doing. He would take his—"

She was interrupted by the clatter of a tray being set down next to Katie's. A skinny, smooth-faced boy in a plaid button-down open over a plain white T-shirt, the standard uniform for suburban alt kids.

Simon Burczyk. Sweet, innocent, and head over heels in love with Alex.

"Am I interrupting anything?"

"Alex was just telling us about her scandalous escapades in a young gentleman's bed last night." Katie somehow always knew the exact wrong thing to say.

"Oh?" said Simon. "Do tell." His voice quavered.

Alex's stare burned on Katie's face. Not that Katie even noticed. "Ugh," Alex said. "It was nothing. Total mistake."

"Two hundred pounds of pure lean man meat of a mistake."

"It's really none of my business," said Simon.

Alex was desperate to change the subject. "Are you ready to work after breakfast?"

"What's this about work?" said Katie with a yawn. "It's Saturday morning."

"Simon's teaching me some basic programming."

"How nice of him," Katie said with a theatrical nudge and wink. "Are you making it worth his while?"

Alex was about to make a rude comment when she was interrupted by a beep of her phone. She checked—e-mail. From her adviser Dr. Strimling, a motherly, soft-spoken humanities professor. It was her third message to Alex about her grades. Alex had opened none of them but made an educated guess that the problem was definitely not that they were too high.

She deleted the e-mail, unopened.

"Katie," Alex said. "Shut up."

Chapter 5

Lisa Frieze woke up with her head against the fiberboard surface kitchen table again, snuggled up to a half-eaten box of General Tso's Chicken, one-quarter of a wineglass of cheap chardonnay, and her laptop, fully drained of battery life.

She picked up her cell phone, which was at two percent, and found through squinting eyes a missed call from—

"Peter," she whispered to herself.

She hated herself a little bit for the fluttering heartbeat, her eagerness in looking at the time stamp—6:57 that morning. It was now just past 10 A.M.

Most of that, she reminded herself, was the loneliness of moving to a new city. She had no friends, not even any acquaintances in Boston outside of work, excepting the ever-elusive Peter Conley. Online dating was too much work for too little reward, and hookup apps were plain depressing.

How does an adult make friends in a new city anyway?

She stood up with a grunt, rubbing her temples, and made a point not to respond to the missed call before taking a shower, which did its intended work of reviving her. She towel-dried her hair in front of the mirror, working its loose auburn curls with her hand, trying to get it into some kind of shape that worked with her big nose, her bony, angular face, before giving up, giving it a shake, and letting it do what it would. She held her gaze on the mirror, now touching her fingers to the shrapnel scars on her left shoulder. The ache still smoldered deep when it was cold, but the memories had finally faded to the point where the anxiety was more like an unwelcome dinner guest than a growling tiger. Then, her bare skin tingling in a cold draft, she rooted through the boxes still scattered around her one-bedroom apartment for the day's clothes.

Some foreshortening illusion made it hard for the fact that she'd already been there a month to sink in, and that she should have enough shame to finally unpack the boxes and get some damn furniture other than the flimsy kitchen table and single, nonmatching chair she'd picked up for thirty bucks (for the pair) at a yard sale. She hadn't even unboxed her kitchen supplies, which meant she was already on friendly terms with all the area's delivery boys. She *had* meant to cook the night before. Instead, she distracted herself with work and ended up calling Hunan Garden for the fifth time in as many days.

All she was missing to complete the pathetic tableau was a cat.

Okay, she thought to herself once she had pulled on her graphite wool pants and blue button-down top. It'd been long enough to convince herself that she was not desperate. She pulled the chair (the one) to the corner of the living room where her phone was plugged into the wall and returned his call.

"Lisa," he said in greeting. "Thanks for getting back to me so quickly."

The smarmy son of a bitch. "Hey, Peter. Been a while."

"Yeah, it really has." She tapped her bare foot on the tile floor. *That's right, squirm in the awkwardness.* "Lisa, I know you must be busy, so I'll get right to the point. I need your help."

She picked at the chipping paint on the wall. "Peter Conley waits until he needs something to call you back. Big surprise."

"I wouldn't be calling if it wasn't—"

"Oh, oh, let me guess," she said with feigned enthusiasm. She reclined against the chair and stretched her free arm. "It's critical, national security, yadda yadda yadda. It could be pivotal in an investigation of—what is it this time? Nuclear weapon? Bioagent? Nerve gas? I don't care. *It's not my problem.*"

"Lisa, I—"

"Don't *Lisa* me. Our entire relationship consists of me doing favors for you, and I'm sick of it."

"But—"

She stood, yanking the power cord out of the phone. She was on a roll now. "Do you understand that my FBI salary doesn't begin to cover this? And I can't take money from you because that would be graft, although God knows I'm already plenty screwed if anyone finds out I've been feeding a clandestine intelligence outfit information for the better part of six months."

"I know you—"

"And I'll have you know that I have things to do. I have a rich, fulfilling life where there's no place for me to keep waiting around for you to call. I have plenty enough going on that has nothing to do with you in the slightest bit. Now will you please just tell me what the hell you want?"

She was left panting by her long tirade. Conley didn't miss a beat.

"A man called Dominic Watson."

She wasn't going to give him the satisfaction of being less quick on the uptake than him. "Doesn't ring a bell. Friend of yours?"

"Corpse. Took a free fall in an elevator at Acevedo Tower yesterday."

"Huh. Doesn't live up to your usual level of insanity."

"Does the prospect of a mysterious deadly conspiracy do anything for you?"

Lisa Frieze looked at the unpacked boxes, the remnants of Chinese food and wine for one. Not like there was anything else going on in her life. "All right, where do I meet you?"

Acevedo Tower. Twenty-one stories of steel and mirrored glass on the corner of Congress and Water, displaying the name of the company in white six-foot letters to the heart of Boston. Frieze found Conley smoking a cigarette, bundled in a parka and leaning against one of the steel and glass pillars that lined the entrance of the building, all six-foot-seven of him, his long, masculine face, strong nose and a jawline sculpted for Hollywood. She couldn't suppress the quiver of attraction in her gut as she laid eyes on him. He waited for her to initiate the greeting with an almost cocky schoolboy aloofness.

She walked straight past him, up the steps that led to the lobby door.

"Hey!" he called out.

"Try to keep up."

He ran up the steps at a jog. "Thanks for coming. I really owe you one."

"You owe me several," she said, without breaking stride. "But who's counting?" She pushed the revolving door to emerge into the warmth of the spacious lobby. Sunlight filtered through the tinted glass, falling on dark blue carpeting, gray patterned panels on the walls and assorted potted palms, which somehow made it even blander than the local FBI office. Yellow police tape cordoned off the two elevators beyond the front desk.

She flashed her badge at the receptionist. "Lisa Frieze, FBI. This guy's with me. Special consultant." Conley handed over whatever fake ID he was using. "I'm here about the elevator accident."

"I'm going to need to call it in," said the young receptionist, picking up a telephone receiver. As she waited for the person on the other end, she said to Conley, smiling just a little too much, "Consultant to the FBI, huh? Must be exciting."

This grated on Lisa.

The girl exchanged a few words with her supervisor, entered their information into the system, and gave each a badge for the turnstile.

Guarding the crime scene was a single square-faced policeman, sitting on a borrowed office chair sipping on a cup of cheap coffee and reading a copy of the *Globe*. Frieze approached with Conley in tow.

"Take the stairs," he said, without looking up from his paper. "Elevator's out."

Frieze cleared her throat. The policeman looked up from his paper, and his pupils dilated when he read the three prominent capital letters on Frieze's ID.

"Lisa Frieze. This is Peter Morris. He's a special consultant."

"Officer Prezelin," he said, fumbling to stash the newspaper under the chair. "I didn't know this case had gone federal."

"I came on a strictly informal basis. Hopefully we can agree that, officially, I was never here."

"Yes, yes, of course. Don't worry about it." Knowing she wasn't supposed to be there relaxed him and gave him the attitude of a co-conspirator. "Is this here more than an accident?"

"I don't know any more than you do. Where's everyone else?"

"Pretty much done. Seemed open and shut, and to be honest nobody was too excited to stick around on a Saturday morning. I'm just waiting for the paperwork to come through so I can release the scene. They've called for cleanup already. I think I heard someone say they're coming early in the afternoon."

Conley broke in, "Are you the only one on the premises?"

"From the precinct. But there's a technician from the elevator company looking at the machinery on the roof."

Lisa punched Conley in the arm. "Ready to leg it up twenty-one stories?"

Grateful that she'd opted for flats, Frieze pounded the concrete, every step amplified and echoing in the endless stairwell. She was pleased to realize that she was in better shape than Conley and would climb just fast enough so that he had to catch up at every landing. Nice to have him chasing her for a change.

They met the technician coming down, between the tenth and eleventh floors. He was fat, maybe forty-five, and balding, sporting a thick gray mustache. He had on a heavy gray jumpsuit with a logo embroidered on it—Hornig Elevators.

Frieze showed him her badge. "I'd like to ask you a couple of questions. What's your name?"

"Upshaw." He had a gruff, raspy voice. "Ask your questions while we walk. I got places to be."

He walked faster than she'd have guessed given his figure, and they had to struggle to keep up and talk at the same time. "What did you find?"

"Elevator went up all the way and the motor didn't stop. Just kept on pulling until the cables snapped."

"What about the emergency brakes?" Conley asked.

"They never deployed. Straight drop down from the top floor."

"I thought they were mechanical. You know, automatic, going off if the elevator hits a certain speed."

"That's how it's supposed to work," Upshaw said.

"So it didn't?" asked Frieze. "What happened?"

"Look, that elevator down there is a big twisted pile of scrap metal. One look ain't enough for me to tell you what happened there. But I'll tell you one thing. Whatever made that elevator act all wonky in the first place, it wasn't mechanical."

"Oh?" said Frieze.

"I tested the motor, couldn't reproduce the error. It stopped every time the program told it to."

"So the problem is the software?" she said.

"That'd be my guess. The computer folks should be going over the electronic records now."

"Could we get a copy of those records?"

"You'll have to check with the boss. They tend to be pretty territorial about what they show anyone, so I wouldn't be surprised if they asked for a warrant. But call 'em up. You never know."

"Mind if I take your card?" Lisa asked.

Upshaw stopped at the landing on the fifth floor. He reached into his pocket and handed her a business card with a greasy, sweaty hand.

They parted ways at the lobby, the technician moving off toward the exit while Conley and Frieze hung back.

He was all business. "If we go over there soon maybe we can—"

"No, you can do that yourself," she said. Man, it felt good saying no to him. "I need to go if I want to keep my job."

"They won't talk to me." He laid his knobby, masculine hand on her shoulder. "Not without you."

She shoved his hand away. "Tell you what. I'll call Hornig from the road and see what I can do."

She turned her back on him.

"Where are you going?"

"To do my job." She dropped her card at the turnstile and walked out into the street.

Chapter 6

"This is a debriefing session for operation number 1032A-3. Subject is Daniel Morgan, code name Cobra, internal designation AZ27-F. Speaking is Diana Bloch, AZ04-D. At my side are Paul Kirby, AZ43-I, and code name Smith, AA-004."

Clear, crisp, and professional, Diana Bloch rattled off the information, pretending to look at a script even though Morgan knew she needed no prompting. The prim head honcho of Zeta Division, brown hair in an impeccable bun, neutral makeup on a face set in neutral professionalism, in a classic silk blouse and pearl earrings, sat review-panel style between two others. On her left was Paul Kirby, his back so straight that a broomstick might have run all the way from the chair to his oversized oval head. His chin was raised and his weasel face was at a slight angle, giving him an air of insufferable smugness. To her right was Smith, the inscrutable, with his fastidious short hair, his blank façade, in his trademark black suit, hands lightly clasped on the table. From the far corner of the tiny interrogation room, a camcorder on a tripod recorded him at a three-quarter angle.

"Could we turn down the heat?" said Morgan. The air inside Zeta headquarters felt like a midsummer day. He ran his hands over his still-wet hair from the shower. He'd carried the grime from the Saavedra compound through the airlift all the way here, so they let him bathe in the Zeta gym and pull on a fresh T-shirt and jeans he kept in his locker before the session.

"Surprising as it may seem, the thought had crossed our minds," said Kirby in his usual pissy-polite tone. His forehead, extended by a receding hairline, was glistening with sweat.

"There's some problem with the regulating software," said Bloch.

"Shepard's looking into it. Now, if you don't have any further objections, shall we start?" Morgan nodded in assent. "The purpose of the mission was to gain the trust of Francisco Ruiz, also known as Paco, in order to make contact with the Saavedra cartel, to in turn find their connection in Acevedo International, suspected of involvement in smuggling weapons into and drugs out of Colombia."

"Agent Morgan," said Smith, "please relate the events that transpired yesterday, from last night until your airlift from the Saavedra compound this morning."

Morgan told the story with no interruptions but the occasional request for clarification from Bloch or Kirby. Smith didn't speak at all.

At least until Morgan got to the good part.

"I drew Paco Ruiz's sidearms and shot Saavedra's armed bodyguards."

"And why did you do that, Agent Morgan?"

"The op was blown," he said. "Saavedra was having me sent away, possibly to kill me. I saw an opening, and I took it."

Kirby interjected. "We had the tactical team at the ready to extract you at the first sign of danger. We could have used the connections and information gleaned from this operation to find out more about this Mr."—he looked at his notes—"White. Instead, we lost our only promising thread in this investigation." He looked at Morgan for a response with all the smug superiority of a schoolmarm facing a child caught misbehaving.

"Saavedra is dead, and so is his cartel," said Morgan.

"And another will rise to take its place," said Bloch. "Meanwhile, the Acevedo operator is still at large."

"Do you realize," said Kirby, "that not only does this sever our best lead to connect Acevedo with their arms dealings, but that they now realize that someone is after them? Worse, that someone at Acevedo now knows what you look like?"

Morgan bristled. The heat in the room was suffocating. "It all looks so clear from behind your desk, doesn't it, Kirby? Ever wonder what it's like on the ground?"

Kirby scoffed. "Don't pretend this was a tactical decision. Why—"

"You have no idea—"

Kirby raised his voice. "You are a professional, and you made a decision—"

"—a decision that ended a bloody criminal—"

"Tell us why you did it, Morgan."

"*Because the son of a bitch deserved to die!*"

Morgan gritted his teeth and clenched his fists. Wrong thing to say.

"I think I've heard enough," Smith said. Then, to Bloch: "I want the full report by morning." He stood up and walked out without saying a word.

Kirby held a tight-lipped sneer as Morgan finished his report and stood, collecting his notes. "I'm going to bring up a list of Acevedo employees and associates. Report to the War Room when you're done, Morgan. Let's see if we can't ID your Mr. White."

Bloch motioned for Morgan to stay behind as Kirby cleared the door. She clicked off the camera.

"What were you thinking?" she demanded.

Morgan leaned against the glass. "I couldn't let him get away with it."

She banged her hand against the table. "There is a chain of command. When you subvert it, you put the mission and everyone's lives in danger."

He raised an eyebrow. "No one on our side died, last time I checked."

"You are my weapon." Her voice was sharp, ice-cold steel. "You're here to do as you're told."

"I made a judgment call—"

"You disobeyed a direct order. Rabid dogs are put down. Remember that."

He pushed himself off the wall. Fully upright, he loomed almost a full head over her fragile frame. "Is that a threat?"

Bloch stepped forward, undaunted. Her thin nostrils flared in anger. "It's a statement of fact. We do not work for the US government. We are a clandestine operation, accountable to no authority but a group of anonymous financial backers. It won't come from me and it may not come from Smith, but there are higher powers at work here. If the day comes when their patience runs out, neither of us will be able to do anything to stop it."

Chapter 7

Morgan pulled into the driveway of his two-story ranch-style home after 9 P.M. The suburb of Andover, Massachusetts, was fast asleep. The full moon gave the snowy nighttime scene a sense of unreality, sharpened by the contrast with the carnage he'd witnessed not twenty-four hours before.

The search for Mr. White among the Acevedo employee records had yielded nothing. Kirby said he'd have the analysts look into it and sent him home.

Morgan shut off the engine of his red 1970 Oldsmobile 442 as the garage door ground shut. He squeezed past the boxes that read ALEX on the sides. From the kitchen door came the muffled barks of their German shepherd, Neika. He opened the door and she squirmed through, tail wagging, to sniff and lick at his hand.

"Hey, girl," he said, running his hand through her soft fur. "Did you take care of your mother while I was away?"

She snorted and whined with delight.

Morgan called her in to the dark kitchen and locked the door, resetting the alarms and leaving his heavy coat on the rack. Everything was still, illuminated by moonlight filtering in through the window—the tan striped wallpaper, the white cabinets, the copper pots and pans hanging on the walls. On the black granite countertop, nothing was an inch out of place. He felt his muscles relaxing, knots unwinding, breath growing slower and deeper.

Home. He was home.

He wondered, as he trudged up the stairs, whether Jenny was out, or already asleep. When he reached the upstairs hall, he saw soft light peeking from under the door to his bedroom. He turned the knob and walked inside.

Jenny was on the bed. Not out, and definitely not asleep. She was reclining on the pillows propped up against the backboard, a black negligee and sheer stockings suggesting the outlines of her soft, well-toned body. Morgan's gaze followed the curve of her waist, the smooth lines of her legs, and the angle of her shoulders. Her light brown eyes were devouring him, heavy-lidded with desire.

"I stayed up," she said, red lips curling into a teasing smile. "I couldn't wait to see you."

Two weeks of heat and mosquitoes, of stink and sleaze. This was his reward. And worth every minute of it.

She crawled toward him on the bed. He bent down to give her a kiss, taking in her warmth, her fragrance, basking in the animal fire of being in her presence.

Without drawing her lips away from his, she stood up from the bed and pushed him against the wall, her body flush against his, her skin hot where they touched. She tugged at his buttons with desperate fingers.

"I missed you." Her breath hot against his ear. "Damn it, I missed you."

He pivoted, lifting her by the waist. She wrapped her legs around his powerful abdomen as he pinned her against the papered wall of their bedroom. They clawed at each other in a whirlwind of frantic desire, as if trying to pull each other closer than was possible to make up for the distance that they had endured.

Later, they lay in bed together, Morgan's exhausted muscles drained of tension. Jenny was curled up against him, her brown hair spread on his chest. He ran his fingers along her scalp.

"You," she said, eyes closed, voice tinged with sleepiness, "are the best."

They kissed. Morgan enjoyed the closeness, being off his feet, and the comfort of his bedroom.

"How have things been around here?"

"Mmmm, lonely," she said without opening her eyes. "Better now that you're here. But I've been keeping busy. Work all day, party all night."

"Hussy," he said, tickling her ribs.

She squirmed and giggled. "Stop that, you ass."

They kissed and Morgan lay back on the pillow. "How's Alex?"

A dark cloud hung over the question. Neika, asleep on the floor, stirred and emitted a series of tiny yelps. Dreaming.

Jenny drew herself up so that she could face him, head resting on the pillow. "Still having a tough time."

"Does she still hate me?"

"Your daughter doesn't hate you, Dan. Good grief."

"She told me. In so many words."

"Words are sometimes not about telling the truth," she said, running a comforting hand over the hairs on his chest. "She wanted to hurt you. It was her dream to work with you at Zeta, and you thwarted it. You can't expect her not to be angry. And then with the accident, her leg, and the motorcycle being totaled . . . It hasn't been an easy time for her. She lashed out, that's all."

"Do you think I should have let her join?"

Jenny raised an incredulous eyebrow. "Absolutely not."

"I mean, she had the offer. And I can't stop her if some other agency wants her."

"For her to do that, she'll have to graduate college at least. Which at least gives me three years plus before I have to worry about her the way I worry about you." She snuggled up against Morgan. "Just my luck that the two greatest loves of my life are reckless storm chasers."

Morgan winced with guilt.

"Don't, Dan," she said, sensing his tension. "You're living the life that you chose. But even then, chose isn't really the right word, because this is who you *are*. You can't help it." She sat up and took his face in her delicate hands. "Just like I can't help loving you. It was a tough lesson to learn, but by God I learned it. My life is who I am. I'm an interior decorator, and a damn good one. And I'm your wife."

"And a damn good one," he said with a kiss.

"I love you, and that love means I worry and that I go without you sometimes for weeks on end."

"Jen . . ."

She put a finger in his lips. "Shhh. I know one day you might not come back. That's why I want to relish every good moment I can with you. So let's not talk anymore and just enjoy this, all right?"

They lay together by the gentle light of the bedside lamps. Morgan let his eyes wander the familiar setting—the modern chandelier under the off-white ceiling, the arcs and straight lines of the molding, the hypnotic vine pattern of the wallpaper. The comfort of home was carrying him off to sleep when he was yanked to alertness by the ringing of his phone.

"You have *got* to be kidding me," Jenny murmured.

"I don't have to pick that up."

Jenny let the phone ring a few more times before surrendering. "No," she said, exhaling. "The sky's falling and it's time for Dan Morgan to go back into the fray."

He reached for the bedside table and picked up the call. It was Bloch.

"We need you."

Damn it.

"Did you find White?"

"No. It's something else. I'll give you the details on the way."

Jenny was already up and pulling on her comfortable bathrobe. The unsexy one.

"I'll make you some coffee."

Chapter 8

Lily Randall pulled on her fresh black lace panties and dabbed Chanel No. 5 with a delicate brush of her index fingers behind her ears and along the upper line of her areola. She then picked up the sheer silk dress and let it spill over her, caressing her skin as it flowed down to hang delicately from her shoulders.

It was a pretty little number she'd put on the company card. It lay in stark contrast to her milk-white skin and her light red hair, matching the emerald green of her eyes. She took in the effect in the room's full-length mirror—the way it followed the contour of her waist and hips, the coquettish hint of cleavage, the straps with their precarious hold on her slender shoulders, looking like they might lose their purchase at the slightest shrug. Yes, it would do its job.

She walked to the window and pulled open the curtains of her suite at Le Parker Meridien, revealing an illuminated New York cityscape. She tidied up the room, collecting her running shoes from the mustard carpet and stowing them in the closet, and pulling on the red bedspread where she had rumpled it by sitting.

Next she picked up the tiny communicator, skin-colored and about the size of a pea, and pushed it into her right ear. The transmitter she placed in her plain black clutch emblazoned with the Gucci logo in gold, after pushing the button to turn it on.

"This is Agent Randall," she said. "Come in, Zeta."

"Shepard here," came the response, boyish and a little nasal. "You're late."

"Fashionably," she said, striking one last pose in the mirror, giving her shoulder-length hair a slight tousle.

"Let's review the target one last time."

"Roger Baxter, Vice President of Operations at Acevedo International. Fifty-three years old, silver fox type. Suspected of being chest deep in their illegal smuggling operations. Height, six-foot-one, weight—"

"That will do, Agent," came Diana Bloch's imperious voice.

Lily stepped into her black Michael Kors stilettos and drew her keycard from the wall slot.

"Leaving the room and going silent," she said, opening the door. "And Shepard? Try not to interrupt me while I'm working."

She clicked her heels on the patterned floor of the hallway to the elevator, which she took up to the forty-second floor and into the Estrela Penthouse.

"Lily Harper."

The bouncer checked his clipboard and waved her in. Nothing like having rich sponsors.

A waitress in a black dress shirt and white tie held out a tray of champagne. Lily took one, cool crystal against her fingers. Backing up against a pillar, she poured half of the contents into a vase.

Half-full champagne flute in hand, she walked past the coat check to the entrance of the ballroom proper.

Packed with tuxedoes, designer gowns, and tipsy conversation, the Estrela Penthouse had a slick modern design and a 360-degree view of the city. The guests were there pretending to support some sort of save-the-animals charity, although of course their real purpose was to show that they could afford a ten-thousand-dollars-a-plate event and to brush shoulders with others in the same tax bracket.

Lily emerged like a tigress on the prowl. This was a delicate dance, but one in which she was well practiced. If she came to Baxter directly, he would know she had an ulterior motive. No, she had to make him believe he was the predator. What he would want was a woman who could be counted as a conquest, whose face and body he could mount in the trophy room in his mind.

Catching his attention, at least, would not be all that difficult. Unattached young women were thin on the ground here. Baxter, though married with children, would not resist the siren call she was putting out. That much she knew about him.

She walked as if with purpose around the round tables with their overflowing centerpieces and the conversing groups of very fancy people, most of whom were still standing, drinking, and eating canapés. That was fine by her. With free range of the ballroom, she could spot Baxter at her leisure.

She found him about three-quarters of the way to the far window. She caught his eye and maintained contact for just a couple of seconds longer than a proper woman would. He held her gaze, mid-conversation with a white-haired man, before turning back to him with a light chuckle.

Yes, he had noticed. He'd come look for her later. Now, it was just a matter of making herself available.

Finding a spot where she could keep an eye on her quarry, she leaned against the bar near a corner, making lazy circles with her champagne flute, then bringing it to her nose for a whiff. She stole a glance at him the next time his eyes surveyed the room. He noticed. His hair was graying, but still boasted more black than she would've thought for a man on the other side of fifty. He was handsome enough, too, and she could see how a woman who went for older men would like him—a strong, aquiline nose and a discreet but well-defined jawline on a clean-shaven face, aristocratic and carrying the supreme confidence of the fabulously wealthy.

She cornered a waiter carrying a tray of red wine and flashed five hundred-dollar bills in her open clutch.

"I want a little accident to happen with that man. Just a splash on his suit jacket will do."

He nodded and slipped the money in his pants pocket.

Lily watched the little drama she had set up unfold. The waiter, one glass left on his tray, feigned a stumble. The glass flew against Baxter's sleeve. He had some harsh words for the waiter Lily couldn't make out and then excused himself. The waiter looked her way. She tipped her head. He had done well.

Once Baxter disappeared in the direction of the bathroom, she followed. She had already scouted her location—a small nook, half-hidden behind a bamboo palm, within view of the door to the men's room, where someone walking out could not miss her.

She slumped against the rough wallpaper and pinched her inner thigh. Nothing. Coldplay's "The Scientist." Still nothing. This needed more drastic measures.

She closed her eyes and conjured up her parents. The few images she had of them, when her age was in the low single digits, so old and worn that she wondered how much she had filled in the gaps over the years with photographs from around that time, and what other details had accrued from random sources.

Still, they did their job. She pictured her mother, smiling, picking her up, sitting at the dinner table in their London town house. Her father, consoling her while he treated her skinned knee with antiseptic. And then the funeral, being cradled by her gram, or standing alone at their house the day she had cut school to go visit them.

Tears welled up in her eyes, turning the world into an impressionistic light show.

"Miss? Can I help you?"

She knew before she turned to look that it was the wrong man. The voice was too young. There was something smooth about it that didn't fit Baxter's grizzled look.

"I'm fine," she said, turning just enough so that she could see his face. He was even younger than she had imagined, maybe even under thirty, putting him at the category of toddler compared with the average age at this event—at least in the male cohort. His shaggy blond hair covered his ears and framed an unhandsome but still boyishly attractive face, soft-featured and blue-eyed, made alluring through sheer confidence.

"Are you sure?" He offered an inviting smile. "I know this cocktail recipe that's guaranteed to get rid of the blues."

She did not have time for this. "Please go away."

"All right," he said, backing away. "Girl wants to be alone with her sadness. I can relate."

Her irritation almost ruined her hard-won sadness. She fast-forwarded through her routine again to get her back in the zone. The tears returned to her eyes, her lips pouting, her body drooping, forming an image of picturesque sorrow just in time for Roger Baxter to emerge from the men's room, dabbing a paper towel at the sleeve of his suit jacket.

She caught his double take out of the corner of her eye and then felt his looming presence coming closer.

"I'd like to say that your beauty is incompatible with such sadness, but somehow it only makes you more stunning."

Yeah. I know. She turned her head but did not raise her gaze to meet his. Not yet.

"Tell me who caused you to feel this way. I have the resources to have him shot. Drawn and quartered, if you prefer."

This time, she looked at him and let a weak smile break through the sad façade.

"Just say the word," he said with a sly grin. His voice was deep, like a lion's purr.

"Assassination won't be necessary," she said. "But perhaps a drink?"

"Queen's English?" he remarked, catching her accent.

"Drilled into me in public school at the point of a whip."

He offered her his elbow, and they walked together into the main ballroom. "Champagne?" He signaled a waiter.

"Merci," she said as the waiter handed her a flute. Baxter took one for himself. She ended up with her back to a window as he stood closer than decorum would allow.

"Now what could have put you in such a state? No man could have dared upset you like this."

"Not worth talking about," she said with a bashful smile. "In fact, it's becoming less and less clear why it even bothered me so much in the first place."

"Oh?"

She put her hand on his arm, feeling his muscles underneath. "In fact, I find that I can't recall why I was crying at all."

Recognition glimmered on his face. "I could have sworn I've seen you at the Palatine Casino in Monte Carlo."

"I'm certain I would have remembered you. Are you a gambling man, Mr.—"

"Roger Baxter."

"Lily Harper."

"Enchanté." He kissed her hand and held out his champagne flute. "To us."

"Oh, there's an 'us' already?" She clinked her flute against his and then tipped it against her mouth so that the sparkling fluid only tickled her smiling lips without flowing in.

"Does the idea intrigue you?"

An older man and his wife approached Baxter, who raised a

finger to excuse himself and then turned away to greet them. Lily took the opportunity to switch her full champagne flute for one that was half-full, resting on an empty table.

Baxter dispatched the couple. "I apologize for the interruption. It's a bore, but half my job is keeping these fatuous bags of wind happy."

She extended her hand and touched the tips of her fingers to his face, feeling the prickles of his emerging stubble. He closed his eyes and inhaled with desire. His hand shot out and grabbed hers. The strength of his grip made her gasp.

"Not here." He rolled his eyes right and left, checking that no one was watching.

"Then where?"

He produced a keycard and put it into her palm. She tucked it into her clutch. "Diplomatic Suite. I'm going to say my good-byes. Watch for my exit. Stay for another five minutes and then follow. I'll be waiting."

She watched as he walked away to make his rounds before leaving, then retreated to the corner bar. Out of the corner of her eye, she made out a male figure approaching—a round face, a shock of blond hair. He sidled up to her at the bar. *Here we go.*

"Feeling better, I see," said the now-familiar boyish voice of the guy who had come up to her by the men's room.

She turned and shot him a look of practiced indifference. "That," she said, "is none of your concern."

"No, I suppose not." He flicked his hair away from his eyes. "Just like it isn't my concern that you were poised to lure a very particular man coming out of the bathroom. And it isn't my concern that you watered a ficus with Cristal."

The little twerp had been watching her. "A woman has her ways of having fun. Not that you'd know anything about that."

"I know about fun."

"I meant women."

"Touché." He called over the bartender and ordered a whiskey on the rocks. "But you're not here for fun."

"Oh really?"

He stood with his back against the bar and grinned. "In that dress? No, you're all business."

The bartender set the glass of whiskey down on a napkin.

"Which, I might add, is none of yours."

Ice clinked in his glass as he took a sip.

She looked out the window to the sea of darkness that was Central Park. "I'm curious about what you're doing here at all. Tell me, did you have to borrow your daddy's tux?"

He smiled wide. "Why, would you like to meet him? He might be a little more of your target demographic."

"Maybe he is." She cast her gaze around for Baxter. She found him glowering at her from the exit to the ballroom. Jealous. Good. The boy had his uses.

She let the conversation fall into a lull, which he then tried to break. "Has anyone ever told you that you have a lovely accent?"

"You yanks love your accents," she said. "Tell me, does it make me sound smart and sophisticated?"

He chuckled. "No, you manage that all on your own, Miss—"

She shot him a sidelong glance. "Lily."

"A pleasure," he said. "I'm Scott. Scott Renard."

"Of the Poughkeepsie Renards?" she deadpanned.

He laughed, a hearty, wholesome laugh. "I can't figure you out. You're not here for the politics. You're not here with someone who's here for the politics. But I'm not getting the gold-digger vibe, despite your little show. What is your deal?"

"Maybe I'm just tired of men who tell me I have a lovely accent."

"So instead, you want men who have a lovely net worth?"

She watched as Baxter walked toward the elevator, shooting her one last look before he disappeared into the foyer, baring his teeth like a predator.

"So let me guess your—*deal*," she said. "You paid two hundred dollars for that haircut somewhere in Silicon Valley and got shanghaied into coming to this dinner across the country because you're the least socially inept of the partners in your startup, which consists of an application that lets your dog connect with other pets in the area for friendship, romance, and business networking. Am I getting warm?"

He threw up his hands. "Guilty as charged, more or less. Except for the app itself. It's more of an integrated security suite. We've got a good chance of being bought out by Google or Facebook before the year is out."

"I'm sure that must be very exciting for you," Lily said sarcastically.

"It's been boring. I used to program all day. That used to be the job, and I was good at it."

"Now *that* sounds riveting."

"More than you think," he said. "Today, it's all meetings with venture capital and angel investors, PR, management. Not my bag. But that's what the job calls for, so that's what I have to do. Never mind that I'm introverted and have all the social graces afforded by a down-home Midwestern upbringing."

"You seem to be able to hold your own," said Lily. "For an amateur. Little tip: skip the whiskey in social functions. It makes you sloppy, and you wince every time you take a sip. You don't like it and it shows. Get a tonic with a slice of lime. People will assume it's got gin in it. They'll trust you more, and you get to remain sober."

He set the glass down on the bar. "I yield to the expert."

She pushed off, collecting her clutch. "You'll have to excuse me now. This shindig's played out, and I have some grown-up things to attend to."

"I was just about to take my leave anyway," he said. "Condoleezza Rice promised me a dance. But I'll tell you what. I'm just going to put my number in this little purse you've got here." He pulled out a business card, took her clutch and, opening it a crack, slipped the card inside. "You feel like picking up this conversation, I know a great little five-star place that'll give me a table on, like, zero notice."

"I'll consider it," she said, waving him away. What was worse was that she really felt like she might. His young insouciant charm had left her with more of a tingle than she wanted to admit.

She walked out of the event hall and into the elevator, pressing the floor for Baxter's room. In the ride down, she got herself into character. When she emerged into the hallway, she was Lily Harper, *femme fatale.*

She inserted the keycard into the slot on the door to the Diplomatic Suite. It flashed green, and she pushed the door open.

The light poured into the dark chamber, getting lost in its extensive square footage. Its windows opened to the Central Park view, stunning from an unlit space. Her high heels clicked on the hard-wood floor.

Baxter was sitting on a red upholstered armchair, still in his suit, deep shadows cast on his face and body. He puffed on a thick cigar, which lit up red as he drew in. The sweet and acrid smell tickled her nose as she approached him. Lily set her clutch down on a credenza as the door behind her clicked shut and darkness enveloped the suite, letting the cityscape shine through in all its glory.

"Take off your dress," he said, commanding.

She slinked toward him, hips swaying, shoulders thrown back. "Let me make you feel good." She sat on the armrest of his chair, setting a caressing hand on his chest.

"Dress off. Now."

She raised her chin in defiance. "I think that's something you're going to have to earn."

He grabbed a handful of her hair near her skull in his left hand. Her scalp burned. He brought her face within inches of his, smoky from the cigar. "Dress. Off." he growled.

She knew this game. "Yes, sir." He released her hair. She reached back to undo the clasp on her dress. After that, a gentle shake of her shoulders was all that was needed for the sheer fabric to crumple at her feet. He devoured her body with his eyes.

And then his hands were on her, running over her body. They were rough to the touch, grabbing at her skin hard enough to bring her to the threshold of pain. She gasped as he pinched the flesh at her hips.

"I hope you're not squeamish." His breath was hot in her ear.

"Do what you want with me," she whispered, breathless.

He did.

Chapter 9

Morgan parked his Oldsmobile two blocks away from Dominic Watson's Cambridge apartment complex. The time on the dashboard read 11:49. On the night before a Monday, the snowy streets were deserted.

He checked his stainless-finish Walther PPK .380 ACP, made sure that the safety was clicked on, and set it in his shoulder holster, close to his heart. He shouldn't need it, but in his line of work, it was a fine line between *shouldn't* and *did*. He then tucked his lock-picking kit and the leather case Shepard had given him into his coat's inner pockets.

Morgan wrapped a scarf around his neck, high so it covered most of his face, and pulled a beanie down over his head so that only his eyes were exposed. One of the benefits of winter—you could hide your face without drawing any undue attention. He pulled on thin leather gloves and got out of the car into the cold Boston night.

"I'm on the move," he said, boots crushing the fine powder on the concrete sidewalk.

"Remember to approach the building from the south," said Shepard. The technical stuff all fell under his purview, so he was his point man for this mission rather than Bloch. "Skirt the edge of the sidewalk against the fence here to avoid the traffic camera."

"What about the one on the next block?"

"I'll provide a well-timed glitch. Just leave it to me."

Morgan's breath condensed against his scarf as he walked, the still frigid air nipping at his exposed eyes. He passed a couple huddled against the cold who shrank from him as they passed, but otherwise the night was empty, crisp and clear.

Morgan approached the apartment building, a five-story modern red brick, boxy and ugly.

"You've got a camera above the door on your left."

Morgan kept his face down, making a show to huddle against the cold. Standing at the door, he reached into the leather case and pulled out a keycard that connected remotely to Shepard's digital lock pick, inserting it into the slot. The light above the reader flashed red.

"Ready for you to work your magic here," said Morgan.

"Just a second." Morgan heard typing on Shepard's end. "These things are a joke."

The light turned green.

"And you're in," Shepard said.

Morgan drew out the keycard and pushed the door open into the stale warm air of a drab hallway, tracking snow onto the worn carpet.

"There's another camera on the ceiling on the left," said Shepard. Morgan tilted his head down, as if to check something in his right pocket.

"Security video should be relayed through a room that'll be"—there was a pause as Shepard checked—"second door in the hallway to your right."

Morgan found the door and knelt to pick the lock, in full view of the hallway camera. This was the weakest point of the mission, unavoidable as it was. But if anyone was even looking at this feed, it would be a night security guard in a distant facility with a mosaic of who knew how many videos to keep watch on. Security cameras weren't really for surveillance, but rather for deterrence and catching a criminal after the fact.

The lock opened with a click and Morgan slipped into the room, pulling down the scarf and taking off the hat. He inhaled a fresh breath with relief, musty as the air was in the windowless space. He closed the door behind him and flicked the switch next to it. Dim light shone from a bulb hanging from the ceiling by a wire. The far wall held a panel of electricity meters for each apartment, and on the right was a mess of wires for phone and Internet service. A low electronic hum pervaded the space.

A quick scan of the room revealed a box that looked like a large modem with a cluster of thin cables attached to it—the CCTV relay. Kneeling, he inserted a small device from Shepard's case into the Ethernet port.

"The transmitter's attached."

"I'm in," Shepard said a few seconds later. "Video incoming. I'm going to freeze the images as you pass."

Morgan took his position at the door.

"All right, go."

He walked out, closing the door behind him, and down the hall, taking the stairs up to the third floor.

"Hallway's clear," said Shepard.

He crouched at the door marked 3F and drew his lock-pick kit.

"You're alone up there," said Shepard. "Easy does it."

Breaking into the home of a man who had just died had its own particular dangers, not least of which that the police were liable to appear at any moment to search his things. But the lock was simple and the hour was late.

Click.

The door swung open.

Morgan entered Watson's living room and shut the door behind him, holding his right hand against the wood near the knob to stop it from making a sound. He found the light switch and flicked it, bathing the place in too-bright white light. The place looked like some kind of interior designer showroom. It was a clean, modern style, all chrome, white and black leather and mahogany.

"All right, what am I looking for?"

"Computers, hard drives," said Shepard. "Anything that stores data."

Morgan leafed through a pile of mail that sat on a buffet table. There were two credit card bills for different cards printed in menacing reds and yellows. It became obvious how he managed to afford all this. He didn't.

Watson's laptop was in plain view, a brushed aluminum Samsung sitting on a thick glass and metal desk. But there was a problem.

"It's locked to an antitheft chain," he said.

"Look for a bolt cutter or a hacksaw," said Shepard.

Morgan surveyed the apartment, with its fussy decoration and metrosexual sheen. Morgan couldn't imagine Watson would own a hacksaw.

"Something's happening," said Shepard. "There are three men at the building door wearing ski masks. They have guns—I see the bulges under their coats."

Morgan felt his shoulders tensing, the hairs on the nape of his neck standing on end. "Burglars?"

"Maybe, I—what the hell? Someone else is in the system."

"What do you mean?"

"They've hacked the security software, same way I did."

Morgan didn't believe in coincidences. "Can you keep them out?"

"Who do you think you're talking to? I've already overridden the locks. They're not getting in."

Still, Morgan had to work fast. He examined the chain. It connected to the laptop through a cylindrical combination lock that was secured to the metal frame. The cable ran from the lock to loop around the steel leg of the desk. Morgan tested the desk for weak spots, but the welds were solid. He pulled against the lock to warp the aluminum to wrest it free. It held firm, and he was afraid of damaging the hard drive if he applied any more force.

"What the . . ." It was Shepard. "They kicked me out of the system and got the doors unlocked. They're inside the building."

"Morgan." It was Bloch. "Leave the laptop and get out of there."

Not an option. If this was important enough for armed men to come after, it was too important to leave behind.

"They're moving up the stairs," Shepard said.

Morgan's hand went to his PPK. It was him against three armed men, seven rounds and a flimsy door between them, with no time for backup to arrive.

He didn't love his odds.

Chapter 10

"Morgan, get out!"

Sorry, Bloch, but not a chance.

He popped out his earpiece, sticking it in his pocket, and pushed the white leather sofa against the door, dragging it across the hardwood floor. Grabbing two throw pillows, he sandwiched the cable between them. He then slipped his Walther into the crack, muzzle pressed against the chain, and pointed it against the wall.

He fired.

The report was muffled by the pillows. A flurry of down feathers erupted into the air, and the bullet embedded itself in the brick wall. The cable fell slack, sliced in two.

The apartment door rumbled as the men kicked it from the other side. Braced with the sofa, it held firm.

Morgan slipped the laptop into a padded fabric carrying case with a shoulder strap. He pulled open one of two heavy wooden windows, wood scraping against wood. Cold air gusted in.

The door boomed again. Morgan held the carrying case aloft out the window. The building was bordered by an iron fence, recessed from the sidewalk with a hedge in between, bare, leafless but dense with twiggy branches.

Morgan released the case. It fell two stories to land in the bushes with a shuffle of bending branches. Next he looked to either side and spotted what he was searching for.

Three suppressed gunshots. Splinters went flying. A windowpane shattered. A burning pain on Morgan's thigh and blood on his black denim pants where a bullet grazed him.

Time to go.

He retreated into the bedroom, where he pulled open the window and looked to the right to find the black drainpipe, hugging the outer wall, three feet from the window.

The door cracked—the lock had been breached. The couch groaned as they pushed it out of the way.

Morgan ducked, lifting one leg at a time out the window so that they dangled free. He steadied himself against the wave of fear, averting his eyes from the thirty-foot drop.

He heard a final shove of the couch and then footsteps in the apartment.

No more time to hesitate. Morgan reached for the drainpipe with his right hand, getting a firm grip through his glove, and pushed off the window. The drainpipe whined as his body swung, but it held. He grabbed it with both hands, feet against the wall.

He let his hands slide down the pipe like it was a rappel rope. He made it one floor down before one of the attackers stuck his head out the living room window.

"Over here!"

The next time Morgan looked up at him, he was staring down the barrel of a Glock 19.

Oh, hell.

Morgan released his grip on the pipe. He felt the gust of the passing bullet in his hair. And then he fell.

He landed on the bushes, wind knocked out of him.

Another crack of the gun. The slug burrowed into the frozen ground between his legs.

But this time, his hands were free.

He drew his PPK and fired twice up at the window. One bullet found a pane of glass and the other only brick, but it was enough to force the shooter to retreat inside.

Morgan extricated himself from the branches and drew himself to his feet. With an eye on the window above, he squeezed past the bushes to get at the laptop carrying case, a few feet away.

Morgan fired another shot and scaled the fence, leaping over it in under three seconds to land on the snowy sidewalk on the other side.

A bullet hit the iron with a resounding *clang*.

Morgan ran under a hail of gunfire. These guys might be co-ordinated, but they were piss-poor shots. He covered the distance to the end of the block and turned the corner, safe out of the line of fire, and ran the two blocks to his car.

He drove away to the sound of the first approaching police siren.

Chapter 11

Spent amid damp rumpled sheets of Egyptian cotton, Lily Randall watched Roger Baxter as he walked, naked, to the bathroom. He switched on the light and stepped onto the black marble floor, pulling the handle on the shower. Water sputtered and gushed. The sound was then muffled when Baxter closed the stall door.

Lily ran still-tingling fingers over where his savage caresses had left her raw. She'd played these rough games before. She didn't care for mincing or unconfident men. But it wasn't that Baxter was self-assured, or even that he liked to perform the dominant role. He wasn't *playing* at using her. He was using her, full stop. She felt like nine holes at the links. Like wine at a tasting, to be spit out in a communal silver bucket.

But then again, she was also using him.

Lily drew from her clutch the device Shepard had supplied— tiny, squarish, about the size of a dime and with a protuberance that connected to the data slot on a cell phone. This would, upon insertion, install a piece of spyware that would relay all incoming and outgoing communications back to Zeta. As Vice President of Operations, Baxter would be their link to the entire smuggling operation.

She leapt off the bed, walking catlike on the cold hardwood floor, shivering. Baxter liked his room icy.

She found his pants, rumpled on the floor, the belt still threaded through the loops. No phone and no wallet. She tried the jacket next with no luck. Safe was next. She found it in the closet, open and empty. She cast a nervous glance at the bathroom. His phone. Where was the damn phone?

She pulled open drawers in the bedside tables and desk and ran her hands under the pillows. Nothing.

Her gaze returned to the bathroom door. Steam was billowing out, the shower still going strong. She walked to the door and peered in. There it was, on the sink by the shower, on top of a thick leather wallet.

No, you didn't rise to the position of Chief Financial Officer of Acevedo International by being trusting. Even—especially—of the women you sleep with.

She went inside, barefoot, taking light steps. She reached out for the phone and looked back at the shower stall. Baxter had swiped the condensation off the glass and was watching her. She went for a facecloth instead. He watched, stern and impassive. She blew him a kiss over her shoulder as she wet the edge of the cloth.

She was dressed by the time he came out of the bathroom, a towel wrapped around his waist.

"I thought I should get going," she said.

He grabbed her by the waist and squeezed her to him. She ran her fingers through his wet hair as they kissed.

"So, do I get to see you again?" He would like that, of course. For her to ask. It fed into his fantasy of power.

His phone rang before he could respond. He raised a finger to her lips and reached for it.

"Hey, honey," he said, right hand moving along the small of Lily's back. He kept his predator's eyes on hers and pushed her against the edge of the table. "Yeah, everything's all right." His hand moved under her dress, fingertips tracing her thighs. She felt her face flush. "You should be glad you didn't have to sit through this one. How is Sasha?" Lily ran her tongue against her teeth to keep from making noise. *Bastard.* But she had to be what he wanted. He had to want her to return. "Bye, honey. Sleep tight. See you tomorrow." He hung up and set the phone down on the table. He then grabbed Lily by the hair again and brought his eyes level with hers. "Let's make a couple of things perfectly clear. You are not my girlfriend. You will not *be* my girlfriend. And you will *never* be my wife. Keep me satisfied, and I will be good to you. Understood?"

She nodded, whimpering. He pulled her in for a kiss, biting her lip.

"I think we have an understanding then. You may go. I'll call you."

He turned his back on her and dropped his towel. *Dismissed then*, she thought and turned to go. She tasted blood on the tip of her tongue.

Chapter 12

Morgan swiped his card at the gate and drove his Olds down the ramp into the Hampton Building garage. He parked near the forgotten corner lot of the lower floor. He scanned his retinas at the reader hidden behind a panel of circuit breakers. The inconspicuous service door next to the scanner popped open, and he walked into the darkened hallway that led into the subterranean headquarters of Zeta Division.

The corridor lit up when he closed the door behind him. The chamber was bare concrete. In the upper right corner was a black hemisphere containing a high-definition surveillance camera. Ahead of him was a door fit for a bank vault. He scanned his thumbprint now and entered a pass code. The door opened to an elevator, which carried him down to his destination.

He emerged into the Zeta War Room, the heart of their operation. It was about as large as a major corporate conference room, with a large screen overlooking a long wooden table. Opposite the screen, over the door from the garage outside, was the office of the big boss, Diana Bloch. It was a steel and glass cage whose glass could turn from clear to frosted at the push of a button. The decor ran to Bloch's drab, functional tastes, lit very brightly with a combination of white and yellow light that was the closest approximation to sunlight you could get on the market—this was courtesy of the research of Karen O'Neal, their resident numbers analyst, who had read some study that said that people are more alert and work better under these sorts of conditions.

Lincoln Shepard was huddled over his computer in jeans and a T-shirt that read NERD out of some postmodern self-aware impulse, his straight nose and pointed chin inches from the screen as usual.

He had several days' stubble going, and headphones wrapped around his neck, connected to nothing. His messy black hair seemed to stick out in every direction, like a character from a Japanese cartoon. Morgan thought he might be growing it out, although whether for the style or because he couldn't bother to get it cut, he didn't know.

Karen O'Neal was sitting across from him, also in front of her computer. Petite, lean, and half-Vietnamese, she wore her hair short and in a ponytail, bangs hanging over black rectangular glass frames, and followed Bloch's lead with muted professional attire. Little details, however, betrayed her perpetual anxiety—fingernails chewed to stubs, hair mussed, and eyebrows too thin from overgrooming. But today, her usually frantic eyes were vacant, and her hands were resting on the keyboard, not moving.

Morgan put the laptop case on the table. "Special delivery."

"Wonderful," Shepard deadpanned. "You've been very helpful."

He sat down at the table. Neither of the analysts paid him any further attention.

Morgan cleared his throat. "So is anyone going to tell me who this Watson is and why people are invading his apartment at all hours of the night?"

Shepard spoke without looking up from his computer. "Asset. Inside Acevedo. The elevator decided to go kamikaze with him inside. Sorry."

Morgan was going to ask why when he noticed O'Neal was watching him with a scowl. "He installed a worm for us this morning," she said. "A worm that should give us access to the Acevedo servers."

"Designed by none other than *moi*, thank you very much," Shephard interjected.

"Did it work?" asked Morgan.

"It should kick into gear any minute now," he said. "They do a server reboot every Saturday night. Tonight, they're also doing an update—and along with the update, they're installing my worm. If Watson did his job right."

"He did," O'Neal snipped.

"Then my little worm should be burrowing itself in their servers as we speak, and our backdoor into all their dirty little secrets should be available"—he checked his watch—"any minute now, actually. I have it set up to ping my computer if it goes through."

"So how do the people who attacked me at his apartment figure into all this?" Morgan asked.

"I have no idea," said Shepard. "I got the video recordings. I'll throw them up on the big screen."

The monitor that overlooked the table flickered to life, displaying the video from Watson's apartment in a grid. Morgan followed as the men came in from outside and made their way to the apartment door. They moved in a clear formation, covering each other, and keeping watch.

"These guys have tactics," Morgan said. "It's not police or military. Nothing I've ever seen before."

"Private security?" suggested O'Neal. "As in Acevedo?"

"Maybe," Morgan said. "Any chance they knew that he was working with us?"

"If they did, they missed the worm," said Shepard. "I just got pinged. It's active. Running diagnostics now. Looks like our meathead friend wasn't as useless as he looked."

Karen O'Neal stood up from her chair and stormed off.

"What was . . ." Morgan began, but he was interrupted by the click of high heels approaching from the entrance corridor. Lily Randall, the deadly beauty, slinking toward them in a ravishing green silk dress.

"Morgan," she said with a nod.

"Well, if we count your failure we're one for two tonight," said Shepard in greeting. "What happened, did you have trouble sorting out the right end of the cable?"

"I could pop your head right off with my thighs," she said, sitting cross-legged across the table from Morgan.

"Yeah, but what a way to go."

She ignored the comment. "Baxter didn't let his phone out of his sight for so much as a minute. No way I can connect the cable for fifteen. I need something faster, preferably wireless."

"If I could do wireless, I wouldn't need you," he said. Then he turned his screen for them to see. "I present to you the Acevedo company servers." All that was visible was a command line with undecipherable text on it, but Morgan was sure it must have been very exciting for him. He swiveled it back to him. "Beginning data dump now. And you suckers will see I can do more at my desk than all you suckers running around and blowing stuff up."

"How have you been able to stand this little twerp for so long?" Lily asked.

"You learn to tune him out. Eventually, it becomes part of the background," replied Morgan.

"That's weird," said Shepard.

"What is it?" Lily asked.

"Shut it. Let me work." He was typing in command after command, and his computer was returning a noise that sounded like an electronic version of *nuh-uh*.

He banged on the Enter key. *"Why don't you work?"* he screeched.

Karen O'Neal appeared, her face washed, from the inner corridor. "What's going on?"

"It's gone," he said, slumping his shoulders in defeat. "My backdoor is gone. I had it, and now it's gone."

"Were you caught by Acevedo security?" asked O'Neal.

"There's no way those jokers could catch on to anything anywhere near that fast."

"Maybe you're just overestimating how good you are," said Lily.

"Maybe you can shut your stupid face. My code was way beyond their amateur security team."

"I can vouch for that," said O'Neal. "Acevedo's security protocols wouldn't have caught his worm."

"Then what happened?" said Morgan.

Shepard closed his laptop hard and let his upper body sprawl against the table. "I don't know."

"Hello square one," said O'Neal. "I thought it might be longer before we saw you again."

Chapter 13

Simon held his door open so that Alex could take her time getting inside. He lived just down the hall from her—floors were coed, thanks to the university's progressive housing policy. His room was messy in the way boy's rooms are messy, with the trash bin overflowing with soda cans and snack containers, books all over the place, and the clean laundry still sitting rumpled in the hamper, the dirty laundry now accumulating on the floor by the bed. The situation was aggravated by Simon's love of electronics, so that not only was his desk overflowing with peripherals to his laptop, but open hard drives and exposed motherboards and Alex-didn't-know-what-else covered every available surface that wasn't the floor.

The best that Alex could say was that Simon's room had the dubious distinction of not being quite as bad as really messy girls' rooms—like, for instance, Katie's side of their shared room, the floor of which was covered in dirty clothes and which had some hidden cache of empty yogurt cups and moldy ramen noodles that gave the space its distinct aroma.

By some fluke of the housing process, Simon had the room all to himself as a single even though it housed furniture for two, so Alex ended up spending a lot of time there—so much that rumors abounded that they were secretly hooking up. Alex had a strong suspicion of who was spreading the gossip, considering that Katie was the resident miller at the local rumor mill.

She squinted against the morning sun filtering in through the bare branches of the trees outside as Simon pulled up a chair for her at the desk. He helped her sit in his desk chair. She felt the heat of his breath as he hovered over her right shoulder.

"All right," he said. "Show me what you've done."

Alex swiped the touchpad on Simon's Alienware computer, a sleek black laptop with green lights around the edges like—well, like nothing more than an alien spaceship. It came on under her touch and she navigated on his browser to her GitHub page to the project she had been working on. She downloaded the lightweight program and opened it. The user interface was bare bones—the array of buttons consisted of just boxes with badly centered numbers and symbols—but she had finally ironed out all the bugs late the night before.

"Let's see here . . ." Simon leaned over her to type, his gray plaid button-down brushing against her hair, and the smell of his Old Spice made her a little nauseous. He tried a few inputs. Some basic additions, into two, then three, then up to ten digits, which was the limit for the display. "Addition's working okay. Let's check multiplication."

Alex looked on, slouched in her chair, as he tested the various functions of the rudimentary calculator she had programmed. Her attention wandered to the posters that plastered the walls—some things she recognized, like Super Mario Brothers and *Lord of the Rings*, and others that she didn't, like one with a cartoony girl with long pink hair and—another with a guy in a bowtie standing in front of a blue phone-booth-type-thing.

"Whoops," said Simon.

"What is it?"

"Your square root function has problems. Either that or reality is getting really screwy in our vicinity." He hit the *4* button, then *sq rt*. The program display output *–3*.

She took over and tried again, with the same results. "I have no idea why it's doing that. Damn it. I spent so long working on this."

"No worries," said Simon. "Let's take a look at your code." He opened up the text file containing the source code for her program. "Your documentation is still atrocious, I see."

"I know what everything does."

The mock-tension hung between them until it was broken by a frantic knocking on the door. "Guys!" came Katie's voice from the other side as she pounded on wood. Simon pulled it open and she poked her head in, breathless. "Something's happening at Shaw. Come on."

She ran off down the hall. Simon and Alex shared a quizzical look, and then Simon helped her get up and onto her crutches.

"I'll get your jacket," he said.

Outside, Simon held his pace beside her as Alex hobbled across the crunchy snow of Pickett residential quad toward the Shaw Memorial Library. Scores of students were streaming in the same direction like lines of the faithful on a pilgrimage.

Alex was busy negotiating the snow under her crutches, so it was Simon who saw it first, when they were within some four hundred feet from the library.

"Alex," he said. "Look up."

Squinting against the morning light, she let the image resolve in her eyes. Shaw Library, the stately Gothic Revival building, with its cathedral-like stone façade, behind which rose the stacks tower, and from the upper battlements, between the tall narrow lancet windows, something was hanging. It looked like it could almost be—

A person. A man, stark naked, hanging upside down, feet attached to a wooden crossbar. Alex stumbled, trying to walk without drawing her eyes away from the bizarre spectacle.

"Alex! Over here!" It was Katie, at the edge of the crowd. People had their cell phones out, taking photos and shooting videos in a din of gasps and laughter. "Can you believe this?"

Alex looked up again. The distant face resolved into one she recognized.

"That's Jeremy Panagopoulos." she said. He was squirming, but didn't seem panicked. In fact, he was groggy, if anything.

"Who?" asked Simon.

"Chief Investment Officer of the university."

"Not helping," said Katie.

"He manages the university's money. He—an article came out a couple months ago about some shady things going on with the university's investments. Nothing really came of it though."

Campus police were now pushing everyone back.

Alex's phone vibrated in her jacket pocket.

"I guess someone felt a little resentful that he got away with it," said Simon.

"I guess." All around them, phones emitted short beeps in a cacophonous symphony.

"Hey, did anyone else get this e-mail?" said a male student Alex didn't know. She pulled out her own phone and found she had a new message. The subject line read:

Verdict: Guilty.

She opened it.

Jeremy Panagopoulos has been found guilty of financial crimes by the court of the people. Judgment has been rendered and his punishment carried out. We do not forgive. We do not forget. We are the Ekklesia.

"This is insane," said Katie, as Panagopoulos was pulled up by the rescuers on the roof of the library.

"This is amazing," said Alex.

Chapter 14

Lisa Frieze arrived at the FBI office bleary-eyed and hating life. Her body seemed to retain heat like a corpse, and her messenger bag felt like a ton of bricks. A half-glass of Chardonnay and another round of Chinese food the night before was all it took.

She was getting old.

She had to remind herself that this was the journey she had to endure to get to her destination. She was putting in the time. She hadn't been around enough to have any kind of seniority. She was still the most recent addition to the department.

But heck if it wasn't miserable all the time.

She forced herself to take the stairs, which took a little more forcing today, up to the Counterterrorism Division on the third floor.

She was greeted by Gus Loyola's booming voice. "In the office on a Sunday, too?"

"Justice never sleeps," she said, setting her bag down at her desk. "Here for a new assignment. Just got the call from Chambers."

"You don't sound too happy about that," Gus said.

"I don't know how you are so happy."

"I credit that to psychiatric medication," he said.

"Ugh," she said, collapsing on her desk. "Chambers has got me on these piddling cases. Got a homicide. Open-and-shut case, except it had a thread connecting it to a potential terror case, which triggered our involvement."

"Sounds like it could've been promising."

"Yeah, if it wasn't just some couch potato who likes to talk big on the Internet."

"But he was murdered?" asked Gus.

"Home invasion," said Frieze. "Home invasion gone bad. And I had the joy of going to a crime scene where the corpse had been stewing in a heated apartment for three weeks."

"Oof," said Gus. "Yeah, I've had my share of those. The worst was a lady who died in her bathtub. Was there at least a month before anyone—"

"Frieze!" This was Clement Chambers, Agent-in-Charge. Her boss.

"Sorry, Gus, this is truly a lovely conversation, but duty calls."

"Good luck," he said, sipping his coffee.

She knocked on the door to Chambers's office. "Come in!" She pushed it open. "Are you done with the paperwork on the Coutu case?"

She pulled up a chair and sat down. "I've finished typing it up. I was going to input it into the system first thing this morning."

"I have a new assignment for you. I want you on it as soon as your paperwork is done." He tossed a folder in front of her on the desk.

She opened it and leafed through it. There were photos of a naked man hanging upside down against a building that looked like a medieval church. "What is it?"

"Chief Investment Officer at Springhaven University got kidnapped and left hanging from the roof of the school library."

"Dead?"

"Alive and drugged."

"So why am I getting involved?" she asked. "What's the counterterrorism angle?"

"Turn to the third page of the file," said Chambers.

"What is this?"

"An e-mail sent to the entire student body, faculty, and staff of the university," he said. "Along with it was a document dump that's supposed to show he took bribes to put the university's money in shady funds and committed fraud to cover it up. The financial crimes division is looking into it."

The e-mail read:

We do not forgive, we do not forget.

"Vigilantes. I guess we have competition," Frieze said.

"What do you make of it?"

"A bunch of dumb kids playing hero looking to make a splash," she said. "Got a little carried away."

"What if I told you this name, Ekklesia, has been popping up all around the country? It's going to hit the news very soon."

"Yeah? Did they do anything worse than this?" Lisa asked.

"No," said Chambers. "Kidnapping's as bad as it got. It's all in there. You can read about it on your way up there. Think you can handle this?"

"You know I can, Chambers. I came with you to Boston when you got transferred because you know what I can do. I just wish you'd trust me with something more than adolescent pranks."

"A federal case is a federal case," he said.

"Bitch work for the bitch," she mumbled bitterly.

"You're paying your dues, Frieze. Don't give me that attitude. Do the work, be the agent I know you can be, and you'll be having your pick of the cream of cases one day. You don't make your career at thirty."

"I'm thirty-one."

"Don't get cute. Do as you're told. Springhaven University. Go. Today. Right now."

Chapter 15

Lily kept an eye on Morgan's gloved fist, held high to protect his face, while she strode on light feet in circles around him. She moved like a cat, quick and precise. He had her completely beat on raw power—she was a waif compared to him—but she had him on speed and agility.

Their fights usually took all her concentration. But this was a light spar, and the issue was burning in her mind ever since her night with Baxter. Plus, she hadn't even begun to be short of breath. "Can I ask you something?"

"Shoot."

The overhead light flickered over the regulation boxing ring that graced the Zeta gym. Lily maintained her steady movement. She wasn't tired, but the heat was still on the fritz. The temperature made her slow and stupid. Nearly suffocating. It didn't help Morgan, either. Sweat beaded on his brow and his shirt was already half-soaked.

"How do you—oh, God, that stupid phrase. How do you have it all?"

He advanced and she stepped back, bobbing on constantly moving feet. "Do I?"

"Come on, Morgan. Somehow you have the job and the family. How do you pull that off?"

"You looking to get hitched, English?" He went in for a jab and she dodged.

"No. But I'm tired of pretending to want the endless parade of creeps and assholes that comes with the job." Morgan maintained a holding pattern as she spoke, keeping her at arm's length. "I used to think it was fine, that I could rise above it. That I could set myself apart from the character I play, and let her be abused, not me. But I'm not sure that's possible. It's wearing on me."

She came in for a high kick. Morgan deflected it with his left glove.

"Sometimes it does. That's why it's always been important to have something that kept me grounded. Reminded me who I am. For me, that's Jenny and Alex."

Lily came in for a punch. Morgan tried for a grab, but she wrested free.

"You're faithful to Jenny," she said.

"Have been from the day I met her."

"Does that ever get in the way of the job?"

"It's hard to be away," he said.

"That's not what I mean. What about—don't you ever have to have any . . . intimate involvement with any marks?"

Embarrassed by the question, she tried to take it out through violence, kicking at Morgan chest high and hitting his solar plexus, maybe a little harder than she should have.

"Oof," he said. "Got me." He smirked. "To answer your question, I did, back in the day," he said. "I suppose I ended up graduating from that."

"Will I ever?" she asked. "I mean, what am I, other than my face, my body, and my sex appeal? That's my whole game as an agent. What do I have if I lose that?"

"Your brains, crack shooting skills."

Her glove landed on his right cheek.

"And even if you ever lose that, you've still got a hell of a left hook." He took a few steps back and let his arms fall to his side.

"Throw in the towel?" she asked.

"I think I might die of heat exhaustion if we keep at it for another minute." He drew off his gloves and splashed water from a bottle onto his face. They stepped over the ropes and sat side by side on the edge of the ring.

"So, do you have any regrets?" Lily asked.

"Some, but they never stick. I'm doing what I'm meant to do." He ran a towel through his hair. "And I meant what I said about Jenny and Alex keeping me grounded. They give me a reason. Keeps me sane. Keeps me one of the good guys."

"I can never imagine you *not* being one of the good guys."

"I think you'd be surprised." He stood, pushing off the platform. "I'm gonna hit the showers."

"Thanks for the talk," she called after him. She went to the women's locker room to take her own shower—wonderful, refreshing cold water—lost in thought all the while.

She emerged out into the Zeta War Room with purpose, which was almost immediately diverted by Lincoln Shepard.

"Just who I've been waiting for. I've got something for you. For the next time you see Baxter." He held it up.

The object was tiny. It looked like a pill, but inside there was something small and plastic. "It's a wire," he said. "Smallest money can buy."

She took it in her hand.

"You be careful with that," he said. "This baby cost a small fortune. Had to put in a special requisition."

She tossed it in the air and caught it again, just to mess with him. Then she hid it away in her pocket.

"Just put that in the threads of his jacket," said Shepard. "I suggest any pocket that's been sewn shut. It's specially designed to grab onto the fibers like a burr."

"And you can listen in from here?"

"That's the idea," he said. "We'd get only half his phone conversations, but we'd get both sides of anything in person. Nailing him on gunrunning could be the key to bringing the whole company down." He turned back toward the table. "There's something else that I had engineering whip up in the lab for you." Shepard handed her a small cylinder that fit in the palm of her hand, colored in chrome and a deep crimson.

Lipstick. "I appreciate the effort, but this just isn't my color."

He took it back and demonstrated that, at the push of a button, two prongs stuck out from the bottom. A second button caused a snapping arc of electricity to form between them.

"Stun gun," he said. "It's small, so it only really has the juice for one good shock. But it's a good one. Will drop a full-grown man in two seconds flat."

She pressed the button to get a feel for it, looking at the bright miniature lightning. "Lovely."

"Bloch wants you to tell us about your next—assignation, she called it—with Baxter."

"I know," she said, looking at the lipstick to avoid looking him in the eye. What the hell was happening that she was ashamed of this all of a sudden? "Will that be all?"

Shepard held up his hands to say he had nothing more for her.

She left through the garage and got into her car. Once she emerged into the street outside, she took out her phone and dialed a number she never had before.

"Hello?" came the tentative reply from the other line.

"Hello, Scott? It's Lily, from the other night. Remember me?"

He chuckled, and she felt foolish. "Sorry, I shouldn't have called."

"No. No, don't hang up! Of course, I remember you. I just can't believe you're calling me."

She laughed. "I guess I can't, either." They shared a moment of acknowledgment. "So," she continued, "when's the next time you're coming to the East Coast?"

Bloch was waiting for Morgan as he emerged from the Zeta showers. "We have something for you."

He followed her toward the War Room, his T-shirt and khakis in counterpoint to her pressed navy blue blazer and alligator skin Manolos. "From Watson's laptop?"

"Shepard hasn't cracked security on that yet," she said. "No, from the Acevedo servers."

They walked out into the War Room. "I thought that hadn't worked."

"I had begun the data dump when they kicked me off." It was Shepard, sitting at the table, shoveling Cheetos into his mouth. "We didn't get it all, but we got something."

A few chairs down was Paul Kirby, gray suit, red tie, used-car-salesman smile. "Specifically, what jumped out at us was a certain high-priority shipment currently on the way from Mumbai, India, to Abidjan, in Ivory Coast."

"The weigh-in at the port doesn't match their records." O'Neal, completing the picture. "And it's supposed to be consumer electronics, but the volume doesn't match the regional market. There's something in that shipment that's definitely not consumer electronics."

"So I got in touch with some of my contacts in the CIA," said

Kirby. "And we have this man who got on a private jet in New York early this morning. Shepard."

Shepard brought a picture up on the big screen. A thin, bony face, giving the general impression of a skull under a balding head of hair.

"That's him," said Morgan. "That's Mr. White."

"Bertrand Whitman, to be precise," said Kirby. "Special consultant to Acevedo International. Made seven figures from the company in the past year. Currently on a flight path to Abidjan."

"I'm sending you with tactical," said Bloch. "Smith is working on some local assets to provide you with in-country support. Let's try to keep this one on a low profile, okay?"

Chapter 16

It took two hours for Lisa Frieze to arrive at the Springhaven campus. She hadn't eaten anything since the leftover takeout from the night before, and it hadn't been much then, just something to keep the hunger from distracting her as she did paperwork. That same hunger was starting to tug at her insides, but she stamped it down. She had work to do.

The sun was low in the sky, but about as high as it was going to get on a midwinter day. She parked in a lot near the visitor center and used her phone to navigate the campus pathways toward the library. Within sight of the building, she saw a college girl on crutches making her way along the path. An insistent pinprick of recognition poked at Lisa's mind. Then it dawned on her.

"Alex Morgan."

The girl's pixie-like features scrunched up before her eyes widened with surprise. "Lisa? Wow, it's been so long! What are you doing here?"

"Working. You go here?"

"Freshman year."

"Have you picked your major yet?"

"Still undeclared," she said. "But leaning toward criminology."

"Oh really? I could arrange for you to visit a Bureau office, you know. Check out what the work is all about."

"Sure, that'd be great," she said, as if Lisa had just invited her to her community theater production of *Annie*.

Lisa Frieze cleared her throat. "So, apparently a university staffer was strung up on the school library. Would you happen to know anything about that?"

"Only what everyone else knows. I saw him up there, actually, right before they took him down. And I got the e-mail. That's about the long and short of it."

"How has the student response been?"

"Mixed," said Alex. "Some people think it's awful. Others think it's great. It's actually really dividing the campus. People are up in arms about it. Angry editorials in the *Inquirer* and all that. You should check out today's issue, I think they're pretty representative. You can get a free copy at the entrance of most campus buildings."

"I see. Thanks, I think I will. So what side are you on?"

"I don't bother picking sides. I mean, what difference would it make if I did?" said Alex, not wanting to show her interest to the FBI agent.

"You're wise beyond your years, Alex."

"I, uh, need to head to class." Alex adjusted her crutches. "See you around, I guess."

"Make good choices!" Lisa called out, mentally kicking herself for being so lame. She walked the short distance left to the campus library and saw a small cluster of cops at the pointed arch of the door. The whole library had been deemed an active crime scene. A student pleaded with an unyielding policeman that she needed access to her research. Another cop moved to stop Frieze until she showed her badge.

A plainclothes officer, a black man with a shaved head and a well-tended goatee, stepped forward. "Bryce Vickery. Detective on the case. Thanks for coming down." He was gap-toothed in a way that made Frieze look twice. *Hello, Detective.*

"So, tell me I didn't come all the way down here for a prank."

He put his hands on his hips and squinted against the sun. "I've seen kids pull a lot of pranks. Some of them stupid, some very, very clever. But nothing like this."

"How did they get up there?"

"Library stacks," said Vickery. "You know, where they actually keep all the books. The big tower in the back."

"Who's got access?"

"The stacks are closed after eleven-thirty. After that, library and maintenance staff only."

"Until what time?"

"On a Sunday, eleven," he said. "They would've been alone in there."

"But how'd they get out? If they lowered him from up there in the morning, in full view of anyone passing by, how did they manage to escape?"

"Beats me," he said. "Why don't we go inside? I'll show you around."

The inside of the library had a much warmer feel than its stony exterior would suggest, all carpeted, painted in warm beiges with wooden railings on the stairs and balconies.

Frieze looked up at the corniced ceiling. Cameras.

"Did you get the video off of those?"

"I requested surveillance from the campus police," he said. "First thing I did when I got on the scene."

"And?"

"The files are gone."

She frowned. "What do you mean, gone?"

"The files were either wiped from the campus security systems or they were never recorded," he said. "I've put my digital forensics guy on task to discover which one."

"The plot thickens," she said. "Has this happened before? Do the systems fail often? Could it have been a coincidence?"

"Campus security says no," said Vickery. "It'd be a little too much of a coincidence, don't you think?"

"Just covering all the bases," she said. "So we've got an organized group, extremely smart and well-prepared, with access to campus security systems. Does that cover it?"

"Just about," said Vickery.

"This case might turn out interesting after all. How'd they get in?"

"Plenty of possibilities at street level," he said. "But there's only one door to the roof."

"Shall we?" They trekked up six floors and Vickery took out a key ring with at least twenty keys on it. He went through the tags, squinting in the low light, until he found the right one. He unlocked the roof door. Frieze closed her eyes against the harsh blue winter light, giving them time to adjust.

"Was there an alarm?"

"There was," said Vickery, walking outside. Frieze held up her hand, shielding her eyes from the light, and knelt at the door.

"Why didn't it go off?"

"No idea," he said.

Frieze inspected the lock on the door. "Look here," she said. "Glue. Like on duct tape. Looks fresh—hardly any buildup of dirt. And there are scratches on the lock."

"Then that's how they kept it open," said Vickery.

"I'm betting you'll find a door at ground level with the same residue."

Vickery pulled out his phone. "I need crime lab out here. Yeah, in the library."

Frieze turned her attention to the ground on the roof. It was dusty, spattered with bird droppings. The recent activity had left its mark. The snow had been disturbed all over where the rescuers had come. But there was something . . .

"Vickery, how did the responders get Panagopoulos down?" she asked.

"They had a stretcher," he said.

"They brought it up here?"

"Why?" he asked.

"Look." She pointed down. There were two continuous lines leading from the door to the edge, intermittently obscured by footsteps but clearly discernible once you knew what you were looking for. "This is where they dragged him to the edge. How many do you suppose they would need for this?"

"Two for Panagopoulos, which would be kind of draggy, and at least two more for that wooden setup they had. So a crew of at least four."

They looked down together at the dispersing crowd at the entrance of the library.

"What do you like for motive?" Vickery asked. "Do you buy this whole Ekklesia thing?"

"I don't know," said Frieze. "Looks like it's cropping up in other places, too. This isn't an isolated incident."

"So we're talking about an honest-to-God terrorist group?"

"Looks like it," she said, looking out onto the college, this loose accumulation of buildings of various architectural styles, with all its lawns and trees. "What about Panagopoulos?"

"In the hospital. They're running a full tox on him, but whatever they gave him didn't do any permanent damage."

"Can I talk to him?

"Please," said Vickery. "Have at it. He's already lawyered up, what with the document dump the Ekklesia released. Likely to get him indicted for financial crimes. Good luck getting anything useful. I'll let the deputies know you're coming."

Chapter 17

Alex pored over a book of John Donne's poetry, spacing out as she tried to concentrate on the words...

... as yet but knock, breathe, shine and seek to mend.

They held no meaning to her. She couldn't bring herself to pay enough attention for the words to connect to any ideas. But on that day she didn't care. Excitement surged through her body like it hadn't for a long time. She wouldn't dampen it for anything, least of all freshman English.

She walked out of the library and hobbled with purpose out of Pendergrass Hall back to Prather House, up the elevator and then down the hall to the door to Simon's room and knocked.

"Just a minute!" came the response from inside. She pushed the door open anyway—they had long ago disabled the automatic locks since they were in and out of each other's rooms so often. Simon, nude and wet-haired from a shower, scrambled to wrap a ratty blue towel around his waist. His face went a deep crimson. "Jesus, didn't you hear me?"

"Couldn't wait," she said, pushing her way inside.

He looked down at her feet. "You're tracking snow into—"

"Do not pretend to care about wet floors now," she said. "Sit down. Sit."

"I think you'd better sit down yourself," he said, indicating the chair as he sat on the bed, careful that his towel would cover everything. "You're practically jumping up and down. It can't be good for your leg."

She nearly fell over as she situated herself on the wooden dorm chair, which leaned back against her weight. Finally, she steadied herself.

"Burczyk," she said, leaning forward like an insurance salesman. "I have a proposition for you."

"Is it indecent?"

"Har har." She shook off his joke with a wave of her hand. "No. Listen. Those people. The Panagopoulos thing."

"Crazy, right?"

"Crazy *awesome*, I'm sure you mean," said Alex.

Simon raised an eyebrow.

"You seriously don't think so?"

"I always knew you had a screw loose, Morgan, but—"

"No, listen," she said. "It's an opportunity to take justice into our own hands. Out into the streets."

"Okay, Batman."

"I've been looking into the Ekklesia. It's not just here. They're doing this kind of stuff all over the country." She pointed at his computer. "Check it out."

Simon pulled the laptop over onto his towel and searched *ekklesia*.

"It started in the past couple of months," she said. "They've been involved in all kinds of guerilla hacking. They exposed a dog-fighting ring in Florida by sniffing out their identities from their on-line message boards. They also got a child porn producer in Ohio."

"I see here," said Simon. "They have a dirty cop under investigation in New York, based on suppressed surveillance videos. And look, it looks like they've been sabotaging ISIS media and recruitment web pages."

"Isn't that amazing?" said Alex. "They're taking action! Guerilla hacking, doing justice where justice isn't being done."

"I guess it is pretty cool."

"Cool? Simon, we *have* to get in on this."

Simon closed his laptop and stood up, holding his towel at his hip. "That's where I get off the crazy train."

"We need to find out who they are and *join* them."

"I can't count the levels on which that is a terrible idea." She continued to stare at him. "No. There's no way." He turned away from her and made a point to search his drawer for underwear as if he were looking for a particular pair.

"Please," she said, extending the single syllable into three. "This

is one of the most incredible opportunities that will ever present itself to us. This is a turning point, Simon. For both of us. This is how
we escape suburban drudgery. This is how we avoid selling out to
the Man."

"There's a reason people sell out, Alex," Simon said. "Because
it's either selling out or poverty. Although I guess you've added a
fun new category of crazy as a third option."

"Come on, man. Be a pal."

"Why do you even need me anyway?" He slipped on his underwear under his towel. Alex didn't stop herself from taking a peek to
see whether he might flash some skin, but no luck. "You could just
as easily do it by yourself."

"I'm crippled, you asshole!" she cried out, laughing. "Well, that
and I tried Googling and it failed, so I'm basically out of ideas."

"Maybe that should tell you something. Maybe it's a sign from
the universe for you to give up."

"I'm not giving up. Next step is start calling attention to myself
in very stupid ways."

"I'm not your keeper, Morgan." Simon pulled denim pants on
over his boxers and then shook the towel from his hip. "The stupid
things you do are entirely on you." He grabbed a T-shirt from the
hamper of clean clothes.

"Come *on*, Simon. I can't do it without you."

He sat down cross from her. "Then you won't do it at all, which
suits me fine."

"Aw, Simon." She lowered her voice and pulling her chair closer
to him. "I thought it might be a way for us to, you know, do something together. You don't have to be just my tutor, you know."

They made eye contact, full of meaning.

"Alex?" he said.

"Yes?"

"I'm not an idiot."

He stood up, pulled on a hoodie and a parka, and slung his backpack over his shoulder. "I'm off to the library. Lock the door when
you leave. And try not to join any suicide cults while I'm away."

Chapter 18

Lisa Frieze had to elbow past reporters in the hospital lobby who had gotten wind of the story and flocked to try for a snippet of an interview with Panagopoulos. One frizzy-haired woman was insisting with the deputy.

"What's his current status? Sir! Is Mr. Panagopoulos under arrest?"

The deputy, a moon-faced boy fresh on the force, was flustered by all the attention and didn't quite know how to rebuff the entreaties.

Frieze took charge. "Lisa Frieze, FBI!" she shouted, for the whole coterie to hear loud and clear. They fell into silence. "Police have no comment yet on the situation of Mr. Panagopoulos. A press release will be issued in due time. Meanwhile, you can all stay put. I will make a point to *personally* arrest anyone who trespasses into restricted areas of this hospital."

That just sent them into a whole new frenzy of questions.

"Ma'am, is the FBI getting involved?"

"Will Panagopoulos be charged with a federal crime?"

She gestured for the deputy to lead the way. He was all too happy to leave the din behind.

"You new on the force?" she asked as they walked the halls. The smell of hospital disinfectant made her queasy. Her mind rumbled with bad associations, a distant storm of past trauma that she hoped wouldn't be carried toward her.

"Just passed the exam late last year. This is the most exciting thing to happen since then."

"I hope for your sake it remains that way. I find that excitement can get old real fast," Lisa replied.

"This is the room."

She caught the name on the chart at the door. So it was. A private room in the private wing. Didn't come cheap. The deputy opened the door and stood aside for her to come in.

Panagopoulos, whom she recognized from his picture, lay on the bed. She was going to greet him, but was intercepted by a man in a standard-issue graphite suit with an outstretched hand.

"Ramsay Pitman, from the firm of Coleman, Colby, and Splain." He was just at that age where he was on the cusp of making partner, an impression buttressed by his nervous energy. This one was going to be overzealous—in other words, a pain in her ass. "I'm representing Mr. Panagopoulos."

"So I gathered. Lisa Frieze, FBI Boston, Counterterrorism Division."

Panagopoulos sat up, alert, doing a bad job of pretending to look pathetic. The lawyer would be coaching him already for the media blitz.

"I'm very glad the FBI took an interest in this heinous crime perpetrated against Mr. Panagopoulos."

"I assure you we are taking this very seriously."

"And Mr. Panagopoulos offers his full cooperation in finding the criminals who abducted him."

"It's much appreciated," said Frieze. "What can you tell me about the abduction?"

"I was jumped when I was getting out of my car," he said. "I was coming home with a takeout bag."

"You live alone?" He nodded, yes. "How many attackers?"

"At least three," he said. "They stuck me with a needle, uh—" He turned his body and pulled his hospital gown to show a small purple welt near his shoulder. "Right there."

"Did you get a look at them?"

"They wore hoodies and something was covering their faces. All I saw were flashes before they made me turn away, and then I lost consciousness."

"They spoke?"

"One. A man. I couldn't tell you anything else. And then I blacked out. I have flashes of hanging on that . . . thing. I really only woke up here."

"I see," she said. "Can you remember anything at all? Every detail helps."

"That's it."

"I'd also like to try to establish some motive."

"This was a completely unprovoked attack," Pitman broke in.

"Nonetheless, I'd like to ask Mr. Panagopoulos some questions," she said. Then she turned toward the man on the bed: "Do you know anyone who might have a grudge against you? Anyone who might benefit from seeing your reputation tarnished in the media?"

"A man in Mr. Panagopoulos's position naturally attracts the envy of many."

She just kept her eyes on Panagopoulos. He shrugged. "I don't know. I really don't. My ex-wife, I guess. But I don't think she'd be capable of something like this."

"What about these allegations of illegal activities?" she asked. "Has anyone made them before? Does anyone stand out as being particularly . . . ?"

"My client's statement has been submitted to the police," Pitman interrupted. "Now, he is tired and in need of rest to recover from this harrowing experience. Any further questions can be routed through my firm. Good day, Ms. Frieze."

Chapter 19

Alex Morgan lay on her stomach, elbows on the bed, reading everything she could find about Ekklesia. She studied every single news article available, most of which had been copied off the same handful of news agency sources. She then read about the history of the word. It was the ancient Greek council of citizens in the Athenian democracy. Then she went on to the Internet forums to see what people were saying about it.

The Internet went deep. Most of it was complete nonsense. Speculation went all over the place. Her eyes were glazed over by this time, and she was running on caffeine fumes from a large bottle of Diet Pepsi she had polished off. But she hung on, always looking for the next scrap of information. Katie came in after dinner, said hello, and getting no answer, put on her headphones and nestled in bed with a textbook.

Simon came around that evening and found her on her bed—right where he had left her.

"What the hell are you doing?" said Simon.

"Researching."

"Did you leave your room today?"

"Of course I did."

Simon reached over and held Katie's headphones away from her ear. "Katie, did she leave the room today?"

"Not while I was here."

He crossed his arms in judgment. "Are you really this obsessed with the Ekklesia thing?"

"You being chicken won't stop me," she said.

"Ugh," he said, sitting on the bed next to her. "Fine. I guess there's no harm in sending out some feelers. Not like it's going to *work* or anything."

"Really?" said Alex, looking up at him with bright, grateful eyes. She leaned forward and gave his torso a hug. "You're the best! So you know how we can do it?"

"I have an idea of where to start. Move into my room?" He looked at Katie, engrossed in her reading. "Might be a good idea to get some privacy."

Katie sent them off with "Wear a condom!" and they walked down the hall to Simon's room.

"I've been looking at this e-mail they sent," he said. "I had a hunch." He brought up a page of code. "This is the HTML code for the e-mail. Basically what it looks like under the hood."

"I recognize some of this stuff from what you taught me."

"Look, here," he said, pointing to a series of numbers, about four lines of seemingly random digits. "That's not supposed to be there. It's not doing anything on the page, I mean."

"What is it? Some kind of cipher?"

"Would be my guess." He cut it and pasted into a text document.

"What are you doing?"

"Testing it against a couple of decoders," he said. He opened two different programs and pasted the text into each.

"You mean you have those on your computer already?"

"I told you that cryptography was a hobby of mine. Let's see." He chewed on the end of a pencil. "What we need is a key," said Simon. "To decrypt this text."

"It's not there by mistake. They want people to be able to find them, right? Isn't that the point?"

"So it won't be impossible." Simon ran his hand through his hair. "We can try the obvious. Panagopoulos. Justice." He typed as he spoke. "Ekklesia. No, not any of these."

"I was looking into the meaning of 'Ekklesia' earlier," she said. "It has roots in common with the word for 'church,' but it was the council of citizens of Athenian democracy. That's the reference, I'm pretty sure," she said.

"Let's try those," he said. "Athens, a few variations . . . Democracy . . . None of those."

"Hold on," she said. "I think I remember something about the etymology. It originally came from . . . Here it is: *ekkalein*, 'to call out.' This is a call out, right? Try that."

She spelled it out for him. He entered the word. The gibberish resolved itself into comprehensible English.

"That's it!" he said. "How did you get that?"

"Lucky guess." She read the message on his screen.

Congratulations! By finding this message, you have proven yourself knowledgeable and resourceful. If you wish to join the struggle, send an encrypted message with—

What followed were a series of random characters.

"What? How does that work?"

"It's a public key," he said. "Used for encryption. So they're the only ones who will be able to read the message if we send it to them."

He typed a message out on a program Alex had never seen before.

Would like to join the cause. Awaiting instructions.

Simon then ran it through the encryption and hit Send. "It's out there now," he said. "Ball's in their court."

Chapter 20

The Gulfstream G550 carrying Morgan and the four members of the Zeta tactical team touched down in Abidjan at 10 A.M. They were met on the tarmac of Bigny Airport by two shiny black Audi A6 TDI sedans, which drove straight out into the street from the runway, bypassing all customs and immigration.

Which was good, because the luggage they were carrying wasn't exactly legal.

"Who's this we're going to see?" It was Spartan, her legs sprawled in her black denim pants, taking up half the middle seat. Her muscles showed under her T-shirt, and a tattoo of a Greek warrior peeked out under her shirt on her neck under her cropped blond hair. "And whose ass are we going to kick?" Although she was the only woman on the tactical team, she never let any of them forget she was as tough as any of them.

"General Moussa Jakande," said Morgan. "Of the FRCI—the Republican Forces. Apparently he's an old acquaintance of Smith's. As far as ass-kicking goes, I think you'll get your chance."

"Where doesn't Smith have friends?" she said, entranced by the unfamiliar landscape. Spartan wasn't much of a world traveler.

They passed a street market full of stalls set up under black umbrellas, people wearing bright colors carrying large baskets on their heads, and a group of kids playing soccer on a field of dirt. With all the hallmarks of the third world—the decades-old cars, chaotic traffic, and people walking barefoot on the dirty sidewalk—Abidjan also showed signs of recent development, its skyline full of cranes raising new buildings.

The drivers took them to the Deux Plateaux district, where wealth was evident in the new-model European cars and high-walled houses. The Audis pulled into a luxurious apartment complex where security guards performed a full check of the cars, although they didn't ask them to open their luggage.

A servant in a black tuxedo was waiting for them in the parking lot. He escorted them into an elevator to the penthouse.

They—Morgan and Spartan, Bishop, Diesel, and Tango—walked off right into the apartment, appointed with Louis XV furniture, rococo end tables, and cabinets holding collections of ivory and jade ornaments. On the walls were copies of Renaissance masterpieces, skins of exotic animals on the floor. The living room opened up into a vast balcony with an infinity pool. Hand shielding his eyes from the harsh sun, Morgan looked out at the view, making out the ocean in the distance.

The four-man tactical team sat ill at ease on the edge of their seats, like any wrong move might cause something to break. Morgan was used to the luxury—missions often demanded he travel in these circles—but the tac team guys were all ex-military and special ops, more comfortable roughing it in the desert or jungle than this.

"Which one of you is Bevelacqua?"

Morgan turned around from admiring the view to find a serious man in gold-rimmed round sunglasses, gray-haired, wearing a green military uniform, a vintage chrome Colt .45 in his belt holster. Stepping forward, Morgan extended his hand in greeting.

"General Jakande," he said, shaking Morgan's hand. "Welcome to my home."

"We're grateful for your hospitality," Morgan replied.

"Would you like something to drink?" He motioned to a white drink in a liquor bottle. "Bangui. Palm Wine. Our national beverage."

"Thanks," Morgan said, holding up a hand in refusal. The tactical team let him speak for them.

"Myself, I prefer Bordeaux," said Jakande, sitting down on an ornate armchair, all done in gold leaf.

Morgan sat across from him in a plain low-backed wooden chair. "I was told we may be able to help each other."

"Indeed, I believe we can. You are looking for a man. An arms dealer."

"I'm told you know where he is," Morgan said.

Jakande crossed his legs. "He was here in Abidjan earlier today. He arrived in advance of his shipment of weapons."

"How can we get to him?"

"I am afraid it is not that simple. In the city, he is under the protection of General Onobanjo. So are his guns, under heavy guard."

"General? As in the Republican Forces, like you?" Morgan questioned.

"The politics in Côte d'Ivoire are complicated, Mr. Bevelacqua. See, there is a very powerful warlord here by the name of Stéphane Madaki. He has gained power by taking control of illegal gold mines in the interior. They use slaves to extract the gold. And General Onobanjo likes gold."

"Put that way, it sounds pretty simple."

"We live in a delicate balance," Jakande said. "Onobanjo has troops loyal to him and can call on them to fight other battalions of the army if he wants to. He knows nobody wants civil war. And if he allies with Madaki, I am not confident that we would beat them. So we are forced to turn a blind eye as they amass ever greater wealth and power."

"So you have a rogue warlord and a general in his pocket, and you can't do anything about it."

Jakande shrugged. "My hands are tied."

"So that's where I come in, I take it?"

"This shipment of weapons your Mr. White is bringing would give Madaki, the warlord, a decisive superiority. With his numbers and proper guns, he would be able to challenge our national army."

"So you can't fight them head-on and you can't stop the shipment."

"That's right. But perhaps you can. The convoy carrying the weapons left Abidjan earlier this morning. I have their current location, although I do not know where they are going. But they will not be hard to follow. When you have found their destination, you will find Madaki and Mr. White."

"I'm going to need a guide," Morgan said.

Jakande grinned. "I have already arranged one for you, my friend. I think it is better for you two to go alone, for now. You will attract less attention on the road traveling in twos. Other than that, I can give you limited support. I will outfit your men, provide guns and transportation. But it cannot be traced back to me."

"Understood," said Morgan. "Your help is much appreciated."

"I do not want thanks. I want you to kill Madaki. If you do that, it is I who will be grateful to you. Come. We have no time to waste. I have your guide waiting downstairs."

Morgan grabbed his case and opened it for one last check. A MAC-10, his Walther PPK, and rounds for both, plus a sat phone.

He said good-bye to the tactical team. "I'll be in touch," he said to Bishop. "Once I have the location, we'll plan the extraction of Mr. White."

"Good luck," Bishop said, holding his fist out for Morgan to bump.

Morgan went down the elevator, carrying the gun case and his duffel bag. He walked out into the garage, where he was met by a tiny woman with a thin waist and matte skin. She had black curly hair cropped short around her skull and was wearing camo pants. Her chest bore a long diagonal scar that started on her left shoulder, disappearing between her breasts into her black tank top.

"Mr. Bevelacqua. My name is Yolande Ekwensi." She spoke in a French Ivorian accent, with a flat affect, showing no emotion at all. "I am your guide." She extended her hand.

"I think there's been some mistake."

"There is no mistake." She didn't sound defensive, just annoyed. "I was sent by General Jakande to be your guide."

"I was just expecting someone more—"

"Male?" She looked at him with contempt. "There is no one else who will take you. These are dangerous areas. You need a guide with *real* balls." She grabbed at her crotch to demonstrate. "Come. Let us go."

He liked her already.

She motioned toward her dented white Jeep, opening the back for Morgan to put his case and bag in. He then got into the car, which felt a bit off. He wasn't used to being in the passenger seat.

They moved out. As soon as they drove past the security gate and out into the blinding sun, she lit a cigarette. Then she slipped on a pair of Oakley sunglasses. "Do you have guns back there?" she asked.

"Yeah." He put on his own aviators.

"You'll want to keep one on you after we drive out of the city."

They drove along northward on the Boulevard des Martyrs, dodging yellow taxis and cyclists. "Do you carry?" he asked.

"Glovebox."

He popped open the compartment and found a Smith & Wesson MP 380 automatic.

"Just enough firepower."

"It keeps impertinent men in line," Ekwensi replied sarcastically.

He pushed the compartment shut and sat back. It was going to be a long drive.

Chapter 21

Bruce Ansley adjusted his tie in the mirror and then looked for his shoes. One he found where they should be, at the foot of the bed. The other was missing. He looked around the room, his back aching as he bent down to look under the bed. Nothing but a couple of dust bunnies and a lost sock. He grumbled under his breath and went downstairs where Annemarie was making bologna sandwiches for the kids. She was watching the tiny old TV in the kitchen—some talking heads discussing foreign policy.

"Does anyone know where my shoe is?"

"I think I saw Cory with it," Annmarie replied.

"Cory!" he called out. He walked halfway up the stairs. "Cory!"

"What?"

"Do you have my shoe?"

The boy ran to the upper landing of the stairs from his room. "I was playing boat, Dad."

"Well, Dad needs his shoe. Go get it."

On his way back to his room, Cory met Pam, who was just coming out of hers. "Aren't you a little old for pretending shoes are boats?"

"Ms. Lambert says it's good to use your imagination," he said, running out of his room with the shoe held high above his head.

"Ms. Lambert is just hiding the fact that you're actually retarded. She doesn't want to make you feel bad."

"Pam, you'd better stop that. Your sister's just teasing you."

"I know, Dad." He held out the shoe. "Here you go."

"You have your toys," he said, following his son downstairs. "Try to leave my stuff alone, all right?"

Bruce took the milk out of the fridge and glanced at the TV. The cable news network was now showing video footage of Russian tanks. Bruce switched it to a fluffy morning news show on which a blond woman and a bland brown-haired man drank coffee and talked about the weather.

"The kids don't need to be exposed to this goddamn stuff," he said, pouring himself a bowl of raisin bran.

"Pam, did you finish all your homework last night?" Annemarie asked.

"I'll finish it during morning break."

"Pam, I swear, if I get another call from your teacher—"

"I'll take *care* of it, Mom, jeez."

"Don't talk to your mother like that."

"I did my homework, Mom!" Cory broke in.

"That's very good, sweetie. Bruce, could you take care of the gutters later?"

"After work," he said. Then, to his kids: "The bus arrives in less than five minutes. Time to go wait on the curb."

"But Dad, it's cold!"

"You're not making everyone wait because you're cold. Go on. Take your brother. Give your mother a kiss."

The door closed and the house was quiet. Bruce munched on his cereal.

"I saw something so strange on the news earlier," said Annemarie. "Some university official was left hanging from the university library up in Massachusetts."

"Like, hanged dead?"

"No, not dead, just hanging there upside down. What do you make of that?"

"Must've done something."

"Corrupt, they said," said Annemarie. "Took money from the university."

"Allegedly," said Bruce. "They always have to print *allegedly* with stuff like that or they'll get sued."

"Well, he *allegedly* stole several hundred thousand from the school," she said. "Looks like he deserved what he got."

"Still," said Bruce. "There's due process. Vigilantes never know when they might get an innocent man."

"These guys always get away with it. I say he had it coming."

"Well, I have to go," he said as he chewed his last mouthful, putting his bowl in the kitchen sink.

"Don't forget—"

"Gutters. As soon as I get home."

He kissed her and walked out through the garage. On his way into work, he made his usual stop at the post office. He parked and walked inside, pulling out the key from the coin pouch in his wallet. He found his box and inserted the key.

The key had started sticking about five years ago, and had only gotten worse since. He turned it with some effort and held his breath. The usual sense of doom filled him. He swung the door open.

Empty.

He exhaled, closing the post office box, and walked out into the cold winter sun.

Chapter 22

Andrea Nyhan walked up the stairs to the fourth floor of the Acevedo building. It was congested, both elevators being out until they figured out what the hell had happened. Chatter echoed in the stairwell, just business as usual for most people, transposed from the elevator to the stairs. But for her it was different. For her it was something like a solemn duty, some small way of paying homage to Dom.

She opened the door from the stairwell into the office. The elevator—*the* elevator—was cordoned off with caution tape, even though there was also a sign on the call buttons indicating that both elevators were OUT OF ORDER. Some understatement.

When Burt saw her, he opened his mouth, she guessed, to give her the news, but stopped himself. It must have been obvious she knew, from her puffy eyes, maybe still a little watery. Instead he just grimaced. She responded with a sorrowful hint of a smile.

A pall of silence hung over the entire office and seemed to muffle even her footsteps as she walked.

She glanced over at Dominic's cubicle. It was a sort of involuntary tic, a little everyday gesture timed to her walk to her own desk. He'd always been one of those idle office what-ifs, and those glances were always accompanied by ill-defined fantasies of mingled sweat and tangled hair and cuddling up close and tuckered out against cold winter nights. Sometimes she flashed on breakfast, too, making eggs and pancakes for him, or long autumn afternoons of leaning against him with a book as he tapped away at his laptop.

These were airy wisps of fantasy, previously dissipated by the time she sat down at her chair, but now they took on the pungency of bitter regret. The fantasies that left with the dead sometimes pierced the deepest.

Violet Zanger intercepted her before she reached her desk. She was dressed in vast swathes of dark purple cloth swishing with each clomping step.

"Oh my God, honey, did you hear?" she said, laying her arm mother-like on Andrea's shoulder. Andrea resented the assumed familiarity, but she didn't have the energy to tell her to screw off.

"I got the e-mail," she said with a sniffle.

"I was just beside myself when I found out. Did you know I talked to him that morning? Just to think, I might have been the last person to talk to him!"

"Maybe. I think he usually says good-bye to Burt." It felt good to take that away from Violet, that self-satisfaction in the reflected glory of being somehow involved in the thing everyone was talking about. Still, there was something awful about how Andrea's imagination was filling in his last moments. She flashed on him in the elevator, the interminable weightless seconds as the car hurtled to its final stop. "How are you holding up, Violet?"

"I was just in shock. In total shock. Such a handsome young man. What a waste. Can you imagine that poor mother?" She blew her nose on her handkerchief. "But I'm praying for his soul. And meanwhile, we have to carry on, right?"

It was amazing how Violet played out her little private drama in the wake of the death of someone she barely knew and would gossip about in life.

"Anyway, Dominic's funeral will be held tomorrow at nine, at Christ Church, you know in Cambridge? Steve is giving us special dispensation to attend. You know, if you want to pay your respects." She added in a whisper, "Closed casket, of course."

Andrea scowled at the image this brought up. "Of course, Violet. I'll be there. Thank you."

She walked on, but was apparently not destined to make it to her desk, because she ran into Marvin Brainard, who had worked with her and Dominic on network security.

"Did you hear about Dom?" he asked.

"Yeah, I heard." Her voice was tinged with bitterness. "Got cornered by Violet and got all the gory details."

"Look, you need anything, I'm here, okay?"

She acknowledged the offer with a tearful smile. At least he had the common sense not to press her on it.

In spite of herself, Andrea looked back toward Dom's desk. Tears welled up in her eyes. When she reached her desk, she put away the stack of papers on her desk into a drawer. Then she leaned her head down on her desk and wept.

Chapter 23

After some five hours on the paved highway, Yolande turned the Jeep onto a dirt road going northeast. The landscape changed little as they covered ground, alternating jungle and farmland, with the occasional roadside town or village.

Morgan had tried to strike up a conversation with his guide several times since they had left Abidjan, but the diminutive Ivorian gave him nothing. They didn't even listen to music. She just stared ahead at the road and chain-smoked her cigarettes. When he asked if they were going to stop for food, she just said "Peanuts. Glove compartment."

Driving on the dirt road cut down on their speed. The Jeep held up fine to the bumpy ride, but they came upon occasional puddles that spanned the breadth of the road, and they had to pass slowly so as not to get mired.

After the first fork, Yolande pulled over at a roadside shack, where a shirtless old man was sitting, watching the sparse traffic. She tucked her gun in her pants and got out of the Jeep, exchanged a few words with him, and left him with a five-dollar bill.

"He says the truck convoy passed this way," she said, shutting the door and turning on the engine. "About four hours ago. We are on the right path."

They drove on as the afternoon grew late, stopping to ask people along the way if they had seen the trucks. Other than a wrong turn that forced them to backtrack twenty minutes, they were making excellent time.

The sun was low in the sky, with only jungle on either side of them for a long stretch, when they came upon a Cold War–era Peugeot parked lengthwise, blocking the road. Morgan had opened his mouth to ask Yolande about it when he heard movement behind them—three men dressed as civilians, two brandishing revolvers and one an AK-47, coming out of the forest. Another man stood up from behind the car, aiming a Glock 19 at the Jeep.

Ambush.

"Hold on!" Yolande stepped on the gas. The Jeep jerked, the seat belt digging into Morgan's shoulder as they rammed the front of the Peugeot. It swiveled, knocking down the man crouching behind it. The tires of the Jeep skidded on the damp dirt as Yolande tried to get clear of the car.

The tires gained purchase, but Yolande lost control with the sudden acceleration. The Jeep spun on the mud. Morgan was yanked side to side, and lost sense of left and right, up and down. With a final yank, the vehicle came to a stop, and Morgan realized they had tipped over and were upside down. He released his seat belt and fell onto the roof.

The men were shouting and running toward them.

"Yolande!" She was out of it, in a daze from the crash. Her eyes were open but distant and hazy. He put his hand on her shoulder and shook. "Yolande!"

Her eyes focused on him. Morgan pulled his PPK from its holster. He opened the door, using it for cover, and fired on the approaching men. They fired back, bullets hitting the side of the car. They hung back. They had no cover out in the road. But Morgan and Yolande's defensive advantage wouldn't last.

Yolande undid her seat belt. Morgan cast a lingering glance at the gun case, which had landed in the back, far out of reach. The gunmen were coming. They would realize in a moment that they could gain the upper hand by circling the car. Morgan didn't feel like sticking around for that.

"Ready?" he asked Yolande.

"Ready."

He ran out of the car, shooting his PPK at the attackers. He hit one in the shoulder, and the other two ducked for cover. He emptied the magazine to give Yolande time to disappear into the bush, and then he ran after her. They plunged into dense jungle, leaving the Jeep, their remaining guns, all their money, and the sat phone behind. He tossed the empty PPK.

They came to a stop at a clearing, panting in the intense forest heat. Insects buzzed all around them, beginning their evening symphony.

Morgan and Yolande were moneyless and weaponless, deep in hostile territory, lost in the jungle of Ivory Coast.

Chapter 24

"So, Alex." Dr. Strimling steepled her fingers and touched them to tight lips. "Why do you think I called you here today?"

She had her graying hair pulled back in a bun. Her shoulders looked tense and raised under the shoulder pads of her tweed coat. Everything about her conveyed the impression of being wound tight, all corroborated by her office—prim, all the books on the bookshelf pulled out so that they were flush against one another, everything on her desk arranged as if on a grid.

"I guess I have some idea." Alex refused on principle to show any kind of contrition about her current academic dire straits.

"Have you had any trouble getting around with your leg? We have resources for—"

"I know about the resources. And I'll pass."

"Okay. Well. It's just important for you to know that they're there for you."

No, what's important is that you covered your ass by telling me about them.

"Alex, the reason I called you in today is—we need to talk about your academic performance."

"Yeah, I kind of got that."

"I sent you various e-mails about it already."

"Yes. Yes. I saw."

"You didn't think to reply?"

Alex didn't have a response to that. She was annoyed by the whole conversation.

"Your grades last semester were fine," she continued. "A-minus, B-plus. You even managed a full A in your Introduction to Sociology course. And now, nothing higher than a C, and a failing grade in two classes. What's going on, Alex? Is everything okay at home?"

Her voice took on a patronizing tone that filled Alex with gall.

"Everything's peachy, all right? This is not me lashing out because my parents are getting a divorce or whatever."

"How did you break your leg?"

Alex looked out the window. Water dripped from icicles hanging from the eaves.

"I'm concerned that it might have something to do with—"

"It was a motorcycle accident, all right? I totaled my bike just . . . driving down the highway."

"Sometimes, when things are going too fast in life, you look for a way to stop. Sometimes, those things play out in odd ways. Like in an accident."

"Oh, *please.*"

"I'm trying to find the root cause of this change," she said. "Maybe if we can identify it, we can—"

"What, you want to be my shrink now?"

Strimling rested her forehead against her outstretched fingers. "I don't have to be a freshman adviser, you know. I signed up for this because I care."

"Well, don't. You're not very good at it."

Alex could tell that stung and felt a pinch of guilt at having said it. The professor threw her hands up in frustration. "I'm going to refer you to Mental Health Services. If you're having trouble, they can offer you help."

"Wonderful."

"Alex, this is very important. If you don't do this, there's a good chance you're going to lose this entire semester. You're already teetering on the edge of academic probation. Frankly, this is your last chance to avoid it."

"Look, I'll try harder, okay? I'll turn in the paper, bring up my GPA, whatever."

"It's out of my hands and in yours, Alex. It's really all I can say." She pushed herself back from her desk and stood up from her chair. "Do you need a hand getting up?"

Alex braced on her crutches to stand. "No," she said. "I don't."

She walked back to her dorm room in a haze of anger. She opened the door, saw that Katie was absent, and slammed it shut behind her.

She shed her scarf, hat, and heavy coat, tossing them on the floor next to her desk. She rested her crutches against the bed frame, and after some maneuvering, holding on to the reclining wooden chair and bed frame, sat and then slumped onto the bed. She let her eyes wander around the darkened room. Katie had left a dirty bowl with the remnants of mac and cheese on top of the minifridge again.

She shut her eyes, inviting the calm of sleep. Instead, something snapped in her mind. Her despondent anger became an unexpected burst of determination. She pushed herself up, hopped to her desk chair, sat down, and opened her laptop. She created a new Word document and named it Criminology 101, Paper 1. She opened up her folder of sources, papers downloaded from JSTOR, and scanned the titles. She opened one and read from the abstract.

This article assessed the prevalence and extent of prison radicalization among . . .

Her patience ran out after a few lines, and she brought up the document again. She wrote her name, the name of the professor, the title of the course, and the date in the upper left-hand corner and then inserted her last name and the page number on the upper right-hand corner. She adjusted the document to one-inch margins and double-spaced lines. The vague thought of creating a template, which always teased her at this point in the paper, hovered in the back of her mind, but she shut it out. She hit the Enter key after the date and center-justified. She typed:

Adjective noun: something something phenomenon of prison radicalization . . .

So far so good. Enter once more, left-justify, indent.

Since the dawn of civilization . . .

She scowled and deleted it, mashing the backspace key as if she could delete it harder that way.

She chewed on her fingertip until there was a knock at the door. She leaned over to pull the handle.

The door creaked open and a face appeared in the crack. Simon, with a big, dumb smile on his face. He looked like he could barely contain his excitement.

"We've got it," he said.

"What?"

"They answered! We got a response!" He pushed open the door, revealing that he was carrying his laptop like a tray, the monitor open.

Alex swiveled her own computer shut.

"Show me," she said.

He set his laptop on top of her closed one. On her legs, it was lopsided because of her cast. The computer was open to an e-mail, on an e-mail client she did not recognize.

The Ekklesia welcomes all interested applicants to prove their dedication and worth to the cause.

Submissions are to be public and aligned with the interests of the people. Dazzle us, and you may become one of us.

"What do you think that means?" Simon said.

"I think they want us to do something," she said. "Like they did with Panagopoulos."

"You mean—"

"Get your cane, Watson. 'Cause we're detectives now."

Chapter 25

L isa Frieze was driving on I-90 back into the city, trying to keep her eyes open. The day had yielded a whole lot of nothing on the Panagopoulos case. She still had no idea how the attackers had gotten in or out and was no closer to identifying any of them. Still, she'd made a little headway on the Watson front.

She dialed Peter Conley from the road. "I got us a meeting at Hornig," she said. "The elevator company. They have a major office in the city."

"You're the best. Who are we meeting with?"

"Some higher-up," she said. "I don't have a name."

"I'd rather deal with the low-level guys," said Conley. "They know what's going on better than management."

"And that's why management is going to do its best to keep you away from them. Meet you there?"

"How long?" Conley asked.

"Half an hour."

"Okay. Text me the address," said Conley.

"Nina Cotter," she said. "General Manager of Operations here at Hornig. Are you the FBI agent?"

Cotter was in her fifties, with salt-and-pepper hair cropped short, wearing a navy blazer over a matching pencil skirt. Frieze saw a distorted version in her of her own future: professional, high-strung, working twice as hard to get as far as the men in the old boys' club. It might also explain why Frieze had such an instant dislike of her.

"Special Agent Lisa Frieze."

"Is this your . . . partner? Is that how it works?" asked Cotter.

"This is a special consultant working with me. Peter Morris."

"Nice to meet you. I have to say, I'm more than a little concerned that the FBI is looking into this matter." She offered up a look of consternation to match. "Is there any indication that this might be a criminal matter?"

"That's what I'm here to find out," said Frieze. "Mind if I take a look at your accident reports?"

"Be my guest. I can e-mail them to you."

"Actually, could I talk to the technical staff working this situation?" Peter broke in. "It would really help to get into the nitty-gritty with the people who are on the ground. So to speak."

Cotter grimaced, sucking in air through her teeth. "That's gonna be tough. They're tied up with this project. It's extremely high priority for us. I'm afraid I can't spare them at all at this moment."

"Ms. Cotter," said Frieze, "I need to insist—"

"I will cooperate with you, Agent Frieze, to the extent that my people can still do their jobs. If not, I'm afraid you'll have to come back with a warrant."

From Cotter's face Frieze could tell they weren't going to get any further in that meeting. There was no use wasting her time.

"All right," said Frieze. She handed over her card. "I'll look out for that e-mail. Thank you for your time."

"We can find our own way to the elevator," said Frieze.

The doors closed and the car moved down.

"You went a little light on her back there," Conley said.

"She's stonewalling," said Frieze. "It's no use pushing, she'll push right back."

"You think she's hiding something?" asked Conley.

"Most definitely."

Chapter 26

Lily felt a surge of excitement when she found Scott waiting for her at a corner table at Le Troquet. She pointed him out to the maître d', who took her coat and walked her to the table.

There was something refreshing about him. All the stupid pickup books these days told men to treat women like dirt. Well, maybe not dirt, but with little things, like keeping them waiting at the restaurant. Play dominance games. She seemed to have good odds that this was just maybe a decent guy.

He stood up as she approached. "I was concerned you wouldn't show." He held out his hand for a shake as she moved in to kiss his cheek, and they did an awkward kiss shake. Lily giggled.

"So, what brings you to the city?"

"We're courting a developer. Some hotshot upstart. He's the best thing since sliced bread, apparently, so I'm here to lure him with a wad of cash and stock options."

Lily held up a finger. "I propose we taboo any further talk about work."

The waiter set down a breadbasket and gave each of them a menu, all done in rich cream stock and baroque calligraphy. The prices were written as two- and sometimes three-digit numbers, no cents or dollar signs. And the actual amounts confirmed that this was indeed a restaurant for the cream of the crop.

"I think I can live with that," said Scott.

"I find it lets me figure out whether there's anything more to a man than that," Lily commented.

"How often do you find there isn't?"

"If I had a quarter for every man who could only talk about

work, I might be able to get myself a cup of coffee." She bit into a breadstick. "I don't date much."

"I can't imagine why."

"It's a work thing, which . . ." She trailed off.

"Well, we don't have to talk about work at all," he said. "I accept. The topic of work is officially off the table."

"Good. That way I can pretend I haven't Googled your name and read all I could find about you."

He chuckled. "You, on the other hand . . . total mystery. Not a whiff of an online presence. I should recommend you as an example for certain high-profile clients."

"That's veering dangerously close to work talk."

"Apologies," he said. "Let's veer away then. Music?"

"Classic British punk," she said. "You?"

"Prog rock." He laughed. Prog rock was at best the older, stodgy cousin to punk. "Let's move on from that one, shall we?"

The waiter came to take orders for drinks. "White?" Scott asked her.

"I drink red." She flashed a coquettish smile.

"Red it is," he said. Then, to the waiter: "Capanna Brunello de Montalcino, 2010." *Bold choice.* Expensive, but not ridiculously so, which she well knew he could afford if he wanted to. But it was important to her that he didn't have to.

"You said you don't date much," he said, when the waiter had gone. "I find that hard to believe."

"I just don't usually feel like I should inflict my life on someone else."

She couldn't believe she was saying this to him. There was just something about the way he carried himself, the way he spoke, that was utterly disarming. It made her comfortable saying just about anything to him, which was a dangerous quality in its own insidious way.

"That doesn't say much for your self-esteem."

"I'm just being realistic."

"And yet here I am," he said, with his broad smile and big white teeth. "Asking—no, begging—to get to know you better."

"You, Mr. Renard, don't have to beg for a single thing in your privileged life."

"I'm not so sure. Have you ever tried to get coders to do what they're supposed to? Sometimes begging is the only thing that has any effect." She laughed. "So," he went on, "what is the lady having?"

She picked a nice midrange dish, osso buco over polenta, which would pair well with the wine.

"You know," he said, "they have a Wagyu steak au poivre here that you need to try."

She glanced at the menu. The price was three times that of the osso buco.

"Come on, you don't—"

"I swear I'm not showing off. But to come here and miss this opportunity—it just wouldn't sit right with me."

She smiled. "Okay. I'll have that."

"Rare?"

"Blue."

"I like you."

The waiter served the wine. She took a sip, woody with hints of berries. "So is this your routine with all your dates, or—"

Her phone rang in her purse.

"I'm so sorry," she said, reaching for it in the spare seat. "Let me just turn it off." She withdrew it and glanced at the screen.

Roger Baxter.

"Oh, no."

"That doesn't sound good," Scott said.

She stood up. "I know that answering the phone at dinner is most gauche thing you can do, but, I *really* need to get this."

"It's fine."

She accepted the call as she walked to a niche near the door.

"Roger?" she said, keeping her voice down so that Scott wouldn't hear.

"I want you." His voice was husky. Dominating.

"Now?"

"This instant."

"Maybe I'm busy," she said, trying to deflect with flirtation, hoping to put it off just enough to finish dinner with Scott.

"Not for me, you're not. Twenty minutes. The Peninsula." And he hung up. Classic negotiating tactic, not giving her a chance to respond. There'd be no backing out now. Miss this one and she might lose him for good.

At least she was dressed for it.

She looked at Scott, sipping his wine at the table, and cursed Baxter, her job, and the world. She walked back, a look of apology plastered on her face. He stood as she came near.

"Bad news?"

"I'm so, so sorry, but something came up," Lily said apologetically.

"Right," he said. "Was it me? Did I say something wrong?"

"No—Scott, it doesn't have anything to do with you. I was having a lovely time. I just really need to go. Work stuff. I can pay for my half of dinner."

"Oh no, don't worry about that," he said, waving her off. But he was, of course, more bothered than he wanted to let on.

"Look, I'll call you, okay?"

"Yikes. It's been a while since I've gotten 'I'll call you.'"

She was losing him. They'd formed some kind of connection, and now all she saw in his face was a wall. "It's not a line," she said. "I really will."

"Sure," he said. "I'm sure you will."

There was something now or never about that moment, and she decided to go with it. She leaned in and kissed him. "That," she said, "was a promise."

He grinned in astonishment. "Okay," he said, starry-eyed. "I guess you convinced me."

She walked away, leaving a piece of herself behind. At least she left him with a smile.

Chapter 27

"How about we . . . ?" Alex extended the monosyllable in an effort to buy time. "Oh! Here's something! Use of expired food in the dining halls!"

She threw a Nerf ball against the wall of Simon's room and caught it again. Her butt was aching from sitting in the same position for so long, but she had vowed not to move until they came up with one good idea to impress the Ekklesia.

"Bo-ring," said Simon.

"Shut up," she said. "This is a brainstorm. You're not allowed to criticize anything during a brainstorm!"

"All right, I'll put it on the list," he said, with a total lack of enthusiasm.

The ball sailed over her hands. Simon, the long-suffering, got up with a groan and picked it up. He threw it against the wall so that its arc brought it within Alex's reach.

"Nice," she said. "So what have we got so far? Read it back to me."

"People selling course papers and old tests, dining room theft, underage drinking, and now expired food."

Alex emitted a long, frustrated groan. "Pathetic." She hit the ball against the wall, and again it sailed over her head and landed by the door. When Simon leaned over to get it, the door swung open and clocked him on the head.

It was Katie, going full throttle. "Party tonight at Phi Epsilon," she said, looking at Alex with the eyes of a crazed Chihuahua.

"On a *Monday*?"

"It's their famous Midwinter Bash. It's legendary!"

"Don't you say that about a party at least once a week?" said Simon.

"They're *all* legendary," she said.

"Sorry, I didn't mean to step all over your rationalization for partying every night."

"Well, regardless, *you're* coming," Katie said, pulling Alex's arm. "I can't stand your moping anymore."

"I've got better things to do," she said.

"What, stare at the wall with General Revelry here? No offense," she added, for Simon's benefit.

"None taken."

"I hate those parties," said Alex. "Everyone just wants to drink, and you can't hear a word anyone says."

"But you can dance!" said Katie. "I mean, in general, not you specifically. But you can sway, right? Can you sway?"

"Katie . . ."

"Come onnn," said Katie. Her pleading gaze found a new target. "Simon, you want to come, right?"

"I guess it wouldn't hurt to get out a bit," he said, nudging Alex.

"Maybe Devin will be there," said Katie, half-singing.

"On second thought—"

"You know what?" Alex said. "I think it's a great idea."

"Oh, you wanna see Devin?" asked Katie.

"What? No," said Alex. "I'm just tired of staying in. Let's hit it."

"Yeah, we could go," said Simon. He pulled on a flannel button-down over his T-shirt.

"You're going like that?" said Katie.

Alex looked down at her outfit. She was wearing a faded yellow T-shirt, rumpled. There might have been a food stain.

"Grab me a hoodie?"

Katie shrugged. "If you want to go looking like a bum, there's nothing I can do about it." She went to the room to get the hoodie.

They took a campus transit bus to Fraternity Row. The night outside was quiet and peaceful, with the magical stillness of winter nights that feel like being in a snow globe.

As they neared the Phi Epsilon house, the song "Get Low" filled the still air. "To the window, to the wall," came the lyrics. "To the sweat drop down my balls."

"I'm so pumped!" said Katie. "Aren't you so pumped?"

"Woo," Alex deadpanned.

Simon helped Alex up the steps of the porch and they walked inside. The heavy bass and beats of the music, the body heat, and the smell of fresh beer over stale beer hit them all at the same time.

"I already regret this," said Alex.

Katie didn't hear her over the "Wooo!" she was howling.

It took about thirty seconds of their being there for one of the brothers to come up to Alex, red Solo cups in hand. "Beer?"

"I think I'll just have some water." The guy laughed and pushed the cup of beer into her hand. She found a table and rearranged the cups already there to find a corner for hers, which she abandoned to go check out the rest of the party. She peeked into a room that had a beer pong table, where they were playing doubles and a large and loud crowd was cheering every toss.

The main living room was what might be called the dance floor. The music was deafening. This is where she found Katie, grinding on some guy Alex didn't know and guessed Katie probably didn't, either.

When she turned her back to the dance floor, someone put another beer in her hand. She motioned to Simon, who'd been standing nearby, to follow her. She navigated her crutches through the crowded party until they reached the porch outside. The cold was refreshing after the stuffy heat of the inside.

"Jeez, can't hear myself think in there," said Alex. She poured her beer over the railing into a snowbank.

Simon leaned his back against the railing next to her.

"Why do we come to these parties?" said Alex.

"Something to do? I don't know. You're the one who wanted to come."

"Well, I'm over it," she said.

"I was over it before we got here."

"It's decided then. I'm going to go find Katie and tell her we're going."

Alex looked on the dance floor first, but couldn't make out Katie in the strobe-lit mass of writhing bodies. She checked the line for beer, and then the beer pong room. No Katie.

Giving up Alex squeezed through the crowd to the foyer, where she caught sight of Katie. She was stumbling, holding onto the banister of the staircase. A large frat brother, a football player type, was practically holding her up, leading her upstairs.

She did her crutch-walk over to where the guy had just started his ascent—Katie was not quite getting the concept of stairs in her condition.

Alex pulled on the frat guy's arm. "Hey! She looks nearly unconscious!"

He turned his head to look at Alex and offered her an expression that told her she was lower than dirt to him. "Screw off!"

She pulled on Katie's arm. "Hey!" She was unresponsive.

"She's with me," said the guy. "All right?"

"What's her name then?"

"What?"

"If she's with you, then what's her name?" Alex asked.

"It's Debbie, all right? Now get lost!"

Alex held on to Katie's arm and set her jaw in determination. "Let her go or I call the police!"

"What's going on?" It was another very large guy, a frat brother, chest out, muscles tense.

"This bitch is on my case."

"Look at her!" said Alex. "She's practically unconscious!"

"I think it's time for you to go home," the newcomer said, grabbing Alex's shoulders.

"Do not touch me!" she said, flinching.

"Hey, what's going on?" It was Simon.

"Simon, call the police."

"*Simon*, get your skinny ass out of our house," said brother number two.

Simon stepped forward, looking him straight in the eye. "What're you going to do? Beat me up? Let the girl go or I'm getting the police involved."

Alex saw the meathead running the calculus in his brain. Yes, he could flatten Simon. But there were witnesses. There was a boundary here he was not ready to cross.

"Whatever," he said, scoffing. "Take her. I'm over it."

Simon slid his right arm under Katie's armpits to support her weight. She clung to him, her irises rolled up into her eyelids.

"Now get out of our house."

Alex helped however she could, but it was slow going with her on crutches. The brothers watched the entire time. As soon as they had cleared the door, Alex pulled out her phone and dialed 911.

"My friend's almost passed out," she said. "I think she had too much to drink. I need an ambulance. Fraternity Row, number twelve."

They found a bench by the street and Simon eased Katie onto it. Music still blasted from the inside, muffled. Simon sat, looking at the ground. Alex rubbed her hands together and her breath misted in front of her. The night lost whatever picturesque magic it had before. All it was now was cold and cruel.

Katie was mumbling.

"Katie?" said Alex. "Are you okay? Can you understand me?"

She stirred, but her eyes still showed only the whites.

"We're going to get you help, okay?"

The cold chilled Alex to her bones.

The ambulance arrived ten minutes later. Alex stood and waved as it came to a stop by the curbside. Two EMTs came out.

"I'm the one who called. This is my friend here."

"What'd she have?" asked one of them, while the other examined Katie. They were both young, not much older than Alex.

"I have no idea."

"She's lucky you were there." They pulled out the gurney from the back of the ambulance and set to work getting Katie on it. Alex watched as they loaded her in.

"Can I go with her?" asked Alex.

"Are you family?" one of the EMTs asked.

"I'm her roommate."

"Then no, sorry. But don't worry. Her parents will be notified." The EMT closed the ambulance door. It took off toward the health center, lights flashing, leaving Alex and Simon behind in the freezing night.

Chapter 28

Morgan and Yolande trekked through the jungle in darkness, ferns whipping their faces, each step slow and tentative. An ankle injury out here could be just as deadly as a bullet. The music of the insects was now and again interrupted by the screech of monkeys and birds. It was hot and humid, and the sweat that drenched their clothes was not enough to keep the mosquitoes from biting.

They had no water, and Morgan had no idea where they were going. If Yolande did, she wasn't sharing.

"How much longer, you think?" he asked as the first tendrils of light were emerging from the horizon.

"Stop complaining, you pussy. There is a road right up ahead." She mumbled under her breath in French about wanting a damn cigarette.

It was sunrise by the time they came upon the muddy dirt road. Morgan couldn't swear it wasn't the same one they left behind, although Yolande seemed certain it was a different one.

They walked along it toward the northwest until they heard a car approaching from around a bend.

"Hide," Yolande told him pointing to a thick tree by the roadside.

"You don't have a gun."

"If I need you, I will call you," she said. "Now hide."

Morgan hid flat against the tree as the car came closer. He listened as it slowed down and came to a full stop next to Yolande, the motor idling. He heard the voice of a man, who held a conversation with Yolande in French.

After about a minute, Yolande said, "Okay. You can come out."

The vehicle was a Ford pickup truck from the 1990s, dented and scratched and caked in mud. The driver was a half-bald guy with missing teeth in a ratty short-sleeve button-down shirt open to below the chest.

"His name is Henri," said Yolande. "He will give us a ride."

"How nice of him."

"Not exactly. Give me your watch."

Morgan rolled his eyes, but undid the clasp on his TAG Heuer and put it in Yolande's hand. She handed it over to Henri, who inspected it with a broad grin.

"Which way are we going?" Morgan asked. It hadn't occurred to him to discuss this sooner. He assumed Yolande would want to return to Abidjan.

"After the trucks, of course," she said, opening the passenger side door.

"We have no guns. No equipment."

She puffed up her chest, the long diagonal scar prominent on her brown skin. She was sweaty, exhausted, but she wasn't going to let that stop her. "We have a mission."

"It's not yours."

"Shut up. I don't chicken out at the first sign of trouble. Now come on, stupid. Get in the back."

Morgan hoisted himself onto the truck bed where Henri was transporting a number of wooden-handled farm implements. They rattled as the truck set off along the uneven road, deeper into the country, toward Madaki and Mr. White.

Chapter 29

Doctor Schuffman walked into the office and patted Alex on the cast in his avuncular manner. "Everything looks good here," he said. "Relatively speaking. Got any pain, other than the pain in the ass of having to walk around in this cast?"

"Har har," said Alex. "No, no pain, no discomfort. Just kind of itchy." She scrunched up her nose. "And it smells kind of bad."

"Well, that's to be expected," the doctor said with a chuckle. "Just a couple more weeks now. Ready to finally be rid of this thing?"

"You have no idea how ready I am."

"Not much writing on it, I see" he said.

"I haven't been getting out much."

"Well, I guess we're all set. Want a lollipop?" He pulled one out from his coat pocket.

"I'm good, Dr. Schuffman, thanks."

"Good," he said, sticking it in his mouth. "That was my lunch!"

"How long have you been holding onto that one?"

He helped her to her feet and held the door open for her.

"I was saving it for you," he said through the lollipop as she hobbled away. "See you in two weeks!"

"Not if I see you first!" she called out.

She walked to the elevator, but rather than going to the lobby she hit the button for the third floor. The inpatient ward.

"I'm here to see Katie—Katherine Kesey," she said.

"Here we go," the receptionist said, holding up a chart. "Just sign in here." He handed her a clipboard across the counter. "Name, ID number—student ID is fine—the patient you're visiting, then your John Hancock."

She filled out the fields and handed it back to him.

Her stomach felt heavy as she made her way down the hall of the ward to the intense smell of hospital disinfectant.

"Come in!"

Katie was propped up on the hospital bed. There was a teen show on the TV, muted. The other bed was vacant. There was no one else there.

"Hey." Her voice came across drained of its usual energy.

Alex moved to stand at her bedside. Katie, in a hospital gown, had deep bags under her eyes, heavy-lidded, and was Alex mistaken or they were a bit skittish, too? "How are you feeling?"

"Still a little woozy, but okay. They said I could get out of here in a few hours."

"I'm glad. The room's a little too quiet without you."

Katie mustered a weak smile, then her face went solemn and she stared out the window. From the hill that held the student health center, they could see most of the campus, the vast open spaces sprinkled with evergreens and leafless deciduous trees tiny like a diorama, students and professors making their way through the paths to the assortment of red-brick colonial and angular modern classroom buildings.

"Mom's not coming out. She told me it was my fault for drinking too hard. Said she was glad my health insurance covered it, or it was coming out of my college fund."

Alex grimaced in sympathy. "Parents can really suck sometimes." She felt guilty saying so. As much as thinking about her father made her well up with anger, she had to admit to herself that he would always be there when she needed him, no matter what. "How are you doing?"

"Holding up," she said, but her voice cracked as she did. "Barely." Tears welled up in her eyes.

"I don't know what happened," Katie said, shaking her head. "I didn't even drink that much last night. I had, like, half a beer tops. I don't remember anything past that."

Alex frowned. If that was true . . .

"Do you know anyone in the frat, Katie? Anyone who might have wanted to take advantage of you?"

"I barely know any of those guys. I mean, I've seen them around."

Alex looked down at the mottled linoleum floor. She felt so powerless to help her.

"Is there anyone you want me to call? Anything I can do for you?"

"I'd just as soon no one found out. I'm kind of embarrassed."

"Are you sure? It can be really important to have some support—"

"It's fine, really."

"I get it."

Katie's distant expression slackened, and she put her hand on Alex's, which was resting on the bedrail. "Thanks for being here, though."

Alex felt in that touch Katie's deep vulnerability. It was overwhelming to her, who wasn't the picture of stability herself. But somehow it gave her strength, knowing that she needed to be strong for her friend.

She set her jaw. This wasn't going to get any easier, and the clock was ticking. "I'm sorry to bring this up now, but I think you might have been drugged." Katie withdrew her hand, her eyes glazing over again. Alex insisted. "It's really important for you to get your blood drawn as soon as possible, so that—"

"I'm feeling kind of dizzy," Katie blurted out. She put her hand on her head as if to steady it, a little too theatrically.

Alex frowned. She'd lost her. "Do you want me to call the doctor?"

"No, I think I just want to close my eyes for a while."

Alex wasn't buying it. "Katie, this is important. Please. I just want to help."

"Maybe I don't want your help!" She seemed on the verge of a panic attack. "I can't stand all this questioning anymore. What do you people want from me?"

Alex narrowed her eyes and furrowed her brow. "Did someone else come here to ask you questions?"

"This guy. He kept asking these same questions. How much I drank last night. If I had taken any drugs. If I ever drank or took drugs, and if I was a virgin."

"Was he with the police? Campus security?"

Katie shook her head, frantic.

"I won't tell anyone if you don't want me to," said Alex, resting her hand on Katie's shoulder. But her friend flinched at the touch, and she drew it away. "Nobody ever needs to know you're involved. But I don't want to let whoever did this get away with it."

"They'll come after me," she said, near tears. "They said if I talked—"

"Someone told you to keep quiet about this? Who?"

"Please, just leave me alone."

"Give me a name," Alex insisted. "Just a name."

"Out!" she yelled, crying. "I'll scream. I'll tell them you attacked me. *Get out!*"

"I'm sorry," said Alex.

"Just *go!*" Katie screeched.

Alex shuffled off, closing the door lightly behind her. No one out in the hallway seemed to have heard. Heavy with guilt, she limped her way down the ward hall. She had pushed too hard. But her determination to do something only intensified. By the time she reached the reception desk, she had formulated a plan.

"I think I might have missed a number on my ID in the sign-in sheet earlier," she told the receptionist. "Can I see?"

The receptionist handed her the sheet. Alex scanned it for Katie's name. She found it once, next to Alex's own name on the sheet. Then, a few entries above hers, with a matching patient name—

Adam Groener.

Gotcha.

Chapter 30

Lisa Frieze overslept and drove back up to Springhaven University in the late morning, swigging Dunkin Donuts coffee and swerving through traffic. She drove onto campus wired for action.

She found Vickery waiting for her outside the library.

"Nice of you to join us," he said, leading the way inside.

"I was up late last night looking into the other Ekklesia cases around the country," she said. "They've all got similar MOs. None of them took direct action, not more than the kind of prank they pulled on Panagopoulos. All of them claim to be working for citizens' freedom or bringing the guilty to justice. And all of them have a hacking angle."

"But they all happened at the same time," he said. "So there's no way it's the same people."

"We're talking about a massively distributed network of agents," she said.

They were walking downstairs, bare concrete with plain steel railings. "Where are we going?"

"I want to show you something."

He opened a metal door and pointed at the frame, specifically at the strike plate.

"Do you see it?"

"I'm not sure what I'm looking for."

"Here," he said, pointing closer. "What does that look like to you?"

"Glue. Like we found on the door to the roof of the library. So this was their point of entry." She looked through the door. It opened into a tunnel that seemed to go for a mile until disappearing in a curve. A set of thick pipes ran through it, and it was warm and misty.

"Steam tunnels," he said. "They run under every building in the university. It's where the heating comes from." He looked down the tunnels. "It's an awful lot of doors."

"So their point of entry—"

"Could've been anywhere," he said. "Could be students, service staff. Or neither. Someone who could make the camera feeds disappear sure as heck wouldn't have too much trouble gaining access here."

"What's the access system on these doors?" she asked.

"Keycards," he said. "With a manual override key."

"All the tunnels?"

"That I know of."

She thought for a moment. "If we're talking about hackers, it would be more in their wheelhouse to clone a card than to make a copy of the key or pick the lock. I'm guessing any use of the keycards gets logged in a database somewhere."

"I'd guess," said Vickery.

"I want to talk to security," she said. "Maybe we can find a clue in the access logs."

"I've got some paperwork to do down at the station," he said. "But I can put you in touch with the right people." He told her the on-campus address of the security office. "I'll give them a call, let them know you're going to swing by later."

"Thanks."

"Are you going back to the city tonight?" he asked as they walked back upstairs.

"I was planning on it," she said.

"Why don't you hang around? I know a great little bar off the highway. No college kids, just good beer and good music."

Her phone rang. Conley.

"Let me get back to you on that," she said as they parted ways. Then she picked up. "What?"

"Did you look at the service manifest Cotter sent you?" he asked.

"Been busy," she said. "What did you find?"

"Nothing that called any particular attention," he said. "But I had the feeling that it wouldn't. We got it too easily. So I went to the Acevedo building. You know what I found?"

"I suppose you're going to tell me."

"They had a service visit from Hornig two weeks ago."

"Let me guess—it's not on Hornig's logs?"

"No," Conley said. "And I checked the signature on the visitor logs at the building. No match. We had an impostor come in."

"How did you get access—" she remembered the young receptionist who she had no doubt would've remembered him. "Never mind."

"So I went to see if I could find surveillance footage of our guy," said Conley. "And you know what I found?"

"Let me guess," she said. "It's gone."

"How did you know?"

"Do you think Watson's murder might have anything to do with the Ekklesia?" asked Lisa.

Chapter 31

Morgan woke up in the bed of the old Ford pickup truck as Henri pulled it to a stop. His muscles were sore from the previous night's walk and his back was aching from the shovel handle that prodded him through his dreamless sleep. The sun was low in the sky, but sleeping in the open truck bed gave him a nasty sunburn.

They were surrounded by more jungle, but the area seemed wilder, and nature was encroaching on the road as if to reclaim it. In the cab, Henri and Yolande argued in French. Morgan tapped on the window. "What's going on?"

"He will not take us any farther," Yolande said. "He says this is a bad place. Too dangerous."

"What's the danger?"

"This is Madaki's territory. His militia patrol the roads. He says there is a gold mine just beyond the ridge over there."

Morgan hopped off the truck bed onto the dirt road, stretching out his legs. Yolande came out as well. Henri drove away, leaving them with nothing but a canteen of water and two cigarettes, one lit. Yolande puffed away as they walked.

"We should have stolen his car," she said. She finished the cigarette in two minutes flat, lighting the second one with the smoldering butt of the first.

They decided to keep off the roads. They took a right into the jungle, trekking uphill toward the ridge Henri had pointed out.

It was only an hour's hike in the shade, and once they got going, Morgan's sore muscles regained their limberness. More mosquitoes, but not quite as much heat. The top of the hill was dense with trees, but Morgan found a rock that extended up over the canopy.

Using a tree as support, he hoisted himself up, grunting to pull up his weight to the top.

He overlooked the vast country below, jungle sprinkled with the odd family farm. That was all he saw, except for one thing. In the valley, right at the bottom of the hill, the greenery was interrupted by a gash of bare earth. One of Madaki's illegal gold mines. Men, women, and children, numbering in the hundreds, dressed in rags, most shirtless under the punishing sun, digging with pickaxes, sifting, carrying baskets or wheelbarrows of dirt.

Yolande, with her limber frame, climbed on the rock in half the time it took Morgan.

"Mr. White's guns are not there," she said.

No, but they had their own. The upper levels were patrolled by militiamen, dressed in T-shirts, polos, carrying AK-47s, for the most part—the Kalashnikovs were an infestation in politically unstable third world countries, sold off for quick cash after the fall of the Soviet Union—with a smattering of other rifles and SMGs, handguns tucked into the waist of their shorts. Some of them held leashes tied to . . . "Dogs," he said. "I really don't like dogs."

Morgan did a quick count of the guards. For all the people that were working there, there were no more than fifty. Maybe more like thirty-five.

And on one end of the mine, where it connected to the road—cars. Pickup trucks, sedans, nine all told. They were parked near a cluster of buildings.

Morgan heard shouting below. One of the workers, in flip-flops and a maroon shirt, had taken off running toward the road. The guards mustered, aiming their rifles. The *rat-a-tat* of the Kalashnikovs echoed in the valley. The man was hit. He stumbled to the ground, clutching his leg, contorting in pain.

The guards circled him, but didn't shoot. Instead, they loosed the dogs on him.

Morgan looked away. The man's screaming did not last long.

Morgan and Yolande sat down on the rock, watching the sun disappear behind the mountains. He looked at her face, at her rugged beauty, unflappable even here, lost in the middle of nowhere.

"Beautiful country out here," he said.

"It is."

"Are you from around this region? You seem to know your way around."

"I was born at the foot of those mountains," she said, pointing to the east.

"I don't see anything there."

"No. It is not there anymore."

He reclined against the rock. "What's your story? Of all the able-bodied men in his service, how come Jakande picked you for this mission?"

"Do you think he made a poor decision?" she said, in a defiant tone.

Morgan chuckled. "No. I really don't." He swatted a mosquito on his forehead. His skin stung from the sunburn.

"I get things done. General Jakande knows that."

His stomach growled. He took a sip from the canteen and handed it to her—the last of it. "How'd you get the scar?"

She finished the water, letting it drip onto her tongue. "I was a child soldier. Do you need to know more?"

Morgan wanted to, but he could tell she didn't want to talk. He closed his eyes and felt the gust of wind that was rising, letting it cool his sweltering skin.

"We need to go down there," he said. "We need guns and a car. They have both."

"Are you crazy? They will shoot us on sight."

"I don't intend to be seen."

Chapter 32

Scott Renard picked up Lily outside her Cambridge apartment in a white Lexus coupe. She came in out of the cold, red-nosed and chilled, with a huge idiot smile on her face. Why did everything feel so great all of a sudden?

She ran her hands over the leather detailing of the interior. "Is this yours?"

"Rental, while I'm in the city. I'm kind of a car guy."

He flipped on his turn signal and set off.

"Shut up," she said. "I love cars. Well, I love the driving part, anyway. We should race."

"I took a course in stunt driving last year. So you'll have to forgive me if I end up leaving you in the dust."

Lily suppressed a scoff.

"What was that?"

"I said, 'where are we going?'"

"Well, that's a surprise."

"Oh, exciting." She clapped her hands. "You're not going to take me to a *museum*, are you?"

"What's wrong with a museum?" Scott asked.

"Nerd."

"You were under no illusions about that when you asked me out today."

Lily smiled. She was giddy. Giddy! Like a bloody *teenager*!

A car cut them off and Scott missed a light.

"You drive like a girl," she taunted him.

"I'm being *prudent*."

"This is not a car to be prudent in."

They bantered back and forth as he drove past Longfellow Bridge and then Faneuil Hall. It was so different from Baxter's imperious manner, his barking orders. Things flowed with Scott. They felt good.

He turned into valet parking at the New England Aquarium.

"I know," he said. "Kids. Families. Not ideal. But have you ever been here before? It's my favorite place in the entire city. And it's not too busy midafternoon."

She was unconvinced. "I'll suspend disbelief for now."

They got their tickets and Scott pulled her right for the main chamber. When she caught her first look of the four-story Giant Ocean Tank, she changed her mind.

"This is beautiful." They started along the spiral ramp that wound around it.

"I know," he said. "It's my favorite thing in the city." He put his arm around her. "Well, second favorite."

She pulled him in for a kiss. This got them the stink eye from a teacher leading a group of kids on a tour.

"So you haven't told me a thing about what you do," Scott said.

"Uh uh," she said, wagging a finger. "Work talk's still taboo."

"Then you ask me a question."

"How old are you?" Lily asked.

"Twenty-seven."

"My God, you're such a child," she said. A tiger shark passed the window, but Scott was more interesting.

"How old are you?" He furrowed his brow.

"Twenty-eight," she said, laughing. "I thought you Silicon Valley rich guys were all after twenty-one-year-old models."

"The guys after twenty-one-year-olds are the ones who can't get women their own age to believe their bullcrap."

"Is that right?"

"I mean, you can dazzle a college girl if you don't eat ramen noodles for every meal and all your furniture doesn't come from Ikea, as long as you like the right music. It's a pretty low bar to clear."

"And you can get an older girl to believe *your* bullcrap?"

He laughed. "I like someone who can challenge me."

"You don't want a tight twenty-one-year-old body to play with?"

"To the extent that that matters," he said, looking her up and down with wolfish eyes, "I've got all I can handle right here."

They kissed, pulling apart before things progressed past a G rating in a family venue. They walked in silence, Lily clinging to his arm, watching as a stingray passed, gliding through the water.

"So what's your story?" she asked as they neared the top. "What makes you, you?"

"That's a big question."

"Bigger than this fish tank?"

He half-smiled. "All right. I'll give you this. I used to think that being good was about being nice."

"You aren't nice?"

"I try to be kind," he said. "There's a difference. Being nice is not offending people. It's not making anyone feel uncomfortable. But sometimes being nice keeps you silent when you should speak up. It keeps you from acting when you need to do something."

"I hadn't really thought about it that way," she said.

"It's this whole spiritual thing."

"And here my family was happy to attend Anglican services on Christmas and Easter. So you're religious?"

"I like to say I'm Silicon Valley Buddhist," he said with a chuckle. "I know it doesn't have that much to do with real Buddhism, even though we like to pretend it does. But it's a way to live."

The tiger shark came close to the glass, to the delight of the nearby kids.

"I wasn't always like this. When I was, oh, fourteen, I used to play video games all day after I got home from school." His eyes grew distant. "Hardly any friends, maybe none if I'm really honest with myself. I would justify it by telling myself I was doing what I wanted."

"Then what happened?"

"I saw a bird die. I know, stupid, right? He hit a window as I was walking home from school one day and fell to the ground, right in front of me. He twitched for a few minutes and then stopped moving. I watched the whole time. I couldn't move. I couldn't do anything but keep watching, for minutes and minutes after he was dead.

"It could have been nothing. I didn't believe in signs. It wasn't even the first bird I'd seen die. But something just clicked. I was fifteen, and already all I did was kill time. Eat, sleep, video games, zone out at school. That was it. No real hope for something better, no real will to do anything with my life."

"And so you changed?" Lily asked.

"I sold my video game console and all the games the very next day. Made me a cool two hundred. Put it toward some running shoes, free weights, and a couple of books on programming. The books turned out to be mostly useless, but I got into a couple Internet forums for people like me who were learning to code."

She squeezed his hand. "Strange that such a small thing could change your life like that."

"I think it had been building for a long time. One of the hardest things is admitting it. Once I did, things just kind of fell into place."

She leaned into him, head against his shoulders. He enveloped her with his arm.

"What about you?" he asked. "What makes Lily Harper tick?"

Her fake name in his voice caused her a pang of sadness, reminding her of the gulf that separated them that she couldn't cross. It made her want to be open with him.

"I'm an orphan," she said. "Raised by my gram. Kind of a lonely kid. By the time I realized I was pretty, it was too late, and I already wanted to do something with my life."

She trailed off.

"You know what? Why don't we just look at the tank for a while?"

A puffer fish stared at them from behind the glass, wide-eyed and distended. She rested her head against his shoulder, feeling close to him. At least that much she could do.

Chapter 33

Morgan and Yolande waited for hours after nightfall, after the mine guards huddled all the slaves into a warehouse surrounded by barbed wire. They drank around a bonfire, now and then firing bullets into the air just because, and then went to sleep. Only four of them kept a lookout, carrying rifles, walking around the edge of the camp, which was illuminated by lightbulbs hung up on posts, connected to a generator.

Insects were screaming, and the night sky was darker than it could be in any city. The moon lit up the forest, and millions of stars were visible against the smear of glimmering points that was the Milky Way.

Once most of the men had either passed out or gone off to sleep, Morgan and Yolande got down from the rock and began their careful descent. The ground was treacherous, and a false step could mean falling to their death.

They reached the camp within the hour. The jungle extended right up to the edge, where an armed guard was standing. They stopped fifty feet short of his position.

"Go around," Yolande whispered to Morgan. "I'll provide the distraction."

He crept to the right while she went left. One step at a time, he came closer, careful not to make a sound. To draw the guard's attention now would mean putting the whole camp on high alert and there would go their one chance at this.

When Morgan was within thirty feet of the man, he heard a rustle.

The man raised his Kalashnikov. "*Qui est là?*"

Yolande came out of the bush and stepped into the light. She had removed her shirt, breasts bare for the guard to see. Her scar, Morgan now saw, went from her shoulder all the way down to her belly.

This was his cue to move in.

"*Qui es-tu?*" The harshness had melted from the man's speech. His eyes were locked on Yolande.

"*Je suis perdu*," she said. "I am lost."

The man lowered his rifle. "*Vous êtes au bon endroit.*" Morgan could imagine the eyebrow wag that went with that statement. He bent down to pick up a rock, smooth and heavy. Yolande was flashing the guard a coquettish smile. *Poor bastard. Must think it's his lucky night.*

With a nod from Yolande, Morgan raised the stone and brought it hard against the man's head, caving in his skull. He grunted and toppled to his knees, falling at his side. His AK-47 clattered to the ground.

Morgan grabbed the rifle, and Yolande led the way through the wooden shacks. The nearest was a sort of warehouse where Morgan figured the gold was stored. Next was a kennel, where the dogs were kept tied up. Then, the building where the guards slept, from which they heard a choir of snoring. They skulked around it, keeping to the shadows and taking their time.

Morgan looked around the corner at the makeshift parking lot. "I'm going to check the cars for keys," he whispered to Yolande. He crept forward out into the open, taking cover behind a VW pickup truck. He pulled the handle, slowly, making no sound. Locked.

He went for the next one, a Toyota with a door of a different color. He tried this one. It was locked, too. Keeping low, he moved toward the front of the car, looking for the next—

Footsteps. Right on the other side of the car. He bent down to look. Male feet, in sandals. *Shit.* How had Morgan not heard him coming?

The man was moving toward Yolande. She would come into view within seconds. He motioned for her to move, but she was looking away at another guard on the far end of the camp.

Only one thing to do.

Morgan stood up and opened fire. Several bullets burrowed into the man's back and he fell forward, dead.

Yolande looked at him as if to say, *What the hell are you doing?*

"Grab his gun!" Morgan yelled. He ran to the next car, an old Ford Mondeo. He tried the door. Locked.

Gunfire. Yolande, rifle in hand, shooting at the men coming out of the dormitory. Another guard was running toward them from the direction of the mine. Morgan took careful aim. He pulled the trigger. The single bullet found its target, and the man stumbled to the dusty ground.

Guards were pouring out of the dormitory now, each armed, each shooting. Morgan and Yolande took cover behind the Mondeo and fired, trying to hold them back. Yolande, less thrifty with her bullets, ran out in seconds. Morgan kept them away with spaced bursts of the Kalashnikov, but there were too many. As the guards circled them, he dropped his gun and raised his hands, nudging Yolande to do the same. She spat at the ground but complied.

They were surrounded by twenty men, carrying their mismatched weapons, shouting at them and each other. Morgan did his best to appear nonthreatening.

"What are they saying?"

"Well," said Yolande, with her characteristic irrational calm, "they're going to shoot us. They're trying to decide if they will do it now or torture us first."

More discussion. "*Bouge ton cul!*" a man shouted at them.

"What's happening?"

"They decided to shoot us. But they don't want to damage the car. I believe the expression he used translates to *move your ass*."

The man who'd shouted, who appeared to be their leader, motioned with his rifle for them to move away from the car. Morgan looked for a way out. He was unarmed and surrounded by rifle-wielding men who wanted to kill him. Even he had to admit this one looked bad for him.

"Yolande?"

"Yes?"

"Sorry I got you into this."

"Screw your apology. Die like a man."

The woman had a way with words.

Morgan stared at the barrel of the leader's AK. Would that be the one that killed him?

He relaxed. Nothing else to do. Nothing, except to die. There was some peace in that.

Then he heard gunfire—not from the men surrounding them, but coming from the edge of camp, and not automatic fire, but pistols. Everyone's attention turned. Men were coming in from the darkness, dressed in civilian clothing. There was maybe one automatic rifle among them. The rest carried revolvers, or hunting rifles, with the odd semiautomatic. Some, lacking firearms altogether, were wielding machetes or axes.

Morgan pulled Yolande to the ground as the place became a war zone. They retreated behind the VW truck and watched the carnage.

The camp guards were better armed, but the raiders had the numbers, and were mowing down their enemies.

Yolande tugged at his shoulder. "Let's go."

They moved back the way they came, around the barracks, hoping to disappear into the forest. But raiders came out of the woods there, too, cutting off their escape route, yelling for them to move back toward the killing field.

Morgan put his hands up as the gunmen closed around them. Most of the guards were dead, and those that weren't had surrendered. There were around two hundred raiders all told, by Morgan's estimation. A group of them ran off to the slaves' quarters. One man was hitting the lock on the door with an ax.

The raiders were dressed in civilian clothes, much like the mine guards, but they were not all men in their teens or twenties, as the guards were. There were older men among them, even some whose hair was gray or white, and even some women. These were not regular bandits.

"Tell them we're not one of them," said Morgan.

Yolande spoke to one of them men in French. They had a brief exchange.

"They know," said Yolande. "They saw what happened before they arrived."

"Good news then?"

The door to the slaves' quarters opened. The first were scared to cross the threshold, but once the first group had emerged to freedom, the rest poured out, whooping with joy. The raiders collected the guns, and someone found the keys to the cars, which they started loading up with everything they could find. Morgan took a step back as he saw a man carrying a box of dynamite.

One of the raiders motioned for them to move. The group was retreating back toward the road. They were starting the cars, too, filled with supplies and the slaves that were least able to walk.

"Where are they taking us?" Morgan asked Yolande as they moved along at gunpoint.

"I don't know. But at least we are alive. For now."

Chapter 34

"I don't know," said the subchief of security, who was the ranking manager in the office that day. "That's a lot of entries to go through."

Lisa Frieze could tell from the moment she laid eyes on him that he wasn't going to be helpful. He struck her right away as the kind of person who was just running out the clock on his workday—almost over, at five-thirty—and, in a broader sense, his life. She would bet that he made it into this job on seniority alone. And any extra work, no matter how important, just got in the way of doing nothing.

"Plus, you don't have a warrant."

"I was hoping," Frieze said, rubbing her temple, "that you might cooperate with our investigation. That you'd be interested to know whether there's a vulnerability in campus security."

"That's really more of an internal matter."

"Maybe I should come back tomorrow and talk to the chief then? He might like to know how helpful you've been."

He exhaled, signaling that he was not at all happy with the situation. "Fine. I'll sign off on it for you."

She waited half an hour, which she guessed was at least fifteen minutes longer than necessary, until he came back to her with a printed packet of more than a hundred pages.

"Here," he said, dropping it on the counter. "The door access logs for three days leading to the incident. Here you got your door codes, the date and time stamp, and the key code. I'm going to need you to sign this." He handed her a pen and a clipboard with a form attached, and she scrawled her name on the bottom.

She then looked at the packet, at the rows upon rows of numbers and alphanumeric codes, all blending together.

Today was not the day for this.

"Thanks," she said, leaving with the packet in hand.

She checked her phone as she left the building. No sign from Conley.

She scoffed at herself. *Pathetic*, waiting for him to call. She could really use a drink. And there was someone who actually wanted to have that drink with her.

She searched for a name in her phone's address book and made the call. It rang.

"Hello?"

"Bryce? I think I'll take you up on your offer after all."

Chapter 35

It was morning by the time the ragtag group of raiders arrived at their destination, with Morgan and Yolande in tow. The end of their trek was at a camp in the jungle, a mile off the road. It was all tents and makeshift shelters, populated by women, children, and men too old or crippled to fight, who greeted those returning with whoops of joy. Some of them came to greet the freed slaves, too, embracing them with tears in their eyes. Families reunited. Morgan felt a twinge for Alex.

The raiders weren't bothering to keep guns on Morgan and Yolande anymore. It was clear to their captors that the two were enemies of their enemies.

Whether that meant they were friends remained to be seen.

People turned to look as Morgan walked into the camp. The children followed them, staring without any sign of embarrassment. He figured white people weren't too common around these parts. He and Yolande were instructed to sit down on a damp log in front of a fire, where a young woman gave them wooden bowls filled with some kind of corn porridge. Bland as it was, to Morgan, who hadn't had a proper meal in days, it was as good as any steak Jenny had ever grilled.

"I think feeding us is a sign they don't plan on killing us," Morgan said.

"I wish they would give me a damn cigarette."

After they ate, they were taken to a man Yolande identified as their leader, sitting on a rock near the middle of the camp. He was nearing forty, hard and sinewy, with a fresh wound on his face that had been washed but not dressed. They sat down in front of him, a group of young armed guards. Two older men seemed to be there in a more advisory capacity. He exchanged a few words with Yolande, among which Morgan caught *Américain* and *Anglais*. Then the man spoke in English, accented but passable.

"Who are you? What are you doing here?"

Morgan opted for the truth, more or less. "I'm here looking for a man. Goes by the name of Mr. White." Yolande remained quiet— Morgan intuited she didn't want them to know of her connection with General Jakande.

The two men turned to the leader and huddled in to speak. The leader held his hand up for silence. "Are you friends of this Mr. White?"

The correct answer was clear from his tone. It happened to also be the true one. "No. I'm here to make him answer for his crimes. To stop the flow of guns."

"The guns going to Madaki?"

"Yes. I'm here to stop them from reaching him."

"The guns have already reached him. I think you are not doing a very good job." His face erupted into a broad grin and then into laughter. With that, Morgan knew he was in. "I am Etienne Dimka. Leader of this group. We are a resistance army. Our country's military will not rid us of Madaki, so we will do it ourselves."

"I am Anthony Bevelacqua," Morgan said. "I was sent here by my country to capture the arms dealer known as Mr. White."

Dimka grimaced in response. "The great and powerful United States sends one man?"

"This is not strictly official. Still, I have some support in the country. I may be able to get some help. But I need to get in touch with my people, and I don't have any way to contact them."

Dimka rubbed his chin. "I have something that may work." He spoke a few words in French to one of the younger men present. The man ran off with a purposeful gait. Dimka turned his attention back to Morgan. "I know where this White is, and his weapons. We hurt one of the men from the mine until he told us. He is with Madaki. He made his base in an old mansion, twenty miles from here. His army is camped on the land around it."

Not good.

"We are planning an attack in the morning," he said. "We have numbers. There are three hundred here in the camp, plus the slaves we freed last night, but there are more spread throughout the countryside. Madaki has about four hundred men with him. We number more than one thousand." Dimka puffed up his chest with pride.

Poorly armed and poorly trained, thought Morgan. They needed some serious tactics to pull this off.

"Do you know the land where you're engaging the enemy?" Morgan asked. "Do you know if there are sentries posted?"

"They have lookouts," said Dimka. "But we will approach in the dark, like in the mine. We will move silently."

Morgan remembered how many losses they sustained in the mine—two for every man they took down, and that was with overwhelming force on their side. They wouldn't have that at Madaki's camp.

"With your permission," said Morgan, "I'd like to go, along with my guide, ahead of the group. I'd like to take a look at this place. I might be able to advise you about how to use your forces to gain an advantage."

Dimka frowned. He was about to speak when the young man who had run off came back with a familiar handheld device. Dimka took it and handed it to Morgan. "Here you go, Mr. Bevelacqua." It was the sat phone that had been stolen from him on the road two days before. It had been Dimka's men, then, who ambushed them. Morgan hoped he wouldn't be recognized. "Will this work?"

Morgan turned it on. The electronic display lit up. Batteries charged, strong signal. "That'll do it."

"About your request," he said. "I am still not certain you are not a spy. I do not know you will not betray me if I let you move ahead. But perhaps I will send you with an advance team that will keep an eye on you. Is this acceptable?"

"It's fine," Morgan replied.

"Good. Go on. Contact your people. Get what help you can."

With a deferential bow, Morgan stood up and walked away, followed by Yolande. The children, a gaggle of about a dozen assorted girls and boys who had been watching the meeting from a distance, resumed following them.

"What do you think?" he asked.

Yolande was impassive. "He is a dreamer and a fool. They will be massacred."

"This is your chance to leave. I can have my people contact Jakande and send someone for you."

"I do not run from a battle." She broke away from him. "I am going to go find a cigarette."

Morgan found a quiet corner by a grove where he sat in the shade of a palm tree, waving flies away from his face. The children, still on his tail, peeked at him from behind a tent.

Morgan turned on the sat phone. "Zeta, this is Cobra. Come in. Over." He gave it a few seconds and tried again.

"Cobra, this is Zeta." Diana Bloch, relief breaking through even her stony timbre. "We thought we'd lost you."

He related the events since the ambush, telling her about Dimka and his militia. "They're attacking Madaki's camp in the morning," he said. "I'm going with them and try to make my way to White. It's going to be tricky. I need tactical support for extraction."

"General Jakande has secured air transportation and weapons for Bishop and the others. This is an in-and-out mission."

"Understood," said Morgan.

"I mean it," said Bloch. "You owe no allegiance to these people. You do not have to fight their war for them."

Morgan looked out into the busy camp, the displaced families, fighting for their land, for their lives. "They're a means to an end. They'll serve as a distraction while I get to White. That's all."

"Good. I'll alert Bishop to have the tactical team on alert. Keep me updated."

Morgan terminated the call. As he reclined against the tree trunk, he heard rustling from a nearby bush. He looked, expecting to see a child, but instead, it was Yolande, close enough to have heard every word. She was now turning her back on him.

"Hey," Morgan, standing. "Hey! Yolande!"

But she didn't turn around as she stomped away from him, digging her heels into the muddy ground.

Chapter 36

L isa Frieze walked into the FBI field office regretting the night before. She screwed up her eyes to block out the stray images of sloppy drunken make outs with Bryce Vickery that wafted through her mind, but she was finding it hard to focus on anything.

"What truck hit you on the way to work?" Gus Loyola asked her as she walked in.

"I'd rather not talk about it."

She sat in her cubicle with the papers she had gotten from the university the day before, wondering what to make of it.

She had a list of what person held each keycard, identified by a code. She also had a series of maps that showed the code for each of the doors, which she figured out were a combination of four letters or numbers designating the building plus three more designating the particular door.

She wasn't sure whether the subchief of security had given her a printout rather than digital documents out of spite or incompetence. If it had been spite, well, then, kudos to him. He had succeeded in making her life difficult.

She marked the doors that led into the steam tunnels, which inconveniently all had different building codes, with a dot at the end of the row of data. Then she went through each of the people who had accessed any of those doors, highlighting each with a different color.

Her phone beeped. A text message from Conley, finally.

Can we meet?

She texted back.

Half an hour, outside FBI offices.

She returned to her work. It was stupid busywork, but sometimes that was what investigations consisted of.

She was barely a quarter done when Chambers poked his head out of his office. He asked Gus, "Is Frieze in yet?"

"I'm here," she said.

"My office. Now."

"Oof," said Gus as she walked past him. "In trouble?"

She exhaled. "Good it ain't."

"Lotsa luck."

Frieze knocked and entered Chambers's office.

"Close the door," he said.

She did, and sat across from him. He steepled his fingers against his mouth, his chair turned 90 degrees away from her, as if he were reflecting on what he was going to say. Maybe it was his way of torturing her.

"I got a call from someone at an elevator company of all places," said Chambers. "Do you know what they told me? That you've been harassing their people about an accident that happened last Friday."

"I've hardly been harassing anyone. I just had an informal talk with a—"

"Tell me something, Frieze. Did you use your capacity as an agent of the Federal Bureau of Investigation to gain undue access to a case you were not assigned to?"

"I might have mentioned that I was an agent."

"*Might* have? Cut the weasel words, Frieze. Did you or didn't you?"

"I did."

"Would this informal talk have anything to do with a certain accountant with a tongue-twister name?"

"No, sir. I was just following up on a lead, sir."

"A lead about the case you're working?"

"No, sir."

He banged on his desk. "Then tell me, Frieze. What in the *hell* were you doing there?"

"Chambers, this wasn't just an accident. Dominic Watson was murdered."

"The local police, who actually have jurisdiction over this case, disagree."

"They don't have the full picture. The circumstances are extremely suspicious."

"An elevator crashed. End of story!" Chambers yelled.

"A technician came for a service visit that the elevator company has no record of one week before Watson's death. And the camera feeds are just *coincidentally* missing for that day."

"We are done talking about this," said Chambers. "I don't want you near this elevator case. You're on thin ice. Do your job. That's an order."

Frieze walked out of the elevator to meet Conley, who was waiting for her in the lobby. She was angry. She was determined. The bitch would not get away with it, and Frieze would prove Chambers wrong.

"I wanted to show you something I found on—"

"Never mind," she said through gritted teeth. "Let's go find out what Nina Cotter is hiding."

"Now?"

Frieze was in the mood to lash out. No better candidate than the bitch who had caused the mess. "Yes, now."

In her car, Frieze decided she'd come clean. "She called my boss."

"What?"

"Nina Cotter. She called my goddamn boss. Gave him some bull that we were harassing her."

"And so the plan is to go back and *actually* harass her?"

"More or less."

"I don't want to be the one to point out the obvious, but what if she calls your boss again?"

"I'll make sure she doesn't."

"How?"

"I'll put the fear of God into her, that's how."

Frieze pulled into the parking space outside the building that housed the Hornig offices, tires squealing, and pressed ahead as Conley stayed behind to put change in the meter.

He caught up with her in the lobby, where she was already flashing her badge to the receptionist.

"FBI. I'm here to see Nina Cotter."

"Hold on just a minute, ma'am," she said. In no mood, Frieze jumped over the turnstile next to the reception desk.

"Ma'am. Ma'am! Hey!" the receptionist shouted after her. "You can't do that!"

"Stop me," she yelled back, pressing the elevator button. She looked back to see that Conley was doing the same. He exchanged a few words with the girl and jogged over to her.

"I think she's dialing security," said Conley.

"I just need enough time to get to Cotter. She won't dare call security on me then."

The doors slid open, and Frieze led the way into the elevator. She pressed the button for six, and the doors closed before security could reach them.

"So, got anything in terms of specifics on the plan?" he asked. "You know, just so I can play along."

"No." She was furious beyond self-doubt. "I'm winging it."

"Oh," said Conley. "Good to know."

She held on to her righteous energy, trying not to let it deflate. A cartoon carrot played on the elevator's video screen. Some kind of ad for toothpaste or something.

The elevator reached the sixth floor, went straight past it, and the display marked 7. The car showed no sign of slowing down.

"What the—" said Frieze. She pressed the button for the sixth floor again, but the elevator kept going up, now at the eighth floor.

The name *Dominic Watson* played vaguely in her mind about half a second before the words came on the screen, black on white.

HELLO, LISA FRIEZE.

Chapter 37

Faced with the screen that was now addressing her, the reality hit Frieze. This was a trap, a trap like the one that killed Dominic Watson. She felt like the elevator walls were closing in around her.

"What the—" said Conley.

She looked around. She had to think fast. She tried the emergency button.

The reader changed from *9* to *10*.

"How many floors on this building?" she said frantically as she pulled out the receiver on the elevator emergency phone. It was dead.

"The buttons," said Conley. "*19*."

Then the screen read:

You Two Have Been Very Inquisitive.

She shut the text out of her mind and focused.

"What do we know about what happened to Watson?" she asked, and then, answering her own question: "The elevator went all the way to the top floor and the motor kept going until the cables snapped with the force."

Now The Game Is Over.

Adrenaline pumped into her veins. Her body buzzed with energy. Time slowed down.

She looked at the elevator doors. No. No way to get the door open, no way to get out even if they could.

The reader said *13*, then *14*, as the elevator continued to rise.

"Shepard," Conley was saying. "Shepard, come in, Goddamn it!"

There was no time to call anyone. Frieze looked up at the ceiling. Six panels, each with its own light fixture. And above that—every elevator had a service hatch.

"Conley. Help me out here."

He gave her a boost and she put one foot on the railing below the mirror. She laid her hand on the crossbeam for the panels, testing its strength. It would hold.

THIS IS THE END FOR YOU.

She then pushed up the panel on the right back corner. It wasn't screwed on and opened easily to reveal a mass of wires and smooth metal above. Wrong side.

She looked at the reader. It read *17*.

She climbed down and motioned for Conley to help her up on the other back corner. He pulled her up again and she pushed up the panel to find exactly what she was looking for.

There was the service hatch. She reached for it, but the handle was beyond her reach by inches.

"Push me up farther!" she said.

With a grunt, Conley lifted her another foot. She grabbed the handle and released the lock on the hatch. She pushed it open, then held onto the sides as she strained her biceps to pull herself up with Conley's help until she was sitting on top of the elevator.

The whirring of the motor echoed, closer and closer. She looked up and saw a fast-approaching girder. On instinct, she lay supine, flat against the elevator.

The car crashed into the side beams, a din of metal against metal. Frieze was in the gap above the car, her nose inches from the crossbeam that held the motor. It was roaring, straining the cables. Metal groaned as it bent, practically in her ear.

"Conley!" she yelled out. "Come on!"

She didn't have to tell him. He was already lifting himself onto the railing in the elevator car.

The first cable snapped, swinging back against the metal roof of the elevator like a whip.

She moved over in the cramped space under the girder to give Conley room to come out.

Then the second cable snapped. This time its edge sliced into her left arm.

"Augh!"

She didn't even look at the wound. No time for that now.

"This is not going to hold!" she yelled over the motor. "Grab onto something!"

Conley held onto a supporting beam. She reached out for another, but her arms weren't long enough. She inched her body along the surface as the elevator jerked. She smelled the burning of the engine.

The last cable gave out.

As the elevator let loose, Frieze reached out and grabbed the crossbeam. The car plummeted, leaving her legs loose and kicking in air, a sudden weight on her arms.

A roaring wind filled the tunnel in the wake of the plunging box. There was a crash, and Frieze flashed on the image of her body down there, crushed by twisted metal.

She turned to look for Conley and was relieved to find him hanging beside her.

"How you doing there?" she asked, breathless.

"I'd rather be somewhere else."

They clambered along the central I-beam. Frieze, being closer, reached for the service ladder, and once she had a firm hold, activated the door-opening mechanism. It slid open to reveal a carpeted office on the nineteenth floor.

Frieze eased off the ladder onto the floor and Conley followed close behind. She checked the gash on her arm. It was deep, but she'd survive.

Then she turned her attention to the office into which they had emerged.

The scene had frozen at the moment they had stepped out. Every single person was staring at them. A secretary, phone in hand, mid-dial, a man with a coffee mug half-raised for a sip. All eyes were on them.

"I suggest we get out of here," Conley whispered to her.

"Okay," she said. "On one condition."

"What's that?"

"Let's take the stairs."

Chapter 38

"Problems," was the first word out of Lincoln Shepard's mouth. Lily swore to herself that she'd make him regret it. "What is it this time?"

The heat was still suffocating, even in her black tank top. Shepard was reclining deep in his chair, resting his red All Stars on the War Room table. Lily wondered that Bloch never gave him an earful about treating Zeta headquarters like his bloody living room.

"This guy is more paranoid than we thought," he said. "Our device has been disabled. Given the patterns of its final transmission—the data went all screwy—I'd say he ran his clothes through an electromagnetic field generator. Fries any electronics stuck in there."

She sat across from him, legs crossed. "Do you think he knows?"

"My guess is he does this every day. A preventive measure to fry any bugs that might have been put there. Paranoid bugger."

"This is going to make things hard."

"Which is why I have something new for you." He swung his feet off the table and laid out two pieces of equipment he pulled from his pocket. It was a matching set in black plastic—one about the size of a pack of cards, and the other one tiny, squarish, about the size of a dime and with a protuberance that connected to the data slot on a cell phone.

"You still have to get your hands on the phone," he said. "But you don't have to have it for as long. Thirty seconds is all it takes. And all you have to do is attach the tiny bit to the data jack. Just the transmitter. The real work is done by this little baby here." He patted the card-sized device. "They connect wirelessly. Instead of a full data dump, which is what we were going for before, it'll install a little bug that'll reroute the phone's backup to us."

She palmed the devices and examined them.

"Think you can do that?"

"I'll manage."

She called him from her Porsche as she drove out into the evening traffic.

Chapter 39

Simon and Alex were sitting up against opposite sides of his bed in his room, with pillows against the hard frame, legs overlapping in the middle. They were immersed in their online search. Alex had at least ten tabs open on her browser.

"Here he is," said Simon. "Adam Groener. Assistant football coach at the university. There's not much about him online, but he's been at the university for a long time, it seems. I found an article from when he was hired . . . twelve years ago."

"I'm looking for the guy from last night," Alex said.

"I didn't get a good look at him," said Simon.

"Well, I did," said Alex. "I'm not always the best with faces, but I've been learning to force myself to pay attention to the particular features. He had a square face, with a forward-jutting chin and deep-set eyes. His cheekbones were wide and just a bit salient. His brow ridge was pretty heavy, which makes him look just a little like a Neanderthal, but his eyebrows are not particularly thick. Light brown hair, hazel eyes."

"That," said Simon, "is pretty specific for someone who's not the best with faces."

"Thanks," she said with a smirk. "I try." She scrolled through photographs from the football team website and found a group photo. She then scrutinized each of the faces until she found what she was looking for. "Look," she said. "This is him, there near the middle." She swiveled her computer on her lap and showed him the photograph.

"Are you kidding me?" said Simon. "You don't mean Matt Klingensmith, do you?"

"Who?"

"Star cornerback on the team." He typed something on his computer. "Everyone thinks he's a shoo-in for the NFL when he graduates." He turned the screen for her to see a feature article about him entitled *Springhaven's Football Wunderkind*. "Alex, this guy is a big deal on the team. I mean, if even *I've* heard of him . . ."

Alex navigated to his Facebook profile and searched through the latest postings. "He's not shy about drinking," she said. "Kind of a party animal, actually. The kind of guy that could get out of control. Doing something like that could be a real black eye for the team. Simon, are you thinking what I'm thinking?"

"The assistant coach is covering up his players' bad behavior."

"This is it," she said. "I think we have our case."

"Are you kidding? Alex, this isn't a game. It's criminal behavior. Like, felony-level. You need to go to an authority with this."

"Oh yeah? Why haven't they done anything yet? Plus, they won't believe me anyway. I have no evidence except what I saw."

"Katie—"

"Won't talk," Alex interrupted. "She's been avoiding me ever since I went to see her at the health center. Plus, nothing actually happened to her. And even if they do a tox screen and find whatever he gave her, how do we draw that connection?"

He pressed his lips together and ran his hand through his shaggy hair. "But it would show that a crime has been committed. It would put the right people on alert."

"Honestly, Simon, I don't trust the university to do the right thing in this case. Not for a second. I mean, at least one official is complicit in covering it up. Who's to say there aren't others?"

"If that's true," said Simon, exasperated, "what do you think *you* can do about it?"

"Find our evidence and then make this very, *very* public."

Simon shut his computer. "Alex, I think this is going too far."

"*Too far*? Simon, what did you think this was all about? Homework? A hobby? It's about getting up and *doing* something."

"There's a difference between doing something and getting ourselves expelled, or worse. And then there's Katie. There's a reason she didn't want to talk. We're just going to make it worse for her."

"We'll keep her out of it."

"Whatever we do, she's going to be a part of it. If you go poking around this particular thicket, they're going to think she blabbed, even if she didn't."

"Well, what about the next girl? It could have been me. It could still be, if we don't do anything about it."

"Don't try to manipulate me," he said. "You're not that good at it. Yet."

She put her hand on his arm. "Simon. This is important to me. It could be the most important thing I've done in my entire life."

Simon screwed up his face. "Fine. I know it'll bite me in the ass, but I'll help."

Chapter 40

Conley drove his black Camaro Coupe south on I-93 while Frieze examined the wound on her arm. The elevator cable had torn her shirt to shreds. She had at least two deep cuts, but it was hard to assess the extent of the injury.

This wasn't her first time seeing her own blood, or even the first time sustaining damage like this. Still, it made her woozy. The pain fueled a conflagration of rage inside her.

"I'm going to nail the Hornig people."

"It wasn't them," said Conley. He wasn't looking at her, which meant he was ashamed. He was hiding something.

"What?"

"Trust me. Whatever she's hiding, it's not this. Hornig had nothing to do with what happened to Watson or to us. Not directly, anyway."

The bastard. What did he know that he wasn't telling her? "Then who did?"

"It's complicated." His handsome face was blank. As usual, she couldn't get anything past that wall.

"Whatever." She wasn't in the mood. There would be a reckoning. Later. Now, she was bleeding. "Do you have anything I could use to—?"

"First aid kit in the glove compartment. How's the cut?"

One thing about that man: he paid attention when it mattered. "I'll survive," she said, opening a packet of gauze.

"That was some quick thinking back there."

"Yeah." She wasn't eager to relive it. Instead, she focused on cutting what still held together of the sleeve of her shirt.

"Seriously," he said. "I probably wouldn't be alive if it weren't for you."

She poured rubbing alcohol over the wound, winced, inhaling through her teeth as she cleaned away the drying blood with gauze, exposing her quivering flesh. Fresh blood welled up from the cut. "Don't mention it." Then she added: "Really, don't."

She opened another packet of gauze and held it against the gash as she rolled the bandages around it as tight as she could.

Conley pulled off the highway somewhere near Quincy.

"Where are we going?"

"We have a safe house set up for this kind of situation," he said. "More than one, actually."

They were driving into a middle-class residential neighborhood, all ranch-style houses and minivans. Not the first place you'd look for a clandestine intelligence operation's safe house.

"What? I need to go into the office and file a report. I don't have a moment to—"

"We can't afford to be visible right now. You especially, since it seems they know you by name. If you go where you're expected, they're going to try again until they succeed. The only thing that saved us this time is that we knew how Watson died. Do you think they're going to make the same mistake next time?"

"I'm in the FBI," she said. "I don't run from a cheap threat like—"

"The organization behind the attempt on our lives is far more dangerous than the FBI. No offense, but the Bureau won't save you."

He turned into a single-story house that stood out for being built out of bricks—better, she supposed, at resisting gunfire. He pulled the Camaro into the garage and punched in a code on a keypad at the door, which unlocked with a beep.

Conley held the door open for her.

On the inside, the house was furnished just as a rented house might be. Cheap pine furniture, upholstered with rough chenille. Walls whitewashed and bare. Old brown carpeting. Impersonal and depressing.

Frieze was sticky with blood, smelling of iron. First order was to wash her hands. The pipes hadn't been used in a while, and it took a few seconds after she opened the faucet before the water in the bathroom sink sputtered out, and yet a few more for the brown rust to turn clear. She washed her hands and arm and examined her face in the mirror. Somehow she had gotten blood on her face and neck, too.

After washing up as best she could, Frieze emerged from the bathroom. She felt light-headed, as if, having done everything there was to do at the moment, her mind found its opportunity to check out.

She collapsed onto the scratchy couch.

A strange euphoria crept up on her. When faced with death, it had a way of coming into sharp focus. She was alive. It was beautiful. It was a miracle. Colors grew more vivid and her whole body tingled with sensation. Even the sting of the gash on her arm felt glorious.

And the world itself seemed transformed. Usually, being alive was usually just a background fact, like sunlight, and everything around her receded into the background, all but whatever was relevant to her current objective. But now, she was noticing *everything*. The colors and the texture of the faded furniture, the cracks on the walls and spiderwebs in the corners, the way the sunlight that peeked into the room and projected onto the wall flickered as the wind outside moved the branch of a tree.

She was filled with the beauty and exhilaration of it. She was high on *being*.

Peter Conley came out of the bedroom, where he had been washing up in the second bathroom.

"You're going to need stitches on that paper cut."

Frieze couldn't take her eyes off him.

"What?" he asked. "Do I have something on my face?"

Without breaking her gaze, Lisa Frieze got up and kissed him, running her hands through his hair. Startled, he settled into the kiss, putting his arm around her waist.

She was breathless when she broke away from him.

"Lisa, I—"

"Shut up." She pressed her lips to his. This time he leaned into it, pulling her in close.

She tugged at his shirt, breaking the buttons, fumbling in her haste to open the last ones without breaking from their kiss. He reached behind her and undid her bra through her shirt with a swift practiced motion.

She ran her lips over his neck, kissing him, tasting his skin salty with sweat. She pulled his shirt down off his shoulders, revealing his lean and sinewy upper body, scarred by past violence, and the tattoo of the cougar on his arm, curled and ready to pounce.

She gasped as he kissed her ear, grabbing at the skin on his back and feeling the movement of his powerful muscles.

Every touch, every scent, all her senses were magnified by their near death. With Peter Conley, she lost herself in a whirlwind of sensation, in a state of grace of being alive.

Chapter 41

The university athletic building bore all the signs of its recent renovation—shiny new floors, flags and pennants hanging from the ceiling, a ten-foot-tall graphic of the Springhaven Raptor. Straight through were the athletic facilities. Through a set of glass doors on the right was the athletics office. Its walls were adorned by team pictures, recent and vintage, and a trophy shelf ran along the entire extent of the room, a few feet off the drop panels of the ceiling.

"I'm here to see Coach Groener."

The student receptionist, a junior or senior whose muscular frame told that she was an athlete, checked a list on a clipboard. "You're from the *Inquirer,* right?"

"Right."

"I have a friend in the Arts and Entertainment section. Isabel. You know her?"

"Yeah, definitely," she said. "I mean, she doesn't know of me. Just a freshman and everything. And we're in different sections. But her new haircut looks great."

Alex had done her homework.

"Doesn't it though?" She smiled. "Go right ahead. He's expecting you. Just knock on his door before you go in."

Alex crutch-walked over the new carpets to a door that read ASSISTANT FOOTBALL COACH ADAM GROENER and knocked.

"Come in!" said a gruff voice inside.

She opened the door. The coach, sitting behind his desk, was a thickset man in a polo shirt bearing the school's colors, maroon and gray. His square face, sitting on a thick neck, was accented by a buzz cut, still a full head of hair, but the first gray hairs appearing on his temples. He extended a meaty paw to invite her to sit down.

"So you're from the *Inquirer*?" he asked.

Alex leaned the crutches against the desk and sat. She was all smiles. "That's right."

"They have a website, you know," he said, making a show of scrolling through a website on his computer. "You're not on the masthead."

She took his suspicion in stride. "I'm a freshman. Started this semester. Reporters don't get on the masthead until induction, and that's not until April."

"I thought that might be the case." He fixed his gray eyes on her. "So I called the office. And you know, it's the darndest thing. They've never even heard of you." He leaned forward and hissed. "So what is it you want?"

That's what it was going to be. She dropped all pretense of friendliness. "I'm here to talk to you about Katie Kesey."

"I've never heard the name." He stood up. He was short but broad-shouldered and barrel-chested. "And I don't like liars. It's time for you to go."

"What did you say to her in the hospital?"

"I'd really rather not call security on a girl with crutches."

"So you didn't go see her in her hospital room? Your name's not on the guest log?"

He leaned forward, hands on the desk, the weight of his upper body resting on his shoulders. "I'll remind you that patient files are confidential, and it's a crime to look at them without permission."

"How many players have you protected? How many rapists did you get off the hook by threatening victims?"

"I'm calling security." He picked up the phone.

"But you made it your business, didn't you?" she said, standing. She leaned forward so that their faces were inches apart. She could hear his tense breathing, see his flaring nostrils. His cheeks bloomed red with anger. "You wanted to make sure she wouldn't get any ideas about going to the police about your star cornerback."

"That's enough. Get out of my office. Get out!"

Simon was waiting for her in the door niche outside the athletic center, cowering from the cold.

"Did you get anything?" he asked as they walked together back to the Prather House.

"No. He's careful. A hidden recorder isn't going to be enough to hang him. We'll have to find some other way. But you had to see his reaction, Simon. We're on to something."

Chapter 42

Lily waited at the corner of Garden and Philips, travel bag in her hand, shivering in the cold. Baxter sent an executive taxi to pick her up—he would never take time out of his busy schedule to come himself. She was delivered like a parcel to the airport, where she was whisked past security and out onto the runway into the company Learjet 85—three thousand–mile range, Pratt & Whitney Engines, expensive as hell.

Baxter sat with a glass of whiskey in his hand, ice tinkling as he swirled. Next to him was a thickset man in a light gray suit and a cowboy hat.

"About time," Baxter said.

"Now, that's no way to treat such a pretty lady," said the man. "What's your name?"

"Lily, sir." Baxter insisted on the *sir*, even when it wasn't addressed to him.

"A Brit! How about that?"

"This is Duke Bertrand," said Baxter.

"And this is the new toy," he said, leering at her. "The plane, I mean." Lily knew what he meant.

"She gets the job done when properly motivated."

Baxter felt up her dress. The flight attendant closed the cabin door.

It was going to be a long flight to San Francisco.

Baxter left the hotel room for whatever business he had in town early the next morning, leaving her with his credit card and "Get yourself something pretty. Show it to me later."

Lily took a long shower, scrubbing whatever she could of him off her, rubbing the sponge against her skin until it was red and raw. She spent an hour working out her anger on the treadmill in the hotel gym, then took another shower—a quick one to get the sweat off.

Next she called Zeta on her secure cell phone.

"No luck yet," she said. "He won't let his cell phone out of his sight."

"Keep trying," Kirby said.

"I don't know how long I can keep this up," Lily said.

"We're counting on you."

She hung up.

Alone in the empty room. She looked at Baxter's credit card on the desk. Shopping with it felt slimy, like a tacit acceptance of this filthy bargain.

"Sod this."

She took out her phone and made another call.

"Scott? I'm in town. Let's do this."

"I was in the middle of a meeting of upper management."

"Oh, sorry, shall I call back?"

"That's all right, upper management is basically three of my old college buddies. Our meetings tend to devolve into hanging out anyway, and we're just about at that time. Shall I send a car?"

Lily didn't want anyone at the hotel seeing her leave with another man, so she took a cab to the nearest Best Western, where she waited in the lobby until Scott pulled into the drop-off area in his Infiniti Q60. She opened the passenger door, but he climbed out and tossed her the keys.

"I figured you might drive this time. If you can manage driving on the *correct* side of the road, that is."

She grinned.

Lily tore down Interstate 280 in the tight little coupe. It was a wonder—a feisty, sensitive little thing, responsive to the slightest turn of the wheel.

"So where are we going?"

Scott just shrugged. She laughed.

"You and your secrets."

"You'll like this one, I promise."

"Hey, I loved the aquarium. All those fish and . . . more fish. I think I saw a penguin, too." She laid her right hand on his knee.

"Well, today's going to be a bit of a change of pace."

She turned off the highway at his direction and took another right until they were on a narrow desert road. On this flat expanse was an oval racing track. Lily brought the coupe to a drifting stop and got out, not quite believing what she was seeing.

There, waiting for them, were two Formula One cars.

Lily was speechless.

"So. Want to take one for a spin?"

Chapter 43

"I count three hundred that I can see," Morgan said.

Morgan passed the binoculars to Honoré, who was leading the reconnaissance mission. He was an excitable and idealistic young man who had lost his family to Madaki's soldiers. He might have been handsome if his face wasn't disfigured by a scar, extending from the corner of his lip up to his right temple.

They were lying prone on the crest of a hill, overlooking the house Madaki had occupied for his base of operations. It was a French colonial mansion, paint peeling, wood falling to pieces. The perimeter of the estate was marked by a crumbling wall that had collapsed in two places that Morgan could see. The jungle reached into the long-untended estate toward the house. The preliminary survey was encouraging. Plenty of cover, not much need to fight out in the open.

By the fading light, Morgan saw Madaki's men walking around their camp, eating their dinner. The convoy of trucks, four in all, was parked near the house.

"The crates are still on the trucks," said Honoré. "White's weapons are not with the men. They are carrying old revolvers and Kalashnikovs."

"We hit the trucks then," Morgan said. "We jump the wall, over there, where the jungle is thickest, and move in on the trucks, setting enough dynamite to destroy the shipment. Meanwhile, we send our main force in three different groups to set the rest of the explosives along the perimeter. They divide the enemy forces while we move into the house and take Madaki hostage." *And Zeta tactical will come in to extract me and Mr. White, leaving everyone else to fend for themselves.*

They returned to sit with the rest of the dozen men who comprised this makeshift squad of commandos, all with their pick of the better weapons in the camp. Honoré had Morgan's stolen MAC-10. Morgan ended up with a Star 30M, a bulky, heavy, no-nonsense semiautomatic, and a knife. It wasn't a real combat knife, just a black-handled kitchen knife in an improvised leather sheath that he wrapped around his calf.

But it was sharp. That's all he needed.

Morgan shared a piece of jerked meat with Honoré. It would be hours before Dimka would arrive with the rest of the troops—and Yolande, who had not spoken a word to Morgan ever since she overheard him speaking to Bloch.

Honoré grinned as he chewed, showing extra teeth on his right where his lip had been mutilated. "In the morning, we meet our victory. And I am going to be the person to put a bullet in Madaki."

Morgan raised his canteen. "I'll drink to that."

Chapter 44

San Francisco Four Seasons, Executive Suite. Roger Baxter stretched in postcoital bliss, hands interlocked behind his head, and closed his eyes. Lily lay back naked, body aching, head swimming with the tail end of her drunkenness, relieved that he was done with her. The luxury of the hotel room around her, marked with shadows cast by the bedside lamps, was a cruel mockery with its comforts, its modern decor, the stupid phallic glass ornament on the coffee table the size of a football, the blackout curtains keeping out the afternoon light.

When she was sure he wouldn't notice, she curled away from him. She let a single, silent sob escape her unflappable veneer—all she could afford. She couldn't do this anymore. She couldn't. Her body would rebel. She would vomit, faint. Anything to stop *him* from touching her again.

Now, lying on the bed, facing the closet door, she waited.

She had plied him with alcohol.

She was a drinking heavyweight, and taunted him about not being able to keep up, although he made her pay for it later. Drunk, Baxter was crueler than ever.

Lily wondered about the other women before her, and what they endured to give him the impression that they enjoyed what he did. Or maybe that wasn't it at all. Maybe it was that Baxter believed he possessed some irresistible allure that gave him *carte blanche* to do as he pleased. And for whatever reason compelled them, these women, like her, kept coming back.

It was no small consolation that, if she succeeded, Baxter was going to be put away, probably for the rest of his life. He wasn't going to do this to anyone else, ever.

She heard the faint wheezing snore first. She listened for a few more seconds to his breathing. Then she turned around and saw that he had his eyes closed, and his facial muscles were slack. Finally, for the first time, he was sleeping after one of their trysts.

This was her chance.

She rolled slowly so that her legs hung off the side of the bed and planted her feet on the floor. Digging through her clutch, she found the pillbox that held the device Shepard had given her. She shook it out onto her palm and held it between her manicured fingernails.

Now for the phone.

The bedsprings creaked as Lily shifted her weight to her feet. She looked at Baxter, who stirred but didn't awaken. She tiptoed around the bed to his side, taking careful, measured steps. His phone was right there on the bedside table. Baxter's nose twitched, and she froze. Satisfied that he was still unconscious, she crept on. Once it was within reach, she extended her arm, inch by inch, until her fingers met the cool glass screen. She pulled it off the table and held it in her right hand.

Okay. Courage. It's just thirty seconds.

She walked to the bathroom on tiptoes, pulled the door closed and locked the door. She then inserted the device into the cell phone data slot.

The gadget did its work, hiding a worm in the device's subroutines, which would send all the data in his phone to Shepard back at Zeta the next time it was backed up.

The light stopped blinking, indicating that it was done. She removed the device and slipped it between her hip and the elastic band of her panties.

All she had to do now was return the phone.

She turned off the bathroom light and opened the door as slowly as she could manage. Baxter was still in bed, still wheezing.

She tiptoed to the bedside table and set the phone down, nudging it to get it in the exact right position. Then she turned to check on Baxter again.

His eyes were wide open, staring at her.

She moved to turn and sprint away from him, but he sprung out of bed and grabbed her by the arm. His touch caused her revulsion.

"What are you doing?" he demanded.

"I just wanted to make a phone call—"

"You have a phone," he hissed.

"My batteries were dead."

Still holding onto her arm, he reached inside her clutch, which lay on the bed, and pulled out her phone. He hit the power button and it glowed, on the start screen, the power meter reading sixty-eight percent.

Crap.

She kneed him in the groin and hit him hard with her flat palm against his nose, feeling a crunch as it broke. That was enough for him to release her, but he recovered fast enough to swing his fist, hitting hard against her right cheek.

That, she thought, *was a mistake.*

She rolled to the other side of the bed, where she was within reach of the minibar. She grabbed a glass of whiskey and threw it at his face. It shattered.

He looked at her like an enraged animal, his face marred by deep cuts, with remnants of glass embedded in his skin glinting in the lamplight.

Not so handsome anymore.

He jumped on the bed and she leapt away. What she wasn't counting on was that he would dive headfirst onto her. His weight knocked her down. He held her arms against the floor and straddled her abdomen.

She lost herself in panic. He was too heavy for her. Too strong. She flailed her arms, trying to scratch him, anything to hurt him enough that he would get off her.

But he was drunk and mad with rage.

Looking into her eyes with triumph, he held down both her hands with his right and wrapped his left around her neck. He squeezed, closing her windpipe, cutting off circulation to her brain.

"Time to die," he growled. Then he moved his face in close to hers. A drop of blood fell from his lacerated cheek onto her bare chest. Her throat throbbed under the constriction. Her lungs seared.

"You won't be the first bitch I kill," he whispered in her ear. "But I'm going to remember this moment for a long, long time."

Air. Air. She gasped for it but none came.

"This is what it means to be a powerful man."

Darkness slowly engulfed her, and her body seemed more and

more distant. All the pain was washing away, and death seemed more and more like comfort.

No.

He wasn't going to beat her. She wouldn't let him.

She gritted her teeth and wrested her left hand free from his grip. She scratched at the wounded side of his face. A stabbing sting as a tiny shard of glass burrowed under the manicured nail of her middle finger.

He roared in pain, which was intense enough for him to release her right hand. Out of the corner of her eye she made out the sleek black shape of her Michael Kors stiletto. She reached for it with her right hand and brought it down hard, heel-first, against his head. Then again. Then again.

He released her neck and brought both hands up to protect his face. She gasped for air, wheezing. It came at such a rush that it made her light-headed. She dropped the shoe and went at his face with both hands, sinking her thumbs into his eyes. Baxter bellowed.

But she couldn't get out from under him. No matter how much damage she did, he was bigger. That was the whole game, and she was on the losing side.

Blinded, eyes bleeding, he grabbed the hideous glass ornament from the coffee table and raised it above his head. He was going to bash her head in.

A knife came out of the darkness and plunged into Baxter's neck. The gloved hand that held it gave it a final thrust and then pulled it out, bathing Lily's exposed chest in blood. Baxter dropped the ornament onto the carpet. Then he collapsed on top of her.

Screaming, she shoved him off her and dragged herself on her heels to a corner of the room. Then she looked at her savior. He had a ski mask on, but she was very sure, even in this state, even in this light, that she did not know him.

He wiped the knife on a rag, which he stuffed in his pocket.

Woozy from the lack of oxygen, she stumbled to her feet, putting too much of her weight on a chair and tipping it over. She fell against a side table.

"You weren't supposed to be here," he said, as she regained her footing.

"It was supposed to be just Baxter. No one was supposed to see." She staggered to the bed and fell onto it, rolling on her back. Dazed from the oxygen deprivation, she flopped like a dying fish. Appropriate. She was about to be gutted like one.

"I'm very, very sorry for what's about to happen."

He walked over to the bed at a relaxed pace. Her hands closed around the small metal cylinder, the device disguised as lipstick.

The man stood over her with the knife.

"Really, it's nothing personal. I should have let him do it himself, but it seemed distasteful. Well . . ."

He raised the blade, which glinted as it caught the light. She plunged the stun gun against the turtleneck sweater that covered his waist and hit the button. Electricity cracked as the little cylinder delivered over a million volts to her attacker.

The shock scrambled communications between his brain and his muscles, and the man dropped like a sack of potatoes.

Lily willed herself to her feet. She had the presence of mind to wrap herself in a hotel bathrobe before exiting the room. She ran down the hallway, as much as her shaky legs allowed, and then down the stairs. She checked herself before going out into the lobby. The pearly white robe hid most of Baxter's blood, and the fabric was thick enough that only tiny spots had seeped to the outside. Nobody who didn't look too close would notice. She hoped.

She came out and kept close to the wall, walking fast but not enough to attract any undue attention. She got her share of stares for simply being in a bathrobe in the lobby. She stayed out of people's radar long enough to grab an unattended coat from a baggage cart near the revolving doors and pull it on as she exited the lobby.

She plunged out into the afternoon light, power-walking down Market Street, barefoot and bloody. People stared at her as she passed, but no one seemed too concerned. A man wearing nothing but a lime-green Speedo and a bicycle helmet to match roller-skated past her, and it dawned on her that the city's residents were accustomed to weirdness.

A Muni trolleybus came to a halt as she passed the station, and she hopped onto it. As it took off, she looked back through the rear window to see her attacker running out of the hotel, cell phone in hand. He looked both ways, but, at a loss, made the wrong guess and walked in the opposite direction.

There was no ticket inspector on the car, but she was faced with another problem. Passersby on the street were one thing—they had a couple seconds, tops, to look at her. In the trolley car, people had a chance to examine her, and they were drawn to the blood as it peeked out of the fur coat, to the bruises that must be showing up on her neck. She could feel the murmur as people seemed to be trying to decide what to do about her. She had to do something.

Since she couldn't hide, she got up on a seat, holding onto the handrail.

"Hey!" the driver yelled. "Get down from there!"

"The fur industry kills millions of innocent animals every year!" she shouted, opening the coat to reveal her bloody chest. She watched as the previously concerned passengers rolled their eyes. Just another crazy.

"Fur is murder!" she screamed. "Fur is murder!"

The trolleybus pulled into its next stop and she ran out as soon as the doors opened, pushing past the other passengers and disappearing into the foot traffic.

She crossed Market to Battery Street, where she ducked into a diner and sat at a corner booth.

The waitress didn't seem fazed by Lily's current condition. "What can I get you, hon?"

"Some tea, please," she said. "Do you have any Earl Grey?"

"Sugar, we got Lipton's."

"That'll do." Then, as she walked away: "Please, do you have a phone I could use?"

"In the back."

She went to the old-style wooden phone booth. In these days of cell phones, it was more of a curiosity than anything. She dialed Zeta first, collect.

"This is Shepard."

"Give me Bloch," she said.

"Lily? Holy—Hold on."

A grating MIDI rendition of *Für Elise* played for about three seconds, which was three seconds longer than Lily cared to endure it at that moment, and then Bloch picked up. "Talk to me, Agent Randall."

"I'm fine," she said, then corrected herself: "I'm alive."

"Where are you?"

She related what happened.

"There'll be security camera footage showing me fleeing the hotel."

"We'll take care of it," said Bloch. "We'll send a cleanup crew. There'll be no trace that you were ever there. Do you need extraction?"

Lily hesitated.

"Agent Randall," she said. "Are you safe?"

"I'm safe. I'll be in touch."

She hung up, took a deep breath, and dialed another number.

"Hello?"

"Scott, please. I need you. Please come get me."

Chapter 45

The sun projected reddish patches through the tree outside onto the wall of Simon's room. He paced around Alex as she bit her nails, wracking her brain. They had cracked open a window, letting in cool fresh air against the excessive heat of the radiator. Lower temperatures, she insisted, led to clearer minds. Other students were shuffling off to dinner, but Simon and Alex had more important things on their minds.

Plus, Alex wasn't too eager to run into Katie.

"How do we even prove something like this?" asked Simon. "How can we if Katie won't talk?"

"This can't have been his first time," said Alex. "It never is."

"Which means there are other victims. Other people who might be more willing to talk."

"We have to find them," said Alex.

"And how do we do that?"

Simon did a headstand on his bed, feet almost reaching the ceiling.

"It's tough," he said. "How do you find victims who didn't come forward in the first place?"

"What would they have in common? They were girls. They drank. They were drugged, which means—"

"That a number of them probably ended up at the student health center," Simon completed. "But medical records are confidential. It'd be hard to gain access to them. Plus, I think it's a felony."

"But visitor logs might be easier to get."

"As long as they still exist," said Simon, still upside down, blood rushing to his face.

"I'm guessing they're at least scanned into a digital database. I don't think they bother to do it just to throw them away later."

"Let me see what I can find," said Simon, flopping onto his bed and reaching for his computer. "We need a login. Maybe I can program a workaround that'll give us access. It'll take a while, until I can figure out the subroutines and I might need you to—"

Alex held up a finger.

"What—"

"Shhh." She looked something up on her computer, then picked up Simon's room phone and dialed.

"What are you—?"

"Shut it. It's ringing."

Someone on the other line picked up. "Health Center, this is Donna."

Alex made her voice nasal and high-pitched. "Hi, Donna, this is Regina, in IT. We're running a security check, and we seem to have a problem with your account, so Albert asked me to give you a call. Have you had trouble logging in?"

"No, I haven't had a problem at all!"

"Maybe our information here is out-of-date. Would you mind telling me your login and password?"

"Sure, no problem!" she said, chipper.

Alex wrote down the data as the woman gave it to her.

"Thank you so much," said Alex. "You've been really helpful."

"Be sure to give me another call if there are any problems."

"Will do!" Alex said, and hung up.

"Here you go," she said, laying the sheet of paper in front of him.

Simon was just staring at her, speechless. "You are really something else."

"The weakest link is always human," she said. "Now, shall we find our patient logs?"

Chapter 46

L ily spotted Scott from the corner booth, where she had been
sipping on her tea for the past forty minutes. His eyes scanned
the room, and as soon as he spotted her he made a beeline to her,
forehead furrowed.

"Scott." She stood and embraced him, holding on to the comfort
of his warmth. He let her, sensing that she needed it. When she released him, he got his first look at her, unshod and naked under a
hotel bathrobe and coat, congealed blood peeking out on her exposed skin.

"Lily, are you bleeding?" His voice was laced with urgency.

"No, it's not mine. You mind spotting me a couple of bucks for
the tab?"

He fished for his wallet in his pocket and set down a ten-dollar
bill. "Let me get you out of here."

Arms around her, he led her to his Infiniti (parked illegally in
front of a fire hydrant), and held the door open for her. As he shut
the door, she felt relief wash over her. His car felt like the safest
place in the world.

He took off down Battery back toward Market Street.

"Do you want to talk about it?"

"I want to tell you everything," she blurted. "But now I just need
to go somewhere else. Please. Can we just get out of here?"

"Of course. I'll take you to my place."

Lily sat on Scott's bed, wrapped in a woven woolen blanket. She
was wearing one of his dress shirts—he was skinny, but it was still
baggy on her. She looked out the gorgeous bay windows, which
overlooked the ocean, tinted by the light of the setting sun. It was a

spectacular view, in one of the most expensive real estate markets in the country. The perks of being a multimillionaire, she supposed.

She absently ran her fingers along where Baxter had choked her. It felt raw. She wondered how bad it looked. She didn't want to look at herself in the mirror to find out.

"The cleanup crew found no sign of Baxter or the attacker."

That's what Bloch had told her when she called. Someone else had gotten there first. No sign of the murder. Nothing in the security cameras. Everything, physical and digital, had been scrubbed clean.

Scott returned from his kitchen holding two cups of hot cocoa.

"I hope Swiss Miss is okay," he said with a bashful chuckle. "I don't really keep any full-time staff. I was never very comfortable with that sort of thing."

She smiled, taking the warm mug in her hand. It grounded her and made her feel secure. And it smelled like home. "It's wonderful."

"How are you feeling?" he asked.

"Better. It feels good to be here. It feels safe."

"You don't even know me that well."

"And yet." She just smiled as she looked into his baby blue eyes, half-hidden behind his blond curls.

"I ordered some clothes for you," he said, fumbling the moment. "Should be here in a couple hours."

"I didn't know you could get clothes delivered like a pizza."

"This is Silicon Valley. You can get anything delivered like a pizza. I went with comfy over sexy, considering, you know."

"Good call."

He sat next to her in bed. "So," he said. "You said you had things you wanted to tell me?" He must have seen her countenance darken because he backpedaled with his next words. "It's fine, you really don't have to."

But he had come to her rescue. She couldn't keep doing this.

"Are you sure you want to know?" she asked. "You're not getting ready to hightail it away from me as soon as you can?"

"Do you see me pushing you out the door? Come on. Try me."

"There's a reason I never wanted to talk about work," she said. She looked down. "Shit. You know how you put something off because you know it's going to be awful, and the longer you wait, the worse it gets?"

This seemed to put him on edge. She felt him move his body away from her, maybe without even being aware of it. "I know the feeling," he said, just a little colder than before.

"I'm afraid," she said, tears coming to her eyes. "Because you've been wonderful. I'm afraid you'll kick me out, and I'm afraid of what you'll think when you find out. That you think I'm awful and dishonest."

He bit his lower lip. "Are you married?"

"No," she said. "That's not it. It's about my work. And with what happened today. And that has to do with the fact that I haven't exactly been exclusive with you." She looked at him to gauge his reaction, but there was no change.

"Are you a prostitute?" he said, then caught himself. "A sex worker?"

She bit the inside of her cheek until it bled. "What if I was? Would that be it for you?"

He rubbed his hand against his temple, mussing his hair. "I hadn't really thought about it before."

"So it doesn't make you hate me that I haven't been faithful?"

He chuckled at this. "I live in Silicon Valley," he said. "Half my friends are polyamorous, free love types."

Lily looked out into the setting sun. "It really is a bold new frontier, isn't it?" She looked back at Scott. "Then you'd really be okay with that?"

He hesitated, looking out the window. "You know, when we consider questions like this in the abstract, we don't really think about the real person they might apply to." He turned his gaze back to her. "But now that it's here, and I know you, it doesn't feel like a problem at all."

She couldn't restrain a smile. It was something. Not everything, but something.

"Did a client do that to you?"

"That's where it gets a little complicated. I'm not a prostitute, really. I'm—I guess you could call me something like a spy."

His eyes widened and his eyebrow visibly tensed. His expression read as something between bemusement and surprise.

"Like, MI-5?" he said. "Spying on . . . *this* country?"

"No! No, nothing like that." She emitted a nervous laugh. "No, we're an American outfit. Sort of clandestine. Honestly, the less you know about the details, the better."

"I see." He sounded incredulous. She was losing him.

"It's true," she said. "The older guy, from the night we met. He was a mark. High-ranking executive in a major corporation."

"Is he the one that did that to you?"

Her hand went to her neck. "Yes. He's . . . dead now."

"You killed him?" She sensed the alarm in his voice.

"No! It was never part of the mission. Someone else showed up—I don't know who. But he killed Baxter—my mark. I only just made it out alive."

He exhaled, staring into the middle distance. "This is a lot to take in."

"I know."

"Is your name even Lily Harper?"

"We use real first names," she said. "Whenever possible. It's nearly impossible to fake a different first name. The response is too automatic, too ingrained. So my name *is* Lily."

"But not Harper?"

"It's Randall. My name is Lily Randall."

"Nice to meet you, Lily Randall. I'm Scott Renard."

"So do you think we can start over?" she asked.

"Why? I think we're doing just fine this time around."

She kissed him and he pulled her close, enveloping her in his arms.

Chapter 47

"Here, I found one!" Simon jumped off the bed in excitement. "Adam Groener! Oh, never mind. Another football player."

The window was closed now against the cold. People were milling about the first floor hallway of Prather House in the usual nighttime bustle. Alex scanned what seemed like the five-hundredth patient log, looking for Groener's name—for a girl he might have intimidated like he did Katie.

It had taken a little sniffing around, but Simon had found the logs in the system. The pages were scanned individually every day. "It's so much more work," said Simon. "All because they don't take a few hours to implement a proper electronic system."

"Lucky us," she said.

"Unlucky us. You'll see."

The unlucky part being that image files were not searchable by word, so that now they were stuck with scrolling through each sign-in sheet for the past six years one by one, looking for Coach Groener's name. It appeared plenty—but mostly it was to visit his players. They hadn't found his name associated with a single female patient yet.

"Maybe this is a red herring," said Simon. "Maybe it was just a onetime thing."

"He's done this before," Alex insisted.

Simon lay down against his pillow. "But maybe it's a break with his usual MO."

"We can only go on what we know," said Alex.

"Maybe this is the wrong approach."

"So many maybes with you," said Alex. "Someone who doesn't know better might think you're stalling to avoid the work."

"Well, what if there's a way to automate this task that I haven't thought of? I mean, maybe if we scan his signature and run a Bayesian probabilistic search with fuzzy—"

"I got one!"

Simon looked almost crestfallen that his scheming was cut short. "Woman?"

Alex nodded. "The name's Hillary Chen."

"I'm looking her up right now," said Simon. "She's graduated already, uh . . . three years ago."

"Can you get me a number?"

"You want to *call* her? Like, now?"

"What the hell do you think this is all about, Burczyk? Get me a damn number!"

"All right," said Simon. "That's easy enough. Here we go, LinkedIn profile. Cell phone. I'm messaging it to you right now."

It popped up on Alex's screen and she dialed.

"Hello?"

"Hi, Hillary? My name is Alex Morgan, I'm a student at Springhaven University."

"Oh?"

"I'm sorry to call out of the blue like this. I write for the *Inquirer*— you know, the campus newspaper. I'm investigating something that happened at one of the fraternities on campus. Phi Epsilon. I was hoping you might talk to me about similar occurrences that might have—"

"I'm going to stop you there," said Hillary. "I don't know what you're talking about. Please don't call again."

She hung up.

"What happened?" Simon asked.

"She hung up when I mentioned Phi Epsilon."

"Too bad."

"No," said Alex. "It's a good sign. It means that we're getting somewhere."

"Ugh," said Simon. "I was afraid you'd say that."

"Back to work, Burczyk."

"I was afraid you'd say that, too."

Chapter 48

"Alex. Alex!" She opened her eyes with a start, disoriented. Simon's room. Night. That much she got. He was showing her the screen of his computer, but her vision was too blurry to make out what it was. She rubbed her eyes.

"What is it, Simon?"

"I found one. I think she's the real deal. Annette Baig."

Alex yawned. She must have fallen asleep. Hunger gnawed at her insides. The dorm was silent, which meant that it must be late. "Spell that for me," she said, pulling her computer onto her lap. "I'm going to look her up."

"I can tell you she wasn't an athlete," said Simon. "I searched her name through all the databases. Got nothing."

Alex searched through the university website, in the enrollment and student information database. "I'm not finding much," she said. "She enrolled at Springhaven six years ago. And graduated..." Alex looked at the graduation announcements from two years before, then from the year before. She even looked at the announcements from three years before, in case she graduated early. Nothing. "Huh. Weird. Looks to me like she never graduated."

"No LinkedIn, no social media presence," said Simon.

"Leave it. We have this one in the bag, and I need some carbs or I'm literally going to pass out."

"Late-night snack?"

"Aw crap, it's past eleven," she said, checking her phone. "The student center's closed."

"Then we go to the Athena."

"Again?" Alex complained. The Athena was the local Greek-themed diner, the nearest restaurant to campus and the only one that was open 24/7. They took full advantage of the monopoly by jacking up prices for mediocre offerings.

"Got a better idea?" he asked. "Let's go. We'll have us a plate of mozzarella sticks."

"Make it chicken tenders and a hot chocolate and you got a deal."

"How exactly do you stay so thin?"

"Have you checked out my muffin top lately?" She pulled up her shirt to reveal the fat poking out of the waist of her pants. Simon reached out and pinched her. "Ow! Ass."

They bundled up and set off into the freezing cold night.

"Wanna call the campus bus?" Simon asked.

"Nah. It takes forever. I'd rather brave the cold."

She regretted the decision about seven minutes into their walk.

"So tomorrow morning we call Annette Baig," said Simon through ragged breaths. "What if she doesn't want to talk?"

"Then we keep trying," said Alex. "We'll find another, and another, until someone is willing to speak up. I'm going to expose these creeps, if I have to track down every single victim. They're not getting away with this."

They walked with teeth chattering, bracing against the cold. Once they got away from the quad, the walk to the Athena took them through a dark and deserted street with woodland on either side. Alex checked her phone.

"Cell reception's dead, for a change."

"It'll come back in a hundred yards or so," said Simon.

The only sound she heard as they walked was the snow crunching beneath her feet until something teased her ears. She turned her head.

"Don't look back," she said. "We're being followed."

"What?" He turned instinctively.

"Don't!"

"You're paranoid, Alex. This is the way to the Athena. It's gotta be just another hungry student."

"Well, I think he's wearing a university hoodie," she said "But I'm getting a bad vibe from this guy."

"There's a fork ahead," said Simon. "The right leads to the Spotswood apartments."

"So we take it and see if he follows." She fingered the knife in her pocket. It calmed her, like a talisman.

The walk was interminable. She pressed on as hard as she could, but there was only so much she could do on crutches, and the guy walked like an athlete, catching up with every step. They turned on the fork, where the road turned flat. Thirty seconds later, Alex saw that their tail turned behind them.

"He's coming after us," said Alex.

"Damn it." Simon checked his cell phone "Still no signal."

"I'm guessing that's why he chose this place."

"What do we do? There's nothing around."

"I want you to run to the apartments," Alex said. "I remember there's an emergency phone right outside the first block."

"I'm not going to leave you alone!"

"I'm not being brave, Simon. I want you to do this because this is the best chance we have. What, you think you can fight him?" Simon didn't answer. "Run and get help while I hold him off."

She closed her fist around the butterfly knife in her pocket. It was time to put her father's training to good use.

"Just hit the emergency button and run back," she said. "On my signal. Go! Run!"

Simon took off, feet crunching snow under his shoes. She turned around and drew the knife from her coat.

She saw the pursuer's face. She didn't recognize him, but she memorized his features in the dim light. Definitely college-aged, with a body for football. He was ready to take off after Simon when his eyes turned to her and were filled with horrified surprise.

"What, did you expect the damsel in distress?" she demanded, brandishing the knife. "Come at me, bro."

He looked at Simon, now far enough away that he wouldn't be able to close the distance before Simon arrived at the emergency phone.

"Come on. Or are you afraid of a woman that's not unconscious?"

This was a decisive moment for him. Could he take the crippled girl with the knife?

Thinking better of it, he spat into the clear white snow. "Stay away from this, bitch," he said, puffing his chest like a rooster.

"Quit sniffing around where you don't belong. You won't see me coming next time."

He turned and ran into the darkness, the sound of his footsteps in the snow receding until they were lost in the stillness of the night. Shaking, turning her head to make sure he wasn't following, and jumping at every noise, Alex walked on until she saw Simon running back toward her.

"Security's coming."

"Then let's get out of here," she said. "I don't want to be here when they arrive. I don't want to draw any more attention to us than necessary. Not while we're investigating."

"What? Are you crazy? You still want to continue after this?"

"We're on to something, Simon," she said. "We can't stop now."

"I don't think joining the Ekklesia is worth putting ourselves in danger."

"It's not about the Ekklesia anymore," she said. "I don't care what it costs me. I'm going to bring these bastards down."

Chapter 49

Morgan was awakened by the raiding party's sentry, who announced the arrival of the rest of Dimka's men, skulking through the jungle to mask their approach. The nocturnal heat was humid and oppressive. Morgan and Honoré walked through the pitch black, each trekking soldier they encountered pointing them in the direction of the leader. They found Dimka bringing up the rear, a rag tied around his head as a headband, AK-47 in his hand. Walking alongside him was Yolande, face set in a look of determination. She refused to acknowledge Morgan.

She had taken on their cause. He should have known. The hardest people can be the most idealistic.

Morgan and Honoré talked tactics with Dimka as they walked, laying out their plan and making adjustments according to the leader's more detailed picture of their capabilities. They split up the dynamite from the gold mine—six sticks for the raiding party, the rest to be divided to breach the walls.

Once they got into position at the top of the hill overlooking the house, Morgan and Honoré spent half an hour looking for sentries. Two were guarding the trucks. Among the others, the ones carrying flashlights were almost too obvious. But they spotted three creeping in the dark, within the camp and around the perimeter. And if they had seen that many, there would be more.

The sky was shifting into a leaden gray, stars melting into the coming light. It was almost time.

Morgan found the raiding party painting their faces red. "They are getting ready for battle," said Honoré, dipping his fingers into a clay bowl of red paint, making a mark like fire rising up from the scar on his lip. Morgan followed suit by rubbing one thick swipe across his eyes. The paint smelled of butter and iron.

Dimka emerged from the forest. "The time has come. Lead the team. The rest will move as we planned. We are counting on you."

Morgan surveyed the raiding party, faces painted red, powerful bodies brimming with energy. He took the lead of his raiding party, with Honoré behind the ten others. They moved single-file down toward the house. They made it within sight of the perimeter wall under cover of forest when they spotted the first sentry.

Morgan held up a fist to indicate for the squad to stop. The sentry was moving in from their left, looking into the dark jungle, where he did not see his approaching death. Morgan waited for him to pass, knife in hand, and bounded out from behind a tree. His strides cracked leaves and branches underfoot, but it was too late for the sentry to react. Morgan plunged the knife into his neck. He collapsed.

Signaling for one of the men to take the guard's Uzi, Morgan scanned the trees growing near the perimeter wall. The wall itself was built out of brick, topped with ceramic roof tiles. He found the perfect spot—a tree that grew diagonally against the wall, with a convenient bough to serve as a foothold. He climbed over, dropping down on the other side.

The camp of soldiers was on their left. They kept as far right as they could while still remaining under the cover of the trees. The whole area was silent and still. The men moved on light feet until they reached the edge of the forest, where tree cover trailed off. Now was the most dangerous part. They had to run one hundred feet out in the open to the trucks, parked in a loose triangular formation.

The two guards were circling the trucks, unaware of the invaders, holding automatic rifles pointing at the ground. Morgan waited until both were out of sight and then ran forward, feet pounding the loose dirt, closing the gap in ten seconds flat.

Winding between the trucks, he circled back around the first, slitting a guard's throat. Then he rolled under another truck, slashing at the passing guard's Achilles tendons. The guard dropped to the ground, too surprised to emit more than a yelp. When he hit the ground, Morgan was ready with the knife.

He signaled to Honoré, and the other nine men of the raiding party moved across the open space single file to the trucks.

The man holding the satchel of dynamite passed it to Morgan, who climbed into the back of the nearest truck, shielded from view of the camp. He examined the crate of guns, cheap wood painted green. The wood had splintered where the nail had held the lid tight.

This crate had been opened. All of them had. He set the satchel down and pulled open the lid.

It was empty.

Morgan didn't hear the approach of the men who surrounded them. By the time he looked up, they were already there—thirty of Madaki's soldiers, in their ratty civilian clothing, armed with a brand-new arsenal of Colt AR-15 tactical carbines.

"*Laisse tomber tes armes!*"

Honoré looked at Morgan for leadership.

Resistance was suicide.

"Do it, Honoré. Tell the men to drop their weapons."

Morgan tossed his Star 30M on the muddy ground. The other guns clattered as the rest of the raiding party let go of theirs.

Only then did he allow himself to be seen. The tall, pale man in the graphite suit, face like a skull. Mr. White, next to a man in military fatigues and a beret who could only be Stéphane Madaki.

"Bevelacqua, isn't it?" said White. "Fancy meeting you here."

On seeing Madaki, Honoré screamed with rage and went for his dropped AK-47. Madaki was quicker. He fired a single shot from his sidearm. Honoré fell forward onto the mud, a bullet in his chest. Morgan looked down at him, inhaling short, shallow breaths, eyes wide, life draining out of him.

Madaki barked orders at his men, and they prodded Honoré's raiding party into the basement of the house, to be tortured for information.

White pulled Morgan out of the line. "Not you. You're coming with me."

They marched him into the decrepit mansion. Morgan had crossed the door into the foyer when the windows rattled with the force of an explosion, followed by two more. Madaki's bodyguard pushed him to the ground, covering him.

Morgan strained to look out the window, where smoke was rising at the perimeter wall.

"They won't save you," said White. "They'll never reach the house."

With that, a cellar door swung open and at least a hundred men poured out, wielding the new AR-15s.

Morgan was yanked toward the stairs by Madaki's bodyguard, a near seven-foot-tall hulk of bone, muscle, and fat. Outside, the gunmen opened fire on Dimka's rebels.

Chapter 50

The fist hit Morgan in the face like lead. The room whirled and dots swam before his eyes. They resolved into the face of Mr. White.

"Who do you work for?"

Morgan spat blood on the dusty hardwood floor of the mansion.

They were in a second-floor living room, where Madaki sat on an old solid wooden chair like a king on a throne. Two men carrying automatic rifles stood guard at the door. Madaki and White were watching the battle rage outside through broad windows, with half the panes missing and the remaining ones cracked.

Madaki had sent a battalion of his men with the new AR-15s to hold a few miles away. They waited for Dimka's troops to breach the perimeter and then moved against them in the jungle, while the group that had come from the cellar fought them on the property. Dimka's men were stuck fighting on two fronts.

They were getting massacred.

"This little rebellion won't last long," said White. "With their new weapons, Mr. Madaki's men are unstoppable."

"Kill him and have it over with," said Madaki. The warlord was shorter than Morgan had expected, with a snub nose on a chubby cherub's face.

"This man found me twice," said White. "I need to know who sent him."

With a signal from White, Madaki's bodyguard swung his fist again. It sunk into Morgan's gut. He spat up blood.

"This is a waste of time," said Madaki.

"What do you propose I do?"

Madaki pulled out a straight razor from his pocket and held it out, open, for White. "Use the knife. You will see how fast he talks when parts of him start coming off."

White looked at the blade with distaste. Madaki extended it to his bodyguard instead, who took it and ran his finger along the edge. The warlord stood up and grabbed Morgan by the scruff on his shirt, dragging him to the window.

"See how your people die," he said.

The land was strewn with bodies. The rebel soldiers had opted to move inside the perimeter wall, rallying at a defensive position in the ruin of a chapel. They found cover there from Madaki's gunmen, but the latter were moving in with overwhelming automatic fire. It wouldn't be long until Dimka's forces were all dead.

The massive bodyguard pulled Morgan back and, with a meaty hand on his neck, pinned him against a wall. He brought the open razor against the base of Morgan's ear.

White stepped forward. "Are you really going to make me do this?"

Morgan tried to speak, but couldn't with the bodyguard's hand blocking his windpipe. White gestured and the bodyguard eased his grip. Morgan only just got the words out in a raspy, guttural voice.

"No. I'm not."

Morgan kicked the bodyguard's leg and they heard the sickening crack of bone. The razor clattered on the ground. The bodyguard screamed in pain. Morgan grabbed the razor and pulled White into a headlock, moving backward and setting the razor against his neck.

"Stay back or I kill him."

Madaki laughed. "I have my guns. You would be doing me a favor." He addressed his two guards. "*Tue-le.*"

Madaki's men raised their guns. Morgan swallowed hard.

The room darkened as two shapes blocked the light from the windows. Then the glass shattered, the two figures broke through, and gunshot resounded in the room. Madaki's guards fell, dead.

There, standing at the windows, were Bishop and Spartan, still attached to their rappel ropes. Morgan made out the sound of a helicopter's rotor turning overhead.

Morgan turned to Madaki, but the warlord was already fleeing the room. Morgan released White to follow him, but Bishop put his hand on Morgan's shoulder.

"Leave him," Bishop said. "He's not getting far. Look outside."

Morgan stepped over the writhing bodyguard to stand at the broken window against the fresh breeze that was blowing inside. Five troop carriers were driving into the property. They parked and men in full Ivorian military uniform poured out, in neat formation. It was Madaki's men, who'd been pressing against the ruined chapel, who were now fighting on two fronts.

Morgan turned around to see Bishop putting White in handcuffs. "Who are the soldiers?" he asked.

"General Jakande sent them. I guess he saw an opportunity."

Morgan turned his attention back to the battle. The army soldiers were advancing. They were minutes away from a rout.

"Morgan," said Bishop. "We need to get up on the roof to leave with the chopper."

Morgan scanned the battlefield below. While Jakande's men were swarming the chapel attackers, another group of Madaki's soldiers was moving back in the opposite direction. Holding them off single-handedly, pinned against one of White's trucks, was a small woman in a tank top, holding an Uzi in her left hand, bleeding from her right shoulder.

Yolande.

"Morgan, we need to go!" said Bishop

"I'll meet up with you later!" He grabbed the AR-15 from one of the dead guards and dashed out of the room.

"Morgan! Where are you going?"

"Go!" He ran full tilt downstairs and circled around the back door. He leapt over bodies as he reached White's green canopied Mercedes-Benz trucks.

The chopper lifted off the roof and flew overhead, moving south. Within seconds it had cleared the property.

Morgan circled the trucks and opened fire on the encroaching soldiers. They stopped their progress, sending a barrage of bullets in response. Morgan kept low and ran to Yolande, taking cover behind the truck cab alongside her. She was nursing a wounded arm.

"What the hell are you doing here? I thought you left in the chopper!"

"Well, I stayed!" The battlefield smelled of blood and burning gunpowder. Morgan peeked around the grille of the truck and fired a volley of bullets from his AR-15. The attackers hesitated, but continued moving forward.

They didn't have long. Not long enough to wait for Jakande's men to save them.

"Okay, genius, you came here to save me," said Yolande. "Now what's your plan?"

Morgan stood flat against the side of the truck, mind racing, when his eyes locked onto something.

The satchel of dynamite, which Morgan had dropped to check on the weapons crates. It was still there, where he'd left it, lying in the mud. Nobody had thought to pick it up.

Morgan crawled forward and raised it off the ground, feeling its weight. He crouched behind the truck and, holding on to the strap, he swung it overhand. It sailed over the truck and landed among the attackers. They yelled and ran for cover. Morgan rolled onto the muddy ground and fired.

The satchel erupted in flames, hot air blowing against his face.

Morgan scuttled back to sit next to Yolande, leaning against the truck's tire. The gunfire grew sparser and more distant as Jakande's men beat back Madaki's.

Morgan took a deep breath. It was over.

He turned to Yolande. "You're welcome, by the way."

"I did not ask for you to come save me." Her lips curled into something like a smile. "But thank you for coming anyway."

Chapter 51

A lex was alone and everything was dark. A figure that came out of the shadows, and somehow *was* the dark, chasing her. Her leg wasn't broken or in a cast anymore, but the more she struggled to run, the slower she seemed to go. The figure just came closer and closer until it knocked her on the ground and climbed on top of her, his face inches from hers, a horrible, twisted face—

She woke up, panting. It was late morning already, but she had stayed up so late the night before out of fear and adrenaline that she only now was pushing herself to get up.

Katie's bed was empty. She had been there the night before, but by the time Alex came back she was already asleep.

Alex was groggy, and the world had taken on the sheen of unreality that followed disturbing events and a night of poor sleep. She looked at the day outside. Gray and snowy. Big surprise.

Still in her pajamas, she knocked on Simon's door. Both had locked their respective doors when they had gotten back as a precaution. Some thirty seconds later, the knob turned and there was Simon, rubbing his eyes.

"Hey," she said. "How you holding up?"

He let her in without a word and they just sat in each other's presence, side by side on his bed. This wasn't the first time she had feared for her life, but she was pretty sure it was for Simon. It had raised the stakes, and she didn't quite know how to deal with it. Neither, it seemed, did he.

Her phone buzzed: an e-mail from Dr. Strimling. She opened it, without thinking, if only to break the awkwardness. She couldn't focus and its contents were a blur, but certain choice phrases jumped out at her, such as *recommend academic probation, by the end of the semester,* and *may be facing expulsion.*

Simon must have caught it as well, because he yanked her phone from her hands and held it away from her. He mumbled the words under his breath as he read them.

"Alex, what the hell is this? Probation? *Expulsion?* Why didn't you tell me?"

"Because it's my goddamn problem, all right?" She grabbed her phone back from him.

"And you didn't think to talk about it with your friends?" he huffed. "Are you talking to *anyone* about this?"

She looked at the carpet and crossed her arms. "I've got it handled, all right?"

"Oh, that is *abundantly clear.*" He swore and looked out the window. "I'm worried about you."

"Forget about this!" she said. "What about the Ekklesia? What about our case?"

"Are you kidding me?"

"We have a purpose, Simon. We have a mission."

"Our purpose is this!" he yelled, motioning all around him. "College. Classes. You know, the reason we're actually here?"

"Girls are being drugged—"

"And we've done what we could. In fact, we've gone way past what is reasonable for someone to do in this situation. But it's over. There's nothing more to be done, except maybe alert someone in a position of authority."

"We can't let them—"

"You can't keep doing this to yourself." He was stern. "I won't let you. You're in a spiral, and I don't know where it ends, but I know it's not good. And I think you're using it to run away."

Painful as it was to admit, he was making some kind of sense. Everything in her life was a shambles. She was close to flunking out of school. She didn't even know what was going on in her classes. She had not spoken to her father in weeks. And her one true friend in college she was using to chase this strange new obsession of hers. Maybe she was holding on to this so that she wouldn't have to face the difficult work of getting everything else back on track.

She broke down in tears. Simon embraced her.

"Alex." His voice was gentle now. "It's time to pull the plug on this."

"Okay," she said weakly.

"I'll help you with your classes. We'll see about getting you a tutor or something in case it turns out you need it. Okay?"

"Okay."

She stood up.

"Where are you going?"

"I just want to be alone with my thoughts for a little while."

He nodded. "Promise you'll call if you need me?"

"Yeah."

"All right," he said, getting up and opening the door for her. "I'll be here."

She shuffled to her bedroom and collapsed onto the bed. A horrible sensation came over her. It wasn't the dull self-loathing she'd been sharing her mind with for the past several months. This was sharper, more painful. It made her want to cry out. To scream. So she put her pillow over her head and did, over and over again, shrieks of pain and anger muffled in memory foam.

And it began to feel better. This was, she realized, what it was like to let go of an obsession. To jog yourself out of something that seemed so important it eclipsed everything else in your life. She had to tear that away, and it took little parts of her with it. But it was also the beginning of healing.

She was startled out of it by her phone ringing in her pocket. She drew it out and looked at the screen: it was an unknown 617 number. She slid her finger across the screen to answer.

"Hello?"

"Hi, Alex, it's Hillary Chen."

"He-hi," she said. "Sorry, I'm just surprised to be hearing from you."

"Yeah. Listen, I lied. I do remember something. Quite a bit, actually. And I'd like to talk to you about it. Can you meet me in Boston?"

"I, uh, have a broken leg," she said. "But I could take the bus—"

"Never mind, I'll drive up this evening. Where can I meet you?" Hillary asked.

And, just like it *was* a drug, she was hooked again.

Chapter 52

Bruce Ansley drove his boxy, steel blue old model Toyota Camry the familiar way home in the noontime sun. He and Annemarie rode together in silence, digesting what they had just been told.

Annemarie spoke first. "So what do we do about Pam?"

"How should I know? I had no idea about any of this."

"We have to talk to her about it. Find out what's causing her to act out."

"I mean, smoking in school?" said Ansley. "Caught *drinking*? What is going *on* with that girl?"

"It's not like she talks to me. But maybe if we sit down with her and offer her a safe space to—"

"She needs consequences. First thing we do when we get back is search her room. I mean *everything*. If she has so much as a piece of candy she's not supposed to have, I'm going to find it."

"We can't!" said Annemarie. "It'll push her away. How is she supposed to trust us enough if she—"

"She needs consequences for her actions," Ansley barked at her. "And that's what I'm going to give her, so help me—I mean, can you believe that two-bit school counselor, suggesting that it's our fault? That we're not *present* enough, that Pam is acting out because she lives in a *hostile home environment*? Oh please."

"Well . . ." Annemarie began.

"Well what?"

"You could try to mellow out," she said. "Sometimes. You yell at her an awful lot, and you don't really give her the space to—"

"Don't give her *space*? She's got all the space she *wants*! She spends all afternoon locked in her room. Doesn't even come down for dinner, and you think she needs *space*?"

"I just mean that she doesn't feel comfortable sharing anything when you're there. She needs to—"

"Oh, *typical* of you to blame me."

"I was just suggesting that you—"

"Like I don't do enough for this damn family. I bust my ass at work, I come home tired every day, and I still have to deal with a sullen teenager and *you* pointing your finger at every little thing I do." He made a brusque turn into the post office parking lot, braking hard at the space. "I have to get some stamps." He got out of the car and slammed the door.

He walked into the post office and opened the post office box.

Empty.

He slammed it shut and locked it again.

As he turned to leave, he saw Annemarie standing there at the door of the post office, looking at him. He wasn't carrying any stamps. Hadn't even gotten in line. She'd caught him red-handed.

"Get back in the car, Annemarie," he growled.

Chapter 53

"It was like a bad dream."

Alex sat cradling an *Americano* across from Hillary Chen at Campus Coffee. She was pretty—not in the sense that she was born with it, although that was also true, but she was one of those women for whom *pretty* was part of who they were and wanted to be. She had a certain bearing, an enviable poise. Alex could tell she was a master at doing her own makeup, too, with a heavier hand with the mascara in a way that complemented her eyes and a subtle and natural blush. Her hair was thick and lustrous. Her clothes were elegant and tailored, fitted to her form without a trace of vulgarity. And what was most remarkable: she had no reason to impress Alex. This, as far as she could tell, was her everyday attire.

Alex, in contrast, was wearing blue jeans and a tank top under her sweater, no makeup, no effort made on her hair except a couple bobby pins to keep her bangs off her eyes.

"I just pushed it out of my mind," Hillary continued. "I thought I could get away from it by ignoring it. And I guess I did. I work, I lead a full life. But it never stopped nagging in the back of my mind. And your call, it brought it all back."

"I'm sorry."

"Don't be. I didn't have the capacity to deal with it then, but I do now. I'm not vulnerable anymore. I'm not afraid."

Alex found herself jealous of Hillary's self-possession. Alex's own shortcomings became embarrassing, and her excuses for not becoming a better person felt petty. She wanted to be strong, like Hillary.

"Does that mean you'll come forward?"

Hillary stared out the window at the falling snow. She sipped her cappuccino. "I'm out of college now," she said. "The bastard can't hurt me anymore." She looked Alex in the eye. "Yes," she said. "I'll come forward. I'll speak on the record."

"Maybe you won't have to do it alone. There's someone else who I think they might have targeted, too. A girl called Annette Baig."

Hillary's countenance darkened. Without a word, she searched for something on her phone and slid it across the table to Alex.

It was an article on Annette Baig—an obituary. Somehow, Alex and Simon had neglected to run a simple Google search. Alex read below the headline. It was dated three years before, which is why she never graduated. It said she—

"She took her own life," said Alex.

"I remember it was a big deal at the time. They found her out in the woods beyond the observatory."

"This was the semester Assistant Coach Groener went to talk to her. Do you think—?"

"We can't know."

No, Alex supposed she couldn't draw a simple line from point A to point B. But—she curled her hands into fists—if Groener had any fault in this, he would pay. She would make certain of it.

"I want to take it to the press first," said Alex. "I don't trust the university not to make this disappear. I want to make it impossible for them to ignore it."

Hillary considered this. "That sounds like a plan."

"I'm thinking of a reporter we can contact. Someone from the *Inquirer*. I've looked into some possibilities. There's this one girl. She strikes me as the kind of shark this story needs."

"Let me know when you know. I'll tell her whatever I can to help."

Alex smiled, and her eyes nearly welled with tears. She had it. It was within her grasp.

"You know," said Hillary, "I don't know you very well, but I already admire the heck out of you."

Alex choked on her coffee. "Are you kidding? You're, like, this totally amazing woman, making it in the big city. I can barely pass my classes in college." Her shoulders hunched in shame. "I may not."

"But you're doing something harder and more meaningful than any other student at this school," she said. "I wouldn't—I *didn't*—

have the guts to do what you're doing as a senior, let alone as a freshman."

"You have a lot more guts coming forward. It's personal for you. For me it's only a weird fixation."

"Don't minimize this." Hillary stood up from her chair. "You're my hero, Alex Morgan. And I've got your back. You need help getting up?"

Alex waved her off, buoyed with pride. She polished off her coffee, scalding her throat in the process, and stood up without any major disasters.

Hillary held the café door open for Alex.

"So, I gotta get back to the city," she said. "You need a ride anywhere?"

"I'm good."

Hillary smiled. "Thank you again." She moved in and hugged Alex, waving a silent good-bye before walking away.

Alex turned back toward Prather House.

It was time to get in touch with the reporter. She took out her phone and scrolled to the contact she had already saved in anticipation of this moment.

"Hi, Francine? You don't know me, but I have a hell of a story for you. I'd like to sit down and have some coffee. As soon as you can."

Chapter 54

Morgan was dropped off by the driver at the apartment Jakande had set up in Abidjan for the tactical team. It was a three-bedroom, populated with Soviet-style furniture. The tactical team kept it in a state of military neatness. White was sitting on the couch, shrinking under Tango's watchful eyes. Spartan snored, asleep on an armchair in the corner. Diesel was whistling in the kitchen, preparing a sandwich. Morgan's stomach rumbled.

He still had red paint on his face, mingled with dried blood from the beating he had taken from Madaki's bodyguard.

"How you doin', killer?" Bishop asked Morgan with a fist bump.

"Long ride back when you're driving," he said. "Jakande's soldiers secured the house. They got a couple of Madaki's lieutenants. They'll have no problem finding whatever's left of his scattered forces. You guys all right?"

"Fine, except for having to look after Whitey over here." Bishop gave Mr. White a slap on the back of the head.

Morgan pulled up a chair, dragging it close to White, so that their knees were almost touching.

"Hello there, Señor White. Have these guys been treating you well?"

He was trembling. "Wh-what are you going to do to me?" he stammered.

Morgan's mouth broke into a wolfish grin. With all the bruises and paint, he must have been a grotesque sight. "Let me tell you what's going to happen." Morgan slapped a hand on White's knee. "We're going to be friends, you and me. Bee-eff-effs. Isn't that right, Tango?"

"That's right."

"You're gonna come over to my house, and we're going to have a slumber party. Pizza, pillow fights. And then you're going to whisper all your secrets in my ear."

White was sweating and wringing his hands, all color drained from his face. Morgan sat back, putting his feet up on the couch next to White.

"A lot of good men are dead because of your greed. Families driven out of their homes and destroyed. I want nothing more than to toss you in the middle of the people whose lives you destroyed and watch them tear you apart."

White whimpered.

"But I can't do that. You're too valuable to us. I need to know what you know. And if you talk, I pinky-swear that you won't be tried in a state that allows the death penalty."

"I have records of everything," he said, tripping over his words to get them out. "I'll give you everything you need to bury every last person at Acevedo who had a finger in the arms-dealing pie. Drugs, too. I want to make a deal."

"Good," said Morgan. "We're taking you stateside. Some nice men are going to negotiate this deal with you—"

There was a knock at the door.

"Hold that thought."

Morgan got up and opened the door. On the other side was a slender short-haired woman with a scar across her chest, her right arm in a sling.

Yolande.

"General Jakande is here," she said, all business. "He is coming up."

"How's your arm?"

She wouldn't meet his gaze. "It is being tended to."

The elevator arrived on the floor and out came two heavy bodyguards in black suits. They were followed by Jakande, in his military uniform and trademark Colt .45. Yolande stood at attention with military blankness.

"Mr. Bevelacqua," he said with a warm smile, extending a hand in greeting. "Madaki is dead and his forces are routed. I have you to thank for that. All of you," he added, looking at the assembled Zeta tactical team.

Morgan shook the general's hand. "Thanks for saving the day."

"We saw an opportunity to end Madaki's reign and we took it. I pressed the high command, and General Onobanjo did not have the courage to stand against us. He is a rational man, after all." Jakande turned his attention to White. "And I see you got your man."

"He's going to be interrogated. We're taking his whole company down. They won't be bringing guns into your country anymore."

"Good. And we will bring Dimka's uprising under the purview of the army. With their help, we will find Madaki's remaining mines and free the people there. There will be no more slaves in Côte d'Ivoire." He lay his hand on Yolande's good shoulder. "My operative told me of your extraordinary bravery, Bevelacqua. You have my eternal gratitude—and that of my country."

"Maybe we can help each other out again someday."

"I've no doubt. Just one more thing before I take my leave."

Jakande drew his sidearm and shot White three times in the chest.

The Zeta team sprang into action. All drew their weapons, as did Jakande's bodyguards and Yolande. Weaponless, Morgan faced Jakande, who was holding his gun at his side. He could hear the heavy breathing of the team behind him, finger triggers itchy.

Mexican standoff. Morgan's least favorite kind.

Jakande holstered his Colt .45 and raised his hand. Yolande and his bodyguards put away their weapons as well. "Easy," said the general. "I have no quarrel with any of you."

"Stand down," said Morgan. Bristling, the team lowered their weapons. He addressed Jakande. "Why?"

"I am a rational man, too, Mr. Bevelacqua. And when I am threatened by powers greater than myself, I know not to stand athwart them."

"You have an army at your disposal. What power can beat that?"

"Information," said Jakande. Morgan caught a hint of shame in his expression.

"Who? Acevedo?"

"I will not say more. The cars are downstairs to take you to the airport. Don't worry about him." He indicated White's twitching corpse. "It will be taken care of. Just make your arrangements and go."

"Sorry," said Yolande, resting her hand on his arm. She followed Jakande out the door.

"What the hell was that?" said Tango.

"Big man flexing his muscles," said Bishop.

Morgan looked down at the body. They had him. They had what they needed to bring down Acevedo. And it had slipped through their fingers yet again.

"I need to call Bloch," said Morgan. "I need to know what the hell is going on."

Bishop handed Morgan a tablet computer and pointed him to a bedroom. Morgan sat down at a desk with the computer and hailed Bloch.

"Good Lord, Morgan, what is on your face?"

He told her what Jakande did.

"That is troubling," she said.

"He double-crossed us. This can't stand."

"This can and will stand," said Bloch. "If White is dead, there is nothing else to be done. We will not act hastily in reprisal. Jakande may still be a valuable ally."

"He just shot our witness!"

"This is not for you to decide. We will conduct an investigation. In the meantime, we cut our losses and look forward. It's time for you and tactical to go to the airport."

He sat back in his chair, exhaling. "At least after all this it'll be good to go home."

"You are not coming home."

"What?"

"You have a new mission. In Ireland. We'll brief you on the way."

Chapter 55

"I can't believe you," said Simon.

The dining hall was bustling with the dinner crowd, red-faced students coming in ravenous from the cold. Alex tossed a curly fry in her mouth and, before even swallowing, took a bite of her burger, searing hot and juicy.

Simon sat across from her at one of the square tables, agog at what she had been telling him, and not in a good way.

"This is what we were working for," she said through a full mouth of hamburger.

"You're back in."

She swallowed with effort. "I caught a real break with Hillary Chen."

"What about getting your life back on track?"

"I meant it," she said. "I really did. But don't you get it? It's happening, Simon. We're going to do it."

"*You're* going to do it," he said. "I want no more involvement in this insanity."

He got up and stormed off.

"What about your food?" Alex asked, but he didn't stick around long enough to hear it.

She shrugged and took the onion rings from the tray he had left. More for her.

The reporter, Francine Krynick, didn't want to meet over coffee. After Alex gave her the bare bones of her findings, she insisted they get together in one of the private study rooms in the dorm basement. They sat across the beech table from each other. The room had windows to the computer lab that led into it, but it was soundproof, which was one of its main virtues.

Francine had wild frizzy hair, which she didn't try to contain at all so that it ended up sticking out in every direction, some locks curled and some not. She wore, over manic-looking eyes, glasses, square, thick black oversized plastic frames, which she pushed back up when they slid down her face every couple of minutes.

Alex finished relating everything that had happened thus far, ending on her conversation with Hillary Chen.

"That's quite a story," Francine said finally, looking over her notes. "I have . . . questions."

"I would imagine."

She asked more about the party at the frat house. Alex described it in minute detail, being careful to omit Katie's name.

"How did you get access to the visitor logs at the health center?"

"I think we'd better skip that one."

"Illegal then?" Francine shook her head as she jotted down a note on her pad. "They'll come after me to find out how I came by it."

"They will. Will that be a problem?"

Francine laughed. "I'll get word out on the blogosphere. The more the university hounds me for this, the more people will come to my side. And, not incidentally, the more people will read my article and know my name."

Alex knew then she'd made the right choice with Francine. Something she'd learned from her father: sometimes, it's better to have a selfish person who will benefit from helping you than an honorable one who won't.

"To be clear, this girl you're talking about is *not* willing to talk, not even off the record?"

"No," said Alex.

"But"—Francine shuffled through her notes—"Hillary Chen will speak to me on the record?"

"I can guarantee it."

"And you?"

"I don't want my name anywhere on it," Alex said. "As far as your article is concerned, I don't exist. Are we clear?"

"Which means I get full investigative credit."

"Right. Cite me as an anonymous source if you'd like. But that's all. The more you take credit for, the better."

"Not gonna take issue with that."

"So you're in?" Alex asked.

Francine might as well have been salivating. "Are you kidding me? This kind of story could take me on the interview circuit *and* land me a book deal *and* get me an internship at the *New York Times*. Let's get this ready for the next issue."

Chapter 56

Morgan reclined in the seat of the empty Gulfstream jet after his gourmet meal. After a hell of a couple of days, it felt damn good to stretch out in luxury for a few hours, rest his weary legs, and apply cream to the mass of mosquito bites that covered most of his skin. He glanced out the window, clouds white in the moonlight far below. They must be somewhere over Spain. He pulled down the blind. He didn't care for heights.

He closed his eyes for a rest, but that didn't last for two minutes before the flight attendant cleared her throat and set a computer in front of him. "A little dessert, sir."

The screen came on and resolved into the Zeta War Room as seen from around the big screen. Kirby was sitting like he owned the place, at the head of the table. Shepard was in his usual seat at the far end, on the side. Almost every inch of the table was strewn with reams of paper that seemed to have their own chaotic order.

"Whoa, that's not a great angle for you," said Shepard. "Look at the size of those pores."

"How about we get to the point? I'm missing precious sleep for this."

"This is your debrief for your next mission," said Kirby. "Our analytical team has gained access to the data on Dominic Watson's hard drive."

"Yeah? What did you find?"

"Chat logs and forum posts," said Shepard. "Thousands of pages' worth. We've been piecing together the story while you were off tramping in the jungle. Here, I'm sending them to you now."

A folder full of text files popped up on the screen. Morgan opened a file at random. It was a chat log for a conversation between a *capt_omega* and *trackoverflow*. It was mostly gibberish, peppered by the odd *ha-ha* or *lol*.

O'Neal trudged in from the lower right corner of the screen with another ream of paper in her hands, two or three hundred sheets' worth, her light frame bent under their weight. She slammed it down on an empty corner of the table, adjusted her glasses, and swept her bangs out of her eyes. "Here's the last of the trickster convos." Morgan looked through the files Shepard had sent and saw that it was spelled *Trixxter*. "Hi, Morgan."

"Karen. Any of you care to fill me in on why I'm going to Dublin?"

"When we first made contact with Watson, he was spooked," she said, rifling through papers. "He wouldn't say what it was that had gotten him scared, but I got the impression it wasn't Acevedo. He said he wanted to disappear. We promised to make that happen if he—" Her voice faltered, her gaze was cast down. "If he did this for us."

"We knew that Watson was on a number of electronic security forums," broke in Shepard. "People who get together to talk about hacking. Mostly about how to stop it. That's what most of this is."

"I found a conversation he had saved on his computer," said O'Neal, holding up one of the packets and setting it back down in its original place. "That's packet number 27D, for the viewer following us at home. A couple months ago, one of them, a guy whose handle is *tridentkatana*—yeah, I know—shared with the group a security breach he had found in major networks. It could allow a hacker to see certain off-limits information in databases."

"What are we talking about?" said Morgan. "User passwords?"

"That's what he figured at first," said Shepard. "He took it to the group because he wanted their help figuring out if it really was what he thought it was. They could stand to make a lot of money from big tech companies like Google that pay rewards for this kind of thing."

"And was it as bad as they thought?"

"Turns out it was worse," said O'Neal. "It was a vulnerability hidden in the programming language of all the major encryption protocols. I'm talking about something that could give a hacker free range over all encrypted communications. I'm talking government, major corporations, private e-mails. Anything. They were calling it Blackrot."

"Their little circle was sitting on the biggest tech story of the decade," said Shepard. "This could shake the bedrock of Internet security. *Everyone* would scramble to protect their data. Connections would be down for days, possibly weeks. Banking activities would halt. The stock market would take a nosedive. We're talking major panic."

Morgan's brow furrowed.

"But wait, it gets worse," he continued. "Because this gives them access to government communications as well. Watson's group found out that exploiting this breach leaves a signature. And they were finding that signature everywhere. This means someone has been using the Blackrot vulnerability to get where they're not supposed to go. And I mean *everywhere*. For months, at least. Not only e-mails but banking and secret government databases."

"Do we think this had something to do with Watson's death? That it's the same people that attacked me at the apartment?"

"Show him," said O'Neal.

"About a month ago, Watson got this message." It popped up on Morgan's screen.

Being followed. They are on to us. Trust no one.—Meatatron

"Meatatron was Guillermo Santos, native of Albuquerque, New Mexico," said O'Neal. Shepard showed him the picture. "Killed in a car accident two days after that message was sent."

"He wasn't the only one," said Shepard as he cycled through the photos. "Philip Sykes, handle *tridentkatana*. Killed six days later in Liverpool. Asphyxiated by a carbon monoxide leak in his apartment. Elizabeth Nguyen, handle *Trixxter*." The screen showed a chubby woman in glasses and bobbed hair. "Killed three weeks ago in New Jersey. Hit her head and drowned in her own bathtub."

"And Quentin Ferguson, AKA Captain Omega." Thirtyish, black, shaved head. "Killed two weeks ago, right here in Boston."

"Did he have a connection to Dominic Watson?" Morgan asked.

"They were friends," said O'Neal. "Like, in real life."

"You found evidence that they met on the computer?"

"No," said O'Neal. "I knew them personally. I was at Fergie's funeral."

Ah. Her reaction finally made sense.

"That's how we first made contact with Watson," she continued. "Dom told me he was spooked. Fergie'd come up to him a few days before he died. They had gone silent in the forum. But Fergie had found out all their names as an exercise, and he knew that the others had died. He told Dom, and Dom became desperate for a way out. He confided in me about some things, although most of it I'm only learning now."

"And now he's dead," said Morgan.

O'Neal seemed stricken anew with grief and guilt at the reminder.

"Yes," said Shepard. "But we caught a break. There's one left. Séamus Quinn, alias *trackoverflow*. He lives in Dublin."

"That's where I come in?" asked Morgan.

"This is the last member of their circle," said Shepard. "Someone is killing them off for what they knew. If we are to get to the bottom of this, we need that last man."

Chapter 57

Andrea Nyhan frowned as she stared at the list of active processes running on the Acevedo server. It was her job to know each of those scripts backward and forward, including what they did, their priority status, when they were running, and about how much processing power they took up at any given moment.

This was why this particular process was bothering her so much.

"Marvin, come see this."

Marvin Brainard, fat and fussy, pulled up a chair, scraping along the carpet, and set it down next to her. The chair squeaked under his weight. "What is it?"

"It's this weird background program," she said. "Shows up as this, here." She pointed to where it said *btrck.exe.*

"Looks like the backup tracker for XT. There's always a bunch of instances running."

"That's what I thought," she said. "But see the name of the process? It's for the older version of the software. They changed the process name in the latest update. See, it's running here, look." She pointed to another process labeled *ibtrck.exe.* "Somehow they're *both* running."

"Someone forgot to update their tags. That or it's some of the old software that wasn't scrubbed in the update."

"Maybe," she said. "I checked, though. There's nothing left after the update, not even in its original location. And yet there it is. Plus, it's behaving weirdly. The processing patterns are all wrong."

"That's why we call it a bug."

"Maybe." She chewed on her pen. "But if I were to install a worm, this is exactly the way I'd do it."

"Honey, you're paranoid."

"Isn't that what we're paid for?"

"Got me there." He looked at the process log, lost in thought. "Well, I guess there's no harm in running this by Steve. Just in case."

"Later," she said. "I'm going to poke at it and see what else I can figure out."

She ran a number of diagnostics, trying to pin down exactly what it was doing and where it was coming from. The regular tests came out normal. She then tracked the program's location on the drive and navigated to it. If the usual tools weren't working, she was going to decompile it and find out what it did by looking straight at its insides.

She opened her decompiler, hit *Open*, navigated to the program file, and double-clicked it. The computer processed the request for a few seconds and an error message popped up.

FILE NOT FOUND.

"What the—"

She opened the folder that had contained the file. It wasn't there. She refreshed it, made sure that the computer was displaying hidden files, checked for it through different programs. No dice. It was gone.

She banged on her keyboard.

This attracted Brainard's attention. "Your elusive little process giving you trouble?"

"It's disappeared."

"What do you mean it's disappeared?" He bent down over her keyboard and performed a few checks.

"I've done that already," she said. "It's just not there anymore. It's like the program was smart enough to notice that someone had found it out. I've never seen anything like this."

"Could I have some pen and paper? I'd like to jot this down."

She handed him a pen from her cup and opened her top drawer for a scrap of paper. She dug through some important documents and found a sheet from a yellow legal pad. She tore a piece off the bottom and gave it to Brainard, who jotted down the names of the processes and their locations on the server.

"I'm going to look into this on my computer," he said. "I'll let you know if I find anything."

She exhaled, looking at her screen.

Her attention was drawn to the yellow sheet of paper on her desk, the piece missing from the bottom that she'd torn out to give to Brainard. She frowned. She couldn't think of what it might be. It certainly wasn't hers.

She unfolded it. At the bottom was a phone number, and above it—

GET OUT WHILE YOU STILL CAN—D

Andrea was struck by nausea. D? As in Dominic? How long had this been here?

Something was very wrong, and she wondered whether she even wanted to find out what that was.

Chapter 58

The train pulled in to the snowy platform at Wicklow Station, which was a squat yellow stone building with four brick chimneys protruding from its roof. Morgan came out into the cold—a wind more bitter and biting than in Boston—and passed through the station to come to the street on the other side, where Mick Larkin was leaning back in the driver's seat of his 2001 Ford Focus, still baby-faced with his blue eyes reading a newspaper.

He nearly jumped in his seat when Morgan knocked on the window, and then his mouth erupted into a broad grin.

"You don't call, you don't write," he said as he got out of the car. "You stinking gobshite yank!" They embraced like the old friends they were. "How are ya?"

Morgan got into the passenger seat and Mick pulled out so fast Morgan had to grab the handle. Mick was the only bastard Morgan knew who was crazier than he was behind the wheel.

"How's Nora? Ciaran?" he asked, wincing as Mick had a close shave with a low stone wall.

"He's a downright pain in my ass," he said. "Smoking, brawling. You should be glad you have a girl."

If only he knew.

"So, yer here on business, then? Let's get down to it. I found your guy. Lives in Dublin." Mick grinned ear to ear. "Just like old times, eh? So what're we talking? Terrorist? Murderer?"

"Nerd," said Morgan. Mick shot him a puzzled glance. "Stumbled into something he shouldn't have, and now he's marked for death."

"You wanna save him?"

"What I need is to catch whoever's after him. The people behind this have resources. I don't even know how far it goes."

"You never asked if it was dangerous," Mick said. "You just asked if it was right."

"You haven't even asked me that."

"I know you," said Mick. "I don't have to."

"Well, it is. Gonna be dangerous, I mean."

"Good."

"At least let me pay you," said Morgan.

"Fook you," said Mick, extending the words at least three syllables past their regular carrying capacity.

He'd always been a proud son of a bitch.

Mick reached in the back seat and picked up a heavy black duffel bag, putting it in Morgan's lap. "Here's the hardware you requested. Although I don't know how the hell you can afford all this stuff."

"Two words," said Morgan. "Expense account."

"Seriously?"

"One of the perks of working for the private sector."

"You'll have to put in a good word for me one of these days," Mick said.

Morgan rooted around inside the bag. The first thing he pulled out was the Bullard T4Max thermal imager, a handheld device in a blue plastic casing with a lens on one side and a screen on the other that was somewhat reminiscent of an old home movie camera. This was the Cadillac of its class. It felt solid in his hand. Super high saturation temperature, wide field of view, high-res.

"This'll do," said Morgan.

Added to the imager was a handheld parabolic listening device (*good enough*, Morgan thought), a professional-grade lock-pick set, and a gun in its holster along with two magazines. A Walther PPK. He pulled it out to inspect it.

"Put that back inside, you fookin idiot!" Mick yelled. "You can't be seen with that."

"What? We're in the car."

"My car, my rules."

"It might help if you didn't attract the attention of the police by driving like a maniac."

"Like I said, 'my car—'"

"Your rules. Got it." Morgan lowered the PPK into the bag. "Well, thanks for the gun."

"I remember how partial you were to that wee little piece," he said.

"Much appreciated," said Morgan as he inspected the weapon inside the bag. He then examined each of the thirty picks in the kit, each with a different head, and the six different tension tools.

He and Mick talked all the way up to Dublin, about old times and trading war stories they hadn't yet exchanged. It was just under an hour before Mick brought the car to a stop across the street from a low brick apartment, just north of the River Liffey.

"That's it," he said. "Second floor."

"Think he's home?"

"Records show he works at home, gets food delivered," said Mick. "Not much in the way of spending outside the house. This fella doesn't get out much."

Morgan pulled out the thermal imager and pointed it at the apartment.

"I'm getting nothing," said Morgan.

"Are you sure that thing is working?"

He turned the lens to the neighboring apartment. It clearly showed the figure of a woman, in the fluid reds and yellows of the infrared signature. Then he turned it back to point at Quinn's.

"There's no one in there," Morgan reiterated.

"No one alive," said Mick.

"What do you think?" said Morgan. "Move in?"

"After you."

They got out of the car and went to the door of the apartment building. Morgan waited for a lull in foot traffic and drew his lock pick and tension tool while Mick kept a lookout—ready with his police ID in case anyone spotted them. European locks could be a heck of a lot harder than American ones—they tended to come standard with features that resisted lock picking, like mushroom-shaped pins that had false catches. This lock turned out to be that kind. But Morgan had practice. Hard as it was, it still took him under a minute to get it open.

They came inside and Mick closed the door behind them. They crept up the stairs to Quinn's door. Morgan grabbed the lock pick from his pocket, but when he touched the door it creaked open. The lock was busted.

Morgan and Mick walked inside the apartment, and the first thing that was obvious was that someone else had gotten there first. The apartment was completely turned over—all drawers pulled out, all cushions cut open, the floor strewn with papers and objects.

What didn't help at all was that Quinn didn't seem to be particularly neat to begin with. Dishes were piled high in the sink, their smell pervading the apartment, and food delivery boxes were piled on one corner of the counter.

"Christ, this fella really didn't get out much, did he?"

"If there was anything to be found, someone else has found it," said Morgan.

"What about Quinn?"

Morgan took the lead to look at the bedroom and bathroom. "It's clear," he said, relieved. "He's not here."

Morgan walked back to the living room and examined Quinn's computer rig. Three monitors were suspended above the desk, with a very sophisticated-looking keyboard and freestanding mouse pad. The chair was one of those expensive ergonomic things.

Morgan knelt to check the computer. It had been opened and the hard drive removed.

"Bust," said Morgan. "There's nothing here for us."

Mick's phone beeped. "We're not out for the count yet," he said. "We just got a hit on Quinn's car at a traffic camera in a town called Dunboyne."

"Our boy's on the run," said Morgan.

"I'm calling my guys and getting them to cross-reference Quinn with anything in connection to Dunboyne. See if I can get any hits on credit cards or anything like that."

"Meanwhile—"

"We go to Dunboyne," said Mick. "Let's collect our man."

Chapter 59

Alex spent the afternoon going over the *final* details of Francine's story in a dingy room in Thoroughgood Hall, which housed the *Inquirer*'s headquarters. Between stacks of old copies of the newspapers Alex fact-checked the text, on a five-year-old Mac machine, and vouched for its veracity with the editor in chief. It was written, polished, and set to run on the front page of the next day's *Inquirer*.

"Well, kid," Francine said, giving her a pat on the back, "You're about to make my goddamn career."

Alex walked outside feeling victorious. This was going to work. She was going to nail the bastards.

Night had fallen, and Prather was all the way across campus, but Alex was beyond any annoyance or discomfort. Everything paled in comparison to the sense that she had won. She was so exhilarated that she decided to go the long way around, where a series of grassy knolls offered an unreal view of campus in the light of the waning moon.

That turned out to be a mistake.

She paid no heed to the approaching car. Everything was too beautiful. When it came to a stop, she figured the driver was going to ask for directions or offer a ride to the poor crippled girl out there on her own. She smiled, amused by the driver's imagined condescension.

When she turned to look at the driver, she realized too late that the correct feeling at that moment was fear.

Assistant Coach Adam Groener.

She looked around. There was no one to call for help. Not a single person, not a car, not an evening jogger. People were inside, huddled against the bitter cold.

"Good evening, Alex." His voice was friendly and jovial. "Not a very nice one for a stroll, though." She didn't stop, and so he drove alongside her, keeping pace with her halting walk.

"Good enough for me," she responded.

"Where are you going? Why don't you let me give you a lift?"

"I'm fine. It's not far, and I'd rather walk."

"There isn't anything *around* here," he said. "Wherever it is, it's far."

She didn't answer.

"Hey, look. I think we got off to a bad start. I just wanted to talk to you, clear a couple of things up. Some things I think you might have misunderstood."

"I'd really rather not."

"Come on," he insisted. "Hop in!"

"No thank you."

"Get in the car." He dropped his feigned friendliness, and his voice carried outright menace. "Get in the car or I'll make you."

Alex turned away from the car and hobbled onto the grass, going down a hill that was just too steep for comfort. She didn't have a chance in hell of outrunning him even if he wasn't in a car. But if the son of a bitch wanted her, he was going to have to work for it.

"Help!" She screamed, taking out her cell phone. "Help!" She dialed 911. She heard it ring once before a meaty paw snatched it away from her, ended the call, and threw it far away into the snowy slope. It disappeared into the darkness.

"Help! He—" This time he put one hand over her mouth and the other around her waist so that her arms were pinned against her body. Her crutches fell onto the snow as he dragged her back to the car.

She reached for the knife in her jacket pocket, switched it open, and slashed Groener's arm as hard as she could with her pinned arms. He hollered in pain and released her, but without her crutches, she just fell into the snow, ice crystals biting her cheek. He grabbed her again, leaving her father's knife in the snow.

"I'm gonna make you regret that," he growled in her ear, and dragged her all the way back to the car.

He tossed her onto the backseat as if she were a bag of golf clubs. He bound her hands with zip ties and gagged her with a sock. She shifted so that she might at least see where they were going, but her cast made it impossible for her to move without the help of her hands, so instead she got to look at the tan pleather of the backseat, lit up yellow in the passing streetlamps.

"I told you to stay away," he said. "I warned you this wasn't your business. Now you've forced my hand and I have no choice."

"Is that how you justify it to yourself?"

He didn't answer. Alex's mind raced for a way out. She pulled her hands apart, but the ties holding her hands together just bit into her skin and did not give way. Her mind raced for any way to cut them. She regretted pulling her knife on him now. She was hasty. She hadn't thought it through.

"What are you going to do to me?"

He didn't answer. But he didn't have to. There was no going back from this for him.

He was going to kill her.

Chapter 60

The ride was long enough to make Alex's hands numb from the constriction of the zip tie. She didn't speak anymore, and neither did Groener. This suited her fine. She couldn't do anything about the situation now, so she concentrated on keeping calm and honing her focus.

Groener pulled into what Alex assumed was a garage, and the car went dark. It came to a halt and the engine cut out. He opened the door to the backseat, pulled her by her legs, and lifted her to rest on his shoulders. Like she was an equipment bag, he brought her inside the house.

Alex screamed. It was a split second before his hand was on her mouth. She closed her teeth around the flesh of his hand—enough to draw blood and a grunt of pain, but not enough for him to take his hand away.

He tossed her down on a couch. "You know what? Scream all you want. The nearest neighbor is half a mile away."

"What are you going to do to me?"

"You women, you really make it easy for me, even when you make it hard." He opened his liquor cabinet and pulled out a bottle of Wild Turkey. From a drawer, he pulled out a bottle of pills. "You're already depressed. People already think you're crazy. Who's going to doubt that you drank too much one night, took some pills along with it, and ran off into the woods alone to die?"

Alex's heart pounded as he came near, looming above her like he was the only thing in the room.

"Poor, depressed Alex Morgan. Facing the prospect of academic probation and eventual expulsion. It was too much for her." He unscrewed the cap from the liquor bottle, and then from the pill bottle. "They're really going to mourn you, you know. People who hated you are going to talk about what an inspiration you are. People who don't even know your name are going to say you were a great friend. They're going to publish stupid poems about you in the school newspaper. You're really going to be loved for the next week or two. Too bad you won't be around to enjoy it."

"You can't believe you'll actually get away with this." Everything about what he did was stupid. Taking her in his car. Bringing her here. Leaving ligature marks on her wrists. People would investigate this. Her father would. And Groener would go to prison.

And Alex would be dead.

"Nobody is going to look too closely at this. Nobody will care enough. Nobody will even be surprised."

"My dad," she said. "He's gonna come after you."

"Your dad is a mediocre car dealer living in a Boston suburb," said Groener. "Yeah. I know how to use the Internet. Now drink."

He poured the biting, sweet whiskey into her mouth, which she shut tight so that it dribbled down her chin onto her shirt.

"Open up," he said, pushing a greasy, salty finger into her mouth and pouring the alcohol in. It burned her throat and sent her into a coughing fit. Next he picked up the pill bottle.

"It's going to be a peaceful death," he said. "You're just going to doze off and never wake up." She gritted her teeth against his finger. "Don't resist. It'll only make it worse."

Alex bit down hard on his finger and he laid an open-palm slap against her cheek.

"Are you done? You ain't getting away, young lady. So you cooperate, or I make this very, very unpleasant."

He punched her in the stomach, and she bent double on the couch.

"I think I've got a few more of those before I leave anything on you for the coroner to find. What do you think?"

She spit on his shoe.

"Or maybe," he said, "I throw you in the river, so that it looks like you jumped in. I don't even have to weight you down, with that broken leg of yours. I think I could do a lot worse to you before you die when I've got the water covering my tracks." He grabbed her face by the cheeks in his meaty paw. "What do you say?"

This was it. This was her death. Alex felt like she had been preparing for it forever. Now that it had come, a sense of serenity and acceptance washed over her. She had lived. She had tried. She had strived. That was all she could have asked for.

A bottle hit Groener's head with a dull *thunk*, and the muscle-bound body fell to the wooden floor.

Alex looked up at her savior.

Simon.

"You're going to be all right," he said. "The police are on their way. I'm going to get you out of here."

Chapter 61

Mick came back into the car with two shopping bags hanging from his wrist and two medium paper coffee cups. He handed Morgan his and tossed the bags on his lap.

"Tayto Crisps and USA Biscuits," he said. "Something to keep the ol' blood sugar up."

Morgan held the red rectangular tin of USA Biscuits, which were, of course, actually cookies. Separated by a common language indeed.

"How exotic," Morgan said. He examined his beverage cup. "I thought you said you were getting the large coffees."

"These are the large coffees," he said. "Anyway, I talked to my guy back in Dublin. He cast a wider net on our man Quinn. Turns out his uncle owns a cottage here in Dunboyne."

"You know how to get there?" Morgan asked.

"Ever heard of Google Maps?"

Morgan moved his coffee along with the movement of the car to keep from spilling as Mick made the tires sing on tight corners, half-looking at the map on his phone. The directions took them to a narrow country road outside the town, bordered on either side by hedges that were laid bare by the winter, and then into a cul-de-sac lined with identical two-story brick houses.

"Heck of a place for a stakeout," Morgan said. "Which one is it?"

"Second to last on the left."

Morgan drew the infrared viewer. Mick slowed the car down as they passed.

"Someone's in there," Morgan said, looking at the red-orange blob on the screen, large and close, right behind the window. "And he's looking at us."

"Paranoid bugger," said Mick.

"He's got reason to be."

Mick made a three-point turn and they drove back the way they came.

"What now?" he said.

"We come back at night. He has to sleep sometime."

Chapter 62

The police let Alex go in the late morning, after going over every detail of the story with her. They went pretty easy on her, all things considered. They'd caught the coach red-handed, thanks to an anonymous tip. Simon had left as the police sirens approached, at her insistence—it would have been inconvenient for him to explain that he had found her thanks to a phone call from a member of the secret society of vigilantes that they were trying to join. The official story was that she managed to grab hold of the bottle and knock Groener out while he was turned away.

The police gave her a ride back to her dorm after she assured them that there *really* wasn't anyone she wanted them to call, thank you. On arrival, she went straight for Simon's door and knocked. The door swung open. Alex opened her mouth to speak and found that there was both too much and nothing to say. Simon stepped forward and hugged her.

"Thank you," she said. It would do.

"Did you see?" he asked when he finally let go, holding a newspaper out for her. She thought it might be Francine's story, but it was a copy of the *Boston Herald*. The arrest had happened too late for it to make the campus newspaper—it would, she had no doubt, although the police agreed to keep her name a secret—but still, the headline on the front page read:

COACH IMPLICATED IN SEXUAL ASSAULT COVERUP

"You heard it here first," she said. She frowned, patting her stomach. "Are you as ravenous as I am?"

They walked together to breakfast to the dining hall, where she passed a table of glowering football players. She recognized among them Matt Klingensmith, the one who'd tried to herd a doped-up Katie up to his room.

Alex puffed up her chest in a silent gloat. There was nothing they could do now. Any move against her and the police would be on them like linebackers on a running quarterback.

She wondered whether she had gotten that simile right.

She found Katie sitting at their usual table, a copy of the *Inquirer* next to her cereal. She was reading Francine's front-page story. Alex sat down across from her.

"Simon told me," Katie said. "About everything. About last night, too."

Alex rubbed the nape of her neck. She really hated this mushy emotional part. But she really missed Katie, too. "I'm sorry. I shouldn't have pushed you. I should have been there as a friend and nothing more."

"Pshaw." Katie held up the newspaper. "Look at what you did! And you almost got yourself killed, dude!"

"I couldn't let it go."

"You are a total badass."

"Are we good?" Alex asked.

Katie beamed.

Afterward, Simon came by the room, saying he had something else to show her. He opened the deep web messenger program, through which they had contacted the Ekklesia. There was a new message there for them.

You show promise. Stand by to receive your first assignment.

Chapter 63

Mick led the way in the darkness through a barren field, occupied only by a transmission tower. To their right was the row of houses in Quinn's cul-de-sac. It was past midnight and all the interior lights in the homes were off.

They jumped over the wall at the far end of the street, keeping to the shadows, away from the pools of light cast by the lampposts.

Quinn's was the second house from the end. Having talked it over, Morgan and Mick decided it wasn't safe to be out in the open where he might see, even in the dark—Quinn was the kind of paranoid who might very well have night-vision goggles. Instead, they used the neighbor's house for cover. Morgan used the thermal imager to check that everyone in that house was asleep, or at least lying in bed.

They found cover in the bushes bordering a low wall between the two houses. Morgan trained the imager on Quinn's signature. He was sitting up, flush against the back wall.

"What's this?" Mick asked, pointing at a smudge on the imager.

"That," Morgan said, "is a pot of coffee. See the mug here, close to Quinn?" Morgan panned the viewer to scan the house and yard.

"Hold on," said Mick. "Point that thing back over there."

Morgan turned the lens toward Quinn's backyard, farther to the right than before. He made out three distinct figures at the wall, one jumping over, two already in the backyard.

Three, moving in unison. Morgan had seen this before.

"Looks like we're too late," said Mick.

"Looks to me like we're right on time." Morgan ran his hand over the PPK and then the six-inch grooved combat knife that was strapped to his right ankle. Mick had his SIG Sauer P226 semiautomatic and a knife of his own.

"What's the play?"

"We enter through the front," said Morgan. The men were already covering the distance between the wall and the back door. "We engage inside the house. And Mick? Let's try to be quiet about it. The last thing we need is to attract the attention of the Garda Síochána."

Morgan led the way across the yard. They stopped at the front door and Morgan drew his lock picks. This was now a race against the other guy—who could open the door faster. Morgan applied the tension wrench and in fluid haste caught the first, second, third, fourth pin. The lock loosened and he pulled the tension wrench. *Click.* Success.

This wasn't Mick and Morgan's first walk around the park. Morgan signaled for Mick to move through the living room while Morgan took the kitchen route. The back door swung open.

The men hadn't been expecting them, which gave Morgan and Mick the clear advantage.

Mick distracted their attention by shattering a vase in the living room. In the kitchen, Morgan grabbed the biggest knife from a knife block, an eight-inch chef's knife and, pivoting into sight of the three men—all in matching black pants and turtlenecks—Morgan hurled it at the nearest one. It plunged into the man's neck with a spray of blood.

Without waiting for him to fall, Morgan drew his own combat knife and advanced on the other two. As the closer one raised his hands in defense, the other trained his gun on Morgan. *Big mistake.* This left his flank wide open for Mick, who appeared out of the shadows behind him and slit his neck.

The third never got a chance to unholster the Glock 19 he was carrying. Morgan grabbed him by the gun arm and thrust the knife into his belly, upward, pushing until it hit the heart. He was the last to collapse.

"Now let's have a little talk with Quinn," said Mick, among the fallen bodies.

Morgan climbed halfway up the stairs and called out to him. "Quinn!"

"Stay down there!" He threw down a glass ornament, which shattered against the wall at the turn of the staircase.

Well, he didn't have a gun. Morgan could be sure of that. He moved ahead, dodging a book, which sailed above his head.

"I'm here to save you, you goddamn idiot!" Morgan yelled.

Quinn retreated into a bedroom and swung the door shut, but Morgan put his foot down before it closed. His quarry, pudgy and redheaded, retreated into the room. When Morgan opened the door and stepped inside, Quinn, screaming a battle cry, came at Morgan with a letter opener.

Morgan stepped aside to avoid the attack and grabbed the hand holding the tiny blunt knife. With a twist of Morgan's wrist, the letter opener dropped to the floor, bouncing against the carpet.

He then turned Quinn around in a choke hold.

"Would you stop? I'm not here to kill you."

"I won't believe your lies!" he exclaimed. "You're here to kill me like you did the others."

"If I wanted to kill you, don't you think I'd have done it already?"

"You just want to make it look like an accident!"

"I just saved your ass, you ungrateful clown. I'm going to release you, and we're going to have a conversation, okay?"

Quinn grunted in assent.

Morgan let him go. He sprung away and grabbed a statuette from the bookshelf. Quinn swung it against Morgan's head at a sloth's pace. Morgan dodged the blow and swept his foot against Quinn's legs.

He grabbed Quinn's lapel when his head was inches from smashing into the sharp edge of the wooden bed frame. Damn, the son of a bitch was heavy. The statuette hit the floor with a *thunk*. "There's your accidental death," said Morgan. "Would've been that easy. Now do you believe me?"

Morgan pulled him to his feet. Quinn backed away, trying to unrumple his shirt. "Fine, ye don't wanna kill me. That's a pretty low bar to clear. Doesn't mean I should go with ye."

"Morgan, we got company!"

Morgan looked out the window to the front of the house. A car had just pulled up, and the driver's and passenger's side doors swung open.

"What do you say? Are you getting out of here with me or do you want to go with those guys?"

Quinn peered out the window. "Okay," he said. "Let's go." He led the way down the stairs. Mick already had the back door open for them.

"Move your arses!"

They ran out into the yard. Mick ran on ahead, but Morgan had to slow down to keep pace with Quinn. Mick leapt over the back wall as if it were three feet tall. Quinn needed help. Morgan gave him a boost. He heard the back door open and pushed Quinn over the edge. With one impulse, Morgan cleared the wall and landed catlike on the snow, next to a prone Quinn. Morgan extended a hand and helped him up.

They ran together along the wall by the moonlight. Morgan looked back to see the beams of two flashlights going over the wall. They were far away. Even at Quinn's pace, the three of them would make it to the car with time to spare.

Mick arrived first at the car and opened the driver's side door.

"No," said Morgan, grabbing the keys from Mick. "I'm driving."

Mick didn't argue. He ushered Quinn into the backseat and got in next to Morgan.

Morgan hit the gas.

"You!" he barked at Quinn. "Start talking. Who are those people trying to kill you?"

"Who are *you*?"

Morgan kept his eyes on the rearview mirror as he made a tight curve on the narrow road, tires squealing. "Your only friend in the world right now. So you'd better start talking. I know your group found a vulnerability."

"Blackrot. And someone was using it to spy on everything from user e-mail accounts to government communication."

"I know that," said Morgan. "Now tell me something I don't."

"The people who first discovered it. The people who have been exploiting it for months. The people who killed my friends. Who tried to kill me."

"Those men back there?"

"Yes. It's the Legion. The Legion of Erebus." He said it in what Morgan figured was the most portentous tone he could muster.

Mick snickered. "Sounds like something out of one of those Dangers and Dragons things."

"It's mythology," Quinn snipped. "Erebus. God of chaos. Father of Nemesis. Revenge."

"Who are these people?" Morgan said before Mick could derail the conversation with his hysterics.

"Nobody knows. None of them have ever been caught or identified. They're master hackers—they can do things most of us didn't even think was possible."

Morgan took a right to avoid the town. There was no sign of the pursuing car. "What do they want?"

"They call themselves freedom fighters. They style themselves as a kind of resistance against corruption in government and corporations."

"I've heard of that kind of thing before," said Morgan. "I thought that was all bluster. Nerds playing make-believe. No offense."

"There is a lot of that going on, it's true. I always assumed that was it myself, except a handful of groups of white hat hackers who went around looking for vulnerabilities. But clearly it's not."

"How do you know it's them?"

"Because I found them," said Quinn. "I know how they communicate."

"You think you can show my people?"

"I want protection," he said. "These people are powerful. They want to kill me."

"I can get you all the protection you need," said Morgan. He sped forward through the dark country. "The sooner you show us how to find them, the sooner—"

The car came out of nowhere. It slammed into the back of Mick's Focus, sending it into a spin to slam against a low stone wall that bordered the road. The wall gave way and the car plunged down, though the night air, into the Castle River.

Chapter 64

Andrea worked through her lunch hour trying to track down the rogue program. She had to go through the entire registry, correlating the running processes from elements until she isolated the odd one out. It had changed its name to *srvdsktpefr.exe*, which had enough cogent letter combinations to be plausible but as far as she could tell was gibberish.

She was more careful this time. Last time, she had probed the program head-on, and it had slipped between her fingers. This time, she looked for other programs that were interacting with it.

And then she got worried.

It was accessing things even she couldn't. Encrypted databases. Financial, operational, personnel data. That little program was going wherever it wanted to, and none of the usual defenses seemed to be able to do anything to stop it.

This was beyond strange. It was getting uncanny.

Get out while you still can. Those words made her shudder now.

Something was very wrong. She couldn't get the idea out of her head that this program had something to do with Dom's death.

She decided she wasn't going to wait around to find out if she was next.

Wiping sweat from her forehead, Andrea looked around the office. Everyone was busy at their cubicles, no one paying her any attention. She pulled out the yellow sheet and dialed the number on her phone's call function. It occurred to her that it might not be the best idea to make this call out in the open, so she got up from her desk and ducked into the disabled bathroom, locking the door behind her.

Leaning against the white tiles, hand shaking, she hit Send. The phone rang. Someone picked up, but all Andrea heard was the background hiss of the call.

"Hello?"

"Who is this?" A woman's voice. Tough, professional, self-assured.

"My name is Andrea Nyhan. I work at Acevedo International. IT division."

"Where did you get this number?"

"I, uh . . ." She felt stupid. "I work—used to work—with Dominic Watson. He, uh, left this number for me. Something about getting out." The explanation sounded ludicrous to her now. What had she expected?

"Are you scared for your life?"

Well, if she hadn't been before, she certainly was now. "Yes. I am. You can help?"

"Meet me somewhere so we can talk," the woman said. "Do you know where Java Jack's is?"

"Two blocks down on Congress."

"That's the one. Fifteen minutes. Can you do that?"

She checked the time. A quarter to three, but she hadn't taken her lunch break. "Ok. Yes. I can make it."

Java Jack's held a contrasting mixture of professional types reading e-mails on their phones and hipsters typing away on their Macs, working on their novels or Twitter feeds or whatever these people did with their time.

Andrea's eyes cast nervously about the café until they landed on an incongruous pair—a serious-looking woman, about fortyish, wearing a stylish white suit jacket, sitting next to a tall professorial type, maybe a little in too good a shape to be an actual professor, in a denim and a flannel shirt. The woman kept her gaze fixed on Andrea, and seemed satisfied when she moved toward their table.

The woman stood and extended a hand. "Miss Nyhan, thank you for coming. My name is Diana Bloch, and this is my colleague Peter Conley."

Andrea was in no mood to mince words.

"I want to know what's going on," she said as she sat down. "And I want to know who the heck you are."

The man Conley looked at Bloch, who gave him a tacit go-ahead with a curt nod.

"We represent an organization," he said. "An . . . NGO of sorts. We do security and intelligence. We've had our eye on Acevedo International for years."

Andrea's heart sank into her gut. "Had your eye how?"

"We have long known that Acevedo International has engaged in serious criminal activity. Primarily international smuggling of arms and drugs."

"I know about the scandal a few years ago," she said. "I wasn't with the company then. I thought it was just a few bad apples that had been picked out. Over and done with."

"Fall guys," said Conley. "The whole of upper management is rotten, through and through. Our investigations found that they resumed illegal operations almost immediately."

Andrea's head was swimming. It seemed like a reckoning long in the making. Something that had always nagged at the edge of her mind came rushing to the fore. "I'm not surprised at all," she said. "To be honest, I sort of think that's the reason I got the job. People weren't exactly clawing at each other to work at Ace at that moment." She bit her lower lip and looked down at the table. "So what does that have to do with Dom? Dominic. Watson. What does he have to do with anything? Why did he leave me your number?"

"Watson was aiding us in our investigation," said Bloch.

Huh. Dom was a mole. He was the last guy she'd expect would do something like this. He didn't have a political bone in his body.

"On the day he died," Bloch continued, "he installed a backdoor in the security system for us that would allow us to conduct electronic surveillance on Acevedo's servers. We were going to build a case against Acevedo based on the information we got through this opening. Airtight, targeting the entire Board of Directors and all major executives. Take the whole organization down in one swoop."

"It had to be all at once," Conley said. "Anything less, and the rest would just hide the evidence again and we'd be back at square one."

Andrea rubbed her temples. "So the elevator . . . *thing* was not an accident."

"It wasn't," he said.

"So Ace upper management killed him? Is that it?" The two shared a meaningful glance. "What?"

"We don't believe it was," said Conley.

"There's more to this than just Acevedo," said Bloch.

"Does this have anything to do with the note he left me then?" she asked. "*Get out while there's still time.* If all he was doing was spying for you, why does it seem that he knew he wasn't coming back?"

"Dominic was afraid of something. He wanted out—protection. He never told us from what, but we thought it was from Acevedo itself. Now we're sure it was something else."

She shuddered and looked around the coffee shop, as if to look for spies. It occurred to her that she would have no idea how to spot one. "I found a program," she said. "In our security subroutines. It's not supposed to be there. Is that your back door?"

"It could be," said Bloch. "The truth is, we lost control of it."

"Not to us, you didn't." Andrea narrowed her eyes. "Just who the hell is out there?"

"I think," Bloch said haltingly, "that it's better for you not to know."

"And I'm supposed to help you?"

"We can offer you protection," she said. "From criminal prosecution and . . . other things."

"Like you protected Dom?" she said, with stinging indictment.

"We weren't aware of that danger then," Bloch said. "We are now."

"This is not making me feel any more confident in you or the situation."

"It's delicate," Bloch said. "I admit that. A risk remains. But it might be the best option for you. Because before long, the feds are going to roll into Acevedo and scrutinize every dark little corner of that company. Are you sure you want to be there when it happens?"

No. That wasn't possible. She couldn't be that screwed. She hadn't done anything wrong—except work for a company she suspected was criminal. And she was supposed to put her life in danger for this?

But maybe there was something she could do. Maybe she could pivot this to her advantage. "Maybe you just help me, and in exchange I don't tell anyone about you."

Bloch seemed more amused than anything. "Do not threaten us.

We keep our word if we promise to help you. But threaten us, and you lose the last friends you have in this dangerous game."

She wrung her hands. This whole situation was beyond her ken. "All right. Duly chastened," she said. "I guess that's the choice that I have. I'd kind of rather survive, so I guess I'm your girl. Remember, my purpose here is *not to die*. Keeping that in mind, what do I need to do to be part of the team?"

Chapter 65

Morgan walked down the hospital hallway with its dreary fluorescent light carrying a cup of hot coffee. He ran his tongue along where one of his lower left incisors had chipped and had cut into his lip. He nodded a greeting to the armed man standing guard at Quinn's hospital room, one of Mick's ERU buddies from the Garda Síochána, and walked in.

Quinn was lying in bed, his heart rate monitor emitting its intermittent beeps, a heart rate reflecting his deep unconsciousness. They had gotten him to a private hospital, courtesy of Zeta—they weren't going to risk leaving their sole witness in the hands of the public health system. Morgan had gotten off scot-free but for a broken rib and an assortment of bruises, but Quinn hadn't been wearing a seat belt and caught the worst of the accident. He was rushed into surgery for internal bleeding and a collapsed lung. Now he was stable, and they were only waiting for him to wake up to debrief him. They weren't about to take any more chances.

Mick, broken arm in a sling, reclined like a zombie in an uncomfortable chair set against the wall.

"Hey, asshole. I'm here to relieve your shift. Get out of here. Get some sleep."

Mick mumbled something, bleary-eyed, and stood up and shuffled out of the room. Morgan took his seat, still warm, and leafed through the intelligence report he'd received from Zeta, peeking at Quinn from time to time and perking up at any sound. The attackers had failed to kill Quinn before, but they were competent and determined. He questioned whether the armed guards posted in the hospital would be enough to keep them out.

Quinn stirred. Morgan set down his coffee and reading materials and approached the bed. The patient yawned and moved his jaw. His eyes fluttered open. He tried to sit up and groaned in pain.

"Easy there. You shouldn't be exerting yourself."

"Where am I?"

"Hospital," said Morgan. "We were driven off the road. You took it a little harder than Mick and I did. The nurse will give you all the gory details later. But I can tell you the doctors say that the prognosis is good."

"Am I—"

"You're safe. We're paying for your treatment, and we have you protected." *I hope.* "How do you feel?"

"Thirstier than a camel's arse."

Morgan poured him a cup of water from a pitcher by the bed. "Quinn, I know this is sudden, but I need you to tell us what you know as soon as you can. The faster you do, the sooner we can go after the people who are after you."

He polished off the cup with a smack of the lips. "Think I can get a cigarette?"

"No. But I can get you a nicotine patch if you need one."

"I'm good," he said, with a weak wave of his hand. "We can talk. Being that I'd prefer not to die, maybe sooner rather than later might be best."

"That's the spirit."

"It was after we stopped talking to each other, the group. They all wanted to leave it alone. I kept digging. And I found a pattern in the data. In the way they were using Blackrot. It allowed me to track their usage."

"Did you find them?"

"I got close. But with a little more time, I know . . . I . . . can . . ."

Quinn trailed off and his eyes rolled up into his eyelids.

"Quinn?" He'd fallen asleep midsentence. Morgan patted his cheek. "Quinn?" No, something was wrong. Morgan hit the nurse call button.

The intervals on Quinn's heart monitor grew longer. He was unconscious, going into a state of deep relaxation.

And then it went beyond relaxation. Morgan knew a dangerously low heartbeat when he heard one.

He leapt to the door of the room.

"Nurse!" he yelled out.

He turned back to Quinn. Internal bleeding wouldn't do it, nor would a stroke. He really had just gone to sleep. As if—

Morgan's attention moved to the IV needle attached to Quinn's hand, and the control, attached to the panel behind the bed, that operated the morphine pump. It had been set on a tray next to the bed, out of Quinn's reach. And yet, the heart rate monitor beeped at greater and greater intervals.

Morgan tore out the needle from Quinn's hand. Seconds later, two nurses came running in and pushed Morgan aside. As they were checking his vitals, his monitor went dead, playing only a single, long tone.

The nurses applied CPR, and Morgan divided his attention between the inert Quinn and the heart monitor. But it was too late. Séamus Quinn was dead, the heart rate monitor stuck in its incessant monotone.

"What happened?" one of the nurses asked Morgan.

"He just fell asleep. It looked to me like a morphine overdose."

"Impossible!" exclaimed the plumper of the nurses. "It's all run by computers! The program won't let the pump deliver more than is safe for a patient! It's just not possible!"

Right. The program that regulated the morphine pump ran on networked computers. The kind a group of superhackers might have no trouble gaining access to and controlling, instructing it to deliver a lethal dose to a patient with a few keystrokes.

The Legion of Erebus had found its latest victim.

Chapter 66

Alex and Simon walked off the library elevator on the fifth floor with trepidation. She had always found the book stacks eerie and unnerving. Up from the silent but busy library proper, the stacks were dark and almost entirely deserted. The lights were hooked up to motion sensors and were usually off, which left long dark passages between the bookshelves. Just enough people walked them to startle her out of her pants whenever she was convinced that she was alone.

It was, she had to admit, a heck of a good place for a clandestine meeting.

The man from Ekklesia had told them to meet him among the mathematics shelves, topology, in particular, Dewey Decimal code 514.

"This is it," said Simon.

They were among shelves in the corner of the floor, where a study table sat against the wall along with three wooden chairs.

The lights in their corner went out and a man's voice spoke from behind her. "Please, sit down, Alex." Calm. Controlled. Alex nearly fainted.

She sat down by the light that filtered through the shelves from the main hallway and looked at the man from the Ekklesia. She could tell very little about him except that he was about her height, standing, and wide set, but not fat.

"Were you the one who called me to save Alex?" Simon asked.

"Yes. I was."

"How did you know where I was?" she asked.

"I've been following your progress."

"How?" Alex felt sure they hadn't been tailing her.

"We have our ways. We are very interested in you. Both of you. What you achieved here is a serious accomplishment. You took more risks in the past week than most people take in a lifetime. And you, Alex, did it all with a broken leg. My hat is off to you. My question now is, are you ready to go after the big boys?"

"I'm ready," said Alex.

"Bring it on," said Simon.

"Then stand by for instructions. They will come very soon."

He turned and walked off, footsteps echoing in the empty corridor.

"Hey!" Alex called out. "What's your name?"

"You can call me Polemarch."

Chapter 67

Morgan scanned the passport for his British alias at Logan International Airport Immigration. He didn't trust using his own ID anymore. If the Legion had that kind of reach, they'd be watching the Department of Homeland Security databases for everyone who came in and out of the country. Worse yet, travel documents might be the very thing that exposed him, that would tell them who he was.

He had nothing apart from his carry-on bag with a few changes of clothes in it, so he went right past baggage claim to the terminal. It was early morning, and the airport was already bustling with travelers. He crossed the walkway to the covered parking lot where he'd left his car.

Something was tugging at his attention as he moved. His training had long ingrained in him a vigilance that he kept up at every moment. And in this moment, his sense was nagging him. Soon he figured out what it was.

He was being followed.

Morgan had spotted him inside the terminal, where he might have been just another of the people making their way to the parking lot. But Morgan recognized the signs: the cagey movements, the halting walk, the sunglasses indoors.

He wasn't much of a professional, either. Morgan would never have been spotted like this. It didn't fit the profile for the Legion. Acevedo? Too amateurish for them, too.

Morgan knew what Bloch would have him do: stall and call for backup, let the tactical team do the heavy lifting. But he was restless. The loss of Quinn had left him bothered. He wanted someone to take it out on. He wanted action.

He plunged into the mess of vehicles in the lot. Winding through the cars, Morgan contrived to put a large white van between them. On the other side was a raised Ford Expedition. *Perfect.* Morgan pushed his bag under the SUV and laid on the ground, which was ice-cold and smelled of motor oil. He rolled underneath the truck and waited.

He didn't have to wait long. Soon enough the man's ratty sneakers approached. Timing it carefully, Morgan pushed out his bag just as he passed. The man tripped and fell forward.

Morgan rolled out from under the Expedition and stood. The man, dazed from his fall, went for a gun in a shoulder holster under his coat. Morgan twisted his arm and kicked the gun under the van. He raised the man to his feet and pinned him against the van.

"You and me are gonna have a little conversation," Morgan said.

But the man kicked Morgan's shin and head butted him, hard. This was enough for him to wrest free and push Morgan against the Ford.

The man ran off, feet pounding the pavement of the parking lot. *Shit.*

Chapter 68

After phoning in the attack, Morgan sped through midday traffic to get home. He pulled the Olds in at an angle in the driveway and ran inside, relieved to find Jenny busy vacuum-sealing packets of homemade ravioli, while Neika was sitting and watching, hoping for a scrap.

"Well, look what the cat dragged in." He grabbed her and kissed her flour-dusted lips. "Yeah," she said, breathless. "I missed you, too." He caught her eyeing the seat belt bruise on his chest, then his ragged mouth.

"Is that a chipped tooth?"

"Among other things."

"So. Was it one of *those* trips?"

Jenny knew him too well. "Someone tried to kill me."

"Must be Tuesday."

"Maybe you should get out of town for a while," Morgan suggested, concerned for Jenny's safety.

She tossed a wooden spoon into the sink, where it clattered against the metal. "Except not such a *maybe*, right?"

"It isn't safe to be around me."

"Is it ever?" She turned on the water in the sink and rinsed off her hands.

A fair point he didn't feel like discussing. "Zeta's going to arrange for someone to pick you up. They'll get you somewhere out of the way. No electronics, no communications of any kind."

"What about Alex?"

"She's okay, for now at least. They haven't ID'd me yet."

"But the minute this gets dangerous for her—"

"That girl," Morgan said, "is my life. And I would give everything to keep her from coming to harm."

Jenny brought a glass of water into the living room and sat down on an armchair. "Any idea when I'm coming back? I should let my clients know."

"You know how it is."

"I'll remember to load up my e-reader then."

"Do I even have to tell you?"

She really didn't. Diana Bloch's face, looming over him, said it all. Her stiff white shirt collar made her seem all the more severe.

Lincoln Shepard, at the other end of the Zeta War Room table, was submerged in his computer stuff, earphones in, bottle of Mountain Dew on the table next to him.

"I took a calculated risk."

"You shot from the hip, with a predictable outcome. Again. And so you force me to play out this headmistress routine."

He snickered. "Are you going to punish me?"

"Don't give me lip. I can't do much to punish you. But if you continue on this path, when the consequences come, they will be devastating. You'd do well not to forget that. Now do your job and deal with your damn mess." She walked away, heels clicking on the floor.

"Harsh," said Shepard, mussing his wild black hair and making a face. The little bastard had been listening.

"Shut up. What have you got?"

"I've pulled up surveillance footage," he said, throwing it on the big screen from his laptop. "We have your guy leaving here." It was the hooded figure who had attacked him, running out of the parking garage. "No good pictures of his face, though."

"I remember his face."

"I'll pull up the mug shots then," said Shepard. "Brace yourself for a long night ahead."

"What have you found about this Legion?" Morgan asked as Shepard compiled the database.

"Oh, I've known about the Legion for, like, forever. They're this group of hacker vigilante freedom fighters. They're supposed to stand for civil rights, against government intrusion, yadda yadda

yadda." He rolled his eyes and made a jacking-off gesture with his hands. "This holy band of white knights. Only one problem."

"What?"

"It's a myth," said Shepard. "Pure and simple. Just some hacker wet dream, nothing more." He changed the image on the big screen to the mug shot database. "Here. You know the drill."

"Let's set a couple of filters," said Morgan. "Can you do that?"

Shepard merely scoffed in response.

"Sorry to doubt your prowess," Morgan said apologetically.

"Just give me the parameters."

"Make it in-state. Maybe add in the bordering states to be safe. But there was something Boston about him. I wouldn't put him too far from the city."

Shepard typed. "Keep talking."

"White male, dark hair. He had a few gray hairs, so I know he wasn't dyeing. Let's put his age at between thirty-five and fifty-five, to be on the safe side."

Shepard entered the data. "Some sixteen thousand hits. Care to narrow it down some more?"

"Filter out the ones in prison, 'cause this guy's obviously not."

"Done."

"And order them by violent crimes first."

"And done. Hey, we're down to about eighteen hundred. Looks doable." He handed Morgan a tablet computer with a set of mugshots already on it, the first of his list. Morgan swiped each wrong hit away.

"Quinn seemed pretty sure it was the Legion," Morgan said, eyes glued to the screen.

"Quinn found *something*," Shepard said. "A group of master hackers? Sure. They'd have to be to pull that stunt with the morphine pump. Dangerous and deadly? Beyond question. But the Legion? Eh?" Shepard popped a piece of gum into his mouth and reclined in his chair.

"Madaki said the people who had him kill White had information. It's suggestive."

"It's speculation."

"Tell me more about them. The Legion," Morgan said.

"Well, there are lots of things they're supposed to be responsible for. There are people who'll say they were behind any of the major document leaks in recent years. They have followers, too. Groupies. People who want nothing more than to join them. There are societies devoted to nothing more than finding out every scrap of evidence there is about them." He tipped the bottle of Mountain Dew against his lips. "But the real kicker is their leader."

"Oh?"

"Guy's known as Praetorian, you know, like the Roman emperors's elite guards? Yeah. What an asshole, right? Anyway, he's supposed to be the greatest hacker that ever lived. No one knows who he is. No one knows where he came from. No one has ever found him. No one has ever seen a picture of him. He's untouchable. Ruthless and efficient. Completely devoted to the cause."

"Kind of fits this group's profile, you'd have to admit."

Shepard burped in response. *What a charmer.*

"This guy I'm looking for," Morgan said. "I don't think he was one of them. He was stupid. Sloppy. Far more than any of the other thugs I encountered. Not too young, either. The kind of guy who has a criminal record."

"See," he said. "This high-omnipotent Legion is supposed to have sent a bumbling contract killer?"

"It's a weird break in MO. All the others were these supercompetent three-man teams."

"Maybe someone else wants to kill you," Shepard said.

"Wouldn't be the first—hello there." The face at the screen jumped out at him. "This is him."

"Are you sure?"

"Positive.

Shepard raised a mocking eyebrow. "That guy kicked your ass?"

"He caught a lucky break and slipped away."

"Whatever you have to tell yourself, man."

Morgan swung his chair to face the skinny, glass-jawed Shepard. "Wanna test out how you'd do against me?"

Shepard cleared his throat in response, deflecting. "His name is Louis Vincent Merullo. Known as Lou. Did six years down in Lewisburg for aggravated assault. He's been picked up for a couple murders—organized crime stuff—but they didn't stick."

"Maybe I ought to pay Lou Merullo a visit."

"Not alone, you're not." It was Bloch, from the door to her office above them. "You're taking tactical with you."

"I don't need my hand held."

"You're treading close to the edge here. If I were you, I'd avoid moving any closer."

"Whatever," said Morgan, walking off toward the locker rooms to change. "Just tell them to be ready in half an hour."

Chapter 69

Lou Merullo lived in a neighborhood of leaning, rusted chain-link fences, houses long overdue for a paint job, and enraged dogs straining against their chains.

Morgan was riding shotgun in the van. Bishop, a black beanie covering his shaved head, was behind the wheel. The rest of the team was huddled up in the windowless back. The cover du jour, in the form of a sticker on the side of the van, was a licensed clip art of a World War I fighter plane. *Red Baron Plumbers: Bomb out blockages!* Morgan had no idea who came up with this stuff.

Morgan spotted Merullo's house half a block ahead. "That's it right there."

Bishop pulled in across the street, two houses up. They were looking at a one-story structure, the front yard littered with trash and overgrown with weeds. A coat of paint and a trim of the garden might fool someone into thinking it was a fixer-upper, but all signs pointed to this being a veritable dump.

"Would've been better to do this at night," said Bishop.

"No time," said Morgan. "We need to move on this." Then, to the back of the van: "Give me infrared."

A woman's hand—Spartan's, broad-palmed and calloused—handed him a tablet from between the front seats. It showed the house and a tall, broad red shape. "There he is," said Morgan.

There was a smaller red shape moving around Merullo's feet. "Dog," said Morgan, showing it to Bishop. "Medium build. Think he's cuddly?"

"Man, I just really hope it's not a pit bull," said Tango. "I hate pit bulls."

"Doesn't help things either way," said Morgan. "Have we got audio?"

Spartan handed over the parabolic listening device. Bishop pointed it at Merullo's house and adjusted the dial. Then he plugged the jack into the tablet, which played a bluesy guitar riff and then Hank Williams Sr.'s languid voice.

"Nice soundtrack for a home invasion," said Morgan. "So here's how we play this out. I go in alone, with someone to provide a distraction. Once I have him secured, you move in."

"Bloch told us to move in force," said Bishop.

"We do that, and we have a higher chance of gunfire. Attract the attention of the neighbors, the police, and give us a much bigger headache than I'm looking for here. Let me try to finesse this one."

"'Cause Dan Morgan is known for his *finesse*." Bishop flashed his white grin.

"I know what I'm doing."

"Fine." Bishop held his hands up. "But this goes south and it's your funeral."

Morgan ignored him. "All I need is someone for an assist."

"I'm in," said Spartan.

Morgan came out of the car and waited for Spartan to come out the back. A thick black turtleneck was molded to her squarish body, and above her broad shoulders, a round face bordered by close-cropped blond hair.

Morgan took the lead with Spartan following, their guns securely in their holsters. They came onto Merullo's property through a gap in the chain-link fence. Once they were flush against the house, Morgan signaled for Spartan to go around while he waited by the back door, gun drawn.

The window on the other side of the house shattered. The dog barked his ass off.

"The crap?" said Merullo inside. Morgan heard the rustle as Spartan hid from view of the window. The dog did not stop barking on the other side of the door.

"Shut the hell up!" Morgan heard a knock, the dog whimpered and stopped barking.

Morgan heard the turning of the key in the lock. The door opened and Merullo emerged behind the barrel of a sawed-off shotgun. Morgan pushed the shotgun against the door and held the muzzle of his Walther to Merullo's head.

He tugged at the shotgun, and Merullo, seeing no choice, let go.

"We're gonna go inside, nice and slow. And we're going to have that chat you ran away from yesterday. Nod if you understand."

Merullo nodded.

"Good. Now march."

Merullo backed up inside to the kitchen and Morgan shut the door behind them. Merullo's kitchen was grimy, the floor covered in food stains and dog hair. A single wooden chair, covered in crumbling baby blue paint, sat at an old table of peeling linoleum.

"Sit," Morgan said.

Morgan heard a rhythmic thumping and clicking against the wooden floor of the house. His attention turned to its source, at the door to the living room.

The dog, black and tan with a thick snout and big scary teeth.

Rottweiler.

"Oh damn it."

Morgan leapt back as the dog lunged and avoided losing his fingers by inches. Merullo took the moment to attack. He wrested Morgan's gun away, letting it fall to the ground, and then broke free, running for the living room. Fluffy made another try for Morgan, who grabbed an oven mitt from the counter and waved it in front of the dog's face. Crazed, it grabbed the mitt between its teeth, shaking it from side to side. Morgan ran after Merullo.

The mitt didn't distract the dog for long. He let go of it and ran for Morgan again, nails clicking against the floor, picking up speed as he crossed the kitchen. Morgan kicked the kitchen door closed. It shuddered on its hinges as the dog hit it with a bang and a whimper.

That would hold him.

Morgan turned his attention to Merullo just in time to see his fleshy fist coming at his face. He took the punch hard, staggering back. But while Merullo had street smarts and instinct, he also had no training, and in this, Morgan had him beat. Morgan dodged the encore, snapping to the side and grabbing Merullo's arm in a lock, which he negotiated into a choke hold.

Merullo winced with pain, but he didn't cry out. That didn't bode well for interrogation.

"If you're gonna kill me, just get to it," Merullo said. "'Cause I ain't talking."

Morgan pushed him against the wall and bound his hands with disposable plastic restraints. Then he sat the meathead down on his ratty old sofa.

"Your house stinks," said Morgan. "You know that? This is a goddamn dump. You bring women back here?"

"Your mother sure didn't complain when I screwed her last night."

Morgan brought his heel down on Merullo's kneecap. Merullo hollered in pain.

"Who hired you to kill me?"

"Don't I have rights?" Merullo demanded. "I want my lawyer!"

"I'm not a goddamned cop, Merullo. I am, in fact, a very pissed-off man with no accountability. Who happens to be the man you tried to kill yesterday. So are you going to start talking or are you going to piss me off even more?"

Merullo snorted and spat brown phlegm onto Morgan's black sweater.

Morgan came back hard with a slap to his face.

"Let me make it clear how this works," he said. "You talk, or you die. It's that simple."

"Law of the streets," said Merullo. "If I talk, I die. And I don't think you have the balls to kill me."

This was going nowhere. Merullo was smart enough to know where his interest lay. Morgan wasn't going to kill him in cold blood, and he had no doubt that whoever hired him would.

Morgan's attention was drawn to the dog scratching at the door from the kitchen, letting out the occasional bark. He looked around at the house again. Beer cans lying around the floor, ashtrays and dishes and takeout boxes filled with cigarette butts, the smell of dog piss pervading the air. No, Merullo hadn't had anyone over in a very, very long time. If Morgan had to guess, it would be that Merullo was a lonely man with a single friend in the world.

Morgan wound up for what he was about to do. It required precision to the millisecond.

He opened the kitchen door like a toreador.

The dog sprung into action, taking a running jump. Morgan

swung out of the way and pushed the dog against the wall, just hard enough to stun it. The dog hit the wood with a bang and whimper and fell to the ground, dazed. Morgan put his right boot against the dog's neck, careful not to press too hard.

Sorry, you old mutt. It's not your fault your owner is an asshole.

"You'd better get talking," said Morgan. "Or else it's not going to be you who gets it. It's going to be Sparky here."

"You can't do that!"

"I'm not police. I can do whatever I want."

Morgan pushed harder against the dog's neck. The dog whimpered.

"I think you have one good thing in your miserable life, and that's this dog." Another push, another whimper. "So let's get talking."

Morgan saw him cast his gaze about the room for some way out of the cuffs. He found a serrated knife that lay in an empty pizza box on the floor.

"Don't even think about it," Morgan said. "I've got people on us. You're not getting out of here."

"You're full of it."

"Spartan?"

She heard him through the comm. Another window shattered, this one in the kitchen.

"All right? So behave."

Merullo's eyes were on the dog. "It's all right, Nancy. I'm not gonna let the bad man hurt you."

"Then you'd better start talking."

"Look, I got the assignment over the Internet, all right? That deep web bullshit. I never met anyone face-to-face, never even heard a voice."

"You got something to show me?" Morgan asked. "E-mails? Chat logs?"

"You think I keep them?"

"And how did you contact them?"

"They contacted me," Merullo said.

"How did you get paid?

"You ever heard of Bitcoin? It's untraceable."

"He's right," said Shepard over the comm. "If these people are as professional as they seem to be, there's no way we'll trace that deposit."

"All right," said Morgan, shoving the subdued dog into the kitchen and closing the door, relieved he didn't have to follow through with his threat. He then walked over to Merullo and rested his boot on the couch next to him. "Here's what we're going to do. We're going to monitor your phone. Any communication you get from them comes to us as well. And when there's a hit, you stay out of the way. Understand?"

"Yeah."

Morgan drew a burner phone from his pocket and tossed it on Merullo's lap.

"Keep this on you at all times. We'll be in touch."

Morgan turned to leave.

"Hey!" He held up his hands, still restrained. "You gonna leave me like this?"

Morgan opened the front door. "You're a tough guy. You'll figure something out."

Chapter 70

By the time the single working elevator dinged its arrival on the nineteenth floor of the Acevedo building, everyone but Alex Morgan had already gotten off.

"I'm here to see Mr. McGovern," Alex said to the receptionist.

She peered out the window, from which she could see the Charles River in the distance. The Acevedo building towered over most others in downtown Boston, and she was very near the top.

As a Deputy Vice President, her quarry, Leonard McGovern was an important man.

"Oh, are you the student?" The receptionist was perky and friendly and there was a slight condescension to her voice. Good. Being underestimated was its own kind of power. "Please, take a seat." She motioned at some leather office chairs to her left. "Can I get you anything while you wait?"

"I'm good, thank you so much."

Alex nestled into a comfy leather couch, arm around her purse at her side. She had nothing of her usual sporty look today. Instead, she looked the part of a student angling for an interview—gray herringbone pantsuit, hair in a neat clip, and even—*gasp*—makeup.

Alex's phone vibrated. Message from Simon.

Is it time yet?

She typed back to him:

Hold your horses. I'm still waiting to be called in.

She felt the familiar flutter in her gut, that blend of fear and excitement she lived for. She distracted herself by taking in the surroundings. The office this high up was a long way from the ply-wood and gray walls of the worker drones. Through her mother's pro-fessional eyes, Alex saw everything that made the decor expensive: the bold color scheme in clashing metallic colors, furniture made out of real wood, and the sprinkling of flowers, orchids and crocuses and Spathiphyllum.

"Mr. McGovern will see you now."

The inner office had an open plan, with a couple of closed-off conference rooms and private offices against two sides of the build-ing, among which was McGovern's, light streaming through the floor-to-ceiling windows on Alex's right.

Alex played up the difficulty of walking on her crutches as the receptionist led her to her destination. Another rather surly recep-tionist opened the door marked with McGovern's name.

"Please, come in," McGovern said. "Alex, right?"

McGovern was a bald man with yellowed teeth and a shiny nose. He had a friendly but overeager manner. Alex liked him right away, which didn't make the assignment any easier.

"Thank you so much for seeing me, Mr. McGovern."

McGovern's office had a sprawling view of the North End's chaotic mass of red brick buildings and the water beyond, shim-mering in the sun.

The receptionist pulled out the chair for Alex—an Eames Mesh, if she wasn't mistaken. Worth about fifteen hundred each.

"It's always a pleasure to talk to an alumna. Go Raptors!"

Alex pumped a fist. "Boola boola."

"Would you like anything?"

"Oh, I don't want to impose."

"Oh, goodness, it's no imposition! Agnes, get me a coffee, and for Alex . . . ?"

"A water, please. Thanks so much."

Agnes left to collect the drinks and McGovern turned his full at-tention to Alex, resting his jaw on the heel of his hand. "Now, what can I do you for?"

Alex played the role of the enthusiastic future corporate climber. "I have so many questions, I'd hardly know where to begin."

"You're interested in management as a career, is that right?"

"I just like to get things *done*." She did her best simulation of starry eyes. "Like, give me a spreadsheet and data and watch me entertain myself for hours."

Agnes returned to the office and set a mug of coffee in front of McGovern and a glass of water for Alex.

"Well, that's certainly good to hear." He put two lumps of sugar in the coffee, just like they'd told her he would. "It's a never-ending challenge," he said, stirring the liquid with a spoon. "There's something new to deal with every day.

"I'll bet."

He took a sip of his coffee and exhaled hard. "Hot."

She reached in her pocket and sent Simon the signal message they'd prearranged.

Seconds later, McGovern's cell rang. Polemarch had rigged it so that the call would appear as coming from the CEO.

"I'm sorry. I'm going to have to take this. Could you just give me a minute?"

Alex shifted, making a big show of collecting her crutches, making herself seem about fifty percent more incompetent than she really was. "You know what?" he said as he stood. "Stay put. I'll take this outside. Would you excuse me?"

He walked out of the office. That was her cue.

She reached into her purse and opened the mint tin inside. She popped the lid and turned it over onto her palm. The tiny pill rolled in the grooves of her hand. She took it between her finger and thumb and, stretching forward, dropped it into the mug of coffee. She picked up the spoon and stirred, watching it dissolve as readily as the sugar had.

Alex started in her seat when the door opened. *Amateur.*

"How strange," said McGovern to himself. "Anyway, where were we?" She watched as he slurped his coffee, ending with a lip smack and an *aaah.*

"You were just telling me about the challenges of working in management."

"Ah, yes," Another sip of coffee, which Alex now noticed he used to stall for time as he was thinking of something to say. That's what her father might call *actionable information.* Ask complex questions, make him drink. "You have to have the creativity of an artist, you know, and, and"—another sip—"and the discipline of a long-distance runner. You know what I mean?"

"I think I get the picture," she said. "So what would you say is your favorite part of this job?"

"Helping people." *Slurp.* "It's knowing that my work is going to impact the lives of the literally millions of people that benefit from the products that we ship around the world." *Slurp.* "But the best part is the work we do with the US military. We provide support for—for operations in—"

Sweat was forming on his bald head. He kept rubbing the nape of his neck and fidgeting with objects on his desk. She could hear his breathing as it grew shallow and rapid.

"Are you okay, Mr. McGovern?"

"So sorry," he said, just about jumping to his feet. "Excuse me for a moment."

He sprinted out of his office. Alex saw Agnes stand at her desk and stare as he ran down the hallway. Alex didn't see him go into the bathroom as the door to his office swung shut.

She was alone. McGovern wouldn't be back for a few more minutes, at least. And there it was, his computer, open and logged on. *Yahtzee.*

Alex turned the monitor to face her and pulled the wireless mouse and keyboard where she could use them. She opened a browser window in private mode and then typed in the complex URL she had committed to memory for the purposes of this mission.

She hit Enter.

The screen only flashed the text THANK YOU, and the browser window shut itself down.

The door handle turned and Alex looked up, startled. It was Agnes, the receptionist. Alex looked guilty as hell, keyboard on her lap, monitor turned 180 degrees from its usual position. No use acting innocent.

"Um, I'm sorry, I just really needed to check my e-mail," she said. "Phone went dead." She held up her cell phone with a helpless shrug.

The assistant looked at her with narrowed eyes. Had she seen something? Did she suspect?

"You kids," she clucked. "Can't disconnect for five minutes."

"I've just been expecting this e-mail—"

"Don't explain. Just don't do it again." She seemed nervous, like she was afraid her boss would blame her for not preventing Alex's transgression. "I'm afraid Mr. McGovern appears to be ill. He asked whether he might be able to reschedule another day."

"Oh, no problem at all," she said. "I'm sorry to hear he's not feeling well."

"Do me a favor and don't leave any sign that you used his computer," she said. "Mr. McGovern is very protective of his privacy."

"Oh, of course. Not a trace, I promise."

"All right, dear. Can I help you with those?" She motioned toward the crutches.

"Oh, no, I've gotten pretty good at it. Watch." She got up off the chair in a half-graceful motion. "It's done wonders for my upper arms."

Agnes held the door open for Alex. "Thank you so much," Alex said as she hobbled through. "Should I e-mail about setting up another date?"

"Please do. We'll be in touch."

Alex grinned as she moved away. "Most definitely."

Alex settled into the passenger seat of Simon's beater 1996 Corolla. Her skin was tingling, but she kept her poker face while they were still in view of the Acevedo Tower.

He set off down Water Street.

"Did you do it?" he asked.

She waited until they reached the corner and laughed in exhilaration. "It's done, baby."

"Wow." Simon took a left on Kilby. "We really did it. Were you scared? Did he—"

He was interrupted by Alex's ringing phone. "Shut up, it's gotta be Polemarch." She answered in speakerphone. "Hello?"

"You've done well. We've gained access to McGovern's computer. This is an important piece in our ongoing operation. With your help, we're going to bring down Acevedo."

"Heck yeah," said Simon.

"This is all I'll need from you at the moment. Stand by for further contact."

He hung up. Alex squealed in joy. "Simon! We're *in*! We're *doing it*!"

Things had never felt more right for Alex Morgan.

Chapter 71

Morgan woke up in the Barracks—what they called the room lined with bunk beds adjoining the Zeta gym. With nothing to go home for—Jenny gone, Neika at a dog sitter's—he had spent the night there. It must have been morning, but underground that didn't mean much.

He took a shower and was pulling on denim pants when Shepard called him from the hallway outside. "Come out when you can. I've got something for you."

He put on a shirt and walked out into the War Room, where Bloch was waiting, arms crossed, leaning on the table by Shepard. "Merullo got in touch with us earlier this morning," she said. "The Legion has made contact."

"Can we trace them?" Morgan asked.

"No," said Shepard. "Not even the NSA can crack deep web encryption."

"What did Merullo say?"

"They want to meet," Bloch said. "Today. In about an hour and a half at the Common."

"It's a trap."

"It's definitely a trap," said Shepard, swiveling in his chair.

"So we set our own," said Morgan. "We scatter tactical around the Common and see what crops up when I show. Unless," he said to Bloch, "you've got a problem with this."

"I've already called in tactical," she said. "I know when a risk is worth taking, Morgan. And this one is."

The sun shone, lighting up the snow on Boston Common. The trees, bare for the season, were frosted with powder as well, and the whole scene gave the impression of a snow globe before shaking. People bundled up in winter coats went about their daily business, crossing the park for convenience or for the view. Morgan walked the path at a leisurely pace, shoes sinking into the snow, looking around and letting himself be seen.

"I have a really bad feeling about this," said Bishop over the communicator.

"I think that's a healthy attitude to take," said Shepard. "Given the circumstances."

"Keep the channel clear. Essential communication only," Bloch said, always the professional.

Diesel and Spartan, the best sharpshooters on the team, had taken positions atop neighboring buildings so that between the two of them they covered the entire expanse of the park, with significant overlap. Tango and Bishop, meanwhile, were pacing the square, keeping their distance from Morgan and their eyes on all passersby.

"Anyone see anything?" Morgan asked. "Eagle's nest?"

"Negative," said Diesel.

"Hard to know what we're looking for." A woman's voice— Spartan. "We've got about fifty people total on park grounds. Nothing suspicious yet."

"No snipers up in the buildings either," said Diesel.

"Ground crew?"

"Nothing," said Tango.

"Not a goddamn thing," said Bishop.

Morgan considered what they were looking for. He didn't for a minute believe that someone was here to meet Merullo, but he looked the part anyway—blue sports jacket, sneakers, and a yellow beanie, all taken from Merullo's not too fragrant wardrobe. Morgan was roughly his size, and in the winter, it might be enough for someone who'd never met either of them to take one for the other.

But Morgan was preparing for an attempt on his life. He wore Kevlar under the jacket, and his Walther was tucked into its shoulder holster under his jacket. He kept his peripheral vision clear, looking out for tails. Having the Zeta tactical team getting his back didn't hurt, either.

He spotted a man walking alone coming the opposite way on the same path. Their eyes met and lingered for longer than normal. White male, between twenty and thirty. Was this their guy? They exchanged glances as he drew nearer. "I think I've got him," said Morgan. "Lone man, moss green parka, about six two, coming my way."

"Copy, Cobra," said Spartan. "I have a visual."

The man approached and put his right hand in his pocket. Morgan tensed and slipped his hand inside his coat and wrapped his fingers around the grip of his Walther PPK.

"Hold," he said.

The man pulled out a handkerchief from his pocket and dabbed at his nose, passing Morgan without incident.

"Stand down."

"*Peekaboo.*" An unfamiliar voice over the communicator.

"Who was that?"

"Who was what?" Bishop asked.

"*They can't hear me. Only you.*"

Morgan looked around for the source of the voice. Too many people whose mouths were covered by scarves.

"Shepard, someone's patched into our frequency."

"What? How do you know?"

"He's talking to me." Morgan's gaze jumped from person to person, trying to find anyone who didn't fit.

"*Now that wasn't very polite.*"

"Who are you? What do you want?" He crossed out the couple at ten o'clock, the three kids at eleven.

"*I wanted to meet you. Just like I told the incompetent Mr. Merullo. Who, I think you may not be too sorry to hear, has met with a regrettable end.*"

So they had killed Merullo. The stranger was right. Morgan couldn't work up too much compassion. "Come out then, if you want to meet me. Say hello."

"*I think this is close enough for me.*"

"Cobra, keep talking to him," said Shepard. "I'm trying to isolate his signal."

"*Tell Shepard it's not worth the trouble. He won't be able to.*"

Three people on their own on the pathway that would meet his to the right. It could be any one, or none of them.

"How did you get to Jakande?"

"*Everyone has something to hide. We found his something. Several somethings, actually.*"

"Why did you want White dead? I thought we were on the same side."

"*We are not,*" the voice hissed. "*You serve the status quo. We fight for something more.*"

"Who are you? Praetorian?"

The man laughed as if Morgan had said something very stupid. "*He wouldn't bother with an insect like you. And don't bother looking. You won't see me.*"

"It's like the signal's jumping around," said Shepard. "I can't zero in."

"I wouldn't be so sure."

"*You mean your team? Two snipers on the roof, two patrolling the Common?*"

Shit. They are still two steps ahead. "So, what now?"

"*Soon, you will see a sign of our power. Give up. Stop looking for us. You've failed every step of the way so far. Keep trying, and you won't only lose. You will die.*"

"Who are you?" Morgan shouted. Nearby pedestrians maneuvered around him. Crazy man on the Common, best not to get too close. "What do you want?"

But the voice had vanished, leaving behind only white noise on a now dead radio channel.

Chapter 72

Morgan jogged down the Zeta entrance hall, responding to Bloch's 911. Shepard, Kirby, and O'Neal sat around the conference table. Leaning against the far wall was Peter Conley. They weren't quite the picture of urgency he expected to find. Kirby was his usual stiff self, texting on his phone and taking notes on a file folder. O'Neal was biting her nails, the spreadsheets on her computer reflected on her black-framed glasses. Shepard had his feet up on the table and looked like he was playing a game on his phone. "What's going on? Where's the fire?"

The door to Bloch's office opened as if in response. She walked out onto the staircase, but not alone. With her was the stolid Smith and another man, of about sixty, with a full head of white hair, and the shape and bearing of a military man.

"This is General Alan Strickland," said Bloch. "He's here to oversee our operations."

Morgan knew him by reputation. Four-star general. Commanded a cavalry regiment in Desert Shield and Desert Storm, served as Deputy Commanding General in Operation Enduring Freedom. His official uniform was plastered with countless awards and decorations.

And he was, it seemed, one of the people pulling the strings of Zeta Division and its umbrella program, Project Aegis.

"So," said Morgan. "The powers that be show themselves."

"Dan Morgan." Strickland approached, as he reached the landing, offering a hand. "I've heard so much about you. And there's a lot to hear."

Morgan shook his hand. He couldn't get a read on the man. He was more personable than either Bloch or Smith, which Morgan found far more dangerous.

Shepard swung his legs off the table and got to his feet. "Gather round, gather round!" he called, like a royal herald. Strickland took his seat at the head of the table across from the big screen, a space usually reserved for either Bloch or Smith, when the latter was present. They flanked the general instead. Morgan pulled out a chair and sat at a distance from the table. All eyes were on Shepard.

"I've just confirmed that our worm is active. It's just that we're not the ones using it. We have a new asset inside Acevedo who got us intel that shows it's being used to extract information and monitor Acevedo's operations—everything we meant to use it for. And I'll have you know it's working perfectly."

"Except for someone else," O'Neal deadpanned, eyes locked on her screen.

"Regardless," continued Shepard, "it works, which can only mean one thing."

"The Legion is going after Acevedo," said Morgan.

"It fits the profile," said Conley. "Big, corrupt corporation with close ties to the government. They'd be a prime target for hackers."

"I say let them," said Morgan. "Someone else wants to do our job for us? I don't see why we should interfere."

General Strickland broke in. "The Acevedo investigation is extremely sensitive. These people who are targeting them are supposed to be anti-secrecy freaks. Their modus operandi is to go public with everything they find."

Morgan raised an eyebrow. "I don't see how anyone would be worried unless they had something to hide."

Strickland's eye caught Morgan's. "Would you have everything there is to know about this operation laid bare to the public at large?" Yes, the man had more depth than he was letting on.

"Critical as that is, it's not why I called you in," said Bloch. "Our asset has given us new access to the Acevedo networks. We've made a breakthrough."

"The Acevedo Board of Directors is meeting with their top executives in two days," said Shepard. "Yours truly has designed a rootkit that, once installed in the Acevedo wireless network, will infect all computers that are connected to that network. In one day, we gain access not only to their servers and official data, but the private communications of every single individual that logs on to that network."

"How would that be different than access to the servers?" Strickland asked.

O'Neal broke in with her faltering voice. "Personal communications will be more likely to show or hint at illegal activity, which will not be recorded on the servers. Probably."

Strickland raised his eyebrows. "That would be quite the coup for Zeta."

"What's my role?" Morgan broke in.

"I want you to command tactical support," said Bloch.

"What do we need tactical for?"

"Dominic Watson was killed for his cooperation with us," said Bloch. "I'm not about to let the same thing happen to our new asset. I already have a twenty-four-hour protective detail on her. I don't want her targeted in our most sensitive operation."

Chapter 73

Andrea Nyhan opened the door to the twenty-first floor of the Acevedo building from the stairwell, sweaty and out of breath. No more elevators, never again. She had manufactured a reason to be on the floor that day—a virus scare on one of the assistants' computers. The call came a full hour before, giving her more than enough time to do what she had to do—except cut shorter by the long march upstairs.

"You really oughtn't be so superstitious about these things, Andrea dear."

The snag was that, given the importance of the day's meeting, they decided to call up two people.

She didn't like a single thing about this plan. She didn't like that she was committing a crime. She didn't like that she was sabotaging her employers. She didn't like that Brainard could catch her if he was paying any attention to the goings-on. She didn't like that some unknown terrorist organization, which happened to have killed her friend, was watching the servers and would likely detect exactly what she was doing.

And she didn't like that Violet was on her ass because she was not competent enough to do anything on her own. So she stood behind Andrea as she worked, alternating between asking what she was doing and offering inane suggestions. Meanwhile, Andrea had to pretend not to know what she was doing, because even Violet would be able to tell that what she intended to do wasn't what she was supposed to do.

She tried suggesting that Violet check another computer or consult with some of the staff, but after a number of unsuccessful attempts, Andrea decided on a more direct approach.

"Violet, would you shut the hell up and let me do my job?"

"Well, how rude!"

That was enough to get her to wander off looking for someone to tell. Good. Andrea's reputation didn't matter anymore, and she felt rather good about leaving these people behind thinking she was a bitch.

Violet's absence gave Andrea the opening she was looking for.

She opened the network settings for the floor wireless and accessed the router through the terminal. She set up the proxy connection according to Bloch's instructions, routing it through the program she had supplied.

People were trickling in as she worked, high executives in pricey tailored outfits and shoes worth two or three times her weekly salary.

She had so forgotten about the communicator in her ear that she nearly jumped when a voice, Diana Bloch's, said, "Report in, Nyhan."

She checked that she was alone. "Almost done."

Board members were coming out of the elevator by twos and threes now. The meeting was about to start, and she needed to get gone. She ran the firewall bypass executable, and that was it.

"It's done."

"Testing. Stand by."

The last of the board must have arrived, because they were closing the frosted glass doors to the conference room.

"We're good to go," Bloch said. "Get out of there."

Andrea went for the door to the stairwell, leaving Violet behind. She had a long and anxious climb down ahead of her.

She pulled the door open, and as she crossed the threshold the lights cut out. The elevators dinged, both at the same time, and men with guns spilled out into the office.

Chapter 74

"There are men here," said Andrea Nyhan over the communicator. "They have guns."

Morgan, in his Oldsmobile across the street from the steel and glass Acevedo building, sat up in his seat. Conley, at his side, was already checking his gun. "Come again?"

"Andrea, this is important," said Bloch. "What's going on?"

"The lights just went out and a group of men came onto the floor through the elevators. Both, at the same time."

Morgan and Conley exchanged a look that said everything they needed to know. Both opened their car doors at the same time.

"Send in tactical!" Morgan said. "Cougar and I are mobile."

"Tactical, stand by to move in."

Morgan and Conley ran through the lobby door and flashed their fake badges at the welcome desk, leaping over the turnstiles.

"National Security Emergency!"

They were gone before the receptionists could react, halfway across the lobby floor, toward the stairs. No elevators—they had learned that lesson.

Andrea pushed the door open further so that she could see what was going on by the light coming in from the windows.

"Nyhan," Bloch asked. "What's your position?"

"At the stairwell door."

"How many men are there?"

"I didn't get a good count, but I think eight or nine. They're all dressed in black, and they have guns, sort of like Uzis. A couple of them were carrying bags, too. Do you think they might be explosives?"

"I don't know. Andrea, our people are coming to help. But we need you in there to be our eyes and ears for a little longer, okay?"

She put her back against the concrete wall of the stairwell. Her heart was beating a mile a minute, and she was sweating. She took a few deep breaths. "Okay," she said. "All right." She opened the door again, just a crack, so that she could look through. "They have everyone who was on the floor in the conference room now. They're saying something, but I can't hear."

"Could you move in closer?"

Andrea closed her eyes, trying to hold on to her courage. "Okay." She slipped inside the office, crouching behind a desk, moving closer to the conference room. On reaching the frosted barrier, she crouched, touching her ear to the glass.

"Put these around your necks," said a man's voice. "Do not be alarmed. We only want to take a photograph. We are making a political point. We mean you no harm."

Andrea crawled to the door that led into the conference room, which was ajar, and looked through.

"They're nooses!" Andrea whispered. "Each member of the Board of Directors is wearing a noose!"

Chapter 75

Morgan burst in through the stairwell door in time to hear the shattering of the mirrored windows that bordered one side of the conference room. Andrea Nyhan, on all fours by the conference room door, stared at him with terrified eyes.

Morgan motioned for her to leave, and she quickly obliged, slinking off into the stairwell, mouthing *thank you* as she disappeared behind the door. With Conley close behind, Morgan crept to where Andrea had been and looked inside. All the board members were lined up against the window, which now opened into gray sky, snow fluttering in. Each had a rope dangling from his or her neck, hands restrained behind their backs; twenty-two captives in a row.

With uncanny coordination, the armed men pushed each hostage over the edge into the open air in quick succession. They screamed, and each of their screams came to an abrupt end as their rope was drawn taut.

Screams—the office staff, all huddled in the far corner.

Morgan turned to Conley. "Here's how we play this. We overturn the desks here for cover, leaving them unguarded. Meanwhile—"

"Morgan," Conley broke in. "We can't take them. Too many, too well-trained, too heavily armed. We're not prepared for this. Not even the tac team is."

"We're the only ones—"

"And we'll be dead, too, and no good to anyone. We trust each other, right? Well, trust me on this. This is a losing battle."

The armed men were standing at the edge of the window, looking down at the city below like they owned it. *Bastards.* It would be so easy to open fire. He'd be sure to take down two or three—

One turned to look at the hostages and saw him. He yelled to the others, and eight men spun around, Daewoo K1 submachine guns locked and loaded.

"Oh shit!"

Morgan and Conley ran and jumped over an office desk as all of the attackers opened fire at the same time. The walls of the conference room shattered in a torrent of broken glass.

"I'm going to call this one," Morgan shouted as they huddled under the cover of the desk. "You were right!"

They made for the stairwell, staying low until they had cleared the heavy fire-resistant door. Morgan struggled to keep up as his longer-legged partner took four steps at a stride.

"We need to intercept them downstairs!" Morgan said. "Shepard, any word on the police response?"

Sound of a keyboard clattering. "Nine one one has been flooded with calls," said Shepard. "They're getting reports from all around the city. Explosions, shooters, all sorts of things."

Morgan's heart sank. "Are they simultaneous attacks? Hitting several targets at once?"

"No," said Shepard. "I'm looking at Twitter and Facebook now. The Acevedo thing is the only one there with pictures and real reports. People at the other sites are saying that it's a hoax."

"Diversionary tactics," said Morgan. "To keep responders away from here. Looks like we're all there is. Is tactical at the ready?"

"In the van," said Bishop.

"Keep the motor running," said Morgan. "We'll cut the shooters off downstairs."

Chapter 76

Morgan elbowed through the screaming crowd that funneled toward the front door of the Acevedo building, emerging from the suffocating throng into the cool outside air. He ran for his car, leaving Conley, who couldn't get past the crowd, behind—there was no time to wait. He couldn't resist a glance up at the broken window above at the distant corpses, dangling from ropes just over the enormous Acevedo sign that graced the building. It was gruesome, and it was meant to be.

Morgan jumped into the Olds and turned the key, starting the motor.

"Anyone have a visual on the getaway vehicle?"

A white van cleared two feet off the ground as it roared from the garage ramp, scattering curious onlookers and smashing into a car as it turned. The reinforced Ram ProMaster looked like it could more than take the hit.

"Never mind," said Morgan, tires singing as he floored the accelerator. He was joined in the pursuit at the next intersection by the Zeta tactical van, black and fragile looking compared to their quarry. They sped down the narrow Water Street.

"That you, Cobra?"

"Affirmative."

They circled back to Court Street, which merged onto Cambridge. Within a few blocks, police cars were following, sirens blaring. The Legion van barreled on ahead, undeterred. In fact, it seemed that all lights were turning green to let it pass.

And then the squad cars were swerving off the road, crashing into parked cars and buildings. One ramped off a parked sports car and landed upside down on the sidewalk.

"What the—"

"They're hacking into the cop cars!" said Shepard. "They're disabling everything connected to the electronics in the car."

In his 1970 Oldsmobile, Morgan didn't have to worry. Every single part of it was mechanical except for the radio.

The van was another story.

"I'm losing control!" came Bishop's voice. "We're gonna crash!"

"Brace for impact!"

The van plowed full speed into a parked car, pushing it some thirty feet before stopping.

Morgan pushed the gas pedal harder. The white van was a full city block ahead.

"Shepard, get them on the traffic cameras!"

At the next intersection, the cars from the cross street advanced before he passed. Morgan swerved, narrowly avoiding a crash.

"What the heck?" They were turning the cross lights green as they passed. Morgan held the horn at the next intersection, passing inches from an oncoming car.

They were cutting it closer themselves, Morgan noticed, turning the light green before even they made it through.

"Traffic cameras are all dead!" Shepard exclaimed.

Morgan sped past one more city block, but cars were moving in from both sides. He pushed down on the gas to make the gap—

The crossing cars overlapped. Morgan slammed down hard on the brakes, letting the Olds drift sideways, losing speed until it came to a stop with nothing but a nudge to the nearest car crossing the intersection.

Morgan got out of the car and watched as the white van traveled down Cambridge Street until it disappeared onto Storrow Drive.

Chapter 77

Alex Morgan's heart fluttered when she saw the mention of Acevedo on her news alert. She opened the article on the first news aggregator site on the list.

22 Dead in Downtown Boston Terror Attack

She read on.

An anonymous source claiming to belong to the Legion of Erebus has released a statement explaining the motive of this brutal attack.

She clicked on another link for an article labeled ON THE SCENE. It was dominated by pictures, taken on phones by people who'd been there, or still were. Each image bore a warning for graphic content. She opened the first. The bodies were barely visible, hanging far above street level. She felt her stomach heaving. She clicked the next, and the next. This last photo was taken by a camera with a proper optical zoom, the bodies shown just close enough to make out the faces. Among them, clear as day, was McGovern.

Not mobile enough to reach the trash can, she threw up on the floor next to her chair.

"Ew!" said Katie, who'd been highlighting a textbook on her side of the room.

"Sorry," Alex said, pushing herself to stand. "I'll clean it up."

"It's all right," Katie said. "You're crippled. I can get it."

"No," said Alex, "stay." She walked to the door. "I'll get some toilet paper."

She walked past the bathroom and went to Simon's room instead. He was sitting at his desk.

"Simon, did you see?"

"Yeah."

"McGovern was one of them," she said.

"I saw." She only now noticed that he seemed oddly calm.

"The Ekklesia—they're just a front for the Legion."

"I know."

She leaned in closer and brought her voice to a whisper. "Simon, we're *accessories to murder*. We could go to prison for a long time for this."

"I know."

She threw up her arms. "Well, I'm glad you're feeling so relaxed about the whole situation."

"I don't care, Alex. For once, I feel like I'm doing something. I feel like I'm useful."

"Are you crazy?" She pointed at the gruesome scene gracing his computer screen. "You call this *useful*?"

"All this studying and hard work, and I only had a life of nine-to-five to look forward to. Best-case scenario, I'd work for Google and have free sushi for lunch. Tiny cog in a huge machine of doubtful utility. Now, that whole idea seems suffocating. Rats on an exercise wheel, pushing a bar for rewards."

"Simon, *people are dead*."

"Exactly. This is real. This is meaningful. It's a drop of sense in this world that makes none."

"Look at the damn pictures and tell me this makes sense."

"I'm not a sociopath," he said, averting his eyes from the screen. "I don't take pleasure in it. But my empathy also tells me that we did the right thing. Have you read the statement? Did you look at any of the documents they released? Do you know what these people were doing? Drugs. Weapons to cartels and warlords. Buying governments and fueling civil wars. The death and suffering they've been causing to pad their bottom line? They're not human beings, Alex. These people are animals. They don't deserve any better than what they got. Ugly as it is, this is justice."

Alex felt like she might throw up again.

"I need to go to the bathroom," she said. "I'm not feeling well."

Simon bent down and looked her square in the eyes. There was something cold and intense in them that wasn't there before. It frightened her.

"Be brave," he said. "We're doing something. We're making our difference. Fighting for a cause. We have to be steady in our purpose. Unwavering."

"Yeah," she said. "I'm not wavering, I promise. It's just a lot to deal with."

"Give it time," he said. "What we did was right. You'll see."

Chapter 84

Praetorian had gotten free of his handcuffs. Morgan wondered how long he sat on that trick, waiting for the time to act.

He looked at the gunman and figured he liked his chances against Praetorian better.

Morgan pivoted to get behind Praetorian, but the bastard was quick and pushed him. Morgan stumbled backward. Falling would have put him in a vulnerable position he couldn't recover from.

Praetorian followed up with a lunge toward Morgan, bodychecking him and landing a quick one-two punch before Morgan could block him. Morgan gasped at the sharp pain in his broken ribs. Damn, the bastard was fast. The next blow pushed Morgan against the steel table with a clatter of instruments.

Morgan grabbed a scalpel and swung at his opponent. Praetorian raised his arm to deflect and Morgan slashed, long and deep. He followed it up with a left hook and moved to stab him again, but Praetorian spun and knocked the scalpel from his hand.

Out of the corner of his eye, Morgan saw the gunman, tense and watching, waiting for an opening to shoot. At all costs, Morgan couldn't give it to him.

Praetorian picked up a dentist's probe. Morgan grappled with him for it. They turned, vying for the weapon until Praetorian kicked him away, propelling Morgan to the middle of the room. Praetorian's confederate had a clear shot.

Morgan picked up the chair he had sat on and tossed it full force against the gunman, who raised the MP7 to block it. Morgan took the opening to run in the only direction that was left to him—to the catwalk and the prisoner holding cells.

His running steps echoed in the vast open hull of the ship as he

Chapter 78

Morgan stopped at the newsstand down the street from the Hampton building, which housed Zeta headquarters, to grab the morning papers. The *Boston Herald* carried photographs of the board members and high executives hanging over the Acevedo sign, while the *Globe* opted for a more respectful black cover.

Neither had reprinted the manifesto, but they didn't have to. It was everywhere on the Internet.

> All corporations that make their money on the blood of the innocent . . . Yesterday, they were among the most powerful men and women in this country. Today, they are dead.
>
> So it will be with all the corrupt, the unjust, the oppressors.
> —Legion of Erebus

Morgan slapped the paper down on the Zeta War Room table.

"Fine, I was wrong," said Shepard. He looked pale and worn, his hair wilder than usual, his skin more pale. "But you're late. Karen has been getting her I-told-you-so's in for hours."

O'Neal was sitting at the corner of the table, pulling at her bangs, her tiny frame seeming diminished by stress.

"Did you get any sleep last night?"

Shepard took a drink from a bottle of Mountain Dew. "What do you think?"

Bloch came out of her office, followed by General Strickland. "Morgan," she said. "Thank you for coming. I'd like to brief the two of you on new information brought by General Strickland. I'll let him do the talking."

"Thank you," said the general as they took their seats around the table. Strickland stood, leaning with both palms resting on the table's surface. "The Legion of Erebus has finally come out of the shadows and identified itself. Yesterday's display should be enough to dispel any doubts not only about their existence but their capabilities as well. Today, I'd like to discuss the legendary leader of the Legion. A man known only as Praetorian."

"I'm willing to believe in the Legion," said Shepard. "But *Praetorian?* Come on."

"Praetorian is real," said Strickland.

"How can you be so sure?"

"Because we caught him two months ago."

There. There was the bombshell. He had already told Bloch, judging by her lack of reaction, but Shepard was stunned.

"Impossible."

"We have him in custody now," said Strickland.

Morgan broke in. "And you've been sitting on this fact while we've been killing ourselves trying to find out anything about the Legion?"

"If there were relevant intelligence to share, I would have shared it."

"Bullshit. We should have gotten access. We should have gotten interrogation tapes. Anything!"

"Let me tell you what happened last time we acted on intelligence offered by Praetorian. In exchange for a few comforts behind bars, he agreed to give us the location of the safe house of one of his followers' cells. The location was booby-trapped with explosives. We lost three operatives."

"We'd double, triple check," said Morgan.

"Another time, we gave him access to a computer so that he might help us track some of his people. It took him about thirty seconds to shut down the system in the detention facility for three days. Prisoners were out of their cells. It was chaos." Strickland rubbed his face with his hand. "We moved him to a more secure facility. He hasn't spoken a word in about six weeks."

"But if you know his identity—"

"I didn't say we knew his identity. We have the man, but we haven't matched him to any information in any known database."

"It's impossible that you have nothing at all," said Morgan.

"If anything, we have less. He might be playing us even in what we think we know."

Morgan stared into empty space, trying to assimilate the news. "So why this? Why now?"

"Yesterday's events have made it clear that we need to take greater risks and intensify the hunt for the Legion," said Strickland. "I understand you are one of the most experienced and successful interrogators here at Zeta."

"Are you suggesting what I think you're suggesting?"

"I believe so," said Bloch. "Morgan, we'd like you to talk to Praetorian yourself."

Chapter 79

Lisa Frieze came home at noon after spending more than twenty-four hours in the office. She was maybe the most tired she had ever been. It was not a pleasant surprise to find Peter Conley waiting for her outside her building. Once the sheen of their near-death experience had worn off, the wrongness of their tryst came into sharp focus. Much as she wanted him, she also knew he took what he needed from her, all the while keeping vital secrets.

"Tell me you haven't been waiting there for hours," she said as she unlocked the front door to her building.

"I knew you were coming home," he said. "We have—"

"I don't want to know," she said, opening the door. He just stood there. "Well? I don't think you came just to say hello."

He followed her inside and up the stairs. She held her apartment door open for him. "Come in."

"Excuse me."

It was funny. She'd imagined him in her apartment on so many lonely nights. Reality was so stark and ugly in comparison.

"There are boxes everywhere," she said as a kind of halfhearted apology.

"It's fine."

"So what are you here for?" She made herself busy putting away silverware from the drying rack as if it were urgent, as if the rest of her apartment wasn't a total mess. "I mean, you must want something."

"Actually, I really only wanted to talk about yesterday."

"Ah," she said, tossing the dish towel on the sink and crossing her arms. "You mean the terrorist attack that coincidentally happened in the same building where we were conducting a bizarre in-

vestigation into an elevator-related death"—she paused for breath—
"during which not only was I nearly killed but got into a lot of trouble with my boss, thank you very much."

"I wanted to tell you about the investigation. I wanted to tell you what it was all about. I just couldn't. It was classified." There he went, with his puppy dog eyes. But Frieze wasn't falling for it.

"Meanwhile, you pump me for privileged information, right?"

"You have no idea how much I wanted to tell you everything."

Frieze screamed in frustration and kicked a box that was stacked on top of another. It fell with a din of clanging metal and breaking glass.

"What *is* this freak show of you and me?"

"I wish you wouldn't talk like that," he said, moving toward her. She backed away from him, averting her eyes. God, she couldn't even look at him.

He picked the box up and set it on the table.

"I was just hoping we could talk. I think we have something here, if we could just—"

"Get out, Peter." He didn't move. She yanked the apartment door open for him, so hard that the doorknob slammed against the wall, leaving a dent in the plaster. "I mean it. I'm done."

"Lisa, I—"

"Go," she said through an upswell of tears.

He walked out and turned, still trying to talk. She slammed the door and broke down on the kitchen floor, crying from exhaustion and heartbreak.

Chapter 80

The chopper touched down at sixteen hundred hours. It was night already in the black waters of the Bering Sea. The frigid air filled the cabin as the doors slid open, carrying with it flurries of snow.

Morgan stepped onto the helipad out into the bitter cold on the deck of the oil tanker *Aurora Borealis*.

The chopper lifted off as he reached for the iced-over railing of the steps that led down to the deck. Morgan was met by a couple of surly men wrapped in thick parkas holding MP5s in one hand and the railing in the other. They were swaying with the ship.

Morgan followed them inside the bridge through an external hatch. The two men took off their parkas. The taller of the two said, "This one's yours," and took off without another word.

The other was ginger, red-haired and freckled, with a short nose and high forehead. The overall impression was that of a little troll. "Jim Oehlert," he said, taking off his parka. "Part of the long-term team here on the Good Ship Hellhole."

"Dan Kinch," said Morgan. Alias. Standard procedure.

The inside was not too much warmer than the outside, but Morgan took the cue and took off his jacket, shaking the snow off at the door.

"Sure you are," said Oehlert. He stowed his H&K MP7 submachine gun in the armory and locked it with a key that he put back in his jeans pocket. "Well, welcome, I suppose. I got stuck with the task of showing you around. I may not sound very enthusiastic, which is because I'm not. But it beats the whole lot of nothing that most of us get to do on this ship."

"You miss dry land?"

"Just every goddamn minute," said Oehlert, holding on against the tilting of the vessel. Morgan didn't and stumbled against the wall. "Because there is not one where this bathtub is not swaying like it's at a Phil Collins concert."

"Oil tanker, huh," said Morgan, regaining his footing. "I expected a military ship."

"Everyone expects a military ship for a clandestine operation," said Oehlert. "Which is exactly why this is not one."

"Clever," said Morgan.

"Would you like a tour of the facilities? Of course you would. Why would you be here otherwise? Come on, I'll show you your bunk first. Give you a chance to drop off your stuff."

Oehlert led Morgan through a bulkhead and down a long alleyway. "We have a chronic excess of vacancies up here, because as you might imagine, we're a skeleton crew." He stopped and opened a steel door with a creak. "The upshot is you get your own room."

The cramped room held two berths. Morgan tossed his duffel on one. Nothing valuable there, just a few changes of clothes and toiletries, so he had no problem leaving it behind.

"Come on," said Oehlert. "I'll show you what you really want to see."

They went down three ladder wells. Morgan felt the humming of the engines, which became more and more intense as they went down.

He calculated they were about halfway to the bottom hull of the ship when they turned fore, toward where the oil tanks would be on a regular tanker.

Oehlert unlocked a heavy steel door, which opened up into an enormous tank, an echoing emptiness. They moved forward on a suspended catwalk toward a room held up by steel beams disappearing into darkness on either side, Morgan assumed to attach to the hull.

Oehlert scanned his fingerprint on an electronic door, a strange contrast against the rough steel of the environment. The door admitted them into an anteroom, from which Morgan could see the interrogation room beyond through tinted reinforced glass. A man in rubber overalls was washing the floor with a massive hose, the water draining off toward the sides of the room.

"This here's Gillevet," said Oehlert.

Definitely not his real name, Morgan thought.

Oehlert pressed a button on a panel and spoke into a microphone. "Gillevet, why don't you come meet our newest guest."

Gillevet gave them a thumbs-up and slung the head of the hose on a hook. He walked to the door out of the interrogation room.

Something about him gave Morgan chills. The way he moved was unnatural somehow. Inhuman. When he got close, Morgan looked into his eyes and saw only death. He reminded Morgan of Elvis, the hatchet man for the Saavedra cartel.

"This here is our interrogator," said Oehlert.

Ah, that explained it.

"Might be good to get acquainted," said Oehlert. "You guys might be spending some time together working on Praetorian."

"Thanks, but I'd rather work alone."

"Suits me fine," said Gillevet. "Tough nut to crack. Haven't gotten a thing out of him in two months. Not a single word. Still, I'm taking my time. Working up to more . . . extreme methods."

"Any insights you can offer would be valuable." Morgan meant it more as flattery than anything else.

"The guy's a goddamn brick wall. How's that for insight?" Gillevet laughed, a hollow, metallic sound. "Wanna check out the facilities?"

Morgan motioned for him to lead the way. He put on disposable slippers, and Morgan did the same. Then he followed the torturer into the chamber.

Morgan had seen this kind of thing before. The interrogation room.

The lights hummed, harsh and cold, an uncompromising white. All surfaces inside were chrome: racks, a gurney, an operating table, a support table for instruments. The floor was of the seamless surgical type. The industrial cleaning hose still dripped from its hook overhead.

The central feature, under operatory lights like in a dentist's office, was the stainless steel Navy chair, with built-in steel loops for hand and ankle cuffs.

"We have the autoclave over here, and our . . . *instruments*." He opened the door to the expensive-looking sterilization device. Hot humid air blew out. On the shelves inside lay assorted medical and dental equipment. Sharp edges and points were a recurrent theme among them.

"Everything is sterile in here during an interrogation," said Oehlert. "Wouldn't want the inmates to catch any infections and die."

"Is that common?"

"Not under my watch," said Gillevet.

"It's true," said Oehlert. "Dr. Tuttle always sings the praises of Gillevet's technique. Very clean. Let's move on. There's more to see."

The interrogation room held another door on the far wall. They left Gillevet behind as Oehlert undid the heavy crossbar and swung it open. This led into a long catwalk toward the front, enclosed as far as Morgan could see by an arch of steel mesh.

"That guy gives me the creeps," Oehlert said when they were out of earshot.

They walked forward until they came upon two chambers, on either side of the catwalk, suspended in the massive tanks, much like the interrogation room.

"These are cells. Whenever we take any prisoner out, we have their handcuffs attached to this rail," he said, pointing up at the metal rod above them that followed the catwalk from the interrogation room all the way down.

They passed the first two cells. Morgan peered in to the one on his right, but couldn't get a good angle and didn't see anyone inside. They approached the second pair of cells.

"On the right is one of our *permanent* residents," Oehlert said. "Been here at least twenty years. We bring him around for *enhanced interrogation* now and then. But it's really more for old times' sake."

He banged on the door, which resounded with a series of deep metallic *clangs*, seeming to echo throughout the expanse of the hollow ship. The old man startled awake, mumbling.

"How you doing, Sergey?"

"Lick my balls, Oehlert." He spoke through a thick Russian accent. His voice was hoarse and ancient.

"Nice guy," said Oehlert.

They walked past a couple more cells with nothing more than their footsteps on the catwalk to mark their progress. Oehlert seemed to get more nervous the farther they went—something about the quality of his steps, the way he carried himself.

It was undeniable. Oehlert was scared.

They stopped in front of a cell marked *11*. He banged on the door, but noticeably less hard this time.

"You nerd bastard. Come out of the shadows and meet your new friend."

Morgan peered in through the tiny Plexiglas window on the cell door and saw a figure looming in the darkness in the corner of the cell.

"Want me to turn on the floodlights?" asked Oehlert. "We use 'em when we don't want to give them the luxury of sleep. They should give you a good look."

"Don't worry," said Morgan. "I'll see him soon enough."

Morgan stared into the darkness that held the enemy, this man that had become part of the blackness, as insubstantial as the shadow that held him.

But no. All men had bodies and so did he. And all men could be broken.

Chapter 81

Morgan watched through the two-way mirror into the empty interrogation room. The weather had calmed and the boat rocked gently, but being in the enclosed space was still wreaking havoc on his inner ear.

The steel door to the cells was unlocked and opened. Two guards pulled a chained man in an unmarked orange jumpsuit, a rough-spun burlap sack covering his head. He stumbled as he walked down the corridor, which prompted the guard in front to yank him so hard he stumbled again and nearly fell.

"All yours," said Oehlert.

"Can you turn off the cameras?" Morgan asked.

Oehlert shook his head. "Not even General Strickland can get you that in here."

Praetorian was made to sit down on the Navy chair with a kick to the back of his knee. The two guards secured his hands first and then his feet. They left the room, locking it behind them.

"He's all yours," said Oehlert. "Return him in relatively decent condition to us when you're done. Otherwise, have at it."

Morgan put on the disposable cotton slippers over his socks—a ridiculously dainty act, given the circumstances—and walked into the interrogation room. Oehlert shut the door behind him.

The closing of the door muffled all noise from the outside, except the occasional groan from the ship.

Morgan circled the man, who was motionless, head still covered by the sack. He could hear the man's breathing, just barely. It was even. No fear. No physical arousal. For all he knew, he was about to be tortured, but this man didn't seem to feel a thing.

And somehow his organization was working on the outside, even while he was in here. And somehow, months of interrogation yielded nothing from him.

This was a frightening man.

His body was slight, but powerful. Morgan could tell by the definition of his muscles. This was recent, too—this man had been working out in his cell.

Praetorian's right hand was bandaged, Morgan noted. Blood had seeped through, leaving red spots on the gauze. Amateur work. Was this Gillevet's doing? Had to be.

Morgan had watched the tapes the day before. It was hours and hours of no reaction. Threats and pain meant nothing to Praetorian. Violence didn't elicit any kind of emotional response. Not so much as a wince.

Morgan checked the handcuffs. They were secure. The ankle cuffs as well.

Morgan had lain in his bunk the night before, nausea washing over him as he thought about what he would do at that very moment.

Morgan pulled the sack off Praetorian's head.

His features were distinctly Korean—jet-black hair, greasy and unwashed, hanging straight down to about his high cheekbones, face bony and more angular than average. And through the hair, the black, black eyes looked back at Morgan, or past him, with an unnatural calm, as if he were contemplating infinity.

Morgan checked his body language for the standard signs you look for in an interrogation. They were all missing. No attempt to avert his eyes, to turn away, to shut himself in. Whatever was happening in his head, Morgan knew one thing: this man knew no fear.

Morgan pulled the second chair from the corner of the room and set it in front of Praetorian's.

He sat down, looking the Korean straight in the eyes. For minutes, he watched, taking the measure of the man—the abyss, which gazed also into him. He thought he saw something, hardly a twitch.

That was it. That's what he was looking for. The chink in the armor.

Curiosity.

Morgan got up and banged on the door to the viewing room.

"I'm done," he said.

The door opened. Gillevet was on the other side of it. He closed and locked it. The other door to the interrogation room opened, and the two guards walked in to put Praetorian away.

"What was that? You didn't even touch him!"

"Is that what you did in your first session with him?" Morgan asked. "Rough him up?"

"What do you think?"

"Well, how did that work out for you?"

Later, Morgan lay in his bunk, still getting used to the swaying of the ship, trying to let it rock him to sleep. Exhaustion washed over him like waves, but when he closed his eyes, he saw the dead eyes of Praetorian staring back at him.

Chapter 82

Day 2. Morgan waited in the interrogation room as they brought in Praetorian and sat him down. As on the previous day, Morgan waited for the guards to vacate the room before he removed Praetorian's hood.

Morgan sat facing him again. They looked at each other for minutes on end. But this time, the man spoke.

"You are different." His speech was refined, precise. He might have attended a New England preparatory school for all the accent he had. "Not like the usual animal that comes in here. Who are you?"

"Take a guess."

"You are CIA," said Praetorian. "Maybe some other intelligence agency. I recognize the arrogance. You do not fear the law or anything else. You may have been ordered here, but that's not why you came."

Morgan gave him stony silence, which seemed to amuse him.

"Do you think you are a good man?" Praetorian asked.

"I try."

"Yes, you do." Morgan felt like he was the subject, and Praetorian some kind of scientist. "You don't like being here, unlike the petty sadist Gillevet, who takes his small pleasures where his government lets him. But you are also not just here to say you did your duty. You don't think it's enough to just show people you tried."

"I care about what happens to the next people your organization plans to kill."

"So the Acevedo initiative went as planned then? I am glad to hear it."

Damn it. That was careless of him, to let that slip. But he had also learned something. Praetorian was proud. This was a fault line, something to exploit.

"Tell me," said Praetorian, "was it spectacular?"

"It was . . . something," Morgan said. "Was it your design?"

Praetorian just grinned.

Morgan pressed. "Were the unrighteous punished?"

Praetorian burst out laughing, an unsettling, mechanical sound. "I am not a messiah. I am not an avenging angel."

"Then what are you?"

"What are *you*?" he retorted. "We have established that you believe you are a good man. But you see the corruption of this world. You see, just as you give your life to the eradication of the enemy, that the rot has taken hold of the roots of your own side and is slowly climbing up that tree. How does that make you feel?"

"No side is perfect," he said. This wasn't good. Praetorian had him on the defensive. "I can be a patriot without—"

"And yet you fantasize, don't you? About being let loose. About leaving behind the shackles of your duty, of your *ethics*, and simply doing what you must. What you know in your gut is right."

Morgan swallowed hard. "Is that what you do?"

"I am the logical conclusion of you," he said. "I am what you would be if you were truly free. I am what you may one day become. If you have the courage."

"I'm exactly who I want to be."

"Do you know what your superiors *do*?" he snarled. "Those petty bureaucrats in the Pentagon? Oh, if I could show you every filthy secret I've dredged up. Not the country-saving lies. The ones told for money and privilege and sex. Or worse, for respect of their peers, one more rotten than the other. Are these the people you want to serve?"

Morgan motioned to Praetorian's hand. "Did they hurt you?" he asked.

"Is this what makes you different?" he asked, emitting the horrible mechanical laugh again. "That you *care* enough to ask about my hand?"

"It's just a question," said Morgan. "Maybe I can help."

"And what would you want in return?" Somehow Praetorian still talked as if he had all the power in the room.

"You know," said Morgan. "I need information."

"I'll let you in," he said. "I'll let you know me."

"And in exchange I get Gillevet to stop hurting you?"

"Sure," Praetorian said, not appearing particularly interested in the prospect.

Chapter 83

"You're later in coming today."

Praetorian spoke as if they were meeting for afternoon tea. Morgan wondered how he could possibly know the time. He had no light, no access to watches, and he hadn't gotten any meals since their last conversation.

But that, too, was calculated. There was nothing magical about this man, Morgan reminded himself. He was intelligent and methodical, but not superhuman. When he seemed so, it was because he had meant to. There was a rational explanation—something he could hear, a light that seeped in, even just an especially good circadian rhythm, by which he could tell the time. That was it.

But damn, did the man know how to push people's buttons.

"They are starving me." From another this might have seemed like a desperate plea for help. He spoke with the matter-of-factness used when talking about the weather.

This was Gillevet's idea. The idiot insisted. Thought it might give Morgan an edge in the interrogation.

Morgan walked around Praetorian's chair in a loose circle. "That can stop."

"Hunger gives me clarity. Hunger makes me strong."

"You said you were going to tell me things."

"Why do you care about them? Normal people are pigs. They live in their own slop. They enter into their stupor and never have the nerve to climb out of it until they die. They never test themselves. Never know what they are capable of. They cannot, because they think their purpose is pleasure." He released an unnatural guffaw. "Even that they are not good at. They fill themselves with fat and sugar and alcohol and despise those who have cocaine-fueled orgies, who give themselves to heroin or any other kind of hedonism, pretending that the problem is petty morality and not their own envy. They kick their dog for a sprinkle of satisfaction and resent the man who takes a family's home to make millions. Are those the good people you protect?"

"And you're different?"

"I have no envy. I have no resentment. I have clarity of purpose."

Morgan continued to circle around the Navy chair, coming around now to see the perfect serenity of his face. "And what is your purpose?"

"To be as I am," he said. "To live out my nature. To burn bright until I burn myself out."

"Maybe everyone does, too," said Morgan. "Maybe it's just in their nature to be decent. To care about others. To have ideals and allegiances."

"As you serve your country?"

Morgan leaned his head in assent. "It's worth fighting for."

Praetorian laughed again. "I happen to know who sent you here. I know who you are fighting for."

"I find it hard to believe even you would know that."

"I will tell you a name," said Praetorian. "In return, all I want to know is if I am correct."

What the hell was he playing at? "Okay. Take your guess." He completed another full circle to face him again.

"Does the name Strickland mean anything to you?"

Damn. And he has seen Morgan's reaction. There was no denying it.

Praetorian grinned. "That is all the answer I need. Do you want to know how I knew?"

Morgan didn't answer. This little victory made him uncomfortable. He didn't want to indulge him further.

"There is only one man who would be so persistent," he said. "Only one man who cares this much about me. Have you asked yourself why?"

Morgan pulled up a stool and sat in front of Praetorian. "He cares about his country."

"General Alan Strickland cares about one person only, and that is General Alan Strickland. Use your head!" Praetorian swung his forward, whipping his hair over his face. "Why is this man so concerned with me? Could it be he has something to hide?" Praetorian's mouth formed an *o* of phony shock.

Morgan wasn't going to bite. Anything he gave had an ulterior motive. "I don't think you much care about General Strickland."

"And what do I care about?"

"You want to be known. You want to be recognized. In the Legion, you had followers. All of them had to look on you like a god. It was the nature of the thing. From everyone else, you had to keep who you were a secret, or you'd end up"—Morgan motioned around them—"in a place like this. But for some reason, you respect me. You think that I can see who you really are."

"And maybe you can," he said. "On opposite sides though we might be."

"Whose side are you on?"

"My own."

"You're being cagey," said Morgan. "It's beneath you. If your purpose is to live out your nature, then what is your nature?"

"Chaos. The essence of my being, my calling in life, is to cause pain and destruction."

"I don't think you'll have much opportunity."

Praetorian's face stretched into a hideous grin. "I am going to kill a lot of people. I am going to bring down the government of the United States, and the world will be mayhem."

"I don't see how you're going to accomplish that in here."

"And I'm going to kill *you*, too."

"This session is over," said Morgan. A raw assertion of power was necessary to put the prisoner in his place.

Morgan walked over and knocked on the window to be let out.

A hash buzz sounded, and both the door to the control room and to the holding cells clicked open. There on the threshold to the control room stood Gillevet. It took Morgan a moment to figure out what was wrong with him, to assimilate the look of dumb surprise on his face. A moment later, Gillevet stumbled forward and fell to the ground, blood spreading on the clean floor.

Behind him was a man holding an MP7 from the armory, one of the replacements who had arrived in the latest transport.

He heard Praetorian speak behind him. Close. Too close.

"I think it's not."

made his way to the far side, away from Praetorian. There was only one problem.

Ahead of him was a dead end. With the last two cells on either side, the catwalk ended.

An alarm blared and this was no longer the greatest of his problems.

All the doors to the cells opened at once. Prisoners who had been drawn to the commotion were taking tentative steps out onto the catwalk, blinking in the relative brightness outside their confinement. Men in beards and long hair, whose eyes told a story about how long they had been there. Two emerged from the far cells on either side of him. Morgan stood back against the wire mesh that closed off the end of the catwalk.

While they looked at the way out, several of those pairs of eyes (although in at least one case, it was a single eye) noted Morgan's presence, and saw that he was unarmed. Most made their break for the exit, but two, whether to neutralize a threat or out of sheer revenge, turned on Morgan. One was Middle Eastern, about Morgan's age, with thick black hair and a scraggly beard, and the other was young and Eastern European, with light blue eyes and dirty blond curls in a tangle. These two walked against the current of escaping prisoners toward Morgan.

Through the aches that were settling in from his struggle with Praetorian, Morgan wound himself up for a fight. His muscles tensed and his hands curled into fists at his sides. These were tight quarters. He was cornered, but they could only approach one at a time. And given their situation, Morgan should be by far in better shape.

The kid rushed him first, sloppy and hasty. Morgan grabbed his arm and swerved, dislocating the boy's shoulder, and then kicked down to break his leg. He screamed and fell to the metal floor.

The other, Morgan could tell, had more experience. He held a solid stance and advanced guardedly. But he had slaughter in his eyes.

"I'm not the enemy," said Morgan. "I never put you in here, I never did you harm. The way's free and clear. Go."

But whether he didn't speak English or was enraged beyond words, the prisoner didn't make a sign of having understood. He just moved forward.

Well, if that's how it's going to be . . .

The attacker lunged, throwing a heavy punch. Morgan dodged and came back with a kick to his chest. The man stumbled back but recovered. He was strong, solid, and thick. A direct attack would leave them grappling, which Morgan had no certainty of winning. His approach to such an opponent would be to circle around him, stay on the move, and look for an opening. The tight quarters gave him a solid advantage of focusing his defense.

The man charged. With nowhere to escape to, Morgan positioned himself to mitigate the force of the blow.

The man brought him down, and Morgan used the momentum of the fall to push him off and back.

Morgan stood up before he did. Before he could attack, he heard footsteps behind. At the end of the catwalk was Praetorian's gunman.

Think. Use your environment.

The man charged. On instinct, Morgan jumped and grabbed the railing that ran above the catwalk, lifting his body. The prisoner charged past him and he dropped back down on the catwalk.

The gunman opened fire.

The Middle Eastern prisoner took the hail of bullets as Morgan ducked into the far cell on his right. He heard the heavy thump as the prisoner fell onto the catwalk.

He'd been saved from that attack, but what now? Footsteps clanged on the catwalk as the gunman drew closer. Morgan was trapped, with nowhere to go. Then—

"Let's go!" It was Praetorian.

"But the interrogator—" the gunman began.

"Leave him. Let him sink along with the ship."

Morgan heard footsteps on metal receding as the gunman walked back toward the interrogation room, and then the clanking of the door to the catwalk being locked.

This was not good.

Morgan lay in wait in case they came back, running the scenario in his head. They were sinking the ship.

He had to get out of there, which meant that first he had to get out of this damn cage.

He waited it out until he was sure they had gone. Then he emerged from the cell and ran to try the only door out of there. Locked, of course. He examined it. It was airtight, with a window into the interrogation room made of glass reinforced by wire mesh, too small for Morgan to crawl through in any case. It was dead-bolted from the other side. There was no hope for him to get out that way.

He then looked around the door. The mesh ran the entire length of the catwalk in an upside-down U. Morgan ran his hands against it. It was thick, ten-gauge wire, welded rather than woven. It was welded as well to the walls of the interrogation room and the floor of the catwalk. With something to batter it, like a fire extinguisher, he might, with enough time, be able to hammer it loose. He had nothing of the kind, nor enough time to accomplish it.

He walked back down the catwalk, taking in the details of the structure, looking at the fault lines. All were as solid as those around the door. He reached the end of the catwalk and examined the cage there. All welded tight.

The young Eastern European man was still moaning on the floor, clutching his broken leg. He looked at Morgan with sheer hatred.

Morgan looked at the area around the catwalk. On one end it was attached to the interrogation room, but it was otherwise in the void of the cavernous oil tank, attached by massive chains, three to each side, evenly spaced, that ran off into the dark recesses of the chamber. More, Morgan figured, although he couldn't see, would be holding up the cells.

The place was, of course, built to be a maximum security holding facility. But, he reasoned, it was also meant to be watched twenty-four/seven, which left the possibility that something might have been overlooked that could give him the advantage. He saw a glimmer of hope. If he were able to pull out a toilet, he could—

BOOM.

Morgan was knocked off his feet and thrown against the mesh cage. Metal screeched, and Morgan lost his sense of up and down. He tumbled, disoriented, until he hit something soft.

It was the dead prisoner, still bleeding from a dozen gunshot wounds. It took him a moment to figure out what had happened. There had been an explosion. The catwalk and cells had been knocked loose from their chains on one side. The whole superstructure had been torn away from the interrogation room and was now hanging on by a thread. The far end, where he now found himself, was resting against the bottom of the ship.

Lights flickered.

There was something else, too, and he heard it as soon as the ringing in his ears subsided.

Water. Thousands of gallons of water, cold and black, gushing inside through a gaping hole in the hull. Below him, dark water washed over the bottom of the tank and rose fast.

But Morgan had an opening now. A goal. He was stuck at the bottom of a tubular cage, but the other end of the catwalk, torn from the interrogation room and now a steep upward climb away, promised escape. He began his ascent. The mesh made for fine hand- and footholds. The water was rising fast, but he could move faster.

As he passed the door to the first cell, a hand reached out and grabbed his leg. He looked down to see the Eastern European kid whose leg he had broken, already half submerged in water.

Morgan kicked, trying to wrest himself free. The water rose to touch Morgan's foot. The kid was getting desperate. He grabbed Morgan's leg tight, terror on his face as the water came closer and closer to covering his nose and mouth.

He was condemned. There was nothing that Morgan could do to get him out of there. Morgan wrested himself free, leaving behind a boot, and continued his climb, legs now sodden and heavy.

The water reached the lights, which shorted and fizzled out, plunging the chamber into total darkness. Morgan pressed on, barely outpacing the water.

He was now nearing the top, which brought another problem. Where would he go from there? The door to the interrogation room would still be shut tight. He didn't know whether there were any other openings into the upper decks. There was only one opening to the outside that he knew of for sure. It was down, where the bomb had torn open the hull.

Morgan reached the top just ahead of the rising tide and went right to the business of shedding every article of clothing on his body—they were dead weight to him. He took a few deep breaths as his shins were submerged. He filled his lungs one last time and climbed over the mesh, plunging into the icy waters of the Bering Sea.

The cold was nearly enough to knock all the air out of him, but he kept his wits about him and held it in. He grabbed the wire mesh, from the outside this time, and began the climb down.

Fighting buoyancy was easier than fighting gravity. Reach, grab, pull. Reach, grab, pull. As his fingers grew numb, the grab became trickier, but he pressed on. Reach, grab, pull.

Thirty seconds later he was at the bottom, and this is where things became difficult. He had only the vaguest idea of where the hole was, and he was about to lose the guide of the catwalk.

As the mesh curved down, he reached out. He visualized the bottom of the boat as he had seen after the catwalk collapsed. There was a girder that ran from fore to aft along the central spine, and others that ran up the sides like ribs. He found one of these latter ones and pulled himself toward the middle, his legs dangling upward.

This is when he released the air in his lungs. This gave him a minute, ninety seconds tops, before he was toast. He had to get out of there.

Deadened as his sense of touch was, he found the middle girder. In the complete darkness, with compromised feeling, one thing told him where to go. He had to move against the current. As he got closer to the hole, it would only get stronger.

The current shifted as he moved, moving from his twelve o'clock to one, then two, until it was to his three o'clock. The tear was off center, then. He reached for the cross-girder and found one some five feet ahead.

This pull was the hardest. His lungs burned, and the current threatened to tear him away from his handhold if he didn't fight against the paralyzing cold hard enough to maintain his grip. He could feel nearly nothing now. One false grab would do him in.

Reach, grab, pull. Until he reached—and there was nothing to grab, only an overwhelming current, going upward. He had reached the hole.

This was the last challenge. Morgan had to push himself off and clear the hole, catching the outside hull on the other side or he'd be sucked upward toward the top of the oil tank, where he'd die, trapped against the ceiling.

He pushed. His back hit the lip of the hole on the other side, and the current pulled him back inward.

He reached out for anything that might hold him back. He didn't know what he found, just that his right hand found purchase, and he brought his left hand to brace against the relentless force.

He pulled, as hard as he could, muscles screaming with pain and his lungs begging for air.

And then he was out, tumbling against the outer hull of the tanker. Buoyancy pulled him up, faster and faster. A dull pain filled him, and he wondered what kind of damage this might be doing to his body. But only one thing mattered.

He emerged into the air and took in a deep, wheezing breath. For half a minute, all he did was breathe.

Through stinging eyes, he saw the wall of the ship beside him in the moonlight. A helicopter flew past overhead—Praetorian, making his escape.

The ship was half-sunk. He needed to get as far away from it as possible before it sank completely, or it would suck him down as it went under.

The cold had penetrated to his bones, and his limbs were barely responding. But he swam away from the ship, using energy he did not have.

He was a little over one hundred yards away, by his estimate, when the night was lit up by a second explosion. He looked back at the ship. It was up in flames.

Debris dropped into the water all around him. He dove as deep as he could to avoid direct hits and stayed as long as his breath allowed.

He resurfaced amid scattered pieces of the ship. With the last of his strength he swam to a floating barrel and draped himself over it.

He blacked out to the warm glow of the fire on the sinking ship and the bobbing of the waves.

Chapter 85

"**H**e's coming! He's coming!"

Valkyrie had the familiar glint in her eyes. Centurion had almost forgotten what it was like, how Praetorian brought this out of her. It burned at his insides, how close he and she had gotten in the past few months, all that they had shared, and still, she never once during that time seemed as excited about anything as she was now.

He followed her outside to the misty morning, looking out into the Appalachian Valley, the sea of evergreens poking out of the snow, the sun just peeking out between the mountains behind them.

All this beauty, and still Centurion's eyes were drawn to Valkyrie, her purple-highlighted dark brown hair, her fine pale white features like a china doll's. And her eyes, large, beautiful and blue, looking only at the chopper approaching in the distance like the faithful awaiting salvation.

Centurion sat on a frigid rock as the minutes ticked by and the helicopter drew closer, but Valkyrie didn't move. It was as if she wanted to reach out, to run so that she might see him a few seconds sooner.

The helicopter touched down in the clearing a couple of hundred feet down and Valkyrie sprinted down to meet it. To meet *him*.

Centurion waited, imagining as Valkyrie embraced Praetorian, kissed him, gave herself wholly to him. It was better than seeing it firsthand.

They appeared from between the trees as they walked up to the house, the mercenaries taking the lead.

And there he was, just ahead of Valkyrie, a manic smile plastered to her face. *Him*. The beautiful. The terrible.

Praetorian.

He looked haggard. His hair was longer, his beard overgrown. But there was triumph in his eyes.

"Greetings, brother," Praetorian said. "Sister Valkyrie tells me you've been a good lieutenant in my absence."

Centurion bowed. "My allegiance is with you. Welcome back."

Behind him was someone else. Someone Centurion had never seen before. But he knew exactly who it was. And he knew that Praetorian's mission had been a success.

Chapter 86

Morgan woke up chilled to the bone in a hospital bed, hooked up to wires and with an IV stuck in his arm.

His arms were bandaged from shoulder to fingertip, with only patches of skin showing here and there. Another bandage was constricting his upper abdomen. "Hey!" He yelled out to a passing nurse. "Hey! I'm awake!"

She came into his room. "There's no need for that," she said, and he put her accent in the Pacific Northwest. "You have a call button, see?" She pointed to the little green button on the side of his bed.

"Where am I?"

"University of Washington Medical Center," she said. "You came in last night with severe hypothermia."

"How did they find me? Who brought me in?"

"That I don't know," she said. "But why don't you rest, Mr. Bevelacqua. I'll see if there's anyone here for you."

Morgan pushed himself to a sitting position, but felt light-headed and had to lie down again. He looked around the room, but saw nothing of his there. It was a private room, expensive. That and the name Bevelacqua pointed to Zeta.

He wondered whether Jenny or Alex knew where he was.

The person who came in through the door of his hospital room was Diana Bloch.

"How are you feeling?"

"Not my best self," he said. "But alive."

"You were pretty torn up and nearly frozen to death when they found you."

He remembered his upward dive, scraping the side of the ship. "How did they find me?"

310 • *Leo J. Maloney*

"A nearby ship came when they saw the explosion," she said. "They sent a rescue helicopter and found you floating on a piece of debris."

"Any other survivors?"

"None."

Urgency surged within him. "Praetorian! We need to—"

"He's escaped," said Bloch. "Vanished. The trail's gone cold. Morgan, I'm going to get a full debrief from you in time. But for now, I need you to rest up."

"Jenny—"

"Is fine," said Bloch. "And so is Alex. But this isn't the end of Praetorian's plans. And if he's already accomplished this from the inside of a secret prison, I shudder to think what he's going to do now that he's on the loose."

Chapter 87

When Morgan arrived home he still hadn't shaken the cold. It seemed like it might take a couple of days for the warmth to seep in. He pulled up to his house in his Olds 442, which had been parked at Zeta during his expedition, switched off the engine, and exhaled. This had not been a good day. In fact, *not good* was the understatement of the damn century.

And Jenny was out, hidden away by Project Aegis. Not even Neika was home. He had an empty house to look forward to.

At least he'd be able to take a long and very hot shower and sleep.

He opened the door to the kitchen and set down his keys.

He pulled open the refrigerator and scanned it for anything edible when he heard a noise upstairs.

There was someone in the house.

His gun was in his bedroom. There was no other gun downstairs, and he'd left his carry weapon at Zeta.

Stupid. Sloppy. He'd let his exhaustion get the better of him.

He closed his fist around the handle of a seven-inch chef's knife and drew it slowly from the knife block so that it wouldn't make a sound. He used his feet to take off his shoes and crept in his socks, his footfalls making only the faintest of sounds.

He tightened his grip on the blade. This was his home. Nobody was going to invade his home.

Knife in hand, he took the steps one by one. Slow. Steady. He turned into the hallway to the bedrooms.

A shadow, and then a figure emerged. Morgan tensed to strike.

Alex.

His knife arm fell slack at his side. "Jesus, you scared the hell out of me."

But her expression didn't mirror his relief. "Dad, I think I've done something really stupid."

Morgan's expression darkened. "What is it?"

"I'm in trouble," she whispered. "They might be listening."

Morgan held a finger up to his lips.

He pulled a bag of popcorn from a cupboard and tossed it into the microwave. He turned it on. He then took out his cell phone and set it on the counter, motioning for her to do the same. Once she did, he opened the door to the garage. They walked out to the sound of corn popping and got into Morgan's Olds.

"Dad—"

"Not yet."

He pulled out onto the driveway. Once they hit asphalt, he spoke. "Okay, tell me."

"I thought I was doing good," she said. "I swear I was. But then all those people *died*, and I—"

"Hold on," said Morgan. "Start from the beginning."

Morgan's heart sank as she told him about her involvement in the Ekklesia. Morgan let her speak, but he had already filled in the blanks in his head when she got to the meat of the matter—her unwitting complicity in the murder of the Acevedo Board of Directors, and the discovery that the Ekklesia was part of the Legion all along. The many, many ways in which this was bad unfolded in his mind. The fact that she could face a life sentence at the hands of an unsympathetic judge was not among the worst things, which did not say much for her situation.

One thing was for certain: Alex had been, however indirectly, complicit in the Legion's act of terrorism.

"That's it," she said, sniffling. "When I heard about what happened, I told my roommate I was coming down for a surprise visit, and here I am."

He gripped the steering wheel. The silence between them hung like—well, like the Board of Directors of Acevedo, come to think of it.

"I'm ashamed," she said. "And I feel guilty. I thought I wanted excitement. And now I have blood on my hands." She looked out the window. "Where are we going?"

"I'm taking you in to Zeta," he said. "That's the only place I know you'll be safe for now."

"I get to go *into* Zeta?" she asked. That excitement, in spite of everything. He hated that tone in her voice.

"Yeah," he muttered. "Today you do."

Chapter 88

A lex held her breath as she stepped through the door to Zeta headquarters.

She knew she was here as a visitor. This was where her father could keep her safe, and he'd whisk her away as soon as the danger had passed or he could find some safer corner to stuff her in.

But at that moment, it felt like stepping into a new life.

It was more than she'd ever imagined. The optical scanners in the parking garage, the security elevators, the hallway that opened up into the high-ceilinged War Room, overlooked by Diana Bloch's office, that suspended box of frosted glass. She imagined everyone sitting around that table during a crisis, under Bloch's able leadership, as she assigned missions.

She was so excited she could scream.

She was met with concerned stares from people she didn't recognize. Then, a familiar face: impeccable maroon suit jacket over a silk blouse, hair in a neat bun with not a lock out of place, prim and muted makeup, and a look of pure steel.

Diana Bloch.

"Hello, Alex," she said. "It's wonderful to see you again."

The last time had been over coffee, when Bloch had offered Alex a sort of traineeship at Zeta, which her father had nixed, forcing her to go to college instead.

Her father now spoke to the Zeta director in low tones, and by Bloch's intermittent glances at her Alex could guess what the subject was.

"Hi," said a woman of about thirty, with bangs and black-framed glasses and a round face. The shape of her eyes and nose suggested she was part Asian. "I'm Karen. It's nice to meet you." Her intonations were off, not from a foreign accent, but from someone who maybe understood numbers better than she did people.

Her father and Bloch seemed to come to a resolution, and the Zeta Director approached her. "Alex, we need you to tell us everything about your involvement with this . . . activist group."

Alex felt a twinge of shame. She had known this was coming. Though she was looking forward to relating some things with pride, she did not relish the prospect of having to rehash every stupid thing she did over the past couple of weeks.

Bloch sensed her hesitation but didn't get why. "We're not the police," she said. "We're not here to incriminate you. We just need to know so that we can fight these people."

No use putting it off. "When do we get started?"

They sat her in a room with a mirror covering the upper half of one wall and a camera set up on a tripod. A man with a supercilious manner who introduced himself as Paul Kirby sat across from her. He tried, Alex noticed, to hide his receding hairline by combing his wispy blond hair forward.

"I'm going to ask you some questions. Are you comfortable with that, Alex?"

"Yes," she said in her best all-business voice. "Do I need to look into the camera?"

"Wonderful," he said. "First, I'd like you to tell us, from the beginning, everything you remember about your contact with the Ekklesia."

She pretended her father was not watching through the mirror in front of her. "Hold on to your butts," she said. "It's a long story."

Chapter 89

Morgan stood and watched through the two-way mirror as Alex told her story. He cringed as she related each risky decision, each juncture that had brought her deeper into her current quagmire. He felt the urge to whisk her away, to hide her where no one would find her and she'd be protected from everything.

"I'll tell you one thing," said Bloch, sitting to his left, farther back from the window. "She's a remarkable young woman."

She was. Of course she was.

"I don't want to tell you how to raise your daughter—"

"Then don't."

He sensed her presence at his side. "I'll tell you a story then," said Bloch. "Of when I was young."

"Hard to believe you were ever young."

Morgan kept his eyes on Alex. He knew the story, but he was still proud of her composure in telling it, her poise under hard circumstances.

"I was a wild thing," Bloch continued. "My father wouldn't let me out of the house after six p.m. No boys, no sleepovers, no outings with friends." The resentment in her tone was palpable. "So I snuck out at night. I lied about where I went. I talked to boys on the phone under the covers and he would yell at me about the phone bill."

"Teenage rebellion isn't really the same as—"

"I'm not finished," she said. "I was smart enough not to challenge him directly while I was a minor. But I saved up, and the day I turned eighteen, I cashed out my bank account, hopped into my much older boyfriend's car, and left."

Morgan turned his chair so he'd face her. "Let me guess. Things went sour, you came back, you and your father had a tearful reconciliation where you thanked him for caring and he promised he'd be more lenient?"

"No." Her eyes were blank as she submerged herself in the memory. "I never went back. I didn't see him for years after that. My life got real bad for a time. Things could have gone a very different way." She sniffled. Were those tears in her eyes? "But eventually, out of money and tired of a bad relationship, I got serious. Got a job, enrolled in community college, studied hard. No government agency would have me with my history, but I went into the private sector and attracted the attention of the right people." She seemed to return to the present now. "I turned it around, but I live with the consequences of that period of my life to this day."

Morgan rolled his eyes. Vulnerable as she had made herself, he still got a vibe of barefaced manipulation from the story. "What's the lesson of this little morality tale?"

"My dad didn't let me have a boyfriend, so I went out and got the worst boyfriend I could find. You don't let Alex pursue her calling—"

"I get it," he said. "The answer is still no."

Bloch laid her hand on Morgan's shoulder. "You can't stop her. The harder you squeeze, the more she'll squirm. And when she gets free, she won't come back."

He shook off her grasp. "I don't care."

"With that kind of wits, guts, and spunk, think of what she could do under our guidance, with our resources."

"I contacted a journalist," Alex was saying. "That was my way of telling the story without my direct involvement."

"My daughter," he said, through gritted teeth, "is going to have a safe, *normal* life, do you understand?"

"That may not be possible anymore."

Morgan ground his teeth and watched as Alex narrated how she had put laxatives in an Acevedo executive's coffee in order to install spyware on his computer.

Bloch got up from her chair. Morgan watched as she left the viewing room and opened the door to the interrogation room.

"Alex, that will be all for now," she said. "Except for one last question: do you still have active contacts in the organization?"

"I do. The man who gave me the mission, who called himself

Polemarch. I can get in touch with him through a secure deep web messaging service."

"Could you show us how?"

"Of course."

"Wonderful. Alex, I'd like to make a proposition. At the moment, you stand as our strongest link to this organization."

Seeing where this was going, Morgan sprang from his chair in the observation room.

"I'd like you to help us ID him, run surveillance, and hopefully smoke out the—"

Morgan burst into the room. "This is not happening."

"Morgan, this is an opportunity," said Bloch. "Alexandra is in the unique position to—"

"No," said Morgan. He brandished his index finger in her face. "No!"

"Dad, stop. This is my decision." Then, to Bloch: "What would I have to do?"

Bloch was unfazed by Morgan's anger. "Set up a meeting with this man and go. That's it. We'd be responsible for the rest."

"So I would be bait."

"Chum in the water to attract the shark," said Morgan. "Don't even think about it."

"What other choice do we have, Dad?"

"What if they've already figured out who I am? What if they've already connected me to you?"

"They've killed more than twenty people and it's partly my fault," she said. "Dad, I need to do this."

"I won't let you."

"Morgan," said Bloch. "Alex is an adult. She can make her own choices."

"I'll fight you," said Morgan. "I'll go up against all of Zeta and anyone else who gets in my way."

"What about me?" asked Alex. "Will you fight me? I'm going to do this, whether you like it or not."

Who was this Alex, so bold, standing up to him like this? She had her chin raised, her chest out, and it seemed like she was taller than him. He saw, then, something magnificent about his daughter.

He was also furious. He stormed out of the room, slamming the door behind him.

Morgan made his way into the gym, which was dark and abandoned. He slammed into the punching bag, pummeling it as hard as he could with bare hands until he left bloody spots on the red leather.

Morgan sat down on the edge of the ring, panting. Only then did he notice that Lily was standing silhouetted by the door.

"I heard about what's happening with Alex. I gathered you wouldn't be too happy."

"She has no idea what she's getting herself into."

"Nobody ever does, Morgan. Did you? I didn't. But would you have done things differently?"

"Wouldn't you?"

Her right hand rose to her bruised neck. "No," she said. "I don't think I would."

"If she gave college a chance—gave a normal life a real chance—I think she'd feel the same."

"I think she did give normal life a chance," said Lily. "It made her miserable, until something extraordinary found her."

A light flickered out in the hallway.

"She's your kid whether you like it or not," said Lily, standing up. "You can try to stop her and fail, or you can be a part of her life and try to steer her in the best direction you can." She walked away, her footsteps echoing against the wooden floor, stopping at the door. "It can get pretty hard to figure out on your own."

With that, she left him alone, in the dark.

Morgan returned to find Alex in the War Room, talking to Lincoln Shepard. Bloch stood at the corner of the table, arms crossed.

"I've wired your phone so that you can receive calls down here," Shepard told her. All of Zeta was built inside a Faraday cage, which provided protection against wireless surveillance and EMP attacks, but which came with its own drawbacks. "The signal's going to be relayed through a tower in Andover, so that anyone who might be monitoring the call will think you're home or thereabouts."

Shepard caught sight of Morgan and pushed with his feet, rolling away to give him and Alex privacy. But Bloch did not look away.

"Look," he told his daughter, "I can't stop you from doing this. Or the next stupid thing you decide to do. I can't fight you on this right now, because there's nothing I can do that won't make this worse. So I think what I—"

A phone rang—Alex's. She held up a finger to Morgan and walked over to the table, holding the screen up so she could see.

"It's him. My friend Simon."

"Remember what we talked about," said Bloch. "He can't know we're listening in."

Alex nodded.

"Earphones, everyone," Shepard said, holding out Bluetooth headsets. Morgan took one and heard the hum of the phone's ringing. All eyes turned to Alex.

"I got this." She picked up the call.

Morgan heard a boy's voice through the headset. "Hey, where are you? Katie said you left."

"Came down to visit my parents. Sorry, I should have told you, but with everything, I forgot I was even coming. I had to run to catch my bus."

"Are you sure this was the best time to go?"

"They'd get suspicious if I didn't show," she said, picking at the fingernails on her left hand. "Believe me, it was the best thing I could do."

"Are you feeling better about the whole thing?"

"Yeah," she said. "I guess I was just a bit freaked. Once I had a little time to let things settle down, things seemed right again."

No sign of the lie in her tone. *The kid is good*, Morgan admitted to himself, a chill running down his spine. Was he responsible for this? Had he raised her to be someone who could tell a convincing lie at the drop of a hat?

Had he raised her to be like him?

"Happy to hear it," said Simon. "I just got a message. *He* wants to meet with you."

"Just me?"

"I met with him today already," he said. "It was supposed to be the both of us, but—"

"I get it," said Alex. "Just give me a time and a place."

Chapter 90

Morgan clutched the steering wheel of his Olds, white-knuckled, even though he was going under the speed limit for a change. He was in no hurry to arrive at their destination.

Alex rode with him, just the two of them. It was a reasonable scenario, in case *they* were watching—a father giving his daughter a ride back to school, nothing more. Meanwhile, the Zeta tactical van was following a couple of miles behind.

The whole ride was tense. Morgan gave her a tube of pepper spray that he kept in the glove compartment and a three-inch folding knife to replace the one she'd lost to Groener. He also took the opportunity to come up with more and more improbable pieces of last-minute advice.

"If you're shot at with a stun gun, remove the wires before they bring you down. And remember, if you find a bomb—"

"Dad, stop. This isn't helping anymore."

They rolled into campus. The weight in the pit of Morgan's stomach doubling, then tripling. Gray clouds loomed in the sky, threatening a blizzard.

Morgan brought the car to a halt and tasted bile.

Alex placed the tiny communicator in her ear canal. Morgan picked up the headset that paired with it.

"Testing," he said. "How's my voice coming in?"

"I can hear you, Dad."

"Headquarters, do you copy?"

"We've got you loud and clear," said Bloch, through a remote connection.

"Come in, tactical."

"Standing by," said Bishop. Morgan spotted the van in the next lot over.

He got out of the car and took Alex's crutches from the backseat. He then opened the door for her and helped her out.

"Okay," Morgan said, holding onto her shoulders with both hands and looking her straight in the eye. "Your priority is to make it out of there *alive*. You hear me? If anything happens, screw the mission and save yourself."

"Is that what you would do?"

Morgan grimaced, deflated.

She walked away toward the entrance of the Gothic-style library. He had the urge to shout out that he loved her, but he didn't want to share that with everyone listening in. Instead, he watched every one of her hobbled steps until she disappeared into the pointed arch doors.

Morgan got back in the car, turned it on to keep the heat going, and took out a newspaper, pretending to read.

"Alex," he said. "Testing, do you copy?"

"Loud and clear."

"Maintain contact," Morgan said. "We need to make sure the communicator is still within range in the library stacks."

Flurries of snow blasted against the windshield.

"In the elevator," said Alex. Morgan tensed up. A *ding* as the car reached its floor. "All right, I'm going in."

Morgan listened hard for anything, but the communicator's microphone was excellent at filtering out ambient noise. The line was silent until—

"Hello, Alex."

Polemarch. The voice was calm, controlled, and somehow empty. Somehow, it was familiar, too. Maybe because it reminded Morgan of Praetorian.

"I'd like to congratulate you on your work. It was key in making our operation possible."

"Glad I could be a part of it," she said.

"Are you really? What did you think of the master plan?"

"I don't like thinking about it," she said. "But justice was served."

Good girl. She knew she couldn't hide her emotions, so she worked with them. Offered up a false confession to conceal the truth.

"You're one of us now," he said. "Not the Ekklesia anymore. The Legion of Erebus. Do you feel that commitment?"

"I do," she said. "I want to know what's next."

"Hold your horses, eager beaver. First I'd like to talk about where you were today."

Alex let escape a nervous giggle. "I was visiting my family down in Andover," she said, stammering.

Damn it, Alex. Keep it together.

"And you saw your father?"

"Yeah." Her voice was concerned now. His tone was filled with menace. Morgan reached into the glove compartment and felt for the snub nose of his .38 Smith & Wesson revolver.

"I'd like to send a message to your father," he said. Morgan's heart beat faster in his chest.

"My father? You know my father?"

Morgan checked his ammo. *Yes, keep the plausible deniability going a little bit longer.*

"I've talked to him before." Morgan almost groaned in frustration. Of course. Boston Common. The mysterious voice. "And I know he is listening to us now."

"Go!" said Morgan, pulling open the door handle. "Move in! Now!"

"Copy that," said Bishop.

"Dan Morgan, we will kill you and your entire family."

Morgan kicked open the door and emerged outside, .38 revolver in hand.

"Your people cannot save Alex."

He glanced at the Zeta tactical van, where a figure, swaddled up in winter clothing, tossed a messenger bag under its near side and took off running.

"Bishop, get out of—"

The bag exploded and Morgan winced against the light and heat. Windows shattered. A split second later, the van was on its side, in flames but in one piece.

Car alarms blared in the wake of the explosion.

Torn, Morgan ran toward the library. His daughter came first. "Tac team, come in!"

"And you cannot save her, either."

Morgan's eyes went wide.

He didn't hear the report of the sniper bullet that hit him.

Chapter 91

Alex was frozen, eyes fixed on Polemarch. She saw his face clearly now by the dim light that filtered in the lancet window. He was older than she had thought he was. Midthirties, at least, with curly hair and several days' growth of beard on his face. His close-set eyes shone with raw menace.

"You showed such promise. Plucky. Determined. My star pupil."

She held her hands up, palms out. "Look, I'll cooperate, all right? I'm involved. I'm guilty, too."

He hovered over her. "It's much too late for that."

"Dad!" she called out. "Dad, help!"

"Your father can't help you. He's already dead."

It was a punch to her gut. Her father. And it was her fault. She threw up, despite herself. Polemarch drew back in disgust.

Alex saw her opening.

She took the pepper spray out of her pocket. He was too far away to stop her. She let loose a stream, straight into his eyes. He screamed in pain and stumbled back.

"Bitch!"

While he was incapacitated, Alex got up, bracing against her crutches, and moved among the darkened bookshelves. "Help!" she called out. No one answered.

She had to hide. She looked at the elevator—too far. Polemarch would be coming for her. She'd never outrun him with her cast on.

She retreated between two bookshelves, clicking off the automatic light as she did. She eased herself onto the ground. Only one thing could save her now. Only one way she could hope to move fast enough to evade him.

She drew her father's knife and flipped open the blade. She pulled her right pant leg over her cast, cutting where it caught. She inserted the blade between the fiberglass casing and the padding underneath. And she began cutting.

The fiberglass of the cast was tough and resisted the blade, but in ten seconds she made a one-inch cut. She pushed it in farther. The knife slipped into her flesh. She muffled a cry. She gripped it harder and kept sawing away.

She looked through the bookshelf, but couldn't see Polemarch.

Alex plunged the knife in deeper, slicing into her skin again. She gritted her teeth against the pain and pushed. The white inner padding of the cast grew stained with blood.

"Come out, little rabbit." Polemarch. Four rows of bookshelves away. She still had some time.

She sliced, pushing faster now, every cut of the double-edged knife piercing her flesh. Past the knee. Push. Push. Push.

Polemarch's footsteps, close. No more time. She grabbed the two sides of the fiberglass casing and wrenched them apart. It broke with a series of *cracks*, setting her leg free for the first time in months.

Polemarch heard. His footsteps made straight for her. Knife in hand, she braced against the bookshelf and stood. She tested the weight on her right leg. Unsteady. But it would have to do.

Polemarch rounded the corner of her shelf and came face-to-face with her, eyes red and watering. She held out the bloodied knife. Still bracing against the shelf, brandishing a three-inch blade, she didn't look like much of a threat.

But he kept his distance.

"You took your cast off," he said, looking amused. "Very resourceful. I should have known better than to underestimate you. But tell me, Alex. Where are you going to run to now?"

"You should take your own advice about underestimating me." She pulled the bookshelf with all her weight. It creaked and tipped over, slamming into Polemarch, who was not ready for it, and then collided into its counterpart, which tipped over in turn, and Alex and Polemarch were wedged tight between the two. A chain reaction ensued in a terrible din of falling metal and books, receding as each new shelf came crashing down.

Alex pushed the books out from between two shelves and squeezed through, emerging free on the other side. Polemarch, too bulky to do the same, was stuck, at least for a while.

Alex ran. She stumbled, her weak leg buckling under the new strain, and fell forward, knocking her chin hard against the floor, teeth clamping down on the tip of her tongue. She tasted blood.

Get ahold of yourself, Morgan. Life or death. Life or death.

Alex stood. The elevator was in sight. Staggering, holding onto the wall, she moved forward with singular purpose, a tunnel vision taking her to her only hope of salvation.

Close. She held onto the bookshelf as the distance between her and the elevator grew shorter, shorter. . . . She pushed her way inside and collapsed against the wall, pushing the button for the lobby. The doors slid together, closing the gap tighter and tighter—

A hand pushed through, and the doors obliged, opening. Polemarch. Battered, gasping, but in the harsh light of the elevator, packed with muscle. In tight quarters, she had no hope of overpowering him. Her knife was gone, along with her pepper spray. There was no escape.

He drew a garrote between his hands.

"Did you really think you could get away from me?" he growled. "Did you think you could stop me?"

"No," came a voice from behind him. "But I can."

Alex's father bodychecked Polemarch, pushing him against the elevator wall and knocking the wind out of him. He reached around him, pulling the garrote back, tight around his neck, cutting off his air. The younger man thrashed, but Morgan had his knee against Polemarch's back and held on tight.

Alex didn't know how long it was—somehow, time seemed both to stop and to run fast-forward at the same time—but Polemarch's eyes rolled up under their lids and he slumped to the ground.

"Dad!" Alex embraced her father. "I thought you were gone."

"Not yet," he said, panting. "Sniper tore my arm real good, but I can still move it, which is a good sign." He grabbed at his right bicep. Alex now saw that his jacket was shredded a few inches below the shoulder, and blood was oozing out, staining the lining and forming droplets on the waterproof exterior.

"Come on," he said, putting his arm around her and pressing the elevator button. "Let's get out of here."

Chapter 92

Alex heard about the bomb under the van from her father on the way to the hospital. Being reinforced, the chassis absorbed most of the damage, but the people in the van—Alex had learned their code names: Bishop, Diesel, Tango, and the incredible Spartan—had suffered a couple of serious fractures each, a few busted eardrums, and assorted bruises and lacerations. They were alive, but out of the game, stuck in bed, under aliases in different hospitals.

Alex had her leg sutured and dressed by a doctor who kept shooting her dirty looks, and then she had an X-ray done. Once they were satisfied that she wasn't at significant risk of refracturing her leg, they let her go with her father, although they insisted on taking her to the car in a wheelchair.

She watched the snowflakes rush the windshield from the darkness as her father drove her back to Zeta. They didn't speak, but in that drive, when it was just the two of them, no mission, she felt a closeness with him that she hadn't felt in months. She watched him, the stubble growing in around his mustache and goatee, healing scratches on his skin, the bandages on his arms disappearing under his sleeves, and the tireless, determined expression on his face.

She had her father back.

Morgan pulled into the garage and they descended together into Zeta headquarters. The whole place was quiet and empty, lit only by the dim LEDs that ran along the walls, which were never off. It was also still pervaded by suffocating heat.

Her father showed her to the barracks, with its row of bunks. She lay down her aching muscles, springs creaking. He was snoring within thirty seconds of hitting his bunk, but Alex, feeling restless, tossed and turned until she gave up on sleeping and went exploring.

Mostly, this was an excuse to test out her leg. It felt strange. Shaky. Even in winter, when no part of her got much sun, the now-mended limb was paler than the other, and the skin was doughy. It was weak and thin, lacking any kind of muscle definition.

But it worked. By God, it worked. It was a marvel, walking. She ran down the hall, whooping at the sheer joy of it. Her leg felt stronger by the minute.

She poked around the facility—the gym; the War Room; Bloch's office, locked; a series of offices off in a side hall, several unoccupied, but one—light under the door and voices, whispering. Alex slowed to a creep as she drew nearer, trying to make out what they were saying.

If she had been a little more alert, she would have stopped there.

Instead, she pushed the door open and saw Lincoln Shepard and Karen O'Neal in a state of undress that made her blood rush to her cheeks. They turned and looked at her in shock.

"Uh. Hi."

"Hey," said Shepard. "You won't, uh, tell anyone, right?"

She mimed a zipper sealing her lips and closed the door. Embarrassed, she made for her bunk and lay in the darkness. But one thing still stuck to her mind as she tried to force herself to sleep.

Simon.

The situation had gotten to his head, but he wasn't this insane person. She couldn't believe he would be okay with what happened. But now he was there, in deep with the people who had almost killed her. And there were only two things that could happen. Either he would keep going until he ran off the deep end, or he would come to his senses and be killed by the Ekklesia—by the Legion.

Guilt welled up in her. She had used him. She had pushed him into this. Whatever happened to him was on her conscience.

Alex crept out of bed and went down the hall to one of the empty offices. She booted up the computer, which whirred in the darkness, and logged on to the deep web, the way Simon had taught her.

On their secret messaging client, she wrote.

Simon, I am here and I am safe. They tried to kill me. I can get you out of this. Please talk to me. Let me help you.

Chapter 93

Morgan huddled around the War Room table with the broken remains of Zeta Division—Diana Bloch, Paul Kirby, Lincoln Shepard, Karen O'Neal, Lily Randall, and Peter Conley, with Smith standing at the head. General Strickland sat at a remove from the table, watching from a chair in the corner.

"An investigation of Polemarch yielded no results," Smith said. "All records of his existence have been scrubbed clean. We've run his photograph through facial recognition software and compared it against the major criminal databases, with no luck. We distributed his photograph to local police departments, but I'm not hopeful that it will give us anything useful."

"So that's it?" said Morgan. "That's all we got?"

"Except for one thing," said Smith, nodding at Lily.

She cleared her throat. "Polemarch is the man who killed Roger Baxter—who almost killed me. Whoever he was, he was an important operator inside the Legion."

"Which still doesn't give us anything to go on," piped in Shepard.

"Meanwhile," said Conley, "they still have their all-access pass to the world's electronic communications."

"I'm afraid the situation is even more dire," said Smith. "I yield to General Strickland."

Smith retreated into the background as the general stood and approached the table. Stormy weather showed on his face.

"There is more to the Praetorian escape than what it seemed. The CIA intercepted a message from the Legion last night—one that, we believe, was meant for us." Shepard moved to speak up, but Strickland preempted him. "Untraceable. Better minds than yours have made sure of that." Shepard scowled, sore at the comment.

Strickland read from a printout.

The locations of all US military black sites and all data
regarding secret and clandestine operations will be released to
the public. Everyone will know all your dirty little secrets.

"It's bluster," said Morgan. "They've got nothing."

"I'd entertain that notion," said Strickland. "But he sent us a taste
of what he had. A small cache of documents. It's . . . troubling." He
cleared his throat. "We now believe that Praetorian allowed himself to
be caught. We believe that his purpose was to gain access to certain
highly privileged information."

"I thought he already had access to everything through Blackrot," said O'Neal.

"Not everything. The most secret government information runs
through different networks and security protocols. It's impossible
to get to them through regular connections. The only way to access
it is—"

"At a government black site," said Morgan.

"That's right."

Morgan swore. "What did he get?"

Strickland balked.

"*What did he get?*"

"The locations of all US secret holding facilities," said Strickland.
"Along with the agents who work there, the identities of the prisoners,
interrogation techniques, and complete records of our black ops initia-
tives, including false flag operations, assassinations—you know the
game, Agent. If this were released, we could expect riots. It would be
pure anarchy. Terrorism would prevail."

A pall of silence fell over the room.

"We've already taken steps to remove the prisoners, but this
creates a serious vulnerability in itself."

"Can't we stop them from releasing it?" asked Bloch.

Shepard broke in. "Not without shutting the whole Internet
down."

Bloch looked at Strickland for an answer.

"We looked into it. He's right. There are countless avenues of de-
centralized communication on the Internet. Once it's out, it's out."

Morgan spoke up. "This is bigger than us."

Strickland furrowed his brow. All eyes were on him.

"We need everything on this. The CIA, the NSA, the FBI, the entire Department of Homeland Security. I'd like to know why you're *here*."

"Zeta has a track record of—"

"Because Praetorian said something," Morgan went on. "During my interrogation. On the last day, right before he made his escape."

The color drained from Strickland's face. "Would you excuse us? Morgan, if you please?" He motioned toward Bloch's office. Morgan followed him up the stairs, and Strickland closed the soundproof doors, giving them complete privacy from the people below.

"You're afraid," Morgan began. "Of what he might have. That it might damn you."

"Listen to me, Morgan." Sweat beaded on his forehead. "We need to present a united front. We can't afford division."

"*You* can't afford it."

"Suppose you bring out something damning against me," said Strickland. "Something that stains my credibility, that of my office, of the entire US military. Is that a victory? Is that good for our country?"

"The logic of a coward."

"You have no idea the decisions that need to be made by a man in my position." His voice was even, but his pupils were dilated and his breathing shallow. Controlled as he was, Strickland was furious. This was not a man who was used to being questioned.

"You're right," said Morgan. "This isn't the time. There are more important things in play. For now."

He walked out the door. All eyes turned to them as he descended the stairs to the War Room, Strickland following. Each sat down in his own seat.

"Well?" Morgan said, slapping the table with both hands. "Don't we have some terrorists to catch?"

Bloch stood on cue, dispelling the atmosphere of curiosity. "We need to lay out a course of action. I want suggestions. Now."

Conley stared at Morgan. They'd been partners for too long, and he could tell that Morgan's suspicions of Conley were undiminished.

Karen O'Neal, fidgeting with her hands, spoke first. "If we aggregate all the data of all their activity, we might be able to find patterns that could give us actionable information. We know they're associated with the Ekklesia now. It gives us a lot more potential data points to work with."

"There might be another weak spot," Lily offered, looking subdued in a black turtleneck and hair in a ponytail. "Anyone we can identify in the organization who might want out or might be willing to make a deal."

"Good," said Bloch. "Keep it coming."

Shepard tossed his pen onto the table. "I'm out of ideas." His boyish face looked aged and pale, and he had dark bags under his eyes. "He's better than I am. Pure and simple."

"This is an enemy beyond any of us." It was Paul Kirby. His eyes didn't seem to focus on anything, just stare into the middle distance. "I'm sorry to say it, but it's true. He's beat us every step of the way. Everything we've done so far has played right into his hands. He's got not only us but the entire government outclassed."

Nobody spoke. The hum of electronic equipment was the only sound. Morgan felt the energy that Bloch had mustered draining from the space.

Morgan broke the silence. "I remember something the magician Penn Gillette said, 'Doing magic sometimes just means spending a lot more time on something than anyone would think is reasonable.'"

O'Neal perked up with interest, the faintest smile glimmering on her face. "I think I know where you're going with this."

"I'm afraid I don't," said Kirby.

"Praetorian's a planner," Morgan continued. "He's been working on these designs for months, maybe years. Playing the long game. These things have been going off all in a row not because he's been conjuring them out of nothing, but because he's been setting up those dominoes for a long, long time. He's always two steps ahead of us because he started moving long before we did."

"How does that help us?" said Kirby. His tone was snippy, his upper lip curled into a sneer. But the others were watching Morgan with interest.

"We've been trying to catch up this whole time. That won't work. He already has his dominoes all in a row. We need to aim at where he's going to be. Look at the big picture, figure out where it's headed, and then knock out the intermediate dominoes. When we do that, the chain reaction stops."

"A nice analogy," said Smith. "But what do we do about it?"

"He's set up an entire network of operatives through the Ekklesia," said O'Neal. "He wouldn't do that if his ultimate goal was to release sensitive information to the public. This might be part of his plan, but it's not everything."

"So he's got a different endgame," said Bloch. "A distributed network suggests that it's big. He'd be able to pull off an attack on a single target as it is, just like he did the prison ship."

"So what are the targets?" broke in Smith.

"The organization is focused on the powerful," said O'Neal. "Assassinations of powerful individuals, destruction of property in major corporations, government agencies—"

"Shepard," said Bloch. "Look for events coming up that might be targeted."

"Oh, I keep an updated spreadsheet." Shepard dove into his computer.

"Karen," said Bloch, "crunch the numbers on the Ekklesia actions. Find me a pattern."

"You got it, boss."

"And Morgan—"

The lights flickered.

"Shepard," she said. "What's going on with the system?"

He frowned. "I have no idea. Let me—"

The big screen overlooking the table shimmered on. It showed, in extreme close-up, a familiar face. Black hair now groomed, face now clean-shaven, but the dark, penetrating eyes unmistakable.

Praetorian.

"Hello, Dan Morgan. Good to see you again."

Chapter 94

All watched in dumb silence as the face of the man they were looking for—their bitter enemy—stared down at them from the screen, his face dominating the entire space.

Praetorian tapped the microphone. "Hello? Is this thing on?"

"This isn't possible," said Shepard. "It just isn't possible."

Morgan looked up at Praetorian, feeling his eyes boring into him, even though the master hacker, of course, wasn't looking at them through the screen.

"Shepard," said Bloch. "Cut him out."

Shepard worked at his computer, going a mile a minute. Morgan could barely tell what was happening on his screen, he was opening and closing windows so fast.

"Don't bother," said Praetorian. "You're beneath me." Shepard's computer screen went blank.

"The heck—"

"He can see us," said Morgan. "How can he see us?" He turned to Bloch: "Where are the cameras?"

"Dan Morgan." Praetorian's voice reverberated through the space. "It took me a lot longer to find you than I thought it would. I have to congratulate your security people on that feat. Isn't that right, Lincoln Nathaniel Shepard?"

"Screw you!" Shepard screamed, half at his own computer. "What did you do, you bastard? What did you do?"

"I'm still getting used to my newfound freedom." The last word was yelled out gleefully. He shook as if in ecstasy. "Still getting back my land legs, you know. The fresh air, the sunlight. I had forgotten how beautiful they can be."

"Break the connection!" yelled Bloch. "Cut the network cables if you have to!"

"Maintenance hall," said Shepard to himself. He ran into the bowels of the facility, yelling back, "Get me tools! Cable cutters, knives, anything!"

"You, on the other hand, have your own imprisonment to consider. And here I mean you in particular, General Strickland."

Alex walked in from the hallway. "What's going on?"

"Enter the daughter!" Praetorian's voice boomed. "Young Alex, responsible for the death of one of my better captains."

"Get out of here," said Morgan.

"Trying to hide her? You think I don't have eyes in every chamber of your little home base?" He emitted his mechanical laugh. "We'll find the lovely Jenny, too. Now that I have everything I could want from the Project Aegis servers, it's just a matter of time."

Morgan burned with impotent rage.

General Strickland stepped forward. "What do you want?"

"From you? To gloat."

"You have us in a bind," said Strickland. "You are in a position where you can make demands of the US government. I can make your case. I can be your voice in the President's cabinet."

"Demands? I don't have any demands. I need nothing from your murderous government except for it to die. And I don't need help to make that happen. I make my first move today."

"What are you going to do?"

"I'm starting with the locations of all your secret detention facilities. Those have no long-term value—I'm sure they're already being evacuated. I'm putting that up on the Internet as we speak. YouTube, e-mail, Bittorrent, deep web—it's massively distributed and you can't stop it. To answer your question, *we* are going to do nothing. We will leave it in the hands of the people. Information wants to be free, General Strickland."

In the hand of terrorists around the globe, Morgan thought, *who want nothing more than to strike this blow at US intelligence.*

"Get the word out," Strickland demanded. "Alert the CIA."

"Won't work," said Praetorian. "You'll never get a single word to the outside. Don't even bother sabotaging the cables. I have everything I want from your little fly-by-night operation. I've done my damage. Now it's time to say good-bye forever."

The screen went black and the lights flickered off. They were plunged into darkness. The whirr of the ventilators and of every other piece of equipment on the premises stopped.

What remained was the silence of the grave.

Chapter 95

Zeta headquarters was dead. That much was clear.

Alex Morgan strained her eyes to see after the lights went out. The afterimage of Praetorian's face remained, and for a few seconds she could see nothing else. As her eyes adjusted, she saw that the odd device that ran on batteries provided a hint of illumination, their glow lost in the expansive War Room. All other equipment was unresponsive.

No one spoke. The faces Alex could make out were somewhere between spooked and defeated.

"Will somebody *do* something?" came the voice of General Strickland.

Bloch stepped in to take charge. "Flashlights first. We can't do anything in the darkness."

"Got it," said Lily, standing and walking into the tunnels.

Alex drew her phone and turned on the flashlight function. Karen O'Neal, who also had hers, followed suit.

"Is there any chance we'll get a signal down here?" Alex asked.

"Not one," said Shepard. "I made sure this place was impregnable. Well . . ." His gaze turned to the big screen, where Praetorian's face had been.

Karen checked her reception anyway, with no luck.

Lily came back in a pool of light, holding a high-powered aluminum-body flashlight in her left hand, three more clutched against her body. Alex's father helped Lily set them down on the table, then turned one on, facing the ceiling. Light dispersed, just enough to see vague features and outlines.

"We need to get out of here," said Strickland.

"Let me try the elevators," Lily said, going into the passage under Bloch's office.

"Would anyone hear if we shouted, maybe through a pipe?" asked O'Neal.

"No," Shepard said. Alex noticed that his attention would turn to his bricked computer every few seconds—she guessed because he was so used to looking at it for answers.

"How long will our air last down here?" Alex asked.

"It'll be at least a week before we run out of oxygen," said Karen. "Of course, we'll start dying from CO2 poisoning long before then."

"Great."

Lily returned in a slow jog. "Elevators are dead, too."

"Is there any other way out?" said Morgan. "Shepard, you know this place better than anyone else. Can we open the doors to the stairwell?"

"I'll check." He picked up a flashlight and went down the same passage Lily had come from.

"The world is burning out there and we're trapped in here," said Strickland.

"Does anyone else smell something funny?" It was O'Neal.

Alex furrowed her brow and sniffed the air. It *was* a funny smell, a whiff so tiny that her brain didn't make the automatic connection to the faint smell of rotten eggs—

"That's gas," said Bloch.

"Everyone get on higher ground!" said O'Neal.

"Nobody make a spark," Morgan said.

"Up to my office," Bloch ordered.

Morgan pushed Alex up first and everyone else followed, filling up the room. The office was spacious, but ten people were still a crowd, even standing against the walls to give each other space. Added to the heat and the anxiety, the constriction was suffocating.

"This buys us time," Morgan said. "But not much."

"Is there any chance anything in here sparks?" asked Strickland.

"How is he even doing this?" Alex asked.

"Every system at Zeta is integrated," said O'Neal. "He might've turned off the pilot light on the water heater."

Shepard did some mental math. "It wouldn't have reached us yet. Not nearly."

"He could've turned up the pressure," said O'Neal, frowning, pupils contracting as she did the math in her head. "That might actually be enough to blow a pipe junction somewhere."

She took a sheet of paper from a pad on Bloch's desk and jotted some numbers by the light of her phone. "If we assume it to be an ideal gas, assume an atmospheric pressure equal to sea level, which is close enough for a Fermi estimate, and ballpark the total internal volume of Zeta at—"

Alex peeked at the paper. She recognized some of the formulas from high school, but she wouldn't know how to begin to apply them here. She wondered if maybe she should have paid closer attention in chemistry class.

O'Neal seemed to come to a final figure, although Alex could barely make out the numbers in her scrawl. "See?"

"That would give us . . ." Shepard grabbed the pen and ran a few of his own numbers. "We'll take hours to suffocate in here."

"Suppose that's not what he means to do," said O'Neal. "Instead, suppose he wants to blow us up. Could he turn on the heater pilot light remotely?"

Shepard's face, drained of color, was all the response they needed. "If he burns up the gas now, he won't get us. He'd wait for the optimal air-to-gas ratio."

"Ten to one," said O'Neal. She scrawled on the paper. "That gives us . . . about ten minutes."

Alex's heart sank.

"We need a plan," said Bloch.

"Where is the gas coming from?" said Alex. "Maybe we can block it off. Somehow."

"There's no way," said Shepard. "There's only one access point to the gas pipes, and that's—the maintenance tunnel! It goes all the way to the garage. Someone might be able to climb up and get out."

"You think it's possible?" said Bloch.

"It's a tight fit," said Shepard. "It needs to be someone small."

"That's me," said Alex. All eyes went to her father.

"She is the smallest here," said Strickland.

"Do it," Shepard said.

Shepard drew her a map, pointing out her path to the tunnel. "Once you're out," he said, "Circle back in through the main entrance. You'll be able to open the stair door from the outside."

Bloch opened a drawer and took out a key ring. She drew three keys and put them in Alex's hand. Two were regular cylinder keys. The third was a tubular key, solid and heavy, of a type she'd never seen before. "The first opens the door to the maintenance tunnel. The second opens the trap door to the garage. Use the third to open the door into Zeta."

She put each in a different pocket of her jeans, memorizing which was which so she wouldn't have to do it under pressure.

"Anyone have a handkerchief or something?" asked O'Neal. "Anything she can hold to her nose."

Shepard took off his flannel shirt and tossed it to Alex.

"Hold your breath as long as you can," her father said. "Take shallow breaths if you have to. We're counting on you."

Alex took a flashlight, pressed the shirt to her nose—it smelled of sweat and Old Spice—and ran.

Her footsteps on the metallic steps echoed in the War Room. She took her last deep breath about halfway down. When she hit ground level, the smell of rotten eggs assaulted her. She had to be careful now. Conserve her breath. Breathing in too much of this air could asphyxiate her. If she lost consciousness, it would be certain death for them all.

She ran across the War Room and into the main hallway of Zeta headquarters, following Shepard's directions to a narrow door just outside the gym.

She pulled out the key from her back pocket—and dropped it. The world swam before her eyes. She couldn't lose consciousness. Not now.

Alex slammed the flashlight against her thigh, still injured from when she'd cut herself out of her cast. Invigorating pain flooded her and brought her back to a keen awareness.

Okay, let's do this. She shone the light on the floor. She bent down, picked up the key, and inserted it into the slot. It slid in. She unlocked the door and opened it.

The maintenance closet did not deserve the name. It was shallow—maybe twenty inches deep, with two thick pipes running from top to bottom.

She shifted the light up. The closet extended upward some forty, fifty feet. She couldn't help noticing that there wasn't a ladder.

Only one way to do this.

Alex put the flashlight, on and facing up, into her right pocket, so that it lit the passage above. It was a snug fit, but that meant it would stay in place. She ran her left hand over the two keys that were still in her pockets. Then she laid her hand on the pipe on the right—and drew it back. It was hot—more like scalding. This pipe brought down the steam that had been overheating the Zeta Division air.

No choice. You do this or everyone dies.

She grabbed the left pipe with her left hand. It was warm, thanks to its proximity to the heating pipe, but was tolerable to touch.

She kicked off the ground and began her climb, pulling herself up by the pipes. The heat burned her right hand with every second of contact, and she resisted the impulse to draw it away.

Her legs weren't in top shape, but her upper arms were a whole other story. They had carried her up a full eight feet before she knew it. Here, the closet became a narrow vertical tunnel into which she wedged herself. Once in, she braced her back against one wall and her feet against another.

Judging it safe, she took a deep breath. Hardly any smell of gas. She stopped to catch her breath until the heat against her skin became so intense that it impelled her to keep moving.

At first, the burn had felt like nothing more than a bad sunburn. Now it was like holding her hand over a burning match.

Still she climbed.

She couldn't rest. Every second that passed was a second closer to the whole facility blowing up.

She didn't know how long it took to make it to the top. She climbed with such single-mindedness that she only noticed she had reached the top when her left hand, reaching up for the pipe, hit a hard surface above.

The trapdoor to the garage was held shut by a padlock. She braced her feet against the far wall, back against the wall. It held up her weight, and her hands were free to work. Alex reached her left hand into her pocket and pulled out the second key. She transferred it to her right hand.

She had underestimated the extent of her burns. Touching the warm metal was like holding a firebrand. Startled by the pain, she fumbled the key.

It dropped straight down the shaft, hitting the ground below with a faint *ding*.

Oh. Crap.

Thoughts raced through her head. How long would it take her to climb down then back up again? Too long. It would run over the ten minutes she had been allotted by at least two. Plus, she didn't know how long she could clutch this pipe before her skin would start to peel from her hand.

There was one other option.

She ran her fingers through her hair and found what she was looking for.

A bobby pin. One single pin. She'd have one shot at this, just as her father had taught her. Everyone was counting on her. Her father's life depended on it.

She stared at the pin by the indirect light shining from her pocket. Bending it back and forth, she broke it in two, right down the middle. She put one-half in her mouth, holding it between her teeth. The other she inserted about a quarter of an inch into the lock and bent it ninety degrees. That half would be her tension wrench. The other would be her pick. Holding the tension wrench in her mouth, she pushed the pick about a sixteenth of an inch in and bent the tip, just a smidge.

Then she got to work, setting the tension wrench in place first, pulling it to the side. Next she inserted the pick. And a new problem: the only sensation she felt on her right hand was burning. She'd have to do this left-handed.

Push, push, click. One pin in place. Two.

Her right hand trembled and the tension wrench fell—onto her abdomen, held by a fold of her shirt. Focusing on keeping her hand steady, she picked it up and reinserted it into the keyhole.

Focus, damn you.

One. Two. Three. Four. She pulled the tension wrench until the padlock clicked open.

Success!

She maneuvered it out of the hole, letting it drop down the shaft, and pushed the trap door open. Cool air! She pulled herself out and flopped onto the floor of the edge of the parking garage. She laid her right palm down, letting the cold concrete soothe the burn as she panted.

Get up, Morgan. You're not done.

She willed herself to stand and ran toward the door to Zeta Division, on the opposite wall some sixty feet away. She found the tubular slot and inserted the third key in. The lock was tough, but she forced it to turn until she felt the dead bolt slide. She pushed the door open and walked in. Beyond the elevators were winding stairs. She ran down—the descent was much easier than going up—until she came upon another door. She inserted the tubular key into the lock and opened it.

The smell of gas was overpowering.

"Come on!" she shouted into the dark passage, coughing. She drew the flashlight from her pocket and waved it, hoping they would see. "It's open!"

She wasn't about to wait to see if they had heard. She plunged inside, coming face-to-face with the others, led by Peter Conley, at the far end.

"Go!" her father, bringing up the rear, yelled to her, wasting precious oxygen. "Run!"

She did, taking the lead up the stairs, the rest of the group following.

She emerged out into the garage. "Keep running," her father called out behind her. "Clear the area!"

She ran without looking back.

As she dashed up the ramp to the street, the floor shook so hard she stumbled to her knees. The rumble grew louder and a fireball exploded from the Zeta entrance, broken metal and wood flying in every direction.

The others were behind her. Most had stumbled, like her. She counted heads. Ten, with her. Everyone had made it out alive.

"Everyone okay?" she yelled out. She scanned people for injuries. Her father first—no bleeding. Bloch was fine, too, as was Smith, Lily, Conley, and—

Shepard. Everyone else stood, but he stayed on the ground. Alive, but . . .

"I'm going to need a little help getting up," he said, grunting.

His left calf was bleeding, caught by a piece of flying debris. Peter Conley lifted him to his feet and helped him walk.

Her father put his hand on her shoulder. "You did good. I'll just say one thing."

"What?"

"I really hope we were up-to-date on our insurance for that place."

Chapter 96

Frieze dialed Conley as she drove, honking her horn against the afternoon rush-hour gridlock. Straight to voice mail.

She had run out of the FBI office as soon as Gus told her about the explosion. She was supposed to have stayed. She had duties in the office that needed her attention during a crisis. She didn't care.

She made the call again and again as she sped her way through downtown traffic, getting voice mail each time. She found a parking spot several blocks away from the Hampton Building and ran the rest of the way, flashing her badge to get past the police cordon. As she approached, she saw that smoke was coming out of the garage.

No. Please.

She ran inside the garage and saw a team of firemen standing around a truck, occupying the parking area that led into Zeta. The wall around the door inside was black with soot.

"Did you find anyone?" she called out to no one in particular.

"No bodies yet," said a fireman, taking his helmet off. "But it's huge down there. I wonder what that was supposed to be."

Tentative relief washed over her. "Any idea of the cause?"

"From the patterns I'd say it was some flammable gas. Probably a natural gas leak."

Frieze wandered around the garage, looking for cameras that could tell the tale of what had happened. There were none, because of course they'd never allow that.

Her phone rang. Peter? No. Gus.

"Where the hell did you go? We have some suspects wanted in connection with the Legion attack on Acevedo. Chambers told me to forward you the profiles, so I'm sending them to your phone."

Frieze pinched the root of her nose. "Sure. I'll take a look in a minute." She moved toward the door to Zeta.

"Hey!" said the fireman she'd been talking to. "That's off-limits until we've cleared it."

"FBI," she said, flashing her badge.

"I don't care if you're the Pope. There are noxious gases down there, and I don't want to deal with the paperwork of a Fed croaking in my fire. So stay right where you are."

Frieze bristled but complied. She wasn't about to die searching through the ruins for Peter Conley's body.

The mental image made her tear up.

She needed to compose herself, get her mind off this for a while, until the firemen had a chance to search inside and give her definite answers.

Frieze found a low concrete wall in the garage where she could sit. She pulled her phone out of her pocket and looked through the files Gus had sent her.

"Oh my God."

She ran back outside as fast as her legs would take her.

Chapter 97

Reclining in the front passenger seat of the noisy 1970 Ford Econoline, Alex poked at her burned hand—second degree, pocked with blisters. She ran a finger over the red skin. It blazed with pain. She took stock of her injuries—the cuts on her legs, the abrasions on her wrists, and now this. But her leg was mended. *Silver linings, Morgan.*

The van was a recent acquisition, Alex found out, in response to the Legion's ability to make any car's electronics go *poof.* Strickland and Smith, along with Kirby, disappeared to do whatever business occupied their time.

Her father was driving and hadn't noticed the burn, which Alex was happy enough about. He didn't need the extra worry, especially not given that his arms were bandaged from hand to shoulder. She'd just grit her teeth and bear the pain, like he did.

"So what are we going to do?" she asked him. "How are we going to strike back?"

"You aren't going to do anything. First chance I get, I'm going to send you with your mother, out of harm's way."

"You heard what he said. Mom's not out of harm's way. None of us is."

"It's going to be more dangerous wherever I am."

Anger rose inside Alex. "I just saved *everyone*," she said, raising her voice. "Where do you get off talking to me like I'm a kid?"

She braced for his rejoinder, but it never came. Whether it was because everyone in the back had just heard her, or because something had really changed in him, he just said, "You're right. I'm sorry."

Twenty minutes later, the van pulled into the garage of a trim brick suburban home in Quincy, south of Boston. Once the garage was closed—reinforced steel, Alex noted, dressed up to look like a regular wooden garage door—they all got out. Conley opened the electronic lock on the door and let them through.

It was a weirdly normal house, even if the furniture was a bit cheesy. Alex flopped onto an armchair, laying her burned hand flat against the armrest, basking in the coolness of the upholstery.

Lying on the couch, leg bleeding, Shepard gave O'Neal directions to open a hidden compartment where he had stashed a pile of preconfigured laptop computers. O'Neal set them on the table with an *oof* and then drew the charger cables, packed in tight figure-eight loops.

"How do we get them online?" she asked. Shepard didn't answer. He had an odd blank expression.

"We can't do it," he said. "I can't fight them on my own on the digital front. They're beyond me." For the confident-to-the-point-of-arrogance Shepard to admit this must have been wrenching.

O'Neal crouched next to him. There was something intimate in the gesture, and Alex remembered walking in on them back at Zeta. She averted her eyes but perked up her head to eavesdrop.

"Hey," Karen said. "Look at me. You are a goddamn badass. You were doing this hacktivism crap when you were in high school. You've graduated past this. So shut up with this self-pity bullshit. You're my freaking hero, man."

"I let them through, and they destroyed it. Zeta's *gone*, Kar."

"It's always easier to destroy. But we're trying to protect. We're trying to make something, Linc. It's an uphill battle for us. But we're going to beat them. Because we're better than they are."

His face brightened. "Damn right we are."

They kissed. Alex nearly squealed.

"Shepard!" Bloch called to him. "We need to set these up. Morgan, Randall, Conley. Over here. Let's powwow."

Alex was left out once more.

Something drew her attention in the corner of her eye—one computer left in the hidden compartment. Karen had drawn out only as many as they needed. Alex stood up, trying to play it like she wanted to go to the bathroom, and bent down to pick it up as she passed.

Once she was locked in the guest restroom, she booted up the computer and logged on to her deep web client, following the procedure Simon had taught her. She opened the messaging service.

There was one new message from Simon. All it said was:

Alex, I'm scared. Please help.

The words wrenched at her heart. Simon. Her imagination exploded with scenarios of what he might be facing, each more horrible than the last. Her breath grew quick and shallow and she grabbed handfuls of her hair as guilty thoughts assaulted her, thoughts of Simon, dead, going to prison, killing people.

Alex gritted her teeth and balled her hands into fists, forcing her breathing to return to normal. She wasn't going to lose it to despair. She grabbed the computer and walked out of the bathroom. They would rescue Simon, and he'd be their key to finding Praetorian.

In her resolve Alex nearly bumped into Karen. "I was looking for that," she said, pointing at the computer with a suspicious glint in her eye.

Alex's stammers of explanation were cut short by someone knocking on the front door of the house. Banging, more like it. Everyone turned to look. Her father reached for his gun and Lily took her position flat against the wall by the entrance.

"Conley!" came a muffled woman's voice. "Conley, open the door! Damn it, please be in here. Conley!"

Peter Conley, looking perplexed, walked to the front door, unlocked it, and opened it.

Lisa Frieze.

"Are you safe?" she said, barging inside. "Is everyone okay?"

"We're fine," Conley said. "There was—"

"An explosion at your headquarters. I know." She was talking a mile a minute. "Listen. You have to get out of here. They're coming for you."

"What?"

"The police are coming for you all. They tracked you to this location, I don't know how. They'll be arriving in minutes."

Everyone looked to Bloch for leadership.

"Get moving," she said. "We need materials. Pack up the computers. Get the guns out of the armory."

Police sirens sang in the distance, growing closer. Lily drew the curtains on the windows closed. Bloch crouched to open a cabinet under the kitchen counter. Inside was a safe with an electronic keypad. She entered a combination.

"There's a tunnel in the basement," she said, opening the door to the safe. "It's well-hidden and leads to the house behind this one. There's a car in the garage. Don't call attention to yourselves and you'll make it out."

She pulled out a bag of money—Alex figured it was at least one hundred grand. Her father opened a cabinet in the living room and unlocked a similar safe, this one much taller. Inside were guns—black handguns and semiautomatics on racks, boxes of ammo stacked on the bottom. Conley brought a briefcase and helped her father load the handguns and ammo.

Police cars converged on the house, tires screeching. Lily looked out through a gap in the curtains. "They're here," she said.

Frieze addressed Bloch. "They know there are people in here. If everyone goes, they'll find us. I suggest some people stay behind. But it's your call."

Shepard was first to speak. "I can't go. I'll just slow you down."

"We need someone who knows how to work with computers."

A bullhorn whined outside. *"You are surrounded."*

"If I go, we all get caught," Shepard said. "Don't make me insist. Playing noble doesn't really suit me."

"Morgan, Conley, Lily, Alex," said Bloch. "You go. We're going to need you on the outside. Karen. You go with them."

"What about you?" Karen asked.

"Come out with your hands up!"

"I'm staying," Bloch said. "You're all more useful than I'm going to be." Bloch wrote down a number on a pad of paper. "Get in touch with Smith." She handed it to Karen O'Neal, who glanced at it, then folded it up and held it out to Morgan.

"I've already memorized it," she said. "Diversify your risks."

Alex spoke up. "Someone's going to check, right? They're going to see that whatever reason they're arresting you for is bogus—aren't they?"

"On a terrorism case, I'm afraid it won't be soon enough," said Bloch. "If we're caught, it'll be weeks at the minimum before any one of us sees the light of day."

"I repeat, come out with your hands up!"

Lisa opened the front door, both hands raised, holding her badge in her right. "Lisa Frieze, FBI!" she called out. "I am in contact with the suspects inside. They are going to come out peacefully!"

"Time for you to go," said Bloch.

Morgan hustled Alex down the stairs to the basement. Conley had taken the lead and was already holding open a wooden panel that held a set of tools and swiveled upward to reveal the secret tunnel. Alex ran headlong into the darkness to the sound of heavy boots invading the house upstairs.

Chapter 98

It was dark by the time Morgan pulled the van up to the parking lot of a rundown roadside motel right off the highway, bordered by forest on three sides. He sent Alex to get the keys to the rooms because among them she was the only one who wasn't wanted by the FBI. Not even sleazy motels were too keen on harboring terrorists.

Alex got two adjoining rooms for the five of them. They shuffled inside, watching for anyone who might see them. They congregated in the same room, which looked like every other cheap motel room in the country—two hard beds with dirty, sticky bedspreads, peeling wallpaper, an ancient TV on a stand, bad art hanging on the wall.

All were so exhausted that they collapsed in place, forming a rough circle, Lily and Karen on the beds, Morgan on the single chair, and Alex on the grimy carpet.

Conley walked in from the adjoining room. "I spoke to Smith. Bloch and Shepard are safe in custody, but it'll be some time before they're free. He's working on lifting our warrants." He cleared his throat. "Most of the CIA prisons were evacuated in time after Praetorian's leak. All but one. Smith wouldn't say where, but it got swarmed by militias. All the prisoners were released. The guards were executed."

The group was unresponsive. They looked like a group of shell-shocked soldiers, with deep bags under their eyes, faces drained of blood, blank expressions. O'Neal was gnawing on her fingernails. His daughter was nursing a burn on her right hand he hadn't noticed before.

Morgan broke the silence. "We're running like rats," he said.

"And all that running gets us is that we're chased into an even worse corner. We need to stop running and start attacking."

"Great, in theory," said Lily. She had washed her face, and this was maybe the first time Morgan had seen her without makeup on. "I'm all for it. Now what does it mean? What do we do? We've got an enemy that always seems to know where we are but we can't seem to find even with all our resources, let alone like this. And whatever we throw at him, he's not only ready for, but uses it against us. What do we do?"

"I say we sleep," said O'Neal, who was barely holding her eyelids open. "We can't make good decisions in this state."

"I want a plan," he said. "Or a shred of something. Anything that will put us on the offensive."

"Simon," Alex said.

"Who?" asked Lily.

"Simon. My friend. The one I pushed to join the Ekklesia with me. The recruiting front for the Legion. He sent me a message. He wants out. He's scared. He could be our way to Praetorian."

"We tried that with you, remember?" said Conley.

"That was different. They found me out because of Dad. And I didn't know anything then, no inside information. But Simon— whatever they're planning, they're going to be using him."

"The kid has a point," said O'Neal, who had given up trying to sit up, and now lay in bed with her eyes closed.

"As long as you know how to contact him," said Lily. "It wouldn't be much use to us if he couldn't find us."

"I already have," she said. Morgan didn't like this at all. More secrets she'd been keeping. More lies. "He wants help. Which I think means he might be able to help us."

"What do you think?" asked Conley, addressing Morgan, who understood it was about more than just finding Praetorian.

"If it's our best plan, then it's the best plan," he said.

"But on one condition," said Alex. "If we go through Simon, I want to make sure he's safe. I don't want to use people anymore."

"That isn't always an option," said Morgan.

"There is no other option," she said. "I'm making this the only one. If we use Simon, we help him as much as we'd do one of ours." She raised her voice to address the group. "Does anyone have a problem with that?"

If anyone did, they didn't speak up.

"All right," she said. "I need a computer."

Conley spoke as Alex wrote her message. "No matter what, if we're going up against the Legion, we need someone who knows their way around a computer," said Conley. "We're up against impossible odds. If they have that large of an advantage over us, there's no hope.

Lily stood up. "I have an idea who we can call."

Chapter 99

Bruce Ansley was having one of his headaches. This one was so bad he could barely drive straight. The night before had ended in a screaming match between him and Annemarie. Cory was sleeping over at a friend's house, but Pam had heard everything and gave him the cold shoulder that morning.

Anger was welling up in him, fueled by the pain in his head, and in his mind it found his usual targets. Annemarie, the nag. Pam, the ungrateful little brat. He'd have words with them today. Oh, he'd tell them exactly what they were.

He called in sick and turned the car around to head home. Through the headache, the familiar anxiety pestered him. The post office. He had to stop at the post office.

He opened the post office box, prepared to give it his usual glance to confirm that it was empty, and that the day he never expected had not come, again.

But this time, it was different. This time, there was a package.

He reached out, hand shaking, and took it. It wasn't large, maybe the size of a children's lunchbox. It wasn't heavy, either. But it now was his whole life and carried the weight of the world.

Dazed, he sat in his car and opened the box. Inside, in foam padding, was a smaller case made of aluminum and a letter, which he opened and read.

The day had come. He couldn't escape anymore. It was here, it was now.

At least, he thought through the pain, it would be the end.

Chapter 100

Centurion sat in his 1979 Buick in the parking lot of the roadside motel. He pulled up next to the van and cut the engine. No need to hide here, not now. No cameras, no electronics. And Praetorian had other things on his mind.

All he had to do was walk up to that room door and knock. It was early, and because it was winter the sun still hadn't risen and the morning was still dark. But they wouldn't turn anyone away with the kind of information he had.

He got out of the car. His shoes hit the gravel, and the moment he stood, someone slammed the car door shut against him, pinning his chest between it and the chassis, and grabbed and twisted his left arm.

"I'm clean!" he protested, wind knocked out of him. "You want money? I'll give you money."

"I want answers." The Boston accent. The in-your-face tone. And Centurion finally got a good look at his face.

"You've been here eyeing that room for an awful long time, buddy. What are you looking for here?"

"Dan Morgan. And I think I just found him."

Morgan pulled on Centurion's arm harder. "You've just made this a lot more dangerous for yourself."

"Wait! I-I come in peace."

"You have five seconds to tell me who you are. This is not a good day to test me."

"My name—they call me Centurion. I'm a lieutenant in the Legion."

Morgan gritted his teeth and twisted his arm harder.

"No! I'm here to help. I want to help you stop him."

"I'm not just going to trust you on this one," he said. "Why today?"

"They've gone off the rails, the whole group. Praetorian, he—I guess he's always been crazy. I just never realized what kind of crazy he is. How far he's willing to go." Morgan eased the force on his arm. "I joined the group because I wanted to do good. I wanted justice."

Some birds cawed overhead.

"You believed in his freedom and openness crap?"

"With every fiber of my being. And I fell under his spell. Here was someone who didn't only want to talk. He wanted to do something—ambitious things. Things that could bring down the whole system. And until recently, I never had a question about the righteousness of what we were doing. About why Praetorian did what he did."

"And you just changed your mind?"

"Would you believe it if I told you it was about a girl?"

"Oh, brother." Morgan took some weight off the door and released his arm. "All right. Let's get inside and we'll talk."

Chapter 101

Morgan roused everyone who was still asleep and they all gathered in the room he was sharing with Conley. He sat Centurion on the bed by the bathroom wall and the rest sat in a semicircle around him. The Zeta operatives seemed tense, like they might jump for a gun as soon as he did anything suspicious.

Morgan was the wariest among them. This could be a trap. Praetorian was elaborate in his plans, that much he knew. But what would've been the point? He'd already sent the police after them. For all he knew, Morgan could be caught at any moment. And if Centurion came to him, Praetorian could just as easily have dispatched an assassin. "Get talking," he said.

Centurion fussed with his hands. He seemed uncomfortable with the attention. "I'm not very good at public speaking."

Morgan rolled his eyes. "What's Praetorian's endgame?"

"You know he has the secret government data from the prison ship," Centurion said. "Well, that's only half the plan. He wants to deal a death blow to the US government. It'll be a two-pronged attack."

"He's using the Ekklesia cells to carry out his plan," said Alex.

"No. They are just a distraction."

"Who are these cells?" asked Lily.

"People like your daughter and her friend. People who were fed up. Who were leading meaningless lives in a system they no longer had faith in. People who wanted to be part of something greater than themselves."

"Why don't these people ever join Habitat for Humanity or something?" said Karen O'Neal. "Why does it always have to be terrorism?"

"Praetorian has a way of bringing people to see things as he does. There's something about him. A strange and powerful charisma. It doesn't matter why they joined in the first place. He will convince them that they did the right thing. They—at least most of them—will join the team as if this had been the plan all along. And they'll love him for it."

Lily snorted in disdain. "People are not that stupid."

"I've seen it done on a smaller scale," said Centurion. "You'd be surprised how much you can convince someone to do, thinking that it's the right thing."

"I would know," Alex said. Morgan winced.

"What's their plan?" he asked.

"They're planting what they think are smoke bombs at various national landmarks. It's supposed to make a point about national security. Except the bombs Praetorian is giving them will be real explosives."

"No," Alex cried out. Then she whispered, "Simon."

"But you said that's a sideshow," said Morgan. "A distributed attack gets every counterterrorism government agency working on overdrive, resources worn thin."

"Exactly," said Centurion. "It's the perfect moment to deliver his real blow. I take it you know that Praetorian let himself get caught?"

"Yes," said O'Neal. "He wanted to get the secure data through the ship's computer system."

"That's only half the plan. You see, he didn't come back alone from the prison ship. He brought someone else with him and left the evidence to blow up and sink to the bottom of the ocean."

Morgan furrowed his brow. Not good. "Who?"

"In the early eighties, the Soviet Union began a program to embed sleeper agents in the US. They were brought in as children, posing as Bosnian refugees. Nine children. They would grow up here until they were adults, raised to follow whatever orders came to them, when they came. There was one man who was responsible for all of them."

The image of the old Russian prisoner came back to Morgan. "Sergey."

Centurion nodded. "Kuklovod."

"Was that his name?" asked Morgan.

"No. It means—"

"Puppetmaster," said Karen O'Neal.

"Excuse me," said Lily, "but *who?*"

"He was a KGB agent, responsible for this program. The only one who knew the identities of the nine sleeper agents in the US. He was caught by the CIA in 1992. Subjected to interrogation and torture over this entire time. He never broke."

"And now he's with Praetorian," said Lily. "Is he talking?"

"More than that. He's collaborating."

"What's his plan?" asked Conley.

"Praetorian is keeping his cards close to his chest," Centurion said. "Nobody but he and Sergey know the identities of the sleeper agents, or what they're supposed to do. But whatever it is, it's going to be big."

"How do we stop him?" asked Morgan.

Centurion shrugged his narrow shoulders. "Heck if I know. But I'll tell you this. Show people who he is, and his followers—the cells—will abandon him."

"How do we do that, if we don't even know who he is?" said O'Neal.

"Because I know his name. His real name. Park Jeongwoo. Look for him, and you'll find out who he is." He looked out the window, blinking his eyes in a nervous tic. "I need to go. He'll notice if I'm missing for too long. I'm already taking a huge risk being here." He gathered his coat. "Find the sleeper agents. Find the cells. Don't let him win."

Morgan opened the door for him. As he walked out, Morgan put his hand on his shoulder. "Just one question. Why did you come to me?"

"He told me about you," Centurion said. "He seemed to respect you. He never respects anyone. I think it says something about who you are."

Morgan watched through the window as Centurion pulled out and drove away.

"This place isn't safe," he said. "We have to move out."

Chapter 102

"That's him," said Lily. She saw the white Lexus when it turned into the parking lot, mostly because she couldn't help looking out the window, waiting for Scott to arrive.

Another day, another motel. Different color carpet, different wallpaper, but everything else just about the same. Lily pined for Europe, where any old roadside inn might be up to a few hundred years old, each carrying its wonderful little idiosyncrasies.

Morgan, Conley, and Alex were out trying to buy cars from dealers who weren't particular about documentation. O'Neal was tapping at her computer in the other room. She wasn't much of a people person, but on hearing this she came to the door that adjoined the two bedrooms. It made Lily wonder what kind of reputation Scott had among those who knew something about cybersecurity.

Lily opened the door before he could knock and threw her arms around him.

"I hadn't had a welcome like that since my dog died."

Lily gave a playful slap against his round face. "Arse."

"H-hi," O'Neal stammered. "I'm Karen. I do computer stuff, too—I'm an analyst. A big fan of your work."

Lily watched with amusement as Karen tried to finesse the situation with the social graces of a jackhammer. She waved Scott inside and shut the door.

"What's your area?"

"Data crunching," she said. "Probabilistic models and machine learning, mostly. As applied to defense and intelligence. I've actually been running an algorithm now that I'd like your input on."

"Maybe you can fill me in first," he said, setting his case down on the bed. "Lily said you needed my help pretty desperately."

"Well, I wouldn't say *desperately*..."

They sat opposite each other on the beds and O'Neal gave him the rundown, tripping over her own words, with Lily adding the occasional aside in edgewise.

"So, to be clear," he said. "We're looking for a handful of sleeper agents no one's heard from in twenty or more years, an unknown number of terrorist cells, and a guy no one has been able to find, ever, except on the one occasion when he wanted us to?"

"That's the gist of it," said Lily.

He drew his computer from its sleeve and booted it up. "Let's get to it then." He set up the laptop on the table across from O'Neal's. "I'm going to log in through our system."

"I am setting up search parameters to identify him by his name," said O'Neal. "That's Park Jeongwoo."

"I'm going to use my computer to relay access to our systems to you," he said. "You can load your parameters onto our algorithms to run on our servers to speed up the process by, oh, some five thousand percent."

"You're kidding me," she said. "You can *do* that?"

Lily couldn't help feeling a twinge of jealousy. "I'm just going to sit here and watch, then."

"So here's what I was thinking," O'Neal said. "Park is one of the most common family names in Korea, so it doesn't narrow the search down much. But the given name is a little better. Korean given names are combinatorial. There's a huge number of possibilities, so there's relatively few of each particular one. Once we narrow it down by name, we exclude any extreme ages—we'll pin the center to thirty-five and let the program search out from there. All that, plus a connection to the US and any known association with criminal activity, hacking, or computer science, although these with low inferential weight."

"Sounds good," he said. "We could also put in web activity related to the name in general. If he's good at hiding, it might not point directly at him, but he might be associated with weird patterns, like a drop-off in recorded activity when he learned how to use encryption and proxy servers in the Internet. Usually happens around age fifteen or so."

"*Genius.*"

Lily could only imagine.

* * *

Morgan pulled into the motel in his newly acquired 1978 Camaro, which cost him double the asking price for cash only, immediate delivery, and no questions asked. The chassis was dented, scratched, and faded, but the salesman didn't know what the car had under the hood. With a little refurbishing, Morgan could have sold the car for four times as much.

Conley pulled in with the bulky van to his left. On the right, Alex brought her new motorcycle to a stop with a drift on the gravel.

"Don't make me regret this," Morgan said as she took her helmet off.

Lily opened the room door to admit them and introduced Scott, who was too engrossed in his computer to pay them any attention beyond an introductory wave.

Conley brought in a bag of burritos they had picked up on the way back. "Anyone hungry?"

Alex took one and picked up one of the idle computers. "I'm going to see if Simon answered my message."

"Conley," said Morgan, drinking water from a bottle. "We're going to need some serious help with this if we get any information. I mean FBI grade help. Do you think you can get in touch with Lisa?"

Conley took a phone outside to make the call.

"This is suggestive," Scott said from his computer. "Park Jeong-woo. Born to a family of wealthy Korean immigrants to the US. We have records of his birth and early hospital visits. Nothing beyond that. Nothing medical, school, all missing. It's like he stopped existing. No record of a death, either."

"Do we have an address?" Morgan asked.

"In Boston."

"I'll go," said Lily. "I'll need a car."

"Karen, Scott," Morgan said. Any luck identifying those sleeper agents?"

"We're running the search," Scott said. "But we haven't narrowed it down enough."

"Keep trying. We also need to find somewhere safer for you to work. Motels are anonymous, but I don't like how exposed they are."

"I have a furnished apartment in New York," Scott said. "We could set up camp there."

"Dad," said Alex, computer on her lap. "I have a message from Simon. It looks like he's in Washington, DC. He's given us a way to track him."

"Then that's where you and I are going."

Chapter 103

A lex sped down I-95 on her used Honda Interceptor. Being on the back of a bike again felt even more like freedom than being able to walk without crutches. It was like flying after a life-time on the ground.

"Slow down," her dad said through the portable communicator he had bought for them. It wasn't the sort of thing Zeta used, but it was enough for them to talk as they drove. "You're leaving me behind."

"How about you keep up?"

They made the suburbs of Washington, DC, in the early afternoon and stopped at a roadside diner before moving into the city. Alex set her computer on the table and ran the tracking program on Simon. "Looks like they're on the move," she said, tilting Coca-Cola into her mouth as ice tinkled in the glass. "In the vicinity of the National Mall."

Her father sipped at a mug of coffee. "Their target could be any number of locations."

Alex checked her watch. "We still have five hours until . . ."

"Let's go after them," he said. "Keep the computer open in the car. You work support. I'll get Simon."

Chapter 104

The shadows of trees were lengthening with the sun's afternoon descent. Praetorian's family home was as old money as old money got—a red brick colonial mansion in Brookline overlooking some serious acreage of the most expensive square feet in the region. Lily pushed the iron gate, which opened with a squeal. She walked up to the oak doors and operated the heavy iron knocker fashioned to look like the head of a lion.

An aged Korean man opened the door. Servant, by his clothes.

"We don't wish to buy anything," he said, in a shaky accented voice, and pushed the door closed.

Lily put her foot down to block the door, which knocked against her toes. She winced with pain.

"Wait! I need to talk to you about Jeongwoo. It's an extremely important matter."

"There is no Jeongwoo here," he said, but his face betrayed his dismay at hearing the name. "Now please, remove your foot."

"It's a matter of life and death."

"Go away," said the servant. "I do not know what you are talking about. Whatever this is, we want nothing to do with it. Go now before I call the police."

Lily withdrew her foot and the old servant closed the door, its mass emphasizing the finality of his dismissal.

She turned to go, mind working on how she'd gain access to what she needed. She assessed the windows for how easy they would be to break in. They might be alarmed, but these houses frequently didn't extend the alarm to the highest windows. It would be trivial to gain access to the backyard, and perhaps she could scale a tree to—

"Stop!"

A female voice, meek and beseeching. She turned to see a beautiful Korean woman, not much older than Lily herself, with long, lustrous black hair, wearing a silk dress—and she looked like the kind of person who would wear silk just to sit around the house.

She came close, obscuring herself from the house windows behind a massive pine tree.

"You were asking about Jeongwoo?" she said.

"Yes, I was."

"Are you against him?"

"What?"

"Is he your enemy?"

Lily didn't know how to play this. But she sensed that the right answer was the truth.

"Yes. He's putting people in danger. I want to stop him."

"There is a diner about two miles down the road. Meet me there in half an hour. I have something to show you."

Chapter 105

"He's on the far side of the Washington Monument," her father said. "Intercept him on your right."

"Copy."

Alex pulled the hood of her sweater over her eyes as she power-walked over the frozen ground. She caught sight of Simon ahead and steered to converge with him. Her mind worked on the problem of how she would make contact.

She opted for ramming him, playing it like she was a distracted pedestrian, hard enough for him to drop his backpack. He gasped as it hit the ground.

"Hey, watch where you're . . ." He trailed off as he registered who she was.

"I'm so sorry," she said, picking up his backpack. It was heavy—must be the bomb. "I was distracted, I—" she brought her mouth close to his ear. "I need to know how your leader communicated with the Legion."

"He's got a special phone on him at all times."

"Can you point him out to me?"

"I'm meeting him now," Simon whispered.

"When's the attack?"

"Tomorrow, nine a.m." Then, in a loud voice: "Watch where you're going next time. Idiot."

Alex continued her earlier trajectory. "Dad," she said. "Did you hear?"

"I heard," he said. "Circle back and stay on him. Don't be seen. Remember like I taught you."

She did remember. She kept her distance, walking at a slight angle to Simon so that no one watching them would have connected the two. She averted her eyes, using only her peripheral vision to track him, and feigned interest in the landmarks that surrounded the National Mall. Alex followed him as far as the Smithsonian before he stopped to talk to another man—short and stocky, with a short-cropped beard and a flattop of black hair.

"I got him," said Alex.

"I see it," Morgan said. She looked around, spotting, to her surprise, that her father had been stalking her. He passed her without making eye contact, and she took the cue not to acknowledge him.

She watched out of the corner of her eye as she pretended to consult a bulletin board. He approached the man talking to Simon, timing his passage to the approach of another couple of pedestrians. He swerved to avoid them and bumped into the cell leader, so softly that it might not even merit an apology.

"I got it," said her father. "I got his phone."

Chapter 106

The Korean woman entered the diner with an elegant bearing. Lily stood as the woman looked around and, catching sight of her, walked over and sat down

"Thank you," she said. "I was afraid you wouldn't come."

The best kind of asset—the kind that thinks she's more interested in you than you are in her. "I want to know what you have to show me. I'm Lily, by the way. Lily Harper."

"My name is Minsoo," she said. "Jeongwoo was—is my brother."

Lily had gathered as much—not mistaking the family resemblance, "Do you have any idea where he might be?"

She shook her head. "I have not seen him in many years. He is not welcome in our house."

"Why?"

Minsoo looked away. "He made my childhood hell," she said. "He was cruel, but he knew how to hide it well. He never left a mark. Never let it show. My parents adored him because he was so intelligent. But all the while, he would hurt me. Torture me, physically and mentally. Threaten me in my bed at night. Tell me awful things. I never had a pet that he did not kill and leave for me to find. But I could never tell my parents. Every time I tried, he hid all evidence—and made sure I was punished for it later."

Lily couldn't help noting the elegance of Minsoo's speech. It was precise and measured, with no sign of haste or hesitation, with only a touch of an accent, which if anything lent her speech class.

"My parents continued to be deluded until he was ten years old. The family dog, a happy little basset hound, was found murdered with garden shears. This time, one of the servants saw him and told my parents. They denied it, but they couldn't. Their son was a monster."

The waitress came and offered them menus. Minsoo thanked her with the utmost politeness and asked for a bottle of mineral water.

"They tried to fix him. They hired the most expensive psychiatrists, psychologists, and neurologists. They wanted a name for what he had and a way to get rid of it. They got him specialized tutors, and then veered into quacks—psychics, so-called shamans, exorcists. Whoever would promise to change what was wrong with Jeongwoo. Of course, nothing ever worked. It was his nature that was wrong."

She kept her delicate white hands on the table, her long slender fingers ending on fingernails manicured with a skin tone nail polish.

"Jeongwoo had always been a gifted child, but in his teenage years he became frighteningly intelligent. He also knew people. He treated them like experiments. He tormented anyone he came in contact with—mostly staff, since my parents did not let him out of the house very often. All learned to avoid him."

The waitress set down the bottle of Evian and a glass. She poured. Minsoo waited and thanked her when she was done. She resumed her story once the server was out of earshot.

"We had a maid at the time—Joonyoung was her name. My father found her dead one day—I won't tell you the details, it is too awful. That was the last straw. My father spent a lot of money to cover it up. A gardener took the blame. He ended up dying in prison.

"To Jeongwoo, my father offered two options. He could go to an institution for as long as father deemed reasonable—and I can tell you now, it would have been the rest of his life—or he could leave and never come back. He chose the latter. I haven't heard from him since, and I thank the heavens every day that I don't."

Lily felt for her. She had undergone a fraction of that—the cruelty of the girls at her prep school, days of hiding in the bathroom and crying. That alone had made her life miserable. To have her tormentor be her brother, an inescapable presence from such a young age . . .

"I have something for you," said Minsoo. She pulled a phone from her pearl-encrusted clutch. She manipulated the screen with a slender finger and turned it for Lily to see.

It was a video. It bore the discoloration of something that had once been on tape. The frame showed a boy. Korean. About puberty. He was sitting on a chair. A fern sat in the otherwise drab background.

"Jeongwoo?"

Minsoo nodded. Lily saw the resemblance.

A voice came from off-screen, with the impersonal warmth of a psychiatrist. "Why did you do what you did to the dog?

"I like it when things die," he said.

"Is that why you killed him?"

"He was annoying."

"Do you think about killing often?"

He didn't answer.

"Do you think about killing a lot, Jeongwoo?"

"All the time."

Minsoo stopped the video there.

"He's a psychopath," Lily said.

"It shows at an early age," said Minsoo. "It did for Jeongwoo."

"Why are you showing me this?"

"Because it's what I have to offer. Because if I can help you find him, catch him, whatever you intend to do, then I will. I want him dead, you see. And if this brings him a little closer to that death, then I do it happily."

Chapter 107

A lex and Morgan had to drive a ways out of the city to find the type of motel they were looking for. All the chain places required ID and credit cards. They had to cross into Maryland before there was a place that would take them.

Alex unlocked the room for her father and set the bag from the electronics store on the table. He set the laptop they had brought along next to it, and then the phone he had stolen from the Legion cell leader.

She pulled the cable from the bag and connected the phone to the computer, which did its usual scratchy noise with the hard drive as it tried to interface. Meanwhile, her father called Scott, Lily's nerdy squeeze (verdict: cute, but not Alex's type).

"Scott," he said. "We're connected."

"All right," he said on speakerphone. "Let me see what I can do."

Her father sat back on the chair. He was getting tired, Alex could tell. Eyes droopy, muscles tense. She wondered if his bandages needed redressing.

"I've got something for you to see in the meantime," Scott said. "I'm sending it to your screen."

A video popped up. Sitting on the bed, Alex leaned forward to get a better view. A child, sitting in a chair. The voice, cold and affectless, unnerved her, even more coming from a child. It was Praetorian, no question. "I guess this is what Centurion was talking about," her father said. "How's it going with the cell phone?"

"I can tell you one thing: I'm not going to be able to get a contact list or anything like that," he said. "All communications are obscured via public-private key. There's just no way, unless we had a hundred years or got a quantum supercomputer."

"How can we get one of those?"

"We'd have to invent one."

Helpful.

The video came to an end. An idea came to Alex. "Scott, can you use the phone to relay a message to all the cell groups, even if you don't know who they are?"

"Could be. I'd have to isolate the—it would take a while. But in principle, it should be possible."

"Prep the video," her father said, quick on the uptake. "We're sending it to everyone in the cells, along with a message."

"I see," said Scott. "You want them to turn on him once they know what he is. You know, realistically, we can't expect everyone to come forward."

"We just need one person in each cell group," said her father. "Just one person to turn after they see this video and tell somebody the location of their cell and what their target is."

Chapter 108

Morgan woke up to his phone ringing. Scott.

He stood up, looking at his daughter, fast asleep in the other bed. It was still dark out. He looked at the time—6:32. Another forty-five minutes till sunrise. The weight of this day was already bearing down on him.

He went into the bathroom to pick up so he wouldn't wake up Alex. "Morgan."

"I've been up all night, but I got it," Scott said. His voice sounded breathy and exhausted. "I've written a protocol that'll deliver a message to the entire network of cells—every individual member."

Morgan looked in the room. Alex stirred but was still in bed.

"All I need," Scott continued, "is the message. Type it up for me and I'll get it sent."

"Good. I'll do that. How's O'Neal coming with the identities of the sleeper agents?" If the diversionary attacks were to happen in a few hours, he had to assume the sleepers were going to strike later that same day.

"Hold on." Too far to make out the words, Morgan heard Scott's voice, and then O'Neal's response. "She says don't bother her while she's working. Get the message written. I'll send you something as soon as I can."

Morgan sat down at the table and opened the computer. The message had to be short and to the point—anything else might risk losing their attention. He typed,

Praetorian is using you. The bombs are real. He is not who you think he is.

He hit Send. Scott texted him:

Got it. Sending now.

It was out there. Now, he had to hope it would work.

Chapter 109

The calls started coming in early in the morning. By the time Frieze arrived, dressed in sweatpants and a T-shirt, which she didn't have time to change out of, the office was bustling with activity.

"What's going on?" she asked Gus, who was on the phone.

"Just a minute," he said into the receiver. "We've gotten two potential terrorists in the city saying they're part of a group planning a bomb attack. I said *hold on*. They say they were deceived, that they want to turn themselves in."

"Two calls with the same story?"

"No. The Bureau's been getting calls like from all over. We're up to something like twenty-five countrywide." He turned his attention back to his call. "Yes, keep him in detention there. We are sending down an interrogator to—"

Frieze sat down at her cubicle and brought up the reports to get up to speed. One of the suspects, a BU student, was in police custody. Similar calls had been made to the police in a long list of cities, including LA, San Francisco, Miami, Atlanta, and New York, with most coming into Washington, DC.

Conley's call to her rang not ten minutes after she walked into the office.

Frieze picked up. She spoke first. "Why was I sure that you'd had something to do with this?"

Chapter 110

Lily met Scott in the morning at his Brooklyn apartment, where he and O'Neal had put together a workspace that had its own chaotic logic. All the furniture in the living room had been pushed up against the walls, and five laptop computers, two tablets, and papers bearing inscrutable diagrams took up the rest of the floor space.

"What is going *on* here?"

"Shh," Scott said and turned back to O'Neal. "What are we doing wrong?"

They were in the zone. This wasn't the time for jealousy. Lily sat down on an orange modern armchair, crossed her legs, and watched.

"We've accounted for a margin of error on each of the established criteria," said O'Neal, pacing over the paper-strewn floor, hands mussing her hair in frustration. "We've filtered through the probable parameters. We've broadened the search functions to include possible errors in the records, misspellings, and ages. But we just don't have enough of a correlation to narrow it down. We need more parameters."

"We've got refugees," he said. "Against age, major cities, job, marital status, ethnicity, income, hospital stays, accounts on all the sites we have records for."

O'Neal let loose a frustrated groan. "What are we missing? What else can we look at?"

Lily had a stroke of insight. "Psychiatric records."

Both turned to her in surprise. "What?" said Scott.

"These people were supposed to be brainwashed, right? Brainwashing is an extreme form of abuse. These are people who are traumatized. They're going to have a record of mental health issues."

"Could work," said O'Neal to Scott with a shrug.

He sat on the floor at one of the computers and navigated the complex user interface. "But psychiatric care databases have a mess of diagnoses. It's going to be hard to search."

"Medication," offered O'Neal, crouching at a computer of her own. "We have a national registry of prescriptions. Let's cross-check our algorithm against anxiety medications, weighted by degree of seriousness."

Lily scraped her manicured nails along the armrest as the program ran. Scott tapped the floor, and O'Neal tugged at her hair.

"I got something!" exclaimed Scott. "Nine hits exactly, two of them already dead. All refugees born within a year of each other. Lily, you're a genius!" He leapt up off the floor and kissed her.

"Uh oh," said O'Neal. "Guys, sorry to interrupt, but this is bad news. Get Conley on the phone. We need to get these names to the FBI *right now*."

Chapter 111

Lisa Frieze ran the names of the suspects Conley had given her. What she saw made her go numb.

She leapt from her chair and ran across the office, which was roiling with the energy of crisis mode. Gus called out to her, but it didn't matter. Nothing mattered.

She burst into Chambers's office without knocking, interrupting a meeting with the Special Agent in Charge.

"Agent Frieze, if you value your job, you'll remember that a closed door means—"

"It's urgent, sir. It could not be more urgent. I will stake my job, my entire Bureau career, on this. I just need you to listen to me for two minutes." She was aware of looking like a crazy person, an impression not helped by the fact that she was wearing sweatpants and a T-shirt in a room with two men in suits.

Chambers grumbled under his breath. "George, if you'll excuse me."

"Sir," Frieze said to the SAC as he left the room looking skeptical.

"You made a bet," said Chambers, "Now show your cards."

"This list of people," she said, putting the printed sheet on his desk. "Now, I know this sounds crazy, but these are Soviet sleeper agents, raised in this country since before the end of the Cold War. All these people turning themselves in, they're just distractions to draw our attention away from the real attack."

"And where did you get this list?"

She opened her mouth, but couldn't think of anything to say. Damn it, why didn't she prepare a lie? "A . . . source."

"I see."

"Look, they all came to the US as Bosnian refugees. No parents. All spent much of their childhoods in the same orphanage. And all of them *just happen* to work for utility companies in major US cities. Do you think that's a coincidence?"

He set the list down on his desk. "Stranger things have happened," he said. "And yet, what I have never heard of is for a group of sleeper agents to spend more than twenty years in deep cover for a nation that doesn't even exist anymore."

Frieze swallowed hard. "I know, sir," she said. "I know how it sounds." She wasn't sure how much even she believed it. But Conley had never lied about something like this. "We need to act on this. They have access to our infrastructure. Put together, they can hit tens of thousands, if not hundreds of thousands, of Americans. If we don't we'll be responsible for maybe the greatest terrorist attack ever to hit American soil. Do you want to be the person remembered for that?"

Chambers looked out the window at the snow, falling thick outside. "I'll tell you, Frieze, you make a heck of a case. We'll do it. I'll send this along the pipeline and vouch for you. But if this goes south, it's your ass." Chambers picked up the phone and dialed. "IOSS? Chambers, from the Boston field office. I need the Crisis Management Unit. Right now."

Chapter 112

"In position."

Lisa Frieze, bundled in a tactical vest, Colt .22 in hand, crouched in the FBI van. The target was in his Arlington, Massachusetts, home, a ground-floor apartment on a calm, sunny street. Their surveillance had shown that the target, Marko Novak, was inside.

"Move out!"

She opened the back door of the van and stepped off, leading the SWAT team toward the apartment. They broke up into two groups, one to take the front door while she led the other to the back door. The battering team got into place.

"On my signal," she said. "Breach and clear!"

They rammed the door, and the team moved in, clearing the kitchen and moving into the hall, Frieze bringing up the rear. They found Novak, thin and black-haired, in the bedroom, trying to escape through a window with a metal box in his hand.

"On the ground!"

Novak ignored her and pushed himself out the window. Frieze took aim. Novak's chest erupted with blood, staining the snow black in the predawn light. The sniper had gotten him.

"Target down!" someone called out

"Area clear!"

Frieze holstered her weapon and went around outside to Novak's body. He had dropped the tin, featureless and as big as a lunchbox, as he fell.

The bomb squad moved in and took the tin into a mobile glove-box chamber. Built out of reinforced steel, the chamber could withstand small-scale explosions and was kept at a pressure near vacuum, so that even in the event of a breach air would only flow in and contaminants could not escape.

Frieze called Chambers.

"We got him," she said. "He was shot down trying to escape."

"The other teams have reported in," said Chambers. "All five other targets neutralized."

"Chambers, he had a box in his hands—the bomb squad is opening it up now."

"It's liquid VX," said Chambers. "Nerve agent. Nasty stuff. Kills you even if you don't inhale because it gets absorbed through your skin. We had an incident in one of the New York operations. The target broke the vial when she saw she had no escape. We have three agents dead and five in critical condition."

Damn. Frieze didn't want to think about how many dead that would have been, even if just Novak had completed the attack as planned.

But she wasn't breathing easy yet. There was still one more sleeper out there, which meant that there was one last vial of VX at large.

Chapter 113

Annemarie was putting away the cutlery from the dishwasher when Ansley came in through the garage door. His home was an alien place now that the mission had superseded every bout of trouble, every effort, every connection he had in that place. It was something other now.

"Bruce?" Annemarie asked, right arm akimbo in her chili pepper apron. "What are you doing home?"

Annemarie felt alien, too. They had been married sixteen years and she did not know him—not the real him. She knew only the shell that he had shed. Only what he had pretended to be for all those years. For decades.

"Honey, are you feeling all right? You look pale." She looked at his hands. "Bruce, you're shaking!" She moved toward him in concern.

Ansley gritted his teeth and grabbed a knife from the dishwasher rack. It carried a six-inch kitchen blade, slender and sharp. The handle was still warm from the wash cycle

"Bruce?" She took a step back. "Bruce, what are you doing with that knife?"

Chapter 114

Morgan and Alex sat in a state of suspended animation in their motel room. There was nothing for them to do, nowhere for them to go. It was all up to other people now. Both were too anxious to eat, too anxious to even talk. Morgan knew how to calm his body and keep still even in times of tension. Alex fidgeted, drumming her fingers on the desk, doodling on a notepad, or playing with the phone cord. Otherwise they just watched, in alternation, the phone and the computer for updates.

The first came early—a series of terse messages from Conley as the sleepers were caught or killed by the FBI. The last one came before 8 A.M., and now, all they could do was wait either for a Hail Mary or for the last terrorist to complete his mission.

Morgan's phone rang. Alex fell off the bed in surprise.

He picked up on speakerphone so that Alex could hear. "Morgan." It was O'Neal, manic and out of breath. "I found it! The last sleeper. He changed his name. That's why they weren't warned about him. His name is Bruce Ansley now. He lives outside DC. In Fairfax."

"What's the target?"

"He's listed as an employee of the Water and Sewer Authority," said Scott. "Problem is, he doesn't seem to stay in any given office. He's a quality inspector, so he's got access to all the water utility installations in the city. He drops that vial of VX into any of them . . ."

"Got it. Text me the address." Morgan hung up. Alex was already standing. "We're on the move. You're going to this Ansley's house, on the off chance that he's still there."

"What about you?"

"I'm going to the city. Whatever his target is, it'll be there."

Chapter 115

A lex parked her motorcycle on the next street over from Ansley's suburban home. She jogged around the corner, passing a
housewife walking a golden retriever. She came up on the house on
foot.

There was a car in the driveway, which held space for two—and
the empty space had an oil stain that suggested another car spent a
lot of time parked there. Someone was out, but someone else might
still be inside.

Alex slinked around the side of the house toward the backyard,
keeping her head low. As she passed a row of small windows, she
raised her head to peek in through one. It opened into the kitchen,
the picture of suburban normality until she caught sight of something that made her gasp.

Not worried about detection anymore, Alex ran around the corner and tried the back door. It was unlocked. She went inside and
headed straight for the kitchen, where she confirmed what she had
only glimpsed before.

A woman—Ansley's wife, she figured. Dead. Murdered in her
own kitchen, a knife wound through her apron, her neck slit.

Alex was reaching for her phone to call her father when she heard
crying. It was faint, but she was certain it was inside the house. Alex
crept, careful not to make any noise. Entering a stranger's home was
an uncanny experience—both intimate and foreign. The Ansleys
seemed normal to judge by how they lived—two-story house, homey,
timeworn furniture, family pictures on the mantelpiece. But one of
the people in those photographs had been killed by the other.

Alex climbed the stairs, following the sound of crying. She
found its source in the first room to her left. A girl. She might have

been thirteen or fourteen, judging from the decoration of her room, a mixture of little girl's items with pubescent interests in pop stars and makeup. She was huddled in the corner of her room, holding her knees, a thousand-yard stare on her face.

A six-inch kitchen knife was on the floor, still bloody. It had stained the girl's pink shag rug. Alex couldn't make out any injury on her. She folded over the rug with her foot to hide the knife from view and stepped closer to the girl.

The girl flinched away.

"Don't be afraid," said Alex. "I'm here to help. Please. What's your name?"

The girl just stared at her. Urgency was making Alex impatient, but she bit her lip and held it back. The last and least helpful thing a traumatized child needed was someone browbeating her into communication.

Alex looked around the room for anything that might help her make a connection. Her eyes lingered on a poster on the wall. "You like Taylor Swift?" Alex said. "She's one of my favorites. What's your favorite song?"

The girl didn't answer. Didn't even look at her. Alex found another potential topic in a photo collage above her desk.

"You like horses? Do you ever go out riding?"

Nothing.

Alex looked around again and her gaze landed on a stuffed giraffe on a shelf. She remembered reading that trauma caused people to regress, to act like they were when they were younger. The stuffed animal looked stained and frayed, which told Alex it had been loved a lot.

Alex took it off the shelf and held it out to the girl. "Hey," said Alex. "Look what I got."

The girl held her stare on the giraffe, then reached out and grabbed it, enfolding it in her arms and closing herself up again.

"What's her name?" Alex asked.

"*H-his* name," the girl said, stammering, "is Tobey."

Alex smiled. "What about yours?"

"Pam."

"Pam, my name is Alex. Nice to meet you. Listen, I just need to make a phone call, but I'll be right back, okay?"

"No!" she cried. "Please. Don't go."

"I'll just be right out in the hall. Okay?" The girl nodded.

Alex left the room with quiet steps and called her father.

"Dad," Alex said, keeping her voice down so the girl couldn't hear. "It's too late. He's gone. He, uh—he killed his wife. But his daughter is here, too. Alive. She isn't hurt, but she's in pretty bad shape. I think she saw something. But Ansley—Dad, he didn't kill her. He brought the knife up here, but I think he couldn't do it."

Alex heard Pam's sobs as her father considered this.

"Alex," he said, "Stay with her and keep the phone close. I might still need you before this is done."

Chapter 116

Bruce Ansley swiped his keycard at the door of the Hayes Street Water Pumping Station, fighting through his splitting headache to focus on appearing normal. He walked inside the vast open chamber, control panels, and meters against the walls. The scream of the eight pumps sending thousands of gallons through their pipes pounded in his brain. He was sweating, rubbing his temples. He couldn't even walk straight.

"Hey, Bruce, are you feeling okay?" someone asked. The identity of the person didn't register with Ansley.

"I'm fine," he growled. He felt for the vial in his pocket and fought through the pain. This was the day. What he was made for, the consummation of his entire life.

He looked at the valve through which he would pour in the VX nerve agent, on the third pipe from the back, accessible through the catwalk. That was his purpose. His mission.

Ansley ran into the bathroom and vomited into the nearest toilet. He was tormented by visions of his family. The face of his wife as he murdered her. Of his daughter, shrinking from him, terrified he'd do the same to her. Cory, who wasn't there—what would become of them? Of his *kids*?

He drew the vial from his pocket. He could just flush the damn thing. It wouldn't cause much harm—the half-life of VX in air was short. The only people in danger would be a few sanitation workers at the worst. He could put an end to this now.

He held the vial over the toilet. It was the right thing to do. The other sleeper agents—if there were any left—might be successful, but he would stop his part. It would end there with him.

Then something else took over, another side of him, cool and hard like the vial in his hands. The mission asserted itself. The mission mattered, and nothing else. He put the vial back in its case, and the case back in his pocket. He waited for the nausea to pass and his breathing to normalize. Then he stood up and washed his face. The mission would continue. He would fulfill his purpose.

Chapter 117

"We've got a hit," said Scott over the phone. "Ansley just used his keycard in a water station. Downtown. I'm sending you the address. Get in there and I'll see what I can do to get you inside."

"I'm on my way," he said, pulling the Camaro out of its parking space. It was a five-minute drive, tops.

"There's something else," said Scott. "That water station—one of the pipes in there leads straight into the Pentagon. If Ansley gets VX in the pipes and the Legion sets off a fire alarm in there, we're looking at more than twenty thousand dead, and the entire Department of Defense wiped out."

Morgan stepped hard on the accelerator, swerving through traffic. The clock was ticking.

He made the Hayes Street Water Pumping Station in two minutes flat, bringing the car to a stop across the street with screeching tires. Like most of its kind, no one would have guessed that this was a utility building. If anything, it looked like a Georgian manor house or gallery. But inside, pipes that a full-grown man could crawl through were pumping thousands and thousands of gallons of water every second.

He picked up the phone and dialed. "Scott. Did you get me a way in?"

"Still working on it."

"We don't have time. He's already inside."

"It's a complex government security system. I'm doing what I can!"

"Too slow." As they were speaking, a woman turned into the

path to the door of the pumping station. This was the time to do something really stupid.

Morgan got out of his car and ran as fast as he could without attracting too much attention, hand on his weapon in its holster. As she swiped her keycard, he grabbed her arm and showed her the gun. The blood drained from her face.

"This is a national security emergency. I don't have time to explain. But I need you to get me inside the pumping chamber. I need to find Bruce Ansley." She was like a deer in headlights.

Morgan stepped inside the well-lit space. The noise of machinery was deafening and constant. A row of eight enormous blue pipes rose out of the ground, each passing through a bright yellow pump twelve feet off the ground and plunging back underground. The pumps were accessible through catwalks that circled the facility.

A man in a blue button-down shirt was standing at one of those pumps. Morgan climbed the stairs to the catwalk, the sound of machines covering up the metallic clang of his footsteps.

He approached Bruce Ansley to find him holding an open vial over the ancillary intake valve on the pump. He seemed to be working up the courage to do it.

Morgan drew his PPK.

"Bruce!" he shouted, barely audible over the noise. Stop!"

Ansley looked up, wide-eyed. His shaking hand brought the vial over the intake pipe. Morgan had a clear shot, but he couldn't risk shooting him and have the vial fall in.

"Don't do it! Step away from the pipe!"

"You step off!" he shouted, voice trembling. "I have to do this!"

"You don't! You'll kill thousands of people, Ansley! You don't have to be that man."

"This is what I am. This is what I'm for."

"You get to choose. That's what it means to be human."

"I killed my wife. Oh God, I killed my wife." His hand shook. His fist closed tight. "Step away!"

With his free hand, Morgan dialed Alex. "Steady!" he said. "Look! I'm not coming closer."

He brought the phone to his ear. "Dad? What's that sound?"

"Is she there?" Morgan asked. "Will she talk?"

"Hold on."

Ansley looked perplexed. "Who are you talking to?"

"Dad," Alex said, "she's here. She's ready."

Morgan held the phone out to Ansley. "It's your daughter. She'd like to talk to you."

Ansley reached out a tentative hand and took the phone.

"Hello? Dad?"

Pam was curled up on her bed with her stuffed animals. Her voice was shaking. Alex, sitting across from her, held her left hand tight.

"Dad, I don't want you to hurt anyone else. Please. Dad, please, don't do it."

At the pumping station, Ansley was tearing up, his face contorted with anguish. "Pam," he stammered. He drew the vial away.

"That's it," said Morgan. "Just put it down."

"No!" he screamed. His grip tightened on the vial.

Morgan adjusted the aim of his gun. "Down! Now!"

Ansley wavered. And then his face set in determination. His hand twitched toward the valve—

Morgan shot. The bullet hit him in the chest.

The vial slipped from his fingers and shattered on the grated surface. The VX pulverized in the air, deadly particles dispersing.

Morgan bolted, holding his breath as Ansley convulsed on the catwalk. He stopped long enough to pull the fire alarm as he passed it on the way down the stairs. The siren shrieked.

Morgan didn't inhale until he reached open air. The fire alarm proved to be unnecessary—if everyone had not already evacuated after Morgan had muscled his way in, the gunfire was enough to do it. Just four employees for the whole facility, counting the woman who had let him in. All were across the street, huddled together. They ran away when they saw him.

Hearing the sound of approaching police sirens, Morgan ran back to the Camaro. He took off, passing the wave of police cars four blocks from the pumping station. They paid him no heed.

Morgan stopped at a convenience store a few miles away to make two calls from the pay phone. The first, to 911, putting in an anonymous tip that there was a nerve agent inside the pumping station. The second was to his daughter, telling her to stay put.

Chapter 118

Morgan met Alex at Ansley's house. They left Alex's motorcycle behind and drove together out of the city, going north. Morgan had a headache from fatigue, and the headlights from the oncoming cars made him squint with pain. But what worried him more was Alex, quiet as a stone in the passenger seat.

"You did good today," he said. "I haven't met many people in the business who can think on their feet as well as you."

She mumbled some vague thank you. Now he was worried. If there was anything that never failed to cheer her up, it was praising how good she was as an agent.

"Is this about the girl?"

"Her mom and dad, dead the same day," she said. "I thought she could save him."

Morgan sighed. "Listen, kid. Things don't always work out. Sometimes things pile on one another, and sometimes one person gets the brunt of it. Sometimes it's an innocent girl."

Alex looked out the window at the suburban landscape, the quiet family homes, all the people who escaped the horror of a homeland attack that day. "Do you think we used her?"

Morgan took her hand in his. "You're going to have to make some tough calls in this line of work. Can't be helped. But to answer your question, no. I don't think you used her. You didn't get her involved in this. You were there for her in maybe her darkest time. And you gave her a chance to turn things around. That was all you could do. Just because you couldn't make it better doesn't mean you were responsible for making it worse."

"Doesn't feel much different."

"Well, it is. And it's important to know that difference when you're involved in this business." He squeezed her hand. "I know you feel guilty. You pushed Simon because you were after the thrill. That was wrong, and I'm happy that you feel bad about that."

"Gee, thanks."

"I'm serious," he said. "It shows you have a conscience. Ethics. It's not such a common thing. And I know it was your conscience that guided you today."

"How do you know the difference?" she asked.

"Practice. And even then you make a mistake now and then."

Alex didn't answer, but Morgan saw that her face had lost the tension it was holding before, and in less than an hour she had fallen asleep. Morgan was considering stopping for dinner when his phone rang.

"Morgan. It's Karen. I looked at the Zeta data dump." She was going a mile a minute. "Everything they took from us before they torched the place. It was a massive load, terabytes on terabytes."

"Karen, slow down. What are you talking about?"

"I tried to track the transfer, but his data packets are relayed pseudorandomly through communications satellites. That has the effect of obscuring where they're coming from and where they're going. But with all this data, I wrote a machine learning algorithm that saw the signal in the noise."

"Karen!" said Morgan. "What are you telling me?"

"We found him," said O'Neal. "We found Praetorian."

Chapter 119

The Black Hawk helicopter flew low over Appalachia, skirting the mountaintops that were catching the first rays of the rising sun. The forest seemed to stretch forever in every direction, a choppy, wavy sea of green.

Morgan held onto the strap, looking forward, trying to make out Praetorian's hideout before it was announced. It would still be a few minutes before it came into view. He turned his attention to Conley, doing his mindfulness practice, and Lily, her pretty face lined with preoccupation. The four other men, on loan from Zeta's umbrella organization, Project Aegis, showed the usual mixture of emotions—anticipation, excitement, dread, a solemn sense of duty.

As for Morgan, energy pumped through his veins. He hadn't slept in at least forty hours, but his body somehow knew to keep him, at whatever cost, strong and alert.

I'm coming for you, you bastard. I'm coming for you.

"Coming up on the drop-off area," said the pilot over the communicator. Morgan checked his equipment—MAC-10 on a sling around his shoulder, Walther PPK in his shoulder holster, snub-nosed Smith & Wesson on his right ankle, and combat knife on his left, flashbang frag grenade. He curled and extended his fingers, checking his gloves for flexibility.

All systems go.

Morgan braced as the helicopter lost speed and came to a hover two hundred yards away from the house. He loosed the rappel rope and was first to push off, sliding down until his boots hit the snow, then leaping away to make room for the next man down.

It was dark enough that Morgan brought down the night-vision goggles over his eyes.

A flash of red.

"Take cover!"

A *fwoosh* filled the air as the surface-to-air missile rocketed toward the chopper and exploded in a fireball that lit up the dawn forest.

"Run!"

Morgan dashed away from the fiery carcass of the chopper as it bore down on top of them. The others scattered.

"Squad!" he said. "Move in!"

They advanced toward the house in the battle swarm formation, covering each other as they moved from tree to tree.

A single gunshot—*BANG*—rang out from the house—rifle fire, though Morgan couldn't make out which. A man fell to the ground and didn't get up again.

"Suppressive fire!" Morgan called. The men loosed bursts from their submachine guns as they moved, in their best approximation of the direction of the gunman.

Morgan leapt out from behind the tree. Muzzle flash. The gunshot caught him square in the chest.

He fell backward, gasping for air. His hand moved to the spot where the bullet had hit. No blood. His Kevlar had held.

He rolled out of the way, and another bullet hit the ground where he had been a split second before. He stood, taking cover against the tree. He felt his chest, bruised and aching but in one piece.

"Hold position!" he yelled.

Something wasn't right. This sniper was getting a reliable shot every few seconds even against suppressive fire. It was inhuman. It was—

Morgan flipped the night-vision goggles over his eyes and switched to infrared. He peered out from behind the tree. He found the barrel, showing bright on the infrared. But there was no rifleman. No human heat signature at all.

The barrel turned toward him. He drew back his head, the bullet whizzing past his ear.

"It's a machine!" Its aim was uncanny, and it stopped only long enough to calculate the trajectory of its next target. "Cease fire!" The bursts of suppressive fire stopped.

Morgan flipped up the heat vision and squinted in the half-light, peeking around the other side of the tree. The muzzle was sticking out of a small pillbox bunker. It turned back to him. He ducked, and another bullet shot past him.

"We need to move together," he said. "Never spend more than five seconds in the open. I want each of you to know where you're going next. In position?" He got confirmation from the five remaining members of the team.

"Move out!"

He ran, pounding the hard frozen ground. *One, two, three, four*—the crack of gunfire.

"Anyone hit?" said Morgan, back to a thick sycamore.

"Just a graze," said Conley.

"Okay, again," he said. "On my mark. Go!"

Morgan ran. *One, two, three, four*—gunshot.

"Augh!"

"Man down," said Conley.

"I'm alive." It was one of the others, who went by the code name Stone. "Bastard got my leg. I'm out of this one."

Morgan gritted his teeth. He was close enough now. He knew what he had to do.

"Cover me. I'm going for it."

He ran out from behind the tree—straight for the gun. Morgan counted—*one*—in his head—*two*—as the rifle turned—*three*—to aim—*four*—straight at him.

Morgan dove out of the way as it fired, and the bullet hit the ground.

The others took his initiative and stopped taking cover, running straight for the pillbox instead.

BANG.

Out of the corner of his eye, Morgan saw a petite female figure hitting the ground with a somersault and getting up again.

Atta girl, Lily.

Morgan was close, but another runner passed him on his right, grenade in hand. He tossed it in like he was dunking a basketball and dropped to the ground. The muzzle turned, and Morgan was looking down the barrel of the rifle.

FOOM.

A muffled burst as the frag detonated. There was no muzzle flash.

Morgan ran, along with the rest of the team, and stood flush against the side of the house. Morgan took stock. Five of them left. He made out the outline of Conley's nose in the half-light. And there was Lily, alive—but clutching her right arm.

Morgan examined the house—boxy, its first story made of stone, the other two built out of logs. The windows were boarded up, and a satellite dish protruded from the roof. Morgan signaled for Conley to lead Lily and one of the men around the left side of the house while Morgan took the right with the remaining member of tactical.

They crept around to the front of the house, where the vista opened to a sprawling valley. Where the hell was Conley?

There was no time to lose. Morgan signaled to the men and kicked in the door, taking the lead inside while the other took the rear.

BANG! BANG!

Two shots in the darkness, and his companion fell, dead.

The room was lit up in harsh, blinding light, and Morgan heard the door behind him slam shut. As his eyes adjusted, Morgan saw that four sets of mobile floodlights had been arrayed around the middle of the room. Dark silhouettes bordered the lights, at least four of them.

"Drop the gun," Praetorian ordered. "*All the guns.*"

He was truly, royally screwed.

Morgan let the MAC-10 clatter on the wooden floor, then un-holstered his Walther and undid his grenade belt.

"The little one, too. Do you think I'm blind? And the knife. Kick them all over here."

Morgan removed the snub-nose and the knife, too. Each scraped along the wooden floor as Morgan pushed them away with his foot.

The floodlights were shut off, each dimming from blinding to a mellow orange as they cooled. Morgan blinked against the after-images, which faded to reveal the figures that surrounded him. Two men, approaching their thirties, he didn't recognize. They were flanking Morgan on either side, each clutching a Daewoo K7. The Russian, Sergey, the Puppetmaster, sullen, crazy-eyed. Centurion he recognized, and next to him a woman he didn't—black hair with purple-frosted tips. Face like a china doll. And next to her—

Praetorian. Clean-shaven, hair cut, in a black turtleneck and denim jeans.

"You clean up good," Morgan said.

"Is this the one who killed my kids?" asked the Russian. He spat on the ground.

"You are a real rock in my shoe," said Praetorian. "I regret not killing you the first time we met."

"As I recall, you tried." Morgan examined his environment—a bare room, taking up the entire first floor of the house, with a wooden staircase in the corner leading up to the second floor, and another on the side corner leading down into the basement.

Praetorian laughed. "You know what happens when I try."

"I stop you. And now I found your little castle."

"Tell me when that starts working out for you," Praetorian said.

"And what do you do now?" Morgan asked. "Your network has turned on you. The sleepers have all been neutralized."

"That reminds me," said Praetorian, picking up Morgan's PPK and shooting Sergey in the head. Despite his light frame, the Russian hit the floor with a heavy thud.

"What I have left," said Praetorian, "Is all the dirty little government secrets I got off the prison ship. All these fireworks, Acevedo, the smoke bombs, even the nerve agent—they're all pageantry." He took something out of his pocket—a small tablet device, about half again as large as a phone. "Here I have absolute control over that information. From this device I can publish any and every secret Uncle Sam wants to keep secret. See, *this* is what makes the world go round. Information. It's what people kill and die for. And it will do more to destroy the US government than any terrorist attack ever could."

"You *really* like to hear yourself talk."

Praetorian grinned. "Don't you want to know what your government is doing? Let me tell you a little story about your friend General Strickland. It's April 2003. The US Army has just taken Baghdad. A squadron of soldiers from the Third Infantry Division is scouring one of Saddam's palace complexes when they come across a group of plainclothes Americans loading a cache of gold bullion into a truck. They confiscate the truck, bring the men in, and make their report. The truck and the men are taken away under Strickland's authority. The men are transferred within the week to combat operations in Mosul, where on their first incursion, the entire squad, all eleven of them, are massacred in a booby-trapped insurgency hideout, during a raid personally ordered by General Strickland. Neither the gold nor the men collecting it are ever heard from again."

Morgan's hands balled into fists. So that was Strickland's secret. Stealing Saddam's gold and killing the witnesses—American soldiers—to cover it up. Morgan felt the righteous fire, the impulse to burn it all down.

"Does that paint a picture for you?" Praetorian scrolled through a list on the screen and then held it up for Morgan to see. "I have a whole file only on him. The original report, his personal order to reassign the squad. I have all of their names here, too."

Morgan locked eyes with Centurion. Morgan's MAC-10 was lying at his feet. He gave a nearly imperceptible nod toward the man flanking Morgan on his right. Morgan nodded back.

"What about *you*, Morgan? Are you in here, I wonder? Will I find a file on Cobra?" Centurion bent down to pick up Morgan's submachine gun, examining it as if it were a scientific curiosity. "What skeletons do you fear will come out of your—"

Centurion slipped his finger against the trigger and opened fire against the man to Morgan's right. Morgan went low to his other flank, sliding on his knees, grabbing the man's gun as he fired and yanking it hard to the left so that the bullets sprayed against the stone walls. Centurion fired again, hitting the second guard several times in the chest. The guard tumbled to the ground next to Morgan.

Centurion then turned the gun on Praetorian.

The knife slipped into Centurion's back before he loosed a bullet against Praetorian.

"*Valkyrie,*" Centurion croaked. His arms fell slack at his sides and he dropped to his knees, then on his side. The woman with the china-doll face stood there, with an expression of righteous wrath.

"That," said Praetorian, "was unexpected." He aimed Morgan's PPK at his head. "I think I'm done with surprises from you."

BANG—a handgun's report, and Praetorian flinched, recoiling his arm. The PPK fell to the floor. Blood spread from Praetorian's hand onto his shirt.

Morgan looked for the source of the bullet and saw Peter Conley coming up the stairs from the basement, his Colt .22 drawn on Praetorian and Valkyrie. Behind him was Lily and the one other remaining member of the tactical team.

"Maybe just one more," said Morgan.

Praetorian's eyes blazed with fury.

"I win," said Morgan.

Praetorian's lip curled into a smirk. Morgan saw why—he was manipulating the screen of the tablet, one-handed, without looking.

Morgan lunged, slamming him against the stone wall. The tablet slid across the floor. Lily ran to pick it up as Conley kept his gun trained on Praetorian, waiting for an opening. He tangled with Morgan without giving him any distance, giving Conley no clearance to shoot. He brought his fists like steel against Morgan's side, knocking the wind out of him.

"In the end," he said, between punches, "I'm just stronger than you."

Morgan gritted his teeth and brought his forehead hard against Praetorian's nose. Praetorian flinched back just enough for Morgan to break free and return with a left jab and an open palm to his solar plexus. Praetorian staggered back.

A gun fired.

Conley. He'd gotten his opening. He hit Praetorian in the abdomen. Conley raised the gun to fire again.

"No!" It was Lily, holding Praetorian's tablet. "Whatever he did," she said, "it's started and I can't stop it. It's uploading the files to the cloud. Once it's out there, there's no way to put the lid on it."

Morgan pushed Praetorian against the wall, elbow at his neck. "How do you make it stop?"

Praetorian just giggled.

"I swear, if you don't stop it, I'll—"

"Do what?" It was Valkyrie, held at gunpoint by Lily. "He won't talk. He withstood the worst torture your government could devise for *weeks*. You know you can't make him do what you want in the seconds you have left."

She was right. Morgan couldn't make *him* talk.

He picked up his PPK and set it against Praetorian's temple.

"But suppose I want to make *you* talk."

This threw her. Her mouth fell slack. "He didn't give me the password." She set her jaw. "It's no use asking me."

"But you know how to stop it."

She clammed up, but her eyes told Morgan everything he needed to know.

"Can you stand watching him die?" he said. "Being without him forever?"

She wouldn't. He saw it in her. He was everything that she was, and without him she was no one.

"Do not do it!" Praetorian screamed.

He depressed the trigger, a millimeter. She flinched.

"Okay!" She cast her eyes down in shame. "Damn it. Okay. Let me do it."

"Valkyrie," Praetorian said through gritted teeth. "If you do this, I will kill you."

"If that transfer isn't cancelled, he dies," said Morgan. "Understand?"

She nodded. "Sorry," she said. "I'd really rather die." Lily handed her the tablet. Her fingers moved deftly over the touchscreen. She was finished in about five seconds. She gave it back to Lily.

"Lily, is it done?" Morgan asked.

"Yes. The transfer's been cancelled."

Morgan took a few steps back from Praetorian and gestured to Valkyrie. "Over there. With him."

She ran over to him, wrapping her arms around him.

Faster than Morgan could react, Praetorian pulled the knife out of Centurion's back and plunged it into Valkyrie's heart. She gasped, eyes wide, and crumpled to the ground.

Morgan fired twice into Praetorian's chest. He stumbled against the wall, sliding down against the rock until he came to rest in a sitting position.

"*Then fall Praetorian*," he whispered. He was still alive, but he was never getting up again.

"We're done here," said Morgan. "Conley, can you call in the chopper?"

Morgan surveyed the bloodbath, the corpses all around him. And the cause of all this, still gasping his final breaths. Justice? Maybe. Maybe not. But necessary.

Praetorian's tablet began emitting an incessant beep.

"What is that?" said Morgan.

"I don't know!" Lily said.

Praetorian laughed, showing bloody teeth. "Open the flashing tab and see," he said.

"Oh my God." She gave it to Morgan.

It read, *Incoming missile.*

"That's straight from the DOD," he said. "Your own people are bombing this place because they're afraid of what I might release. How do you feel about being their agent now?"

Morgan pivoted toward the door. "Run!" He pulled the wooden bar from the door and held it open for Conley, Lily, and the last operative, following them out into the dawning day. They ran as fast as they could downhill, over snow and between trees.

The missile tore the air as it passed. The house exploded into splinters and flying masonry, sending a shock wave that knocked Morgan off his feet. He rolled behind a tree to escape the rain of debris that followed.

As the ringing in his ears subsided and his eyes refocused, Morgan called out. "Is everyone okay?"

"Aye!" Lily called out.

"Roger," said the operative.

"I'm here," said Conley.

Morgan looked at the house, now a foundation and a smoldering pile of rubble to mark Praetorian's grave.

He noticed something in his hand. Praetorian's tablet. He had never let go of it. A device that could single-handedly bring down the entire US government.

He didn't know what was in there. He didn't know what kind of leak could bring down the whole government.

For a moment, he was tempted. Damn it all. Burn it to the ground, if it means the truth will come out. That prospect called to him. It was seductive.

But he had a responsibility. He selected all the files and his finger hovered over the Delete button. Thinking better of it, Morgan unselected one of them, and then deleted.

Then he selected the one that was left and hit Send. A progress bar crept to the right of the screen.

Folder "General Alan Strickland" had been successfully published.

Morgan sat down in a snowbank to watch the sunrise. Conley approached with a limping gait and sat next to him. Lily smoked a cigarette a ways off.

"Beautiful, ain't it?" Conley said.

"Bright new day."

Chapter 120

Lisa Frieze parked in a puddle of slush in front of her apartment, which splashed onto the shoes of a man standing on the sidewalk. She got out of the car, an apology forming on her lips when she saw that it was Peter Conley.

"I know you want me to ask how you know when I'm coming home," she said. "I'm not going to."

He grinned. "I haven't said anything."

She reached into her car to get out her briefcase. "If you're here for a favor, so help me I—"

"No favors, no requests. I'm just saying thanks for sticking your neck out for us yet again."

She squinted against the sun. "It's you guys who ended up saving the day again. I don't think I'll ever put any kind of personal feeling above that."

"I'm only half glad to hear you say that."

"And the other half?"

"Was hoping you'd say you couldn't resist my charm."

She had to smile at that. "You aren't half as charming as you think you are, Peter Conley."

"That's still pretty charming." He flashed his perfectly aligned pearly whites again.

She unlocked the door to her building. "Well, it's not going to work on me anymore."

"If you say so. You want to go get a drink?"

"Now?" she asked. "Nah. But maybe I'll call you sometime."

* * *

Lily pulled the Porsche up to the Hilton, where Scott was already waiting for her, wearing a peacoat over an untucked buttondown shirt and black trousers.

"Hey big boy," she said, drawing off her shades. "Looking for a good time?"

"I don't know," he said. "You look like trouble."

"Get your arse in the car."

He hopped into the passenger seat, kissing her. "Hello you."

"Hello you."

She pulled out of the hotel, tires squealing. "So," he said, "Any new revelations for today? Are you secretly a werewolf? Time traveler from the future? Cavewoman frozen in ice for fifty thousand years?"

She laughed. "I think you know all there is to know."

"Sweetheart," he said, "I don't know a fraction of what I want to find out about you."

An exuberant smile erupted on her face as she drove them west, toward California and the sunset.

Chapter 121

Morgan walked off the elevator on the fifteenth floor of the Hampton Building, where Zeta Division was housed after the headquarters was blown up. The place was bland and boring, but Morgan felt that he could use a little bit of that.

Bloch waved to him and told him to take a seat in her office, no longer the glass and chrome consumed in the fire but a more ordinary wood and faux leather.

"Good to see you got released," he said.

"Well. Jail did not agree with me. Not very sanitary. And people are loud."

"The new digs—"

"Are fine for now, but we are procuring alternative solutions."

Morgan eyed the copy of the *Globe* on her desk—the front page reading, *Top General Arrested After Document Dump.*

"The fruits of your little piece of rebellion." Morgan turned his eyes to her face, expecting stern admonition, but instead he found something that could almost be called a smile.

"Bastard had it coming."

"No comment," said Bloch. "But meanwhile, Zeta lives on. In no small part thanks to your extraordinary daughter."

"I wanted to talk to you about that," he said. "I know the deal here. The way it worked with Shepard and O'Neal. Kirby and you, too, for all I know. Charges get dropped, and people come work here as *very* loyal agents."

Bloch leaned forward, elbows on the table, fingers interlocked at chest height. "What has Alex told you already?"

"Nothing," he said. "But I know she's always wanted to work here, so—"

"Smith has already arranged for her charges to disappear," said Bloch. "Free of any obligation. He said he considered it more than earned for her service."

"So that's it? She's scot-free?"

"On her part, yes. But she did make a similar deal to the ones you brought up."

Morgan frowned. "What do you mean?"

"She did bargain something for her involvement in Zeta for the boy. Simon. The only condition she gave for working with us was for his criminal record to be expunged. Did she have a special connection to him?"

"Maybe," Morgan said. "Maybe she's just learning when to listen to her conscience."

Morgan arrived at home a half an hour later and shut off his cell phone. No calls, nothing else. For a week, at least, he'd be a civilian.

He kissed Jenny, who was sweaty, having just come in from a run. He pulled her close, perspiration be damned, "You wouldn't believe how much I missed you," he said in a throaty whisper.

"I think I have some idea."

He found Alex reading a rainforest survival guide lying on the couch, bare feet up on the armrest. He sat in the armchair opposite her.

"We need to talk about you joining Zeta."

She sat up, countenance gone serious. "Look, Dad, I don't want to get into another fight, but I'm a grown-up now. I can leave the house if you want, and I'll take care of all my own finances if it comes to that, but—"

"No," he said. "I want to apologize. I wasn't being fair to you. I don't know if you were born for this, or I raised you this way without realizing it, or even if that's got nothing to do with it. But this is you, Alex. It's who you are, and I can't get in the way of it anymore."

She beamed and practically leapt off the couch at him, wrapping her arms around him and kissing his head.

"On one condition," he said as she pulled away. "I want you to finish college."

"About that. I, uh—I just saw the e-mail yesterday. They kind of . . . asked me not to come back next semester. Turns out all the excitement wasn't very healthy for my grades."

Morgan sighed and sat down at the dinner table. "You know about this, Jenny?"

"She's your daughter," she said from the kitchen. "You deal with it."

"But Dad!" said Alex, with uncontained excitement. "It's happening! I'm going to get to do what I've wanted for *so long*."

"Yeah, yeah. Just don't look so damn smug about it."

"Aren't you happy, Dad? We'll get to work together."

"Yeah," he said. "Thrilled."

ACKNOWLEDGMENTS

First of all I need to thank my editor at Kensington Publishing Corp., Michaela Hamilton, for being so patient with me and for her support and faith in me over the past four years. She has always been there for me when I have had questions or needed direction and has become a great friend.

Special thanks are due to Mayur Gudka, who is not only my social media guru, but a colleague who takes time to listen and help me in any situation. His advice for promoting my books has been invaluable.

I want to recognize Caio Camargo, who has been my right hand while writing the Dan Morgan thriller series. Our relationship has grown through the years and I look forward to continuing to work together.

To my dear wife, Linda, I wish to express deep appreciation because her encouragement and enduring support have helped me realize my dream of becoming an author.

Finally, I sincerely thank all my loyal fans and supporters who continue to buy and read my novels.

Special bonus!

In case you missed the first Dan Morgan thriller by Leo J.
Maloney, keep reading to enjoy the opening pages of
Termination Orders . . .

Available from Kensington Publishing Corp.

Chapter 1

Three sharp raps at the door yanked young Zalmay Siddiqi from uneasy dreams, and the adrenaline hit him like a kick in the face. He froze with the primitive instinct of a rabbit cornered by a fox, hoping against hope that whatever predator had come knocking would go away of its own volition. He listened. The knocks came in a familiar pattern of three shorts and three longs: Cougar's signal. As his blazing panic subsided, he realized that he had been holding his breath. He exhaled, but the smoldering dread remained. Even friendly knocks were unwelcome in the middle of the night.

He rolled nimbly out of bed and pulled the lanyard on the light fixture above him, spilling the bulb's dim yellow glow onto the sparsely furnished room: a lone mattress on the floor, a plastic chair draped with his clothes, his few possessions huddled in a corner where cracked plaster walls exposed the concrete underneath.

Tugging on a plain Afghan *khameez* tunic and *salwar* trousers made of rough cloth, he hurried out of the bedroom to the hallway door. The knocks were still coming intermittently in their steady pattern. Zalmay gingerly turned the lock, and no sooner was the dead bolt released than the door was flung open, nearly knocking Zalmay back into the wall. A tall, wiry American, a man he knew as Cougar, rushed into the apartment, also wearing Afghan garb and carrying a black duffel bag. His movements were jerky, his voice breathless.

"Grab your things. You've got thirty seconds."

Zalmay's thoughts were forming a protest at Cougar's abruptness, but the urgency in the American's speech stayed his tongue. With a sudden clarity, he asked only, "Am I coming back?"

"No," Cougar responded, and he looked over his shoulder. "Pack only what you can't live without."

Cougar stood at the door, his head cocked like that of a prey animal listening for stalking predators. Zalmay threw his single other outfit and his prayer mat into a canvas knapsack. From under his mattress, he took out a slim roll of cash tied with a rubber band. He reached in again, pulled out a creased old photograph, and hid it, along with the money, in the folds of his shirt. Then he turned to face Cougar, doing his best to look brave.

"I have been expecting this," he said. "I am ready."

Fear and anxiety had marked Zalmay's life since he'd met the American and agreed to help him. Zalmay was well aware of the consequences of being caught. The thought usually kept him awake and tossing on his mattress at night. And on this particular night, his nightmare had finally come calling. He could only feel glad that it was his friend and not an enemy assassin at his door.

"Good," said Cougar, "Now let's . . ." Cougar trailed off and turned his head as if listening for something. Then Zalmay heard it, too, and it stopped him cold. It was the rumbling motor of an approaching car, which came to a halt down below the open window. Zalmay walked to the window to see who it was. Looking down, he saw a black sedan with two men climbing out of it, Americans in Western suits, each with a submachine gun in his hand.

"No, get away from there!" said Cougar.

Too late—one of the men below looked up, called to the other, and pointed right at Zalmay. Both black-suited men dashed for the door of the building. Zalmay's apartment was on the corner, all the way down the hall; the men would have no trouble at all finding them.

"Come on!" said Cougar, motioning for him to go out the door. Zalmay dashed out and was halfway down the hall, past a row of silent, closed doors on his right, when he noticed that Cougar had stayed behind to shut the door to the apartment. He waited, nervously, as Cougar caught up, and they hurried to the stairs. From there, he could already hear the footsteps of the two men scrambling up, closing the distance with each footfall. Zalmay's apartment was only three floors up, so it wouldn't take them long to get there. And there was no other way out.

Cougar drew his weapon from its shoulder holster. "Upstairs," he whispered. "Quietly." He took the lead, and they tiptoed up a flight of stairs, keeping their footsteps as light as possible. Cougar crouched behind the bend of the fourth-floor corridor, and Zalmay ducked behind him, breathing heavily, his mind blank with panic, the way a rabbit must feel when confronting a tiger. The American kept his Glock pointed toward the stairwell as the sound of the men's shoes on the steps grew louder and louder, and then they heard the footsteps receding down the hallway toward Zalmay's apartment.

"Zalmay," whispered Cougar, pulling a set of keys from his pocket, holding them tightly in his palm so they would not jangle. "Take these. I'm going to hold them off. While they're searching your apartment, you run down as fast as you can and start the car. If I'm not the first one down, you take off without me, understand?"

"But . . ."

"Don't argue, just go. Now, after me!"

Cougar walked back down the flight of stairs, quickly and silently, leading with his shoulder, arm extended and gun pointing down, at the ready. They heard a crack as the men kicked in Zalmay's door. Before reaching the landing on the third floor, Cougar motioned for Zalmay to jump over the rusting railing onto the next flight down, so he wouldn't be seen from the hallway. Zalmay clambered over and vaulted down, but his foot slipped on the metal, and his arm smacked painfully on the railing below. A hollow, metallic sound echoed up the stairwell. They heard voices and then the sound of the two men running out of the apartment.

"Go!" said Cougar. "I'll hold them off!"

Zalmay nodded and started down. He leapt down the stairs two steps at a time, one hand clutching the keys and the other the strap of his knapsack, which was slung over his shoulder and slammed against him with every step.

Gunshots, three sets of them, blasted through the hallway upstairs; the single reports from Cougar's Glock were answered by volleys of fire from the two men's semiautomatics. He slowed down and for a split second considered going back to help his friend. Honor demanded it. But no; Cougar had told him to go on ahead, so that is what he would do. He had learned that the honorable thing to do was not always the right thing. He pressed on, and an inchoate, wordless prayer for his friend's survival formed in his mind.

Zalmay raced into the dusty night air, easily spotting Cougar's beat-up jeep, parked at a hasty angle to the building, the headlights left on like the still-open eyes of a dead ox. He pulled the door open and swung into the driver's seat, tossing the knapsack onto the seat beside him. He fumbled to slide the key into the ignition and then turned it; the engine rumbled to life. Gunshots reverberated from inside, but now they came from much closer. Cougar had made his way down the stairs. Zalmay leaned over to unlatch the passenger door and then kicked it wide.

Cougar burst out of the building. He stopped just long enough to shoot out one of the front tires of the men's sedan. Then he ran over and hurtled into the jeep's passenger seat, pulling the door shut as he did in one fluid motion, yelling, "Go, go, go!" Zalmay saw the two men appear at the door as he hit the gas. They sped off under a barrage of bullets. Several slammed into the back of the jeep, making dull, metallic *thunks*, and one shattered the rear window. Zalmay mashed the pedal to the floor. The sound of gunfire slowly faded in the distance and then stopped altogether.

"Are you okay?" Zalmay asked, his eyes on the dark dirt road. "Were you hit?"

"Still in one piece," Cougar said, with ragged breath and looking back. "You?"

"I am fine. Are they behind us?"

"They won't be getting far. Not in that car."

Zalmay exhaled. "Where are we going?"

"Turn here." Zalmay turned the jeep into a narrow side street. "We'll take the inner roads, just to be safe," Cougar added. "It's best to make sure we're not easy to follow."

Zalmay breathed deeply, trying to calm his frantically beating heart. "Where are we going?" he asked again.

"Highway One, toward Kabul," said Cougar, shuffling through his duffel bag.

"We are going to Kabul?"

"You're going to Kabul," Cougar replied pointedly. "And then out of the country."

"You are not coming, then?" Zalmay said, trying his best to hide his anxiety and disappointment. Cougar did not respond, and Zalmay didn't press it. He knew the answer already.

"I need you to bring something with you when you go," said Cougar.

He reached into a pocket and produced a small black plastic chip, no bigger than his fingernail: a camera's memory card. "You know what's in there?" Cougar said.

"Is that what those men were after? The photographs?"

Cougar nodded. "This, and you."

"How did they know?"

"I tried to transfer them electronically, and the files were intercepted. That's how they knew to look for us. Now I can't get them through from here—they're watching every single connection. It needs to be carried out of here. And you're going to be responsible for getting it to the US and into the right hands."

"America . . ." he said in a whisper barely audible over the engine's growl. Through everything that had happened, the dream of going to that Promised Land had never left his mind. But he had never allowed himself to fully believe it was possible. To hear Cougar say it now suddenly made it a reality.

"We'll travel together as far as possible, but it's better if you don't take the jeep. If nothing else, these fresh bullet holes are going to be a tad suspicious. We'll stop where you can find alternate transportation—something less conspicuous."

"But, Cougar . . ."

"We don't have much time, so let me finish. While you're on the road, tell no one your real name. Call as little attention to yourself as possible. If you have any identification, get rid of it now. Burn it, or toss it into a storm drain or down a well. Do what you can to change your appearance. You have some money; here's more." Cougar handed him a wad of bills—American currency. "If anyone asks, you're visiting family in Kabul. Come up with a story, and practice it. And always keep an eye out for tails, just like I taught you. I can't promise you'll make it there safely, between the Taliban and our American friends. But I've done all I can to give you a fighting chance."

Zalmay sat in silence as the morning twilight rose upon the city, making it appear ghostly and unreal. Even now, while they drove alongside light traffic on an arterial road, the scene already felt like a distant memory.

"Why will you not come with me to Kabul?" he asked.

Cougar hesitated, as if gathering his thoughts. "This is the safest way for both of us. I can't get us a flight out of here, not anymore, and I would attract too much attention on the highway, from soldiers and the Taliban."

"The Taliban!" Zalmay bristled. "They would have no love for me, either, if they knew I have been helping you."

"Plus," Cougar added, ignoring Zalmay's interruption, "I have some unfinished business here." He gave a wry smile.

"I will stay and help you," Zalmay declared. "I am not afraid."

"No way."

"I want to stay," he protested, and anger welled up in him. "I want to stay and fight!"

Cougar sighed and took on a stern but fatherly tone. "I need this memory card delivered. I can't do it myself, and there's no one else I can count on to do it. This is your mission, Zalmay."

Zalmay looked away. "It is a coward's mission."

Cougar frowned, and his tone became distinctly one of rebuke. "This isn't about you proving yourself, Zalmay. Delivering those photos is our top priority. People's lives might depend on those pictures getting into the right hands. If you want to do something meaningful, this is it."

Zalmay assented wordlessly. Then he scowled and looked out the window as Cougar proceeded to give him specific instructions for what to do in Kabul. Being sent away like this filled him with shame, because he would be unable to help his friend right there in Kandahar. At the same time, his heart ached with thoughts of America, which had always seemed so impossibly far but was now so tantalizingly close—and that filled him with even more guilt, the guilt of choosing a comfortable life while others like him would remain no better off. Ultimately, he knew that Cougar was right. For now, however, he needed to brood.

With daylight approaching, the city was beginning to show signs of life. They were on the outskirts now, where the streets gave way to Highway 1. This highway was one of the Coalition's most ambitious projects in Afghanistan, cooperatively built by troops from among twenty-six NATO partner countries. Once called the Ring Road, the highway stretched to the capital and beyond, going around the entire country before coming full circle back to Kandahar from the west.

Cougar had Zalmay pull over to the side of the road a short distance from a small bazaar where many drivers stopped for food and tea and to trade information about the conditions of the road before the haul to Kabul.

As Zalmay and Cougar popped open the doors and climbed out of the jeep, the muezzins' voices began to drone over the minaret loudspeakers, calling all Muslims to their morning prayer. Zalmay's hand instinctively went for his prayer mat.

"I'm sorry, my friend, I can't wait for prayers," said Cougar. "But I'm confident Allah will forgive a short delay while you say good-bye to a dear friend."

Zalmay smiled, and they embraced tenderly.

"Thank you, Cougar."

The older man laughed hollowly. "I'm the one who should be thanking you, Zalmay. You did far, far more than anyone could ask for."

"And yet I am eternally grateful to you."

Cougar nodded, and Zalmay knew that he understood.

"I'm sorry you have to go alone, Zalmay. But I promise you, what you're doing is important. I'm counting on you."

Zalmay nodded in assent. "Will we meet again?"

"In the States, if everything goes right. And let's pray that it will. Good-bye, Zalmay."

"Good-bye, Cougar. Peace be upon you."

Zalmay gave the American the keys to the jeep and watched him as he climbed into the driver's seat and started the engine. Zalmay watched him as he drove off, feeling more the loss of his friend than of leaving his home. When Cougar disappeared into the city, Zalmay turned his thoughts to the road ahead: a harsh, dry land punctuated with towns and villages and a thousand enemies between him and his destination.

Chapter 2

Dan Morgan turned onto the small suburban cul-de-sac, the familiar tightness gripping his knee as he forced himself with gritted teeth to pound the pavement harder. *Embrace the pain; love the pain.* He pressed on for the last few dozen yards to his house, feeling the cutting chill of the early-March air in his throat as he inhaled.

Neika, who absolutely would not be tired out, had been straining at her leash to chase a squirrel but now set her sights on home. She let out a frustrated half bark, half whimper, muffled and choked off by her collar. Somehow, she still retained the exuberant energy of a puppy, but he knew she could really do some damage when she was threatened.

"Easy, girl," Morgan chuckled. He broke into a slow trot and then slowed to a smooth stroll as he walked into his front yard. He took a minute outside to catch his breath, letting Neika off her leash. She trotted into the garage to sit at the kitchen door, panting, tongue lolling, and eyeing him impatiently.

Morgan stretched his calves and, feeling another jolt of pain, rubbed his aching knee. "Well, Dan," he muttered to himself as he opened the door and Neika plowed inside, "I guess you're officially not a young man anymore."

As with everything else, Morgan took aging stoically in stride, even now, with forty-one just around the corner. However, those little signs that his body was no longer what it once was always had their own particular sting, especially in the way that they carried a stark reminder of the life he no longer led.

As he walked into the house, he was met by the smell of coffee and frying bacon. His daughter, Alex, was at the stove, cracking eggs on the edge of a skillet. She was as tall as he, and her brown hair had been recently cut shorter, to chin-length. She combined Morgan's athleticism with Jenny's slender frame, and even her casual movements were full of grace.

"Well, this is a nice surprise," he said.

She turned around nonchalantly, looking at him with sharp, intelligent eyes, and gave him a good-natured smile. "Mom's out running errands, so I thought I'd be a good kid and make breakfast." Alex turned back to the counter and scooped crispy strips of bacon from the skillet onto a paper towel.

"Are you sure you should be handling bacon?" Morgan asked, gently ribbing. "Isn't that against the rules?" She had not eaten meat for nearly three months.

Alex laughed. "Whatever rules there are, Dad, I'm the one who makes them."

"So it wouldn't actually be cheating if you had some, just this once?" He grinned with feigned hopefulness.

"And look, eggs over easy, just the way you like 'em," she said, ignoring his comment. She poked the spatula at one of the three sizzling in the pan and then, a bit too abruptly, flipped it over. The yolk began to ooze out from under it. "Ah, crap."

Morgan walked over to her and reached for the spatula. "Here, let me show you."

"I think I can handle frying an egg, Dad." That was his daughter: independent to the bone.

Neika, who had gotten her fill at her water bowl, sauntered over to beg for scraps.

"Nothing for you here, puppy," Alex said. The coffeemaker sputtered, then beeped as the last of the brew dripped into the pot. She poured out two mugs and scooped two spoonfuls of sugar into one. "Still take yours black, Dad?"

"You got it."

She handed him a mug and took a sip from hers. "Ooh, sweet, sweet caffeine."

"So," he said, "big plans for the weekend?"

"Oh, I might meet up with Tom and Robbie later today, if they're around. Nothing definite yet."

While she fussed with the eggs in the skillet, he took a moment to regard her, with her new and yet-unfamiliar chin-length hair. She really was becoming a lovely young woman, charming and vivacious. It was more than that, though: there was something about her that seemed much more composed and self-assured than the moody adolescent she had been even six months ago, when she had turned sixteen. He had always been unconditionally proud of her, but, now more than ever, she seemed to really command it.

"So, your mother mentioned there's a boy you've been seeing," he said, as casually and good-naturedly as possible. He expected her to roll her eyes and clam up, but he was surprised to find not a hint of annoyance in her voice.

"His name is Dylan, Dad. He's a good guy, and I like him a lot."

"That's great, sweetie. I'm happy for you."

"And if you promise to behave," she said, "I might even bring him home to meet you."

He grinned and sipped his coffee. It was steaming hot, and it made him realize how cold he was. "How did you two meet?"

"An APS event."

"APS?"

"You know," she said. "Americans for a Peaceful Society. Remember I told you I joined up?"

"Oh, the peaceniks . . ." said Morgan, chuckling, He sipped more coffee.

"I think the preferred term is *pacifist*, Dad," she said, with an edge of irritation to her voice.

"In the sixties they called them *hippies*." He had meant the comment to be good-natured, but he knew immediately it was the wrong thing to say at the wrong time.

Alex scowled. "I guess it would be too much to ask for you to take me seriously."

Morgan frowned. Things seemed to have taken a turn rather quickly. "I didn't mean . . ."

"I know what you meant," she said dryly. "I know how much respect you have for people like—well, people like me, I guess."

"Of course I respect you, Alex," he said. "But you have to admit, this whole pacifist thing tends to be a bit . . . *unrealistic*, don't you think?" He was trying hard not to anger her, to humor her, this new passion of hers, but he could tell he wasn't doing a very good job of it. *So much for being a master of deception*, he thought.

"Dad, do you know what's happening out there? Do you know how many soldiers are dying in our wars? How many civilians? Just innocent bystanders, at home, going to work or to school? Do you know, Dad, what our government does to terror suspects, many of whom turn out to be innocent?"

He nodded. He wanted to tell her he knew more than she could imagine. He wanted to tell her things he had not only heard about but *seen*. Instead, he bit his lip and let her continue.

"So maybe APS is a small ripple in a big pond. So maybe I can't change the world. At least I'm doing *something*."

Dan bit down harder, doing his best to keep from saying something he might regret. "Maybe, Alex. But the truth is, there are evil people in this world. People who would much rather you and I and everyone we know be dead. It's not like we go to war just for the fun of it. The people who make those decisions always weigh everything carefully, to make sure it's really, absolutely necessary."

She scoffed. "Right. And even then, it still never seems to solve anything, does it?"

"Isn't it ironic," Morgan said, grinning in an attempt to change the tone of the conversation, "that we're fighting over this?"

One of the eggs in the skillet let out a loud pop. Alex sighed. "How about you go sit down, I'll bring breakfast in a minute, and we'll forget I ever mentioned anything?"

It may not have been much, but it was a peace offering of sorts. Morgan took it as an opening. "Truce, then?"

"Truce."

"Hey, listen," he said. "I was saving this until after breakfast, but, you know, the Bruins are playing at the Garden this Friday. I thought you might like to go, too."

"Yeah, Dad," she said, with a measure of genuine excitement in her voice, though still tempered with her irritation. "I'd love to." Sports had always been their bond; whatever the arguments between them, this common ground brought them together. He wondered if it would be enough as she grew older and drifted further and further away. He wanted to tell her that he loved her, that he would do anything for her happiness.

"Okay, then," he said instead, and he turned to walk into the dining room. The table was set for breakfast for two, the silverware slightly askew but with pretensions of luxury, like linen napkins clumsily folded into fans, and a copy of the *Boston Globe* sitting neatly next to his plate. What a sweet kid, he thought, even if she was a little misguided by her own naivety. He sat heavily into the chair, relieving his knees with a sigh, and shivered at the chill of his damp shirt against his skin as he leaned back.

He picked up the paper and flipped through to the National section, which had a long piece on Lana McKay, an up-and-coming senator from Ohio who was making waves in Washington. A fresh face in politics, she had been catapulted into the national spotlight in the past year by her powerful appeals to ethics and political reform. She was bold, had a reputation for getting things done, and had emerged as a presidential hopeful in the next election. Morgan knew well how political fads came and went, and he knew even better that politicians sang a radically different tune inside their cabinets than they did to the press. But even he thought there might be something to this one.

He scanned the article but he couldn't concentrate on the words; his heart just wasn't in national affairs at the moment. Then he looked below the fold to find the smarmy mug of Senator Edgar Nickerson smiling at him. He and McKay were shaking hands at some political event. It made sense, of course, for McKay to be seen with the man widely considered to be the most trusted politician in America. But Morgan's image of her suffered from the association. Nickerson was one of the top players in DC—an old-money aristocrat who had a way of making people trust him implicitly. But Morgan knew better than to believe his public image: the man knew how to play the political game, with a reputation among insiders for masterful behind-the-scenes manipulations that no one ever dared speak of aloud for fear of reprisal.

Morgan decided he wouldn't let politics spoil what was already not the most pleasant of days, so he turned to the sports page for a March Madness update and was immersed in reading when the doorbell rang.

"I'll get it!" he called out to Alex. He walked to the foyer and opened the front door to find a narrow-shouldered man with thinning blond hair and nervous eyes. It was a familiar face, and one he thought he'd never see again. It fell somewhat short of being a pleasant surprise.

"What the hell are you doing here, Plante?"

"Hello, Cobra. How are you?" said the man softly, with an edge of anxiety to his voice. "It's been a long time."

"There's no Cobra here," said Morgan. "Not anymore."

"Would you rather I called you by your civilian name?" Plante asked. "I can do that, if you prefer."

"I would *rather* you tell me what the hell you're doing at my front door," said Morgan. "Or are you here just to catch up on old times?"

"I need to talk to you," said Plante, the apprehension obvious in his tone. "Please."

"Dad, who is it?" called Alex from the kitchen.

"Just a couple of Jehovah's Witnesses, sweetie," he yelled to her. Then he turned back to Plante. "You know what? I changed my mind. I don't care why you're here. Get the hell off my property before I exercise my right to shoot you as a trespasser."

"Won't you—"

"Listen here," Morgan interrupted, lowering his voice to a growl. "I don't work for you anymore. Whatever it is, I don't care. It's not my problem. It belongs to you and the rest of the clowns at the Agency."

"What if I told you it's a matter of life and death? What if I told you no one else could help us?"

"Jesus, it's always life and death with you people, isn't it?"

"You know that better than anyone else, don't you, Cobra?"

Morgan gritted his teeth. "Listen, Plante, my daughter's here, and she just cooked my breakfast. So I'm going in, and I'm going to sit down with her and eat, and you're going to get the hell away from me and my family."

"You won't even listen to what I have to say?"

"There's nothing you can say, Plante. Now, go away." Morgan began to swing the door shut.

"Cobra, it's Cougar," said Plante. The name stopped Morgan dead in his tracks. "Your old partner, Peter Conley. He's been killed. I'm sorry to tell you like this. But now you're the only one who can help us."

Morgan looked at Plante in shock, then took a deep breath.

"Fine. You can come in. But if I find out you're bullshitting me . . ."

Morgan stepped aside to let Plante into his home. And just like that, his past had flooded back to wash away his life of suburban tranquility.

Kippy Goldfarb / Carolle Photography

ABOUT THE AUTHOR

LEO J. MALONEY was born in Massachusetts, where he graduated high school and attended Northeastern University. In the mid 1960s, while in the army, he was recruited to become a deep cover black ops contractor for a clandestine government agency.

While serving his country in the secretive world of black ops for over thirty years, he operated several "cover" businesses, including a classic car brokerage, promotions and limousine companies, and a detective agency. He served as a municipal police officer in Revere, MA, and is still a licensed private investigator in the state of Massachusetts.

After leaving his career in black ops, Leo continued several of his cover businesses, and also had the opportunity to act in independent films and TV commercials. Leo has five movies to his credit as an actor, producer, technical advisor, or assistant director.

He lives in the Boston area. Visit him at www.leojmaloney.com.

"An outstanding thriller that rings with authenticity."
—JOHN GILSTRAP

Patriot. Spy. Assassin . . .

TERMINATION ORDERS

LEO J. MALONEY

SILENT ASSASSIN

A DAN MORGAN THRILLER

FAST. EFFICIENT. LETHAL. . .

LEO J. MALONEY

AUTHOR OF *TERMINATION ORDERS*

BLACK
SKIES

LEO J.
MALONEY

A DAN MORGAN THRILLER

TWELVE HOURS

A DAN MORGAN THRILLER NOVELLA

LEO J. MALONEY